M000204168

Return
to the
Dover Café

Ginny Bell went to school in Dover, never realising at the time what a fascinating and crucial role the town played in World War Two. She is a freelance editor who lives in London with her three children. *The Dover Café at War* was her first novel and there are now four books in the Dover Café series.

Also by Ginny Bell:
The Dover Café at War
The Dover Café on the Front Line
The Dover Café Under Fire

Return
to the
Dover Café
Ginny Bell

ZAFFRE

First published in the UK in 2024 by
ZAFFRE
An imprint of The Zaffre Publishing Group
A Bonnier Books UK Company
4th Floor, Victoria House, Bloomsbury Square, London, England, WC1B 4DA
Owned by Bonnier Books
Sveavägen 56, Stockholm, Sweden

Copyright © Ginny Bell, 2024

All rights reserved.
No part of this publication may be reproduced,
stored or transmitted in any form by any means, electronic,
mechanical, photocopying or otherwise, without the
prior written permission of the publisher.

The right of Ginny Bell to be identified as Author of this
work has been asserted by her in accordance with the
Copyright, Designs and Patents Act, 1988.

This is a work of fiction. Names, places, events and
incidents are either the products of the author's
imagination or used fictitiously. Any resemblance to
actual persons, living or dead, or actual
events is purely coincidental.

A CIP catalogue record for this book is
available from the British Library.

ISBN: 978-1-8041-8333-5

Also available as an ebook and an audiobook

1 3 5 7 9 10 8 6 4 2

Typeset by IDSUK (Data Connection) Ltd
Printed and bound in Great Britain by Clays Ltd, Elcograf S.p.A.

Zaffre is an imprint of Bonnier Books UK
www.bonnierbooks.co.uk

For Sandy, Daddy and Georgina. How I miss you.

And for Trissy, the inspiration for Cissy

Cast of characters

The Market Square

Castle's Cafe
Nellie Castle – Opinionated matriarch of Castle's Cafe
Donald Castle (died in 1927) – Nellie's husband
Cissy Ford – Nellie's cousin

Nellie and Donald's children:
Rodney (31) – Officer in the navy, works at Dover Castle
Marianne (30) – Best cook in Dover, lives and works at Castle's Café
Jimmy (24) – Private in the army, currently stationed at Drop Redoubt on Western Heights
Bert (22) – Also at Drop Redoubt
Edie (20) – Works as a mechanic at Pearson's Garage, married to Bill Penfold
Lily (18) – A trainee nurse at the Casualty Hospital
Donny (11) – Marianne's son (See *The Dover Café at War* for the story of his birth)
Polly – Talkative parrot

Jasper Cane – Donald Castle's best friend, surrogate father to the Castle children
Gladys – Worked at Castle's Café. Nellie took her in after her husband was killed in WW1
Alfie Lomax – Marianne's husband, stationed with Jimmy and Bert at Drop Redoubt
Marge Atkinson – Good friend of Marianne and Reenie's. Is in the Wrens and stationed at Dover Castle. In love with Rodney Castle

Turners' Grocery
Ethel Turner – Good friend of Nellie's
Brian Turner – Ethel's husband
Reenie Turner – Ethel and Brian's niece, works in the shop. Good friend of Marianne and Marge. Going out with Jimmy Castle

Perkins' Fish

Phyllis Perkins – Good friend of Nellie's

Reg Perkins – Phyllis's husband

Wilf – Phyllis and Reg's son. Works as a harbourmaster. Has lived with his parents since his wife, June Turner (Reenie's sister), died many years before

Freddie – Wilf's son and Donny's best friend

Bakery – the Guthries

Mary and Jack

Colin – Mary and Jack's son, missing since Dunkirk. Best friend of Jimmy Castle

Susan Blake – Mary's niece, currently in prison awaiting trial for murder

The Royal Oak

Mavis Woodbridge

Derek Woodbridge – Mavis's husband

Stan – Mavis and Derek's son

Daisy – wife of Stan, good friend of Marianne, Reenie and Marge

Pearson's Garage (Where Edie works)

Clive Pearson – Edie's boss

Bill Penfold – Mr Pearson's nephew and newly qualified pilot with the RAF. Married to Edie Castle

Other Characters

Muriel Palmer – Runs the WVS

Dr Palmer – Muriel's husband

Lou Carter – Runs whelk stall in market square. Local gossip

Terence Carter – Lou's son. Wheeler dealer on the black market

Mr Wainwright – Local solicitor who has helped both Marianne and Lily

Padre Philip Sterling – Army chaplain at the castle, in love with Marge

Roger Humphries – Local constable. Was in love with Marianne

Adelaide Frost – Member of market square community

Mr Gallagher – Runs the news stand

Dot – Trainee nurse and friend of Lily

Vi – Trainee nurse and friend of Lily

Dr Gertrude Toland – doctor at the Casualty hospital

Prologue

The sound of the wind was drowned out by the wailing of the air-raid siren and the crash of bombs as they rained down on Dover. Intermittently, the sky lit up, as search lights sought out enemy planes, and the rumble of the ack-ack guns joined the cacophony.

Seemingly oblivious, a figure scuttled through the backstreets, keeping close to the buildings as they made their way towards Castle's Café. On Church Street, they paused briefly by the wooden gate that led to the café's back door, glancing around to check no one had seen them, then they slipped through and flitted silently across the yard. As always, the back door was unlocked, and in the small hallway they opened the basement door an inch, listening carefully. Nellie Castle's strident voice floated towards them. Satisfied that the family had taken shelter, they tiptoed through the kitchen and up the stairs.

❧

The smell hit Nellie the minute she walked into her bedroom: rose water. So strong that she clapped her hand over her nose and mouth. Her first instinct was to run back to the basement, but with Marianne close behind her, she forced herself to walk in and shut the door.

Inside, she opened the window, then sat on the edge of the bed and looked around the room fearfully. 'Gladys?' she whispered. 'Is that you?'

Chapter 1

March 1941

'She's at it again.' A middle-aged woman wearing a green head-scarf tied tightly under her chin stood in front of the counter of Turners' Grocery Store and nodded towards the boarded-up window, which had once provided a clear view on to Dover's market square.

'Who's at what?' Reenie Turner asked distractedly, blowing a lock of curly blonde hair out of her eyes as she reached up take down a couple of tins of meat.

'Nellie Castle.'

Reenie put the tins down and peered through the strip of celluloid that allowed a modicum of light to shine into the shop. It was early morning on a cold, grey day and even though they'd only just opened, a queue of women already snaked up towards Cannon Street. And every one of them was looking across the square.

The view through the celluloid was blurry, but it wasn't hard to see what they were looking at. Kneeling on the pavement beneath the window of Castle's Café, Nellie Castle was scrubbing at the pavement, her bright red skirt stretched tight across her ample backside. Every so often she'd stop to dip her brush into a bucket of water beside her, then she'd start again.

The woman sniffed. 'Word is she's gone a bit doolally,' she declared. 'And it don't matter how much she scrubs, it's not gonna clean her conscience. Poor Gladys. That woman had a heart of gold, and look where it got her. Murdered right outside the café.'

Reenie's heart sank. She hadn't seen Nellie doing that for some weeks and she'd hoped the worst of her grief at the death of her friend had passed.

'I hope you're not trying to imply that Nellie had anything to do with Gladys's death, Mrs Grantham,' Reenie said.

The woman's bushy eyebrows rose. 'Course I'm not. But she's clearly gone loopy. If we all spent our lives scrubbin' at every bloodstain in Dover, we'd none of us get anything done. Anyway, Gladys died weeks ago, there's no stain there. But I'll tell you where there is one.' She pointed at her head.

'Mrs Castle's taken Gladys's death badly, that's all. And if doing that makes her feel a bit better, then it's not harming anyone, is it?' Reenie said.

'She's making a bloody spectacle of herself,' Mrs Grantham exclaimed. 'An' I'll tell you somethin' else: you won't catch me in the café no more. An' it's not just cos of poor old Gladys. Nellie was harbourin' a spy all them weeks, how could she not have known what that woman were up to? I used to see her, you know – Hester bloody Erskine – out and about at all hours, walkin' around town with young Donny Castle and Freddie Perkins. What woman of a certain age seeks out the company of kids, eh? I said to my Bernard at the time, I said, "That woman's up to something, you mark my words."' She folded her arms across her chest and nodded sagely. 'Turns out I were right. And if you ask me, Nellie should be banged up right alongside Hester.'

Reenie opened her mouth to protest, but Mrs Grantham hadn't finished. 'And look at that big plastic winder over there. The rest of us has to put up with what the council'll give us, but that's not good enough for Nellie Castle. She has to go buy her own. Where'd she get the money from? That's what I want to know.'

3

'I don't think that's any of your business,' Reenie said through gritted teeth.

'I'm not surprised you're defendin' her. You don't want to go offendin' your future mother-in-law, do you?'

Reenie scowled. 'Who says she's my future mother-in-law?'

'Oops, Jimmy Castle a bit slow off the mark, is he? Or maybe he's just out for what he can get, like his no-good brother. If anyone's to blame for Gladys's death, it's Bert Castle. Imagine messin' a girl around so badly, she tries to shoot you! Poor Gladys never hurt a fly, but she's the one what paid the price for Bert's philanderin'. She saved his life that day, but is he grateful? Is he heck. Every time I see the lad, he's got a different girl on his arm.' She shook her head. 'I told my Lizzy, I said, "You go anywhere near that man he'll have your dad to deal with. And mark my words, your dad won't miss."' She chortled.

Reenie gasped. 'That's not funny! Gladys *died*! And it wasn't Bert's fault. That was all down to Susan Blake. She was delusional.'

'You're not wrong there, love. Any girl what thinks Bert'll make an honest woman of her needs their head examinin'. In fact, gettin' mixed up with any of 'em is probably a bad idea, so maybe it's just as well Jimmy ain't proposed. The family's a scandal! Look at Marianne – pregnant at seventeen and no sign of the dad. Then there's Edie, sauntering around in slacks and working at the garage like a common grease monkey. Was up the garage the other day, an' imagine my surprise when I noticed she were getting a bit round, if you know what I mean.' She winked suggestively. 'And her not married more than a couple of months!'

Reenie pursed her lips. Marianne had confided to her that Edie was pregnant and she couldn't deny she'd been shocked. Especially as the baby wasn't her new husband Bill's. She presumed the flashy Canadian airman, who Edie had been seeing before Christmas, was responsible. The poor girl had had a run of bad luck with men, but in her new husband, it looked like she'd found someone who really cared for her.

'Ten to one she's foistin' someone else's kid on to poor Bill Penfold. And him a pilot! He could have had any woman he wanted. I'm surprised Clive Pearson's not sent her packing from the garage, given she's takin' his nephew for a fool.' She leant over the counter. 'Speaking of other men's kids, I saw Donny Castle up near the station the other day. Up to no good by the look of him. Marianne needs to get that boy under control before he gets into real mischief. But I don't see that happenin', what with her bein' as big as a house. Still, at least she's married fair and square this time. That Alfie's a saint, takin' on another man's bastard like that. Seems to be a habit with the Castle girls, don't it?'

Biting back a sharp retort, Reenie slammed down a tin of fish on top the packet of margarine at the bottom of the woman's basket, feeling no remorse when the greaseproof paper split and the marge oozed out. *And I hope it's full of grit when you scrape it off, you nasty old witch*, she thought, holding out her hand for the ration book.

Mrs Grantham handed it over. 'You might not like it but you know I'm right. Them Castles are nothin' but trouble. And then there's the youngest, Lily. Lovely girl, but a little birdie told me she were born on the wrong side of the blanket.' She winked. 'So who's her dad, eh? Well, you don't have to look far to figure that one out. Which means Jasper Cane and Nellie were at it right under her husband's nose – and him not in his right mind. Poor blighter. Take my advice and steer clear of them or you might end up like Gladys – dead on the pavement, a bullet through your heart.'

'Or she might end up happily married to a lovely young man.' Reenie's Aunt Ethel had been stacking shelves, but now she came to stand beside her niece. 'If I were you, Hilda, I'd take your shopping and get out before I throw you out. None of what happened was Nellie's fault.'

'You can stick up for her all you like, but it don't change the fact she were harbouring a traitor in her house for weeks! We could all have been killed in our beds!'

'Every night we could all be killed in our beds, and it ain't got nothin' to do with Nellie,' Ethel responded.

'Or so you believe. And I tell you another thing: I heard that Susan's gonna be on trial for murder in a couple of months, and she'll hang for sure. Poor Mary Guthrie, as if she don't have enough to deal with, what with her Colin dead and now her niece facin' the noose. Funny how just about every scandal that happens in this town has a Castle at the centre of it.' She nodded towards the window again. 'That lot have always thought they're above the rest of us, but I've got my eye on them.'

'Oh, is that why you were sheltering over in their café basement the other day, scoffing down Marianne's biscuits?' Ethel responded heatedly. 'You're a hypocrite, and if I had my way I'd ask you to shop elsewhere.'

'And if I had a choice I'd do it.' She picked up her basket and headed for the door.

'By the way,' Ethel said, 'saw your Bernard with Terence Carter up Providence House the other day when I made a delivery.'

Mrs Grantham turned to face her. 'So? He goes up regular to do odd jobs.'

'Is that what it's called now? Looked more like a smoky room full of men gambling to me, but what do I know?'

Colour rushed into Mrs Grantham's face. 'What are you suggestin'?' she asked.

'All I'm saying is people in glass houses shouldn't throw stones. And if you want to keep your eye on anything, maybe you ought to start with your husband.'

With a scowl, Mrs Grantham hurried out of the door, ignoring the chortles from some of the women who were standing in line.

'Nasty old cow,' Reenie muttered to her aunt.

'She is. But she's had a hard life, married to that no-good Bernard, and the only pleasure she gets is bad-mouthing others.'

'Lots of people have a hard life, it doesn't mean they go around spreading gossip,' one of the other women said. 'And I wish you joy with Jimmy Castle, love. I always liked the lad. Nothing's ever too much trouble for him.'

Reenie smiled. 'Thank you, Mrs Abel. I think he's charming too. Now, what can I get you?'

'What time you off to the match, Reenie?' Ethel asked as Reenie set about filling Mrs Abel's basket.

'Soon.' She checked her watch. 'The team's stopping for breakfast at the café; Jim said he'd come fetch me. You sure you don't mind me going to watch?'

Ethel smiled. 'If your uncle weren't out on delivery, I'd come meself. Reckon I could show them lads a thing or two. Star winger I was for Dover Ladies during the last war.'

'Here we go,' Reenie teased. 'Please tell us all about how you were top scorer in 1916, cos I'm sure you've never mentioned it before.'

Ethel elbowed her in the ribs. 'Cheeky mare,' she grumbled. 'Is Jimmy playing?'

'No. Just a fun thing to do on his day off.'

'Maybe today will be the day.' Ethel winked at Reenie.

Reenie frowned, refusing to show that she hoped it would be too. After Gladys had died, she and Jimmy had grown closer than she'd thought possible. But as yet he'd not mentioned marriage.

'Tell him to get his skates on before someone steals you away from him.'

Reenie snorted. 'Don't think there's much chance of that, Aunt Ethel. I'm thirty years old, and no one's tried to snap me up in all these years.'

Her aunt patted her cheek affectionately. 'Then they're fools,' she said. 'You're a diamond, and the fact that Jimmy's recognised it makes me love him that little bit more.'

'If he don't ask you soon, maybe I can reserve you for my Wallace,' Mrs Abel said. 'He could do with a lovely down-to-earth girl like you when he gets back from war.'

'Over my dead body,' Ethel whispered to Reenie, forcing her to stifle a giggle.

Reenie adored her aunt for being so supportive, but no one could ever call her a beauty. Her face was too freckly, her hair too curly, and despite rationing, she still felt she was too plump. But Jimmy didn't care about any of that. He seemed to love her for who she was.

There had been moments when they'd first started walking out when she'd doubted his feelings; she'd even called things off with him a few weeks ago. At the time, she'd felt he was only with her because she was a comfort after the death of his best friend Colin at Dunkirk.

But then Gladys had died, and they'd found themselves together again. And this time it was different. He'd confided that losing Gladys had jolted him out of his self-pity. He'd always grieve for his best friend, but he had to move forward and find happiness where he could – if only for Colin's sake.

Life was for living and loving, he'd said, kissing her soundly. And it was time he gave himself the permission to do both.

The memory of that kiss, and the many that had followed, sent a little fizz of excitement through her as she thought of what the day might have in store.

Chapter 2

Knees aching from the cold pavement, Nellie Castle sat back and regarded the patch of wet concrete. In her mind's eye, she could still see the dark stain of Gladys's blood. No matter how hard or how often she scrubbed, there it was. And when she'd walked into her bedroom earlier that morning, the scent of rose water making her gag, she'd felt compelled to scrub at it again.

Someone crouched down beside her and gently took the scrubbing brush from her hand. 'Hey, what's brought this on?'

'I've been scrubbin' this pavement for years, Jasper,' Nellie said snatching the brush back.

Jasper sighed. 'You know what I mean. We agreed you'd only scrub once a month. And I know you did it the other day.'

Nellie glanced up at him. Since Gladys had died, his face had gained a few more wrinkles and his bushy hair was now completely white, but his eyes were the same bright blue they'd always been. She started to scrub again.

'What's going on, Nellie?' Jasper asked softly. 'We're all worried about you.'

'There's no need,' she said briskly.

'Look, love, we all miss Gladys, but this has got to stop. Scrubbin' at this same patch of concrete's madness! People are startin' to talk!'

Nellie paused. 'Do you think I'm going mad?' she asked, unable to look at him. In truth, she was questioning her sanity herself.

And if she told him that she thought Gladys was haunting her, he'd probably have her locked up.

Jasper lifted her chin with his finger and gazed into her eyes. 'No, love. I think you're tired and I think you're sad. But' – he gestured towards the queue of women across the square – 'if you keep doing this, *they'll* think you're mad. So come on, the boys'll be arriving soon, and you don't want them to find you like this.'

She nodded. She was sad. Gladys's death had knocked her for six. Her friend had been with her through thick and thin since the last war, and Nellie now realised how much she'd taken their friendship for granted. Gladys had helped her with the children, she'd helped in the café, and she'd helped her with her husband Donald when he'd come back from the first war, his mind shattered . . .

On the day she'd died, they'd made a pact: they would tell everyone the truth about how she and Gladys had inadvertently given him so much poppy head tea over the years that, rather than helping ease his mind, it had driven him further into madness, until, finally, he had shot himself. But without her friend by her side, she simply didn't have the courage.

And she was so tired. She and Marianne needed more help in the café, but there wasn't a soul she could think of who could replace Gladys, even if she could have afforded to do so.

With a deep breath, she pulled herself together and stood up. For a moment she stared into the café, and the blurry face of a woman on the other side of the celluloid window grinned mockingly back at her. Anger flashed through her and, straightening her shoulders, she whirled around to glare across the square at the women standing outside Turners' Grocery. 'Show's over, ladies,' she yelled. Then, picking up the bucket, she strode back into the café.

'If you're not careful, they'll be cartin' you off to the funny farm, Nell,' the woman who'd been watching her remarked.

'If you're not careful, you'll need to find somewhere else to get your breakfast, Lou.'

Lou Carter sniffed. 'Might just do that. Place ain't the same since Gladys died.' She looked around at the rows of dark-wood tables, only four of which were occupied. 'Used to be bustlin' this time on a Thursday mornin', but it's like a morgue in here now.' She slapped her hand to her mouth and widened her eyes. 'Oops,' she said, but there was a sly grin on her face.

'Oh, bugger off, Lou,' Nellie snapped, stalking through to the kitchen, where her eldest daughter Marianne was cutting bread at the large table in the centre of the room. Ignoring her concerned expression, she went into the scullery where she emptied the dirty water into the Belfast sink.

In the kitchen she heard Jasper's hushed voice ask, 'Has somethin' happened to make your mum start scrubbing again?'

'I don't know,' Marianne whispered back. 'She's been strange all morning – well, for weeks, really. D'you think I should talk to Dr Palmer?'

'I can hear you, you know!' Nellie said, coming back into the kitchen, drying her hands on a tea towel. 'If you have any concerns, Marianne, you discuss them with *me*.'

'Nellie,' Jasper interjected, 'you can't blame her for bein' worried. We all are.'

Ignoring his comment, Nellie threw the tea towel onto the table. 'The boys'll be here soon, so we need to shoo some of that dead wood out of the way to make room. You ready, Marianne?'

When her daughter didn't answer, Nellie put her hands on her hips. 'Oh, for God's sake, stop lookin' at me like that. The pavement needed cleaning, so I cleaned it. Like I've been doin' ever since I moved here as a bride of eighteen.'

Marianne and Jasper exchanged a look.

'And don't look at each other like that!' She clapped her hands. 'What have we got for the lads' breakfast?'

'They're getting a sausage sarnie each. But that's it, Mum. It's all I can manage until . . .' She paused and glanced at Jasper. 'Until we put in our next order,' she finished.

Nellie sighed inwardly at the reminder of another problem. 'It'll do,' she said and walked out to the café. 'Your wife chucked you out, Mr Gallagher?' She went and stood beside one of the tables where an old man was smoking a pipe as he read his newspaper.

He glanced up at her in confusion.

'Cos you been sittin' there since we opened, and I think it's time you left.'

'You can't just throw me out. I'm a payin' customer,' he muttered.

Nellie picked up his cup and saucer. 'You've been squattin' over this cup o' tea for over an hour. Get another one or get out.'

Grumbling, the old man stood up. 'You're lucky I still come here, Mrs C, I know a few as won't set foot in 'ere no more.'

'And you're more than welcome to become one of them.' Nellie walked over and opened the door for him. 'Go on, off you pop.'

'All right, I'm leavin'. Next time I'll be goin' to the Pot and Kettle. Least they leave their customers in peace.'

'You do that, love,' Nellie said. 'And be sure to give Mabel and Clarence my regards.'

High-spirited shouting made her look across the square and her heart lifted at the sight of a group of laughing men wearing khaki shorts and shirts making their way up King Street. She squinted, trying to see if her youngest son Bert was among them, but there was no sign of him, although she could see her son-in-law, Alfie.

She waved as they approached. 'Welcome, lads. Come in, come in.'

'Nice window,' Alfie remarked, nodding at the celluloid as he entered.

'Thank you, Alfie,' Nellie said. 'Some people think it's a waste of money.' She glanced over at Jasper, who rolled his eyes.

12

Lou, who was still sitting by the window, tapped on it, making it wobble. 'That's a nice bit of winder, that is. My Terence always knows the best places to get stuff.'

Nellie inwardly cursed Lou's big mouth as Jasper glanced between them, his eyebrows raised.

'Please tell me you didn't get that piece of junk from Terence Carter,' Jasper hissed as she bustled past him.

'I can't see it's any business of yours,' she snapped. 'Now, if you want to help, go get some more cups and saucers.'

Jasper sighed. 'Fine. But this conversation ain't over. Soon as things have quietened down, you an' me are gonna have a chat, cos if you've been buyin' dodgy gear from Terence Carter, then you need even more help than I realised.'

Nellie's stomach fluttered with apprehension. Little did he know just how much help she needed. Problem was, she wasn't sure anyone could help her now.

Chapter 3

'Shit!' Bert Castle leapt up from the mattress on the floor, grabbed his shorts from the dusty floor and pulled them on. He hadn't meant to fall asleep; this was meant to be a quickie to take the edge off his nerves, while he waited for Terence. He'd be here in five minutes, so he needed to get rid of the girl sharpish.

He shook her shoulder. 'Sorry, love. It's been great and all, but you need to leave. My mum's doing a team breakfast at the café and I gotta go,' he said brusquely.

A tousled head emerged from the cocoon of blankets and a pair of blue eyes blinked up at him sleepily. Clutching the blanket to her chest, the girl sat up and pushed her brown hair out of her face. 'Your mum's café? But I thought you didn't go there any more, not after . . .' She trailed off as Bert's expression turned cold.

'After the murder? After the spying?' He thrust his feet into his boots and bent to lace them up.

The girl watched him uncertainly. 'Sorry, I didn't mean . . .'

'I think you did!' He stood up. 'And my mum is not a traitor! if she was, then she'd be sitting in jail alongside that murdering bitch.'

She scowled at him. 'I never said she was. How about I come with you? I'd like to meet the famous Nellie Castle.'

'You can meet my mum any time you like. She's always there. But I won't be introducing you, understand?'

Bert glanced around the room. Like most of the buildings on Liverpool Street, the windows were boarded up, and though he kept the floor swept as best he could, the dust continued to blow through. Still, he'd managed to nick some nice blankets from the café, there were pillows and it was private. And, more importantly, just round the corner from the pub. A tremor of disgust ran through him. No matter how many pints, no matter how many girls, it never made any difference. Nothing chased away the shroud of darkness that had descended on him since Gladys died.

He looked at the girl, noting the hurt in her eyes and felt the familiar pang of self-loathing. 'Sorry, love,' he said more softly. 'Maybe see you around sometime, yeah?'

He watched as she pulled on her uniform, hating himself for making her feel bad. But he was doing her a favour. The last thing she needed was to get involved with a man like him.

You should be ashamed of yourself, Bert Castle. That girl don't deserve this, a voice said in his head. It was Gladys's voice. Always Gladys's voice, reprimanding him as she had when he was a boy.

'I'm sorry,' he whispered.

'Sorry, are you?' The girl jumped up from the mattress and tossed her hair over her shoulder. 'You know what, I don't blame that Susan for trying to shoot you!' She jabbed a finger in his chest. 'If I had a gun, I'd probably do the same.'

Bert smiled sardonically, relieved. He'd rather anger than hurt any day. 'Feel free, love,' he said, holding his arms out. 'The sooner someone puts me out of my misery the better.'

The girl glared at him for a moment, then her expression changed. 'Oh my God, you mean it, don't you?' She reached up to touch his cheek and he flinched away. 'You shouldn't be so hard on yourself,' she said softly.

Bert folded his arms across his chest. 'Just leave, will you?'

Her expression darkened. 'You bloody bastard!' Before he could stop her, she smacked him hard across the cheek, then she snatched up her bag and stamped out, her footsteps loud on the bare floorboards.

'Love you too,' he muttered, rubbing his stinging cheek. He checked his watch; he'd be here any moment. His eyes went to the corner of the room where he'd stashed a couple of jerry cans filled with diesel.

'Wouldn't mind a piece of that meself.'

Bert whirled round and scowled at the man who had crept in. He was wearing a brown coat and brown trilby and his thin lips were curved up in a lascivious smile, revealing crooked teeth.

'You got it?'

Bert gestured to the corner. 'I could only get you a couple. And it's red.'

Terence shrugged. 'Makes no odds. I can filter that out in a jiffy with a gas mask or a piece of bread. What else you got?' He rubbed his hands together.

'Sack of sugar, some tea and coffee.'

'Clever boy. I have to say, I had me doubts about you, but you're turnin' out all right. Next time try and get double, yeah?'

Bert's stomach dropped. 'But the debt's paid. You said this'd be the last time.'

'Did I?' Terence grinned at him. 'Reckon you misheard, mate. This is just the beginning.'

Bert grabbed the man by the lapels and shoved him against the wall. 'No!' he growled. 'I've done everything you've asked. More, even. So this is it, all right?'

Terence laughed. 'I don't think so. You're in too deep to get out now.'

Bert's hands went to the man's neck and he squeezed, wondering if he had the courage to finish the job. He could just leave him here, he thought frenziedly. Chances were the place would be hit by another shell before anyone discovered the body, and then no one would blink an eye.

A sudden burning pain between his legs made him let go and bend over, gasping for breath.

'Any more tricks like that, and it don't matter how many cans you bring me, I'll be havin' a word with your commandin' officer.'

'Go ahead,' Bert choked. 'I'm sure the police would be very interested to know that you're getting soldiers to steal for you so you can line your pockets.'

Terence laughed. 'You misunderstand me, mate. Just so happens, I 'ave a bit of info about your brother Jim he might find interestin'. And I reckon the rest of the community ought to know what sort of man he is and all, don't you?'

With his hands on his knees, Bert looked up at him. 'What the hell are you talking about?'

'What? You tellin' me you don't know your brother's deepest darkest secret?'

'You've got nothing on Jim, and if you want to report me, do your worst. I don't care what happens to me.'

Terence pulled Bert up by his shoulders and laughed. 'You mean to tell me you don't know about your brother's *preferences*.'

For a moment, Bert stared at him in confusion. Then suddenly something Susan had said on the day she'd shot Gladys came back to him. They'd been talking about Jim and Reenie, who had just split up. 'Well, it was never gonna last was it? What with your Jim being a nancy boy.'

He'd disregarded it at the time – nothing that woman said could be trusted – but what if she hadn't been lying?

Terence nodded. 'That's right. Your brother's a ragin' poofter. An' the question I've been askin' is, does poor Reenie Turner know? If not, I reckon she deserves the truth. And what about everyone else? They should know what sort of man he is. Don't worry, it won't take much – a word here, a whisper there, and it won't be long till the whole town knows. How d'you reckon that'd go down with your mum? Not to mention them up at the garrison. I hear they don't like that sort of thing, nor should they. It's disgustin'. An' your brother's got no business messin' with a nice girl like Reenie.'

17

'Like I said,' Bert gritted out. 'Do your worst.'

Terence narrowed his eyes. 'Righty-ho, then. I hear you're all meetin' at the café for a bit of breakfast before your football match. May as well come with you – have a chinwag with your mates and a nice cup of tea. I've got a bit of business with your mum and all.'

Bert went cold. 'Leave my mum out of it!'

Terence grinned. 'You got no idea what your mum gets up to, 'ave you? Anyway, maybe she'll be a mite more cooperative than you when I let her in on your brother's dirty little secret, eh?' He patted him on the shoulder and walked towards the door.

Bert's stomach roiled as he thought about what might happen to his brother – to his family – if Susan had been right. His mum was having a hard enough time as it was, and this would just add to the weight of grief. As for Jim . . . He'd thought his brother was happy with Reenie, but clearly he didn't know him at all, and this filled him with a confusing mixture of anger and sadness.

'Wait!'

Terence turned round, one eyebrow raised. 'Had a think, 'ave yer?'

'You've got no proof.'

'You wanna take the chance?'

Bert's shoulders sagged and he shook his head.

Terence cackled and rubbed his hands together. 'That's more like it. So, same time, same place next week, yeah? And remember, you try to get out of this, you know what'll happen.'

When he didn't answer, the man pulled Bert up by his shoulders. 'Do you understand, mate?'

Keeping his eyes closed, Bert nodded. 'I need more time,' he muttered.

'Next week,' Terence growled. 'Or face the consequences.' Then he left without a backward glance.

Bert waited for a few minutes, his mind whirling at the thought that Susan might have been right . . . If his own brother couldn't trust him with something like that, then what did that say about him? Did the others know? Was it only Bert who'd been kept in the dark? Snatching up his cap, he left the house, blinking back tears of hurt and humiliation. He had meant it when he'd told that girl he didn't care if she shot him. Surely anything was better than the hellish life he was living. But now he was trapped in this deal with the devil, because it wasn't just him who'd suffer if he stopped doing what Terence wanted.

Outside, he ducked into an alley and lit a cigarette with a shaky hand. Drawing deeply, he held the smoke in his lungs for moment, before blowing it out in one long stream. Once he'd finished, he ground the cigarette out beneath his boot, pasted a grin on his face and sauntered towards Market Square, whistling as though he didn't have a care in the world.

As he reached the square, he spotted Jimmy stepping out of Turners' grocery, smiling down at Reenie Turner, their hands clasped. Fury rose within him as he watched them walk towards the café. God, he wanted to kill Jimmy for keeping this secret from him. He'd thought they were as close as two brothers could be, but clearly Jimmy didn't feel the same, and this knowledge left him feeling as though he were alone and adrift on a stormy ocean.

Chapter 4

Once the men had been served, Marianne and Alfie escaped upstairs to the sitting room and collapsed together onto the flowered sofa. Alfie splayed his hand over her stomach. 'You sure there's only one in there?' he joked.

Marianne put her hands over his. 'I've had the same thought myself. Lily's had a listen with one of those thingies and says she can only hear one heartbeat, but I can barely see my feet, and I'm only six months gone.'

He examined her face. 'How you feeling?'

Marianne smiled tiredly. 'I'm fine, love. Honest.'

'And there's been no more trouble? No pains?'

'Of course not. Stop fussing.' In truth, since she'd nearly lost the baby three months before, every twinge and ache made her panic, but Alfie didn't need to know that.

'I'm gonna have a word with your mum. She needs to get you some help.'

'Leave it, Alf,' Marianne said sharply. 'Mum's . . . Well, she's a bit fragile at the moment. She was scrubbing the pavement again this morning. She won't talk about it, but I'm sure there's something going on. She's been acting so weird. After the raid last night, when she went in her room, I heard her let out this little cry, but she slammed the door on me before I could ask what the matter was. I'm really worried about her.'

Alfie blew out his cheeks. 'It's not just her that's suffering though. You all miss Gladys, and she needs to look out for you as well. You can't go on like this.'

Luckily at that moment, Marianne's stomach rippled and distracted. Alfie was right, but how could she explain that she was afraid her mother was going mad? Sometimes, when she couldn't sleep at night, she heard her mother wandering around the rooms downstairs, muttering to herself. And then there were the items she kept finding around the house: her mother's silver hairbrush in the pantry, her sherry glass in the oven, and the lavender bag that usually hung on her door in Polly's cage. When she'd asked about it, her mother had gone pale as a ghost and then shouted at her to mind her own business. She and her younger sister Lily had decided that if this behaviour went on much longer, they would have to take her to a doctor.

'The little madam's busy today,' Marianne said. 'She usually saves all this till I'm in bed trying to sleep.'

'You always say "she". Will you mind if it's a boy?' Alfie asked softly.

Marianne smiled. 'It's a girl. I've seen her. A tiny little thing with bright blonde hair and blue eyes. Just like Daisy.' It had been six months since her friend had died during a shell attack, but she still thought of her every day.

'But what if it's a boy?'

'Don't you want a girl?' she asked, putting her hand over his where it rested on her stomach.

'I don't care what it is, love. Boy, girl, lettuce.' He smiled. 'Whatever it is, I'll cherish them till the day I die.'

Marianne leant forward and kissed him softly on the lips. 'I love you, Alfie Lomax. And you're right. What does it matter? But . . . a girl would be nice, don't you think?'

Alfie rolled her over onto her back, careful not to crush the baby. 'I've got precisely one hour before I have to be back. Will your mum mind if we go upstairs for a bit?' He waggled his eyebrows suggestively.

'I thought you'd never ask,' she whispered.

A sudden sharp kick made Alfie groan. 'How can I have my wicked way with you if that creature is listening in?'

Marianne pushed him off her with a laugh. 'She can't understand, you daft ha'porth! And she's not a creature; she's our baby.'

'Marianne, Alfie!' Nellie's piercing voice made them stare at each other in dismay.

Alfie sighed. 'Looks like it'll have to wait,' he said ruefully, helping Marianne to her feet.

When they got downstairs, Marianne's eyes widened as she took in the sight of a short, thin police constable, with a wispy brown moustache, standing in front of the counter, one hand clutched round the neck of a boy with wayward brown hair. Behind them the soldiers were looking on with amusement.

'Let go of him, Roger!' Marianne snapped, rushing forward to grasp her son's arm.

Constable Roger Humphries scowled. 'You should be thanking me, Marianne. This young man and his equally delinquent friend will end up in jail if they keep going the way they are.'

Marianne sighed. 'And where is Freddie?' she asked.

'I have just deposited him at the fish shop, and Phyllis Perkins told me in no uncertain terms that young Freddie will *not* be going to the football match later.'

'Donny?' Marianne looked at her son, who had so far kept his head bowed and refused to look up. 'What did you do this time?'

When he still didn't answer, Alfie stepped forward and bent to look in his face. 'Don, look at me, mate.'

Reluctantly, the boy's head came up, his grey eyes large and solemn.

'What did you do?' Alfie asked gently.

Donny looked briefly at the constable, then back to the floor.

Just then the door crashed open. 'Panic over, everyone, I have arrived!'

Briefly, all eyes turned as Bert walked in, followed closely by Reenie and Jim.

They stopped when they saw the tableau standing by the counter. 'What's going on?' Jim asked, looking from Donny to Roger Humphries.

Bert laughed. 'Been up to your old tricks, Donny boy?' he asked coming over to ruffle his hair. 'I taught the lad everything he knows,' he said proudly.

'Don't encourage him, Bert,' Marianne snapped. Donny idolised his uncle, so his amusement would only serve to spur her son on.

'This is no laughing matter,' Roger Humphries said pompously. 'Donald and Freddie were caught piling sandbags outside a telephone box on the high street.'

Sniggers from the soldiers made the policeman whirl round. 'You wouldn't think it was funny if you were the one inside!'

Alfie's lips twitched. 'Donny, did you trap Constable Humphries in the telephone box?'

Donny peeped up at him, sensing a softening in his stepfather. 'Sorry, Alfie,' he said.

'"Sorry, Alfie"? What about "Sorry, Constable Humphries"?' the policeman exclaimed. 'I'm warning you, Donald Castle, one more thing, just *one* more, and it's the juvenile courts for you. Think yourself lucky I'm letting you off this time.'

Marianne sighed. 'That's not funny, Donny. People rely on those telephones and your actions were thoughtless and selfish! Now apologise to Constable Humphries.'

'Sorry, Constable Humphries,' he mumbled obediently, though he didn't sound sorry.

Marianne nodded. 'And if Freddie's not allowed to the football, then you certainly aren't either.'

Donny gasped. 'But that's not fair! I *promised* Uncle Bert I'd be there.'

Jasper stepped forward and put a hand on his shoulder. 'Do what your mum says, Don.'

'I was speaking to Mum!' Donny shouted.

'That's it, young man!' Nellie said, reaching beneath the counter and pulling out a wooden spoon. 'You don't speak to your elders and betters like that.' Before Marianne could stop her, she smacked Donny smartly on his behind.

'Ow, Gran! That hurt.' He glared at her.

The policeman put his helmet back on. 'That's more like it. Spare the rod and spoil the child, that's what my mother always said, and it didn't do me no harm. But this is his *final* warning!' Then he turned on his heel and marched out.

As soon as the door closed, the place erupted into laughter as the soldiers came to slap Donny on the back. 'Nice one, son,' one of them said.

'No, it's not a nice one.' Marianne caught her son's arm and pulled him towards the staircase just inside the kitchen door. 'Go to your room and don't come out till you've written a letter of apology to Constable Humphries. And after that, you're going to spend the rest of the day in your room. Do I make myself clear?'

'But, Mum, we only did it cos he's always pickin' on us.'

'Do I make myself clear?' Marianne pointed to the stairs.

Head hanging, Donny nodded and made his way towards the stairs. At the bottom he turned to Alfie. 'Will you come help me, Alfie?'

'Course I will, though I hope you don't expect me to write anything.' He looked at Marianne with a resigned look and mouthed, 'Another time?'

She nodded, grateful to have his support, but furious that once again she wouldn't be able to spend some precious time with her husband.

As they disappeared up the stairs, she rounded on her mother. 'Don't ever raise your hand to Donny again! He's *my* child and I don't hold with that sort of thing.'

'Which is why he's runnin' rings round you,' Nellie said, waving the wooden spoon for emphasis. 'But shall we continue this conversation when we don't have an audience?' She nodded to the men. 'Anyway, you shouldn't worry. Bert were the same as a lad but he's turned out all right.'

Marianne looked over at her brother who was standing in the middle of a circle of men, tall and good-looking as ever, with his dark-brown hair and bright-blue eyes, but he looked thin and tired, his usual sparkle missing. But then, they'd all been missing their usual sparkle.

'Bert wasn't brought up during wartime, Mum. It's different for the kids today; what with no school to keep them on the straight and narrow, most of their friends gone, and them left playing in the ruins of houses or stuck in the caves, knowing that at any moment a bloody great shell could drop out of the sky and kill them and their families. Is it any wonder they're running wild?'

Reenie came up beside Marianne and put an arm around her friend's shoulders. 'It's true, Mrs C. The kids have gone feral round here. Amount of times we've had to scrub graffiti off the walls, and they're always trying to sneak in and nick stuff out the shop. All we can do is keep an eye on them. Freddie and Don are good lads, it's just their lives have been turned upside down. But short of sending them away, what can we do? After the last time, Wilf won't even consider it for Freddie.'

'And I promised I wouldn't send Don away again. But . . .' Marianne shrugged.

'Oh no, you don't!' Nellie exclaimed. 'After what happened last time? We nearly lost him, Marianne, so if you're thinking of sending him away again, it'll be over my dead body,' Nellie warned.

'That's the problem, though,' Marianne said. 'It might just come to that.'

'Stuff and nonsense,' Nellie tutted. 'The boy just needs a bit of discipline. And maybe a job.'

Marianne exclaimed. 'He's only eleven!'

'So? Jasper were eight when he started earnin',' Nellie retorted.

'Those were different times, Nell,' Jasper intervened. 'The old queen were on the throne, and folk weren't the same. And it were just me and Mum. I had no choice.'

'So you think he should just take everything for granted, do you?'

'*Everything?*' Marianne said. 'What? The bombs, the shells, the lack of food, the lack of schooling, Gladys dying . . . For God's sake, Mum! Don't you understand? The kids . . .' She drew in a deep breath. 'The kids have got it worse than all of us.'

'Yeah, you should cut him a bit of slack,' Jimmy said.

'A bit of slack? If we gave that kid any more slack, he'd float across the Channel. What does Wilf think about Freddie's behaviour, Reenie?'

'He don't exactly confide in me. I'm just Fred's aunt, after all. But Wilf can be scary when he's crossed.'

'Exactly. He gets discipline. Which is what I were tryin' to do.'

Marianne snatched the spoon from her mother's hand. 'You've got to let me do this my way, Mum. So if you don't need me, I'm going to go up there to make sure he writes that letter.'

Jasper interjected then. 'Course we don't need you. You go on up, love. Me and your mum will sort this lot out.'

Marianne climbed the stairs, her thoughts spinning. She was well aware Donny needed discipline and education. But above all, he needed to be safe. And it was within her power to deliver all three. If only she had the courage.

Chapter 5

Edie Castle dumped the heavy tea urn on the rickety trestle table Marge had erected at the edge of the field beneath the grey brooding walls of the castle, and pressed her hand into the small of her back. Spending most of her days bent over the bonnets of cars and trucks, or lying on the cold cement peering up at chassis was proving to be more and more difficult. She wasn't sure how much longer she'd be able to keep working at the garage at this rate and she was guiltily aware of the extra burden she was putting on Mr Pearson. Soon she'd just be an extra mouth to feed. Two extra mouths, she corrected herself, swallowing down the sense of panic that thought always brought with it.

If only Bill were here; he was the only one who could calm her fears, but after a hasty wedding and just one night together, he'd left to begin his operational training with the RAF. She stared at the thin gold band he'd put on her finger two months before. If not for this tangible proof that they were married, she might not believe it. But what kept her up at night was the thought that it might be the only time they'd ever have together. She kissed the ring and closed her eyes. 'Come back safe to me, my love. I'm not sure I can do this without you.'

'God's sake, Edie, I said I'd do it. You shouldn't be lifting heavy stuff in your condition.'

Edie jumped as a woman walked towards her carrying a tray of tin mugs. Tall and statuesque, she was elegant in her navy-blue Wren uniform, her red hair bright against the overcast sky.

'I'm fine,' Edie said, only just resisting the temptation to snap. Marge lived and worked at the castle and was one of her sister Marianne's best friends, but she and Edie had grown close over the last few weeks following the bombing of the garage and Edie and Bill's efforts to prove that Mr Pearson – his uncle and her boss – wasn't a spy. Now that she rarely saw her sisters, Marge had become one of her closest friends.

'Really?' Marge put the tray on the table and examined Edie's face. 'Ah, love.' She put her arms around her. 'You missing Bill?'

Edie pulled away. 'I'm fine,' she said again, wiping her face.

Marge looked sceptical, but tactfully changed the subject. 'Look at all this.' She waved her arm at the table, which was crowded with plates of sandwiches and biscuits for them to sell to the spectators, along with jugs of squash for the kids. And the obligatory bowl for donations to War Weapons Week. 'If we did this every time a group of men decided to kick a ball around, we'd have even less food than we already do.'

'I think it's nice that your padre arranged it. And anyway, it's to raise money for the war effort.'

Marge sighed. 'Yeah, bless Phil,' she said, digging in her pocket for a cigarette.

'Don't tell me you've had enough of him already?' Marge and Padre Philip had been going out with each other for a couple of months now, and from what she'd seen, he was no match for her friend, who's fiery hair matched her nature.

Marge lit her cigarette and blew out a long puff of smoke. 'Course not,' she said. 'He's the sweetest man in the world. I just wish he'd remember to be as nice to himself as he is to everyone around him. Still, least he's not a pompous know-all like Rodney.' She grinned.

Edie felt compelled to defend her eldest brother. 'In many ways Phil and Rod are very alike.' She smiled slyly at her friend. She liked Phil, but she'd much prefer Marge and Rodney were together. She couldn't think of anyone she'd like better for a sister-in-law.

Marge let out a brief laugh. 'You've got to be joking?'

'Nope. They're both always trying to do the best for everyone. Just Phil shows it by doing nice things and constantly asking if you want to talk about anything, while Rodney shows it by bossing people around. They're two sides of the same coin.'

Marge snorted. 'Chalk and cheese more like. See, the thing about Rod is, he wants to boss you around *and* he expects you to be there whenever he needs you. Whereas Phil . . . Well, Phil is just plain lovely. There are no sides to him.' She took another puff on her cigarette, then blew it out slowly. 'None at all,' she murmured quietly.

A tall thin man wearing a flat cap and blue overalls ambled towards them from the other side of the field, where Pearson's Garage stood. 'Pour me a cuppa, before I get back to work, love,' he said to Edie. 'Some of us can't spend all day watching football matches and drinking tea.'

'Aren't you going to watch, Mr Pearson?' Marge bustled up to the table and filled a tin mug for him.

'You seen the forecourt?' he asked, pulling a pipe from his blue overall pocket.

'You need more help round here,' Marge said briskly. 'There must be some young lad in the town who's keen to learn how to fix cars.'

'Steady on, Marge. I'm not ready to give up yet!' Edie exclaimed.

'I am on the lookout, as it happens, but I need someone with experience. I can't spend time teachin' as well as all the rest.'

'Oh, Edie can do that,' Marge responded.

Edie snatched up the mug of tea Marge had just poured and passed it over to her boss. 'Weren't you the one just moaning about my brother bossing everyone around and thinking he knows best?'

Marge tutted. 'I was just saying. Anyway, seeing as you're all sorted, I'm just gonna dash back and get Jeanie to join us. I hear

Bert's persuaded your mum to give the army team breakfast at the café. Which sounds a lot better than anything our lot'll get at the NAAFI.'

Edie folded her arms across her chest. 'I wouldn't know what Mum's doing,' she said tightly. 'Nor would I care.'

Marge rolled her eyes. 'Christ alive! Don't tell me you're *still* not talking to her? How long are you going to keep this up?'

'Forever,' Edie retorted baldly. 'And before you ask, it's none of your business, so just leave it.'

Marge shrugged. 'Whatever you say, love.'

After she'd gone, Edie was uncomfortably aware of Mr Pearson's eyes on her. 'What?' she said challengingly.

Her boss took a long sip of tea before saying, 'Whatever it is your mum's done, you're gonna have to forgive her one day.' He nodded at her stomach. ''Cos you're gonna need her soon enough.'

Edie scowled. 'I'd rather live on the streets than accept help from *her*.' She tossed her head and started to walk back to the garage. 'While we've got a few minutes, I'm gonna look at the fuel pump on the Morris.'

Mr Pearson shook his head as he followed her. God knew he loved Edie like a daughter, but he was no substitute for her mother. Especially when it came to looking after babies.

'And don't give me that look,' Edie snapped, her back still to him.

Her boss chortled. 'A man can't even give a look anymore?'

Edie peered over her shoulder and smiled fondly. 'You can give me any look you like, Mr P. All I ask is that you don't mention my mother again.'

Edie's thoughts remained on her mother as she bent over the bonnet of the car. She'd meant what she'd said – she never wanted to speak to her again. She'd lied to her all her life about her father's death, telling her again and again that she hadn't been there. But she had, and now her memories of that day had returned, her nightmares had intensified. Where once she used to dream about a loud bang and blood on the wall, now she saw her father sitting in his chair, his face blown away. And her mother was holding the gun.

Chapter 6

'Time to go, lads!' Bert stood up, and with a flurry of movement, the men pushed their chairs back from the tables and made for the door, rowdily pushing and shoving at each other.

'And where do you think you're going, Jimmy?' Nellie called as Jimmy and Reenie prepared to leave.

Jimmy looked at his mother questioningly.

'Look at this place.' She gestured at the tables, each piled with dirty crockery and overflowing ashtrays. And hovering over it all, a grey haze of cigarette smoke hung like a raincloud. 'Your sister needs to rest, and me and Jasper could do with a hand.'

'It's fine, Nell,' Jasper said. 'We'll manage.'

Casting a quick, meaningful look at Jimmy, Reenie took off her jacket. 'Don't worry, Mrs C, if the four of us do it, it won't take long.'

Sighing, Jimmy nodded reluctantly.

'As long as you're sure, love,' Jasper said. 'We wouldn't want to keep you from your courtin'.' He winked.

Reenie blushed and looked back at Jim who smiled ruefully at her.

'I don't suppose it'll matter if we miss the first half. But you need more help round here, Mum. You won't be able to run the café on your own once the baby comes. You needed help when Gladys was alive. I don't understand why you're being so stubborn about it now,' he said, exasperated.

'We manage, thank you very much,' Nellie snapped.

'Clearly you don't, or you wouldn't need me and Reenie to help now.'

'I been tryin' to tell her the same thing for weeks, but your mum is more stubborn than the mangy old mule up Crabble Hill.' Jasper picked up some plates and walked into the kitchen, chuckling to himself.

Nellie opened her mouth to give him a piece of her mind, but Reenie intervened.

'Chuck me a pinny, and we'll have this sorted in two shakes. You go on up to the castle, Jim, I'll see you there.'

'What, and leave you here by yourself. No chance. Who knows what you might get up to while my back's turned?' He winked and planted a hard kiss on her lips.

Reenie giggled. 'You must know I only have eyes for you.'

Jim snaked an arm around her waist and gave her a squeeze. 'I should think so too. You're not likely to do better.'

She turned into his embrace and put her arms around his neck. 'Do you really want to watch the match?' she asked quietly, casting a swift glance over her shoulder to make sure Nellie wasn't listening.

'Why?' Jimmy whispered. 'What else did you have in mind?'

'Well . . . Maybe once we've got this lot sorted, we could find a quiet spot, spend a bit of time together . . .' She smiled in what she hoped was a seductive manner.

Jimmy lowered his head. 'And why would you want to do that?' he said, his lips twitching. 'I hope you're not suggesting we get up to anything . . . naughty.' He breathed this last into her ear, making her body tingle.

'And what if I was?' she murmured.

'Then I would most definitely think about it.' He lowered his head and kissed her deeply, parting her lips with his tongue.

Reenie responded, her arms tightening about his neck. But a sudden clatter from the kitchen made her jump and cast an anxious look over his shoulder.

'Don't mind me!' Nellie stood in the kitchen door holding a bright pink apron, but although her voice was stern, she was smiling, her good humour restored.

'Sorry, Mum.' Jim turned towards his mother, while Reenie pressed her face against his back, stifling her laughter against his cotton shirt.

'So, when are you gonna make it official?' Nellie asked.

'None of your business,' Jim replied shortly.

'Don't leave it too long, or she'll be stolen from under your nose. And you won't do better for yourself, I can promise you that.'

'Thanks, Mrs C,' Reenie said, peeping round Jimmy's back.

Nellie held the apron out to her. 'I'm only speaking the truth. Now, sooner you finish, sooner you can go canoodlin'.'

Reenie sighed happily as Jim pressed a quick kiss on the top of her head and went to help Jasper with the washing up. It was widely accepted that Bert was the better looking of the three Castle brothers, but Reenie didn't agree. Bert might have the most perfect features and more muscular physique, but he was cocky and far too aware of the effect he had on women. Jimmy was the opposite. He never sized women up as though wondering whether he could get them into bed; he talked to them like human beings rather than a challenge to be overcome, and it made her love him even more.

Half an hour later, the café had been cleared, and with Alfie gone, Marianne had returned to the kitchen to make food for a group of ATS girls who had arrived.

'Off you go, lovebirds,' Nellie said cheerfully. 'Me and Marianne can take it from here.'

Reenie began to take the apron off, then stopped. 'I nearly forgot, have you lost this?' She reached into the pocket and pulled out a small crucifix on a gold chain.

Nellie paled and snatched it from her hand. 'Where did you get this?' she gasped.

'It was in the pocket, so I thought . . .' She glanced uncertainly at Jimmy, who shrugged.

'You better go,' Nellie muttered. 'You don't want to miss the match.'

'If you're sure, Mum? You don't look too good,' Jimmy said.

'I said go!' she snapped.

Reenie jumped, grabbed her jacket from the back of a chair and sped towards the front door, Jimmy following close behind.

Chapter 7

Outside, Reenie turned to Jim. 'What was that all about?'

'God knows. But seems odd, a necklace in the pocket like that . . .' He shrugged.

'Aunt Ethel's worried about your mum. We all are. And she was scrubbing the pavement again this morning. She's still grieving hard for Gladys.'

Jim sighed. 'It's not just about Gladys, though. I reckon Edie's part of the problem. She's broken Mum's heart by refusing to speak to her. I just wish I knew what was behind it. But she won't tell anyone what happened; she just disappeared up the hill and then married Bill without inviting any of us to the wedding. I'd have expected Mum to be up there demanding to be seen, but she's stayed away. I don't know what to make of it. But if I had to guess, whatever it is, Mum knows she's in the wrong.'

Reenie shook her head. 'There's always something with you lot, isn't there?'

Jim looked down at her with a small frown. 'What do you mean?'

'Well, aside from everything that happened with Gladys, Bert and Susan, there was Hester and the spying, and the fact that Jasper is Lily's dad and then there was that bloke that turned up working at the hospital . . . What was his name?'

Jimmy tightened his lips. 'We don't talk about him.'

'But isn't he your brother? Born on the same day as you?'

36

'I said, we don't talk about him,' Jimmy snapped. Then, seeing her hurt expression, he softened his tone. 'Sorry, love, but all that stuff – Dad having another son, Jasper being Lily's dad . . . I try not to think too much about it.' He huffed. 'But yeah, you're right: there is always something. Let's hope we can go a few months scandal-free, eh?'

Reenie took his arm. 'There surely can't be anything else, can there?'

Jimmy grinned. 'I'm pretty sure all the skeletons have been shaken out of the Castle closet.'

'Well, even if there are more, I don't mind. I love you, secrets and all.'

Just then her attention was caught by a tall man with a black beard and shaggy black hair on the other side of the square. His shoulders were drooping with weariness as he walked with his head down towards Perkins' Fish, which stood next door to her aunt and uncle's grocery shop.

Wilf Perkins worked on the lifeboats, and from the look of him he'd had a bad night. Reenie's heart went out to him. Every boat and ship that sailed through the Channel was in constant danger, not only from bombs and shells, but also from the ter- rifyingly fast German E-Boats, not to mention the mines that littered the water. Phyllis Perkins had talked with pride about how many lives her son had saved, but he'd also lost a few. And though they rarely spoke these days, Reenie knew it must weigh on his mind.

On impulse, she stepped into the road, causing a bus to beep loudly and a cyclist to swerve round her. But she barely noticed. 'Wilf,' she called.

He stopped and waited for her to approach.

'Are you all right?' she asked, putting her hand on his arm. Their relationship hadn't been good for many years, but even so, she hated to see him looking so defeated.

Instead of dismissing her as he had so often in the past, Wilf covered her hand with his own and gave it a squeeze. 'I was going to come and see you later. Right now, I need some food and sleep, but after . . .' He shuffled his feet. 'Can we talk?'

Reenie's eyes widened. 'Why?'

He shook his head. 'Later, Reens, all right?'

'Has someone died?' she asked.

He smiled sadly. 'Lots of people have died. And not a thing I could do about it. But no, it's nothing like that.'

'What then? You're worrying me.'

Jimmy walked up then. 'All right, Wilf, mate. Tough night?' he asked sympathetically.

Wilf stared at him with a strange expression then nodded. 'Yeah. Yeah, you could say that.'

'Sorry to add to your woes, but Donny and Fred have been in trouble again,' he said with a slight laugh. 'Your mum's banned Fred from going to the football.'

Wilf grimaced. 'Just what I need,' he muttered shortly.

There was an awkward pause and Reenie shifted uncomfortably, feeling annoyed. Wilf had never been much of a talker, but this felt more like rudeness. Although, his attitude had only changed once Jimmy had arrived, she realised, glancing between the two men in bewilderment.

'Well, me and Jim aren't banned, so we're off there now. But from the looks of you, I'm guessing you won't be joining us,' Reenie said brightly.

Wilf shook his head. For a moment, his eyes seemed to focus on the arm Jim had put around Reenie's shoulder, then he turned and went into the fish shop.

'I hope he's all right,' Reenie said worriedly as they walked away. 'I mean, Wilf's a moody bugger, but he seemed more . . . I don't know, upset, than usual.'

'The things those lifeboat men must see would make the strongest man weep. Churchill goes on about the pilots being heroes, and they are, but that lot going out into danger day and night to save lives are just as heroic.'

Reenie looked over her shoulder; Wilf was standing at the door of Perkins' Fish watching them, though the shadow cast by the green and white awning that stretched over the front of the shop hid his expression. Yes, they were heroes, and she knew Wilf had seen things no one should ever have to deal with, but he'd been doing the job for months now, and she'd not seen him look so disturbed in all that time.

She tried to put it to the back of her mind as she and Jim made their way up Castle Street, but the look on Wilf's face when he said he needed to talk wouldn't leave her. They'd been close when they were younger – more than close. He'd taught her to sail and to fish, and they'd spent hours out on the water, laughing and joking as she helped pull the catch in. She'd loved him so much, and she'd thought he'd loved her too. But in fact, he'd just seen her as a sister at best, a mate at worst. As she'd discovered when he suddenly proposed to her sister June.

She felt the familiar tightening of her throat as she remembered that day; so long ago now, but as fresh in her mind as if it had happened only yesterday. God, she'd been a fool. Her heart went out to her younger self as she remembered how she had cried for hours, her head buried in her pillow as she'd tried to muffle the sound.

Her nephew Freddie had been born soon after the wedding – a little too soon, in fact, so it was clear that while she and Wilf had been spending time together, he'd also been sleeping with her sister.

To be fair, Wilf had never made her any promises, nor had they shared anything but the occasional innocent kiss. But he must have known how she felt. Yet he'd snuck around behind her back and left it to June to break the news to her. Her sister's expression when she'd told her had been a mixture of triumph and malice. How she'd hated her in that moment.

June had died of cancer when Freddie was tiny and, God forgive her, Reenie had felt nothing but relief that she was gone; it was a secret shame that she had never told another soul.

'Penny for them?' Jimmy asked.

She shook her head and smiled up at him. 'Oh, nothing. I was just worrying about Wilf.'

Jimmy's eyebrows rose. 'I thought you didn't like him.'

'I don't,' Reenie said quickly. 'But I've known him all my life. He's family. Anyway, we used to be good friends.'

'Did you?' Jimmy sounded surprised and Reenie realised that during the years she and Wilf had been close, Jim had still been at junior school. In fact, he'd only been ten when she'd left school at fifteen. And when she'd had her heart broken, Jimmy had still been running around in short trousers. She didn't usually notice their age difference, but just then, she felt ancient. Jim was twenty-four now, and she was nearly thirty. Thirteen years ago, he'd been eleven, while she'd been considered an adult. But she'd just been a girl, she thought. With a fragile heart.

'It was a long time ago,' she said airily. She'd never talked about her long-ago feelings for Wilf to anyone – not even Marge or Marianne, her two closest friends. And thank God she hadn't; she wouldn't have been able to bear their pity when he'd married June. Still, there was no point revisiting old hurts, she thought, squeezing Jimmy's hand. Especially as she'd found love again with a man who actually seemed to love her back.

Wilf watched them until they turned into Castle Street and disappeared. Then he made his way slowly up the stairs to his bedroom and slumped down on the bed, rubbing his hands over his face.

He was exhausted, but felt too anxious to sleep. Instead his mind kept going over what had happened that night. What he'd seen . . . *who* he'd seen . . .

What the hell was he going to do? Because whatever he did, he had a feeling Reenie would get hurt.

And God knew he'd hurt that girl enough.

Chapter 8

As soon as they'd gone, Nellie slumped down on a chair, the necklace clutched in her hand. She lifted the apron to her nose; beneath the usual smell of fried food and cigarettes, she could detect a hint of rose water. 'Why are you doing this to me?' she whispered. In her mind's eye, she saw herself outside, Gladys's head in her lap, her blood soaking the pavement. And glinting at her neck was a gold crucifix.

'Nellie?' Jasper came and sat beside her. 'What's going on?'

'I think Gladys is haunting me,' she whispered, unable to keep it to herself anymore.

When Jasper stared at her in disbelief, she held up the necklace. 'It's Gladys's. Reenie found it in the pocket of the apron, but I swear to God, it weren't there yesterday. I launder those pinnies every other day.'

Jasper frowned and took it from her, examining it closely. 'You're being daft, love. These are two a penny. It could be anyone's.'

'Then how did it end up in the apron pocket?' Nellie said, her voice high and shaky.

Jasper shrugged. 'There's bound to be a logical explanation. Maybe one of the customers dropped it and Marianne found it.'

'She'd have given it to me,' Nellie said.

'Maybe she forgot.'

She lifted the apron to her nose again and swallowed back the nausea. 'She's haunting me!' she said again.

'What are you talking about?'

'Smell it!' She thrust the apron under Jasper's nose.

'It just smells like the café. Cigarettes and cookin',' he said, bewildered.

'Smell it again. It reeks of rose water.'

Obligingly, Jasper held it to his nose again, then shook his head. 'Look, it's not that busy. Me and Marianne can manage, so why don't you have a lie-down, love?'

Nellie stared at him mutely. The last place she wanted to go was her bedroom, but she couldn't tell him that – nor why.

'Go on,' he said gently, nodding towards the stairs.

'Can you stay with me this afternoon?' Nellie asked, feeling ridiculous. After all, she wasn't alone here. Marianne was in the kitchen and Donny was sulking in his room. And no doubt there'd be a few more customers. She stared mournfully through the plastic window, willing people to come in. But as had happened so often over the past weeks, few of them did.

Jasper hesitated a moment. 'I've got something I need to do, but I can come back later.'

'What you doing?'

'That's none of your business, woman.'

She examined his face. 'Why do you look so shifty?' she asked suspiciously.

'Shifty?' he said with an innocent smile. 'You know me, Nell, my life is an open book. Give me an hour, all right? I'll be back soon as I can.'

Nellie nodded wearily and stood up, the necklace clutched in her hand, the sharp edges of the cross digging into her palm.

She went into the kitchen and held it over the bin. For a moment she watched it twirling above the rubbish, the light glinting off it. Gladys had treasured this necklace, she couldn't just throw it away. So instead, with shaking hands, she fastened it around her neck, tucking it under the collar of her green blouse.

With Nellie out of sight, Jasper surreptitiously sniffed the apron again. Rose water. He hadn't wanted to lie to Nellie, but he didn't know what else to do. He knew she was struggling – her scrubbing at the non-existent blood outside made that plain enough. But this sudden belief that she was being haunted meant that she was having a harder time than he'd realised.

There were two explanations: either someone had dropped the necklace and one of the others had found it and put it in the pocket. Or someone had put it there deliberately to scare Nellie – although why, he couldn't begin to fathom. As for the scent . . . the only person he knew for sure who wore this scent was Gladys – she used to collect rose petals every summer and make gallons of the stuff. But who else had worn this apron? He thought back over the past couple of days and realised that it could only be Marianne or Reenie.

He let out a deep sigh. So, either Gladys was haunting her or someone was causing mischief. And seeing as he didn't believe in ghosts, his money was on the latter. Was this why Nellie had been so unlike herself recently? Aside from the grief, was someone going out of their way to frighten her? The question was who and why.

Jasper stuffed the apron into his pocket and stood up. Time enough to return to this problem later. For now, he needed to send a telegram. Nellie needed help, and he knew just the person to give it. The problem was, he was pretty sure Nellie wouldn't agree.

Chapter 9

'You might want to do some more stretches, boys!' Marge was standing on the touchline of the makeshift football pitch, watching as the twelve men in navy blue shorts and white shirts stood around chatting aimlessly.

A slim, brown-haired man winked and grinned. 'Like this?' He bent over and looked at her through his legs.

Marge's friend Jeanie let out a loud wolf whistle.

'That's right, Phil, exactly like that. Now the rest of you do it,' Marge called.

Laughing, the other men went to stand beside Phil and bent over.

'What are they doing?' Edie walked up to them.

'We were just encouraging the guys to show us what they got . . . And to be honest, I've seen more meat in the naafi's stew,' Marge said loudly.

'Gotta be better than what you've got!' one of the men said snidely, standing up to glare at her.

Marge raised her eyebrows at him. 'Ah, diddums, did I hurt your feelings? Tough, isn't it, having comments made about your figure? You wouldn't last five minutes as a woman.' She waved her hand at him dismissively.

Edie laughed. 'You are awful, Marge!' God, she loved this woman. How could Rodney have been so stupid to have given up his chance with her?

Marge grinned. 'I do my best.'

'Blimey, Edie, where'd that come from?' Jeanie's eyes were focused on Edie's stomach.

Edie cursed inwardly and buttoned up her jacket. So far, she'd managed to hide her growing stomach under baggy clothes and her donkey jacket. But Jeanie's sly expression, suggested the secret would soon be out, and there'd be more than one person busily counting their fingers and realising that the baby couldn't be Bill's.

She pointedly put her left hand on her stomach, displaying her wedding ring. 'What can I say? Bill's a fast worker,' she said.

Jeanie raised an eyebrow sceptically. 'From the look of you, I'd say you're at least five months gone. And I could've sworn Bill only got back at New Year. So either you're having the biggest baby ever, or someone's got a little cuckoo in the nest.'

'That's enough, Jeanie,' Marge said sharply. 'Plenty of people jump the gun, there's no shame in that.'

'There's jumping the gun,' Jeanie said, 'and then there's straight-up lying. I just hope you're prepared for the consequences, Edie. Cos there'll be a lot of people putting two and two together and getting four once the baby's born.'

'Me and Bill understand each other and that's all that matters,' Edie snapped.

Jeanie held up her hands. 'Keep your hair on, love. You'll get no judgement from me. There but for the grace of God and all that.'

'Amen to that,' Marge said, fishing out her cigarette case.

Edie forced a smile. She hated thinking about her pregnancy. Hated the very fact of it. It didn't matter that Bill accepted it – accepted *her* – despite the baby not being his. What mattered was that *she* hadn't accepted it. She longed to feel the happy anticipation that Marianne felt. But she just couldn't.

This was Greg's baby, and the last time she'd seen him he'd tried to hit her, and somehow, the fury and disgust she felt for allowing herself to be duped by a man like that had transferred to the poor innocent child she carried.

Even if the baby had been Bill's she didn't feel ready to be a mother. Especially now she was motherless herself. She would never admit it to anyone but the absence of her mother – so forceful and dominant – had left her feeling cast adrift. And the baby just made it worse. What she wanted most was to go far, far away and start again with Bill. But she was trapped – not only by her promise to Bill to stay in Dover and help his uncle with the garage, but once she had the baby, she'd be even more stuck because she'd never find a job anywhere else with a baby in tow.

'Want one?' Marge held her cigarette case out to her.

Edie accepted a cigarette and, once lit, breathed in deeply and held her breath, imagining the trail of grey smoke wafting through her veins, spreading throughout her body and slipping into her womb, engulfing the little life inside her until it disappeared. She closed her eyes, and willed it to happen. But then her lungs started to hurt so she blew the smoke out on a long exhale, watching it disperse in the cold air, her mind dripping with guilt. *I'm sorry, little one. It's not your fault.*

'Have you heard from Bill?' Marge asked.

'He's still doing operational training,' she said flatly. 'We got one day and one night after we were married and then he was gone.'

Marge tutted sympathetically. 'He'll be back soon, love.'

Edie looked up at the sky. 'Will he? Planes fall out of the sky every day. Chances are, I'll never see him again.' She took another long drag of her cigarette.

A shout interrupted the awkward silence that had fallen between the women, and they looked over to see a group of men in khaki shorts and jerseys jogging to the centre of the field, a tall, impossibly good-looking man with a ball under his arm leading the way.

'I see Bert's none the worse for wear after Mavis threw him out of the Oak for fighting the other night,' Marge murmured.

'Lord love a duck!' Jeanie sighed dramatically. 'Your brother is one good-looking hunk of a man, Edie.' She fluffed her blonde hair and let out a loud wolf whistle.

Bert looked over and grinned. But when he caught sight of his sister, the smile died on his lips and he turned away.

Trying to disguise her hurt, Edie said dryly, 'I thought you had more sense, Jeanie.'

'I don't want to marry the man!' Jeanie exclaimed. 'But I reckon me and him could have a bit of a laugh.' She nudged Edie's arm. 'If you know what I mean.'

Edie wrinkled her nose. 'Susan Blake didn't try to shoot him cos he was nice. Not that I'm blaming Bert – but it might give you a clue as to why you should stay away from him.'

Jeanie shivered dramatically. 'The whiff of danger makes him all the more irresistible.'

Edie rolled her eyes at Marge, who grinned back at her. 'Don't look at me. I've tried to talk sense into her, but she doesn't listen to a word I say.'

'And why should I? When you've thrown over the deliciously brooding Rodney for St Philip. I mean, don't get me wrong, Phil's a lovely bloke, but he's not the man for you. And the longer you keep lying to him and yourself, the worse his heart will be broken when you finally ditch him.'

Marge pursed her lips. 'Shut up, Jeanie. You don't know what you're talking about. So go ahead, throw yourself at Bert. But don't come crying to me when he walks away before you've had time to pull up your knickers.'

'You're just jealous, cos you know the perfect padre will never give you half the fun in a lifetime as I'd get in one night with Bert.'

'Girls, girls, can you stop talking about my brother like that! Look, Jeanie, go get him, if that's what you want. As for you, Marge, you do know that poor Rodney's been pining for you, don't you?'

Marge's eyebrows rose. 'Pining? I don't think so. Did you know he's asked for a transfer?'

'What? When?' Edie didn't like the thought of Rodney going away. Having him just up the road at the castle made her feel safer.

Marge shrugged. 'Not something he'd tell me. Anyway, he's still here, so maybe they said no. Perhaps you should ask your mum,' she said pointedly.

Edie frowned. 'I better get back,' she muttered.

As she walked back towards the low wire fence that separated the back of the garage from the field, she kept her eyes on Bert, hoping that he might at least acknowledge her, but he didn't even look at her, and she didn't have the courage to approach him.

By the time she clambered over the fence, her eyes were blurred with tears. For all Bert's humour and easy manner, he was as stubborn and hard-headed as his mother – and her if she was honest – so she shouldn't be surprised.

Her thoughts turned to the dreadful day Gladys had died. They'd all been in shock, and while Gladys lay dead on the sofa in the living room, a sudden shell attack had forced them to shelter in the basement.

'It's not your fault,' she'd whispered to Bert as the shells rained down on the market square, making the walls shake. 'We weren't to know what Susan was like.'

His expression when he'd looked at her had been ice cold. 'Oh, I don't just blame myself for this,' he'd hissed. 'We're *both* to blame. But I would never have gone near that girl if you hadn't hatched that stupid plan to lure Susan away from Lily's Charlie. You should have just spoken to Lily and left me out of it. So do me a favour, Edie, and stay away from me.'

He'd not spoken to her since.

Edie blinked back her tears. She had no right to cry. Because everything Bert said was true; it was all her fault. If she'd minded her own business, Gladys would still be here. And her brother would still be talking to her.

In two short days she'd lost her mother and brother. But whereas she felt no regret about her mother; she'd do anything to make it up to Bert.

Chapter 10

The match was in full swing when Jim and Reenie arrived at the field, and a sizeable crowd stood around the pitch. Craning his neck, Jimmy looked over the heads of the spectators.

'Rodney's here.' He grabbed Reenie's hand and pushed through to the front where his eldest brother stood, wearing a dark blue coat over his immaculate naval officer's uniform. Reenie hadn't seen him since Gladys's funeral in January, and Marianne had confided to her that she was worried he was staying away because he was ashamed of them. Having his family associated with treason and murder couldn't be good for a man in his position. But the Castle siblings had always been close, and Reenie knew that no matter what, Rodney would be there for them if they needed him.

So different from her and June, she thought regretfully. They'd fought like cat and dog throughout their childhood. It was one of the reasons she'd spent so much time with Wilf –anything to get away from her sister's nasty remarks. June had always been the pretty one, the one all the boys chased. Whereas she . . . well, she'd believed what her sister had told her. That she was fat and stupid and would end her days behind the counter at the grocery store because no one would want her.

She wondered if things would have been different if their parents had lived. But they'd died during the Spanish flu epidemic when Reenie was eight. Being orphaned so young should have made them closer, but no matter how hard she'd tried, her sister had seemed to hate her. Why else would she have stolen Wilf from her?

Although, Wilf had never been hers to steal, she reminded herself. But he had been her friend. Until he'd married June and everything had changed.

A cheer made Reenie switch her attention to the pitch, and she smiled at the sight of Bert being hoisted aloft on the shoulders of his teammates.

'What's the score?' she asked.

'Three–nil. Bert's scored a hat-trick,' Rodney replied, his eyes wandering over to the other side of the field. Reenie followed his gaze. Ah. She waved, hoping to catch Marge's attention, but her friend was too intent on yelling abuse at the navy's defence.

'If this is how you defend a goal, how do you expect to defend the bloomin' country!' she railed.

Reenie giggled. 'Maybe if Marge was in charge, the navy wouldn't be losing,' she said.

'If Marge was in charge, they wouldn't have made it to the match – they'd all be in the pub!' Rodney drawled.

Reenie glared at him. 'You didn't seem to mind her at Christmas when you were kissing her under the mistletoe.'

Rodney scowled. 'Whatever you're thinking, you couldn't be more wrong,' he responded pompously.

'For God's sake, Rod!' Jimmy pushed his shoulder. 'What the hell's wrong with you?'

Rodney flushed. 'Sorry, Reenie. I didn't mean to be rude.' He looked over at Marge again. This time, she looked back at them, all trace of her earlier passion gone.

It was Rodney who broke the long stare first when he turned his attention back to the game.

Marge put her hands around her mouth and shouted, 'Come on, Phil! Give us four!'

A slim man with brown hair looked over at her and saluted.

Reenie examined him. So that was the famous Padre Philip. Marge had told her about him, but she hadn't actually met him yet. He didn't look like a padre. With his navy-blue socks around his ankles, baggy blue shorts and a white top, his brown hair falling into his face, he looked more like an eighteen-year-old boy, and she'd lay money on him being at least as young as Jimmy. But she'd also bet that Marge didn't give a fig for that, or for what anyone else had to say about it.

Just then, Philip managed to get the ball off one of the soldiers, and set off for the goal, nimbly dodging a couple of tackles and whacking it into the top corner of the army's net. He let out a cry of triumph and, ignoring the congratulations of his teammates, made a beeline for Marge. Grabbing her round the waist, he lifted her up and twirled her round, before lowering her to the ground and kissing her soundly on the lips. The cheering died away as Marge's arms went around his neck and the kiss deepened.

'Bloody hell,' Jimmy whispered. 'Are you sure he's a chaplain?'

Reenie giggled. 'Don't look like it, does it?'

Finally the kiss broke and Phil whispered something in Marge's ear, before jogging back to the middle to restart the game, leaving Marge standing stock-still, her mouth hanging open.

'I've got work to do,' Rodney said suddenly, turning to walk away, his head high and his shoulders stiff.

'Will we see you later?' Jimmy shouted after him.

'No,' Rodney called brusquely over his shoulder.

'God, he's a moody bugger,' Jimmy grumbled. 'I'm gonna check he's all right. Back in a tick.'

Reenie glanced over towards Marge, noticing the way her friend's eyes followed Rodney to the edge of the field before he disappeared round the corner of the garage.

She was just about to make her way over to her, when a familiar sound made her heart sink. She looked up, but all she could see were clouds. Planes raced over Dover all the time, Reenie tried to reassure herself, but even so, she felt unsettled. As the noise grew louder, she looked up again.

Suddenly, as though parting a thick grey curtain, a plane burst through the cloud, its yellow nose bright against the dull sky.

'Christ!' The man next to her started to sprint across the pitch waving his arms. 'Get down! Everyone down!'

It took a moment for his words to register, and then like skittles, players and spectators alike dropped to the ground, arms curled protectively over their heads, as gouts of earth flew up around them, the sound of gunfire drowning out their terrified screams.

Chapter 11

Once the ATS girls had left, the café was quiet and Nellie sent Marianne upstairs to rest. She was looking alarmingly pale, and even though she still had three months to go, it was clear that she wouldn't be able to work for much longer.

'What's to become of us, Polly?' she murmured to the bird, who was sitting in her cage on the counter. Clutching at the crucifix around her neck, she stared out at the blurred outlines of the shoppers in the square. It was no wonder so few people came in anymore. Aside from the scandal that had engulfed them with the discovery of Hester's spying, it felt to her that the café had lost its heart when Gladys had died and she wondered if others, too, had sensed Gladys's restless spirit hovering over the tables.

A face pressed up against the celluloid window, startling Nellie from her gloomy thoughts. Then it disappeared and the door opened.

Nellie pasted a smile on her face, but it dropped the minute she saw who it was. 'What the bloody hell are you doing here?' Although she knew full well why he was there; in fact, she'd been expecting him for some time.

Terence Carter walked into the café, a half-smoked cigarette in one hand. Glancing around, he shook his head. 'Awful quiet in here,' he remarked.

'Just a quiet day. We get them now and then.'

He raised his eyebrows in disbelief.

'What do you want, Terence?' Nellie snapped, although her heartrate had increased and her hands were clasped tightly together to keep them from trembling.

'I miss ya,' he said with a phoney smile. 'An' I'm worried about ya.'

Nellie snorted. 'Right. And Polly here loves a bit of Shakespeare.' She stood up straighter; she couldn't let him see how defeated she felt.

'Who's a clever bird then?' he cooed.

Taking a drag of his cigarette, he came to lean on the counter opposite Nellie, blowing smoke into her face. 'I know you've had your troubles, but I saw your Bert this mornin', and it occurred to me I hadn't seen you for a few weeks. Time was, you an' me used to meet regular . . . '

Nellie wafted the smoke away and pursed her lips.

'Is there anything you want to tell me, Mrs C?' Terence laid his hat on the counter, running a hand through his blond hair, made dark by the amount of brilliantine he'd slathered through it.

'Why would I want to talk to *you*?' Nellie said, relieved that her voice was steady.

'Well, I've learnt that if you don't deal with your problems, you only get yerself into a worse pickle, don'tcha? And so I thought I'd come and offer me help.'

'Right. Cos you're always ready to help those in need,' Nellie hissed.

Terence didn't reply, but his cold eyes never left Nellie's face.

As the silence stretched between them, Nellie snapped, even though she knew it was what he was waiting for. 'Look, I said I'd get it to you soon as I could,' she said.

'That were four weeks ago, Mrs C. And I ain't seen hide nor hair of you since. I've started to wonder whether you're avoidin' me. And I really don't like it when people avoid me. Makes me auspicious.'

Nellie's lips twitched, and the flicker of amusement helped give her courage. 'Ain't nothin' auspicious about you, Terence.'

He narrowed his eyes at her. 'Are you makin' fun of me?'

Nellie held her hands up. 'Look, give me a break, can't ya? I used that food to help the community, and don't you think it'd be a nice gesture if, just this once, you let it go?'

Terence laughed. 'You what?'

'All right, maybe not let me off, but give me a bit more time. You'll get your money.'

'Maybe if that's all it was, I might consider it. But that's not all, is it?' He turned to look through the window. 'Lovely view, ain't it?' He looked back at her. 'An' I'd hate to have to take it away from you.'

Nellie swallowed nervously. 'You couldn't. What use would it be now? All scratched and painted.'

'Oh, I think I'd manage. Always someone desperate for that stuff at the moment.'

'Like I said,' she gritted, 'you'll get your bloody money.'

'Problem is, I don't think I can trust ya no more. If you'd come to me sooner, then maybe we coulda reached an agreement, but . . .' He shrugged and looked pointedly around the empty café. 'How do I know you'll keep your word?'

Nellie sighed. She should have stopped supplying the tea stand in the caves and handing out food parcels to those who'd had their homes destroyed. And she should have listened to all the people who told her to wait before she bought the celluloid. But she hadn't, because she'd simply not anticipated running out of money. And now here she was, in debt for the first time in years – and to Terence Carter of all people. She shuddered. She'd been meaning to sell some jewellery, but she'd been putting it off, burying her head in the sand and hoping it would all go away or that business would pick up again and things would be back to the way they were before Hester had appeared. Before she'd lost one of the best and truest friends she'd ever had.

She glanced at Terence's hard face; his brown eyes had not a glimmer of sympathy and she knew there was no point appealing to his better nature.

'You're just gonna have to wait,' she said firmly.

'I want it now.' Terence held out a grubby palm and Nellie looked at in disgust.

'You ever heard of soap?' she asked.

Terence smirked. 'It's awful pricey these days, and it's hard enough keepin' me belly full, let alone me hands clean.'

Nellie flapped her hand towards the window. 'I'm sure your mum'd be happy to give you a pint of whelks. And by the looks of the it' – she glanced towards Terence's belly, protruding slightly through his black shirt – 'the two of you are doin' just fine.'

'Are you callin' me fat?' Terence snarled.

Nellie smiled. 'Just tellin' it how I see it. In any case, it'd take more than soap to clean your hands.'

Terence narrowed his eyes. 'And what's that supposed to mean?'

Nellie sniffed. 'Oh, I reckon you know exactly what I mean.'

'I reckon I do.' He pointed a finger at her nose. 'An' it's strange you're suddenly so concerned, cos you've never cared before. But just so's we're clear: once you've paid me what I'm owed, you won't never have to deal with me an' me grubby 'ands again. All right?'

Nellie looked away. 'You'll have it soon,' she lied.

The man's eyebrows rose. 'You know, Mrs C, you're not everyone's cup of tea, but I've always liked you, an' Mum loves this place. An' that's why I extended credit. Because I thought you was a woman of your word.' He sighed heavily. 'But seein' as we're such old friends, I'll give you two weeks to pay up. After that I'll 'ave to find other ways of gettin' the money.' He looked at the ceiling thoughtfully. 'Saw your Donny earlier. In fact, see him and his little mate Freddie round town a lot.'

Nellie's brow furrowed at the change of subject. 'So?'

'Well, a little bird told me about him inheritin' a share of Fanshawe's Brewery.' He rubbed his hands together. 'Who'd have thunk it? Little Donny Castle bein' kin to one of the richest families in East Kent.'

Nellie felt goosebumps rise on her arms. 'Leave Donny out of this,' she hissed. 'And anything he inherits is *his*. It's got nothin' to do with the rest of us. Besides, he won't see a penny for years.'

'They must worry about him. Their little heir livin' right on the front line, eh?'

Nellie leant across the counter till her nose was inches from the man's greasy face. 'I said you'll get your money. But know this, that family'd be delighted if Donny disappeared out of their lives. You think they want to share their riches with the likes of him? So if you've got some crazy scheme of usin' him to make money, then save yerself the trouble. In fact, wouldn't surprise me if they paid you to get rid of him. Now get out!' She flung her arm towards the door. 'Get out, and don't come back.'

Terence put his hat on. 'I'll go for now. But *you* should know *this*: I don't believe a word you say.' Then with a nod he walked towards the door, where he paused and looked back. 'Don't forget: two weeks.'

Nellie leant her head on the counter, trying to get her breathing under control. Vaguely she became aware of the sound of a plane and shooting nearby, but she dismissed it. Once she'd thought that the bombs and shells posed the greatest threat to the café, but not anymore. Now the threat felt a lot closer to home, and she had no one to blame but herself.

⠿

Marianne had been supervising Donny's letter to Constable Humphries when she'd heard the bell above the café door tinkle and the hum of voices. Expecting to be called downstairs, she'd left her sulky son to finish his task and crept down the stairs, stopping and sitting on the step as soon as she realised who it was. She didn't want to have any part in Nellie's dealings with Terence Carter.

But as she listened, a growing sense of panic constricted her breathing. She'd had no idea of the trouble her mother was in. If she'd known how deep in debt she'd got, she'd have insisted they stop buying the extras from him long ago.

Her panic turned to outright terror, though, when he mentioned the Fanshawes. She shuddered, praying Terence believed the lie her mother had told him. Because the Fanshawes did care about her son. In fact, they cared far too much for her liking. The only ones who didn't care about him were Donny's no-good father Henry and his bitch of a wife, Elspeth. But, as far as she knew, Elspeth was in prison for treason, along with Hester and the other conspirators. As for Henry, she had no idea where he was. He'd come home for his father's funeral, but he may well have been sent back to the expensive private mental hospital he'd been incarcerated in since he'd kidnapped Donny.

She crept back upstairs to the bedroom she shared with her younger sister Lily, and opened her drawer. Hidden beneath the neatly folded underwear was an envelope. Taking it out, she extracted the letter from inside and stared at it. She'd read it only briefly when she'd received it and had been trying to forget about it ever since.

She lay back on the bed, clutching it to her chest with one hand and rubbing her stomach with the other. She'd never thought she'd have to make a choice. But if they couldn't pay Terence Carter soon, then she would have to confront the issue, or they could lose everything.

Chapter 12

When the plane circled away, Reenie looked up and was hardly able to comprehend the horror that confronted her. Where just a few moments before twenty-two men had been running around full of life, now the grass was littered with bodies. Some were groaning, but others were lying still, their limbs spread at unnatural angles.

Frantically, she looked over to where she'd last seen Marge kissing her padre, and was relieved to see her friend and Jeanie crawling towards her.

Then, like the wailing of a banshee on a dark stormy night, louder even than the cries and groans from the people around her, a high-pitched scream broke into her scattered thoughts. 'Grandad! Grandad, wake up! Granddaaaad!'

She glanced round for the source. Several people, some dragging children with them, were crawling towards the shelter of the garage and the Anderson shelter, although if the plane returned and dropped a bomb, it would be scant protection.

The child's wails rose higher, and Reenie spotted a small boy, no older than four or five, crouching over the body of a man.

She got up and rushed towards him. 'Hey, love,' she said, her voice trembling, as her eyes swept over the boy's grandfather. A thin line of blood trickled down the man's chin and his eyes stared sightlessly at the sky.

Swallowing back the nausea, she held her hand out to the boy, but it was trembling so violently that she had to pull it back. 'Come with me, sweetheart,' she urged.

'I can't leave Grandad!' the boy sobbed. 'Mum'll get cross.'

'No, she won't, I promise.' She moved closer and put her arm around the boy's skinny shoulders.

He stared up at her through tear-washed blue eyes. 'Is he dead?' he screamed. 'Is he dead?'

Reenie wouldn't have thought it possible, but his voice had gone up another octave.

'I don't know, lovey, but he'd want me to get you safe.' She tried to urge him away, but he resisted her. 'What's your name?' she asked gently.

'B-b-bobby,' he managed.

'Right then, Bobby, I'm going to take you over to the garage. And I bet my friend Edie will give you a biscuit for being such a good boy.'

'Will she?' he hiccupped.

'Yes, I promise. But you have to come now.'

Tearfully, the boy nodded and allowed her to draw him into her side. Rising awkwardly, she sat the boy on her hip and began to run towards the garage.

But her steps faltered as she realised that the droning of the aircraft was returning.

'It's coming back!' someone shouted. 'Get down!'

For a moment it seemed like everyone was shocked into immobility. But then panic erupted as people either leapt to their feet to try to outrun the bullets, or dropped back into their huddled position.

Reenie's instinct told her to keep running, but with the added burden of the child, she knew she wouldn't make it.

Then, as the guns started up again, she dropped to the ground, tucking the boy under her.

'Reenie!' A voice rang out above the noise of the aircraft and the screams of terrified people.

Reenie looked up to see Jimmy running round the side of the garage. 'Jim! I'm here!' she tried to shout but her voice came out weak and croaky. So she held up an arm.

Crouching down, Jimmy crawled over to her, his eyes frantic as they travelled over her body, reassuring himself that she was unhurt. 'I thought you were dead!' he said shakily, throwing himself over her.

'You're squashing us!' Reenie groaned.

Jim eased away. 'We're going to try to crawl to the garage, all right?' he said.

Reenie looked up at the whitewashed building just a few hundred yards away. She tried to nod, but she found she couldn't move at all.

'I-I c-can't!' she cried.

'All right, love,' Jimmy soothed, rubbing her back. 'We'll stay here till it's over. It's going to be fine.' He kissed her cheek. 'As long as we're together, everything's going to be fine.'

Reenie could barely hear him now. The panic was fizzing through her, making her ears buzz, and the rat-a-tat of the guns pounded through her head. She could feel her heart, though, thumping hard and fast against her chest. She tightened her arms around the small boy beneath her, wishing she could speak, but her throat had closed up. She tried to drag in a breath, but found she couldn't. Her head started to swim.

'Breathe, Reenie,' Jim's deep voice whispered in her ear. 'Breathe, darling. Come on. I'll do it with you.' Jimmy took in a deep breath. 'Now you.'

Comforted by his steady voice and the warmth of his breath in her ear, Reenie tried to relax her shoulders, and finally managed to drag a breath in.

'B-bobby,' she said into the little boy's ear. 'Can you hear me?'

Beneath her, though, the little boy lay still.

As the plane circled away again, she rolled away. 'Bobby?'

His face was pale, but his eyes were fluttering and his chest moving.

'I think he's fainted,' Jim said. Keeping his arm around her, he helped her up and hauled her into his embrace. 'I thought I'd lost you,' he whispered.

Reenie rested her head under his chin and inhaled the scent of sandalwood which she always associated with him. 'I'm still here,' she murmured. 'I'm still here.' She could barely believe it herself. She pulled away and bent down to pick up the little boy.

'Jimmy!' A figure sped past him. 'Bert's down!'

Jimmy stiffened, his head swinging to look across the grass.

'Go,' she said gently, her eyes darting to the pitch where she could see Rodney scooting to a halt beside a prone body. Not Bert too, she thought despairingly. So handsome, so funny . . . so full of life.

When Jimmy still didn't move, she pushed him away. 'Your brothers need you!'

Jimmy blinked. 'Will you be all right?' he asked.

She nodded tearfully, arms tight around the little boy.

As he ran off, Reenie noticed that several others had followed Rodney's lead and were now on the pitch, attempting to drag the wounded to safety.

Marge reached her just then, her face paper white against her red hair, her arm around Jeanie. 'I've got to go back,' she muttered, looking behind her. 'Phil's been hit.'

'Leave it, Marge,' Jeanie exclaimed. 'There are others to help.'

But Marge just shook her head and turned back to the field.

Reenie wanted to go with her, but Bobby woke and started screeching in her ear, his arms clinging to her neck so tightly she thought he might strangle her, and with Jeanie tugging at her arm, she had no choice but to keep going.

They'd gone no more than a few steps, when, like a recurring nightmare, the plane returned and the shooting began again. 'Jimmy!' she gasped, but Jeanie's grip on her tightened. 'Run!' she yelled.

Eyes screwed shut and lungs burning Reenie tried to run, but her legs crumpled and she sank to the ground.

'Here, give the boy to me.' Jeanie tried to pull Bobby away from her, but he clung on like a limpet, his screams ratcheting up a notch. 'He won't budge!' she yelled. 'Come *on*, Reenie, you've got to move!'

But Reenie couldn't. 'You go,' she managed to gasp. 'Please. I'll be there soon. I just—' She tried to heave in a breath but once again her throat had closed up.

Finally, Jeanie managed to wrench the boy from her, easing her breathing a little. 'I'll be back,' she cried, then sprinted towards the fence.

Gathering all her strength, Reenie began to crawl to safety, her ears ringing with the screams and the deadly tattoo of the machine-gun fire, so close now, she was certain at any moment she'd feel the slam of a bullet into her body.

Finally, though, arms reached out to help her over the fence and she collapsed onto the ground. A moment later, Bobby's small body thumped into her, his arms going around her neck again as he screamed into her shoulder.

Reenie's hugged him tightly to her – despite the screams it was good to have something warm to hold on to.

'Edie, take Reenie and the little one upstairs to lie down,' Mr Pearson said from the tiny kitchen where he was boiling a kettle. The office space was crowded with people, either sitting in shocked silence or sobbing.

'No! I need to know Jim's all right,' Reenie protested.

'You can see from my bedroom.' Edie's voice was shaking and Reenie realised suddenly that Edie had much more to lose. All three of her brothers were out there. Nodding, she allowed her to lead her upstairs.

In the bedroom, she lay Bobby on the bed, and covered him with a blanket, then she went to stand at the window with Edie.

Arms around each other they stood and looked at the carnage in disbelief. Their eyes focused on the three men right in the centre of the field. And beyond them, Marge, whose red hair stood out like a bloodstain against the grass.

Chapter 13

As the plane circled away again, Marge scanned the field, looking for Phil. She'd seen him go down, but her mind was in such turmoil that she couldn't remember exactly where he'd been. And there were so many bodies.

She could see Jimmy and Rodney crouched over a prone figure, and horror rushed over her as she realised it was Bert. But she couldn't dwell on him, because lying by the goal was Philip. And he wasn't moving.

'Please, God, don't let him be dead. Surely he's more use to you here than up there,' she muttered.

What was she doing? God didn't exist. You just had to look around you to realise that.

As she reached Phil, her feet went from under her and she landed with a thud, only just managing to avoid crushing him. Pushing to her knees, she realised with horror that it wasn't just mud that had caused her to slip. She stared at her hands, caked in dark mud, and streaked through it was blood.

She swallowed hard.

Phil's head turned towards her. 'Marge.' His voice was weak, but at least he was alive. She forced herself to calm her breathing and examine him properly. His face was dirty but unharmed. Her eyes travelled down over his torso. No blood. Relief washed through her.

But as her eyes moved down his legs she had to clamp her lips against the sudden nausea, even as her hands reached up to yank off her tie. Then, holding her breath, she wrapped it tightly around his ankle, desperately trying to avoid touching the bone that was jutting out of the bloodied mess that had once connected it to his foot. The foot that just minutes ago had scored a goal. The foot that had carried him towards her, supported him as he'd whirled her round and whispered in her ear . . . .No. She didn't want to think about that right now. Just as she couldn't think about what this injury would mean for him – or where the foot might be.

She pulled the tie tighter, ignoring his feeble groans, and once she was satisfied she could do no more, she grasped his trembling hand. 'You're gonna be all right, Phil,' she whispered. 'Every-thing's gonna be all right.'

He opened his eyes. 'Help me up,' he gasped, lifting his head.

She pushed him gently back and stroked the hair. 'Not yet, love. Wait for the medics.'

'Am I badly injured?' he gasped, teeth chattering. 'I can't feel a thing.'

Somehow, Marge managed to smile. 'Not too bad, love. Bit of treatment and R and R, and you'll be good as new.' She stripped off her jacket and laid it over him, hoping the warmth from her body would soothe him.

He stared at her face, his eyes going over the streaks of mud and blood that she knew must be on her cheeks. 'I . . . never took you for a liar,' he whispered.

'I'm not lying. You *are* going to be all right.' She held his hand tightly.

'Typical of the plane to come just as we're on the way up,' he muttered.

Marge smiled, astonished he could joke, even at a time like this. 'I know. I was just beginning to enjoy myself.'

Phil's eyes fluttered closed.

'Hey, don't go to sleep on me.'

'Just need forty winks,' he murmured.

'Not yet, love.' Marge kissed his cheek. 'Stay with me.'

'Just a few minutes,' he repeated. Suddenly his eyes opened and he looked at her. 'I love you, Marge. I just want you to know that.'

'I love you too, Phil. Please just stay awake a bit longer.'

But his eyes had closed, so she lay down beside him, one arm across his stomach. 'This is how we met, do you remember?' she said tearfully. 'You rugby tackled me to the ground outside the church. Saved my life.'

She felt the slightest movement against her cheek and his eyes cracked open. 'I remember,' he muttered. 'Seems . . . a bit of a . . . habit. Can we try not to . . . again?'

She chuckled, relieved. He was going to make it. 'I'll certainly give it my best shot.'

Sitting up, she looked around. Medics were hurrying across the field and she waved. 'Over here! Quick, please!'

Two men ran up to her. They took in her makeshift tourniquet and the damage to Phil's leg, and one of them patted her on the shoulder.

'Good job, love,' he said. 'We'll take it from here.'

'Marge? Come with me, please!' The tremble in his voice tore at her heart.

'It's all right, mate. She'll come along later. For now, the doc's gonna want to have a look at you.' The man looked over at Marge. 'We'll take him to the castle hospital. It's closer.'

The men picked him up and placed him gently on the stretcher they'd brought with them, then with a brief nod, they left, staggering slightly under their burden.

Marge looked over to where she'd last seen Jim and Rodney, but they were no longer there, and with the field rapidly being cleared of casualties, she realised there was little more she could do.

She tried to stand up, but her legs seemed to have lost all their strength and she slumped to the ground, her body trembling as she pulled her knees to her chest and rested her head on them.

'Come on, up you get.' Someone put their hands beneath her arms and lifted her to her feet, but she kept her eyes shut.

'I can't stand it,' she whispered. 'I can't *bloody* stand it.'

'You have no choice, sweetheart,' the man said softly.

Marge turned into his warmth and put her arms around his neck. 'Make it stop, Rodney,' she said. 'Please, make it stop.'

Rodney said nothing, but his arms clasped her more tightly to him as she sobbed against his shoulder. She felt the brush of his lips over her hair, the warmth of his breath on her cheek, and burrowed closer. And despite the horror and carnage they had just witnessed, a measure of peace came to her.

Finally, she pulled away, wiping her eyes on her sleeve. 'Sorry. I don't know what came over me.' She looked up at him. His face, too, was smeared with blood and his eyes were bleak, and it occurred to her that their embrace had comforted them both.

'How's Bert?' she asked softly.

He sighed. 'Alive. For now. They've taken him to the Casualty.'

'Oh, Rod.' She put a hand to his cheek. 'I'm so sorry.'

He put his own hand up and clasped her wrist. 'And so am I. About your padre, I mean.'

She nodded and took a step back. 'Will you be going to the hospital?'

'I can't. I'm on duty in an hour. I'll call from the office. Come on, I'll walk you back. Philip needs you now.'

Marge's stomach sank with dread. 'I just hope I can be strong enough.'

Rodney pulled her close again. 'You're one of the strongest women I know. He's lucky to have you.'

Marge closed her eyes. He doesn't have me, she thought. He never did. But how could she tell him that now? She drew in a deep breath, wishing she could forget the very last words he'd said to her before the plane arrived.

70

'And you should try not to worry about Bert,' she said, pushing the memory away. 'He's survived one shooting, he'll survive this.' She moved away from him slightly, but without his support, she found her legs were too wobbly to hold her and she staggered.

Rodney put his arm around her shoulder. 'Lean on me, Marge, I won't let you fall.'

And he wouldn't, Marge knew that with certainty. He always stood strong and allowed people to lean on him. And yet when he'd come to her with his troubles after Hester had been arrested and all hell had broken out in his family, she'd been resentful and reacted like a spoilt child. And now it was too late. His trust was gone.

With her head on his shoulder, Marge allowed herself to be led across the field, which was littered with discarded shoes, bags and bloodstained clothing. She closed her eyes against the horror of it, drawing strength from Rodney's warmth and trying very hard not to think about the fact that she had to let go of that small spark of hope that she and Rodney could ever be more than friends. Because as soon as the plane had burst through the clouds and unleashed its venom, everything had changed.

Chapter 14

Reenie and Edie watched tensely from the bedroom window as the medics worked on the casualties.

'They didn't cover his face,' Edie breathed with relief. 'Bert, they didn't cover his face, which means he must be alive. I'm going down to speak to Jim.'

Reenie stayed where she was and kept her eyes on Marge and Phil. She desperately wanted to comfort her friend, but she couldn't leave Bobby to wake alone in a strange place; he was traumatised enough. But when Marge collapsed onto the ground, she nearly left anyway, unable to bear the sight of her in such distress. Then Rodney took the decision away from her. A lump formed in her throat as she watched their long embrace, before they walked away, heads bent close to each other. Any fool could see they were perfect for each other, but they were stubborn, so neither would ever admit it. Maybe this would finally push them together, then at least something good could come out of this terrible carnage.

Now the field had been cleared, exhaustion overwhelmed her and she lay down beside Bobby, putting her hand on his chest. Gradually, the steady beat of his heart and the warmth of his sweet breath on her cheek soothed her and she fell asleep, waking only when the door opened and Jim came in.

He looked terrible; his pale face streaked with mud and blood, and his eyes haunted. She sat up and held out her arms, and without hesitation he came to sit beside her, gathering her into a tight embrace.

'How's Bert?' she whispered.

She could feel his shrug. 'I don't know, they've taken him to the hospital.'

'I was terrified you'd die out there,' she said.

He breathed out a long sigh and tightened his arms around her. 'Then we're even. When the plane started shooting and I was so far away from you, all I could think was that I needed to get to you. I didn't even think about Bert and Edie. I couldn't bear to lose you.' His voice was thick.

Reenie wanted to answer but found her throat was too full, so she turned her face and kissed the side of his neck, hoping it would be enough to show him that she felt the same.

'You mean so much to me, Reens.' He pushed her away slightly so he could look into her eyes. 'I . . . I love you. I honestly just love you.' His beautiful blue eyes were brimming with tears and shining with sincerity.

'Oh Jim. I love you too. I don't think I can even begin to tell you how much.'

He smiled softly. 'If anyone had told me just a year ago that you and I . . .' He shook his head. 'You came to me just when I needed you most. You helped patch up my wounded soul.' He kissed her. 'You've been like an angel in my life.'

Reenie laughed shakily, brushing the moisture from his cheek. 'You don't half talk some rot, Jimmy.'

'But you have,' he said earnestly. 'When I lost Colin . . .' He closed his eyes briefly and took a deep breath. 'You helped pull me back.'

'You pulled yourself back, Jim. You're stronger than you think.'

He shook his head. 'Not without you, I'm not. And I've been thinking and thinking these past couple of weeks, and this has made my mind up. We nearly lost each other today and I don't want that to happen again. We should get married.'

Reenie's mouth dropped open in astonishment. 'What?'

'You and me. Let's make a life together.' With a burst of energy, he dropped onto one knee and took her hand. 'Will you marry me, Reenie Turner, and make me the happiest man in the world?' He smiled tremulously.

The tears that had been gathering in Reenie's eyes started to trickle down her cheeks and Jim caught them with his thumb.

'Are those good tears or bad tears?'

Reenie let out a little cry and threw her arms around his neck. 'Good tears!' she exclaimed. 'Always good tears with you, Jimmy.'

He jumped to his feet, pulling her up with him. 'And I promise that for the rest of your life, I will never cause you to shed bad tears. Only tears of joy and happiness.'

Reenie clasped Jim's cheeks between her palms. 'And I promise the same,' she said. Then, going up on tiptoe, she pressed a gentle kiss to his lips. For a long time they stood, holding tightly to each other, rocking gently back and forth, until a whimper from Bobby forced them to let go of each other.

She sat down on the bed, Jim crouching on the floor beside her.

'One day, we could be sitting on a bed with our own child,' Reenie said softly. 'It's all I've ever wanted. Husband, family. Love.'

'Me too,' Jim said, his voice croaky with emotion. 'I never thought I'd have it, though.'

His words were so quiet, Reenie thought she must have misheard. 'But you're so young. Why would you think that? You could have any woman you want, Jim. You're a wonderful man. And you're not bad-looking, I suppose.'

Jimmy smiled slightly. 'You suppose?'

'Stop fishing, you know you are. So why would you think you'd never have a family of your own?'

He shrugged. 'I don't know, just me being stupid, I guess. But . . . I think we should keep this to ourselves for a bit. Especially given Bert . . .' He drew in a deep shuddering breath.

Reenie nodded. If the worst happened, their marriage would always be overshadowed by grief. Could any marriage survive such a start? And was his offer serious, or just a reaction to what they'd been through? 'Maybe this isn't the right time to make this decision. Maybe we should wait until we're more in our right minds,' she said hesitantly.

Jimmy grasped her hands. 'There will never be a right time, not while this war carries on. And I am in my right mind. I'm shocked, upset and worried, but I know what I want. And what I want is a life with you. Just a normal life with no fear and no tragedy. And a family of our own to cherish. If today has shown us anything, it's that we need to snatch at happiness while we can, Reens, or before we know it the chance will be gone. We've lost so much already, I don't want to lose you too. And if Bert . . .' He swallowed. 'He wouldn't expect us to stay apart because of him.'

It was true. They'd both lost people they loved. He'd lost Colin and Gladys – the woman who'd been like an aunt to him – and she'd lost Daisy. Dear friends, gone forever.

She nodded and rested her forehead against his. 'You're right. Shall we do it soon?'

'Next week?' he said. 'I'll get a special licence.'

She laughed slightly. 'They're a bit pricey. Why don't we get a normal one?'

'Because I don't want to wait, and I don't care how much it costs.'

Reenie tried to reach for the happiness she knew she should feel at his words. But it was buried under the weight of the disaster they had witnessed, and the looming shadow of Bert, who even now might have left them. She wanted to marry Jimmy, but how she wished it hadn't taken the deaths of so many people for him to propose.

To hide her uncertainty, she leant forward and hugged him. 'All right then,' she said. 'Let me know where and when and I'll be there.' They sat in silence for a moment, wrapped once again in each other's arms.

'Why don't you go to the hospital? There's nothing more to be done here,' Reenie suggested after a while. 'I'll see if anyone knows who Bobby's mum is and take him home when he wakes.'

He shook his head. 'I don't think I can stand to hang around there waiting for news. But I do need to speak to Mum.' He sighed heavily and stood up. 'So why don't you and me take Bobby down to the café. Mum knows just about everyone, so she'll probably have an idea who he belongs to and where he lives.'

Jim removed his coat and gently wrapped the little boy in it before picking him up and resting him against his broad shoulder. Bobby murmured softly, but didn't wake as they went downstairs.

The office had emptied now, except for Edie, who was sobbing quietly into Mr Pearson's shoulder.

He looked up at them. 'Will you be going to the hospital?' he asked.

'Not right now,' Jim replied. 'Why don't you go, Edie?'

Edie shook her head, wringing her hands. 'Bert won't want me, and Mum'll be there. I can't.'

'You're not keeping this up even now?' Jimmy said, aghast. 'We need to pull together, not split further apart!'

Edie wiped at her cheeks. 'I don't expect you to understand.'

'Too bloody right I don't understand.' Jim kept his voice low so as not to wake the child in his arms. 'She's your mother! She loves you and you're breaking her heart.'

'And she's broken mine,' Edie responded angrily.

Mr Pearson sighed heavily. 'That's enough! Your brother is gravely injured, people have died in front of our eyes; this is *not* the time for a family squabble.'

Edie looked away, tears rolling down her cheeks. 'I-I'm sorry,' she whispered.

'So come with us.' Reenie held her hand out.

For a long time, Edie looked at the outstretched hand, then shook her head. 'I don't expect either of you to understand. If he's awake, tell Bert I love him.' Then she got up and went up the stairs.

'Do you know what?' Jim muttered. 'I don't give a fig anymore. After what we've just been through, the fact she can just walk away . . .' He stalked out of the door.

Reenie stood uncertainly for a moment. 'Will she be all right?' she asked Mr Pearson.

The man rubbed his eyes wearily. 'Between you an' me, Reenie, I'm not sure. But don't go tellin' your man that. He's got enough to worry about. Meantime, I'll look after Edie.'

Reenie nodded and impulsively leant forward to kiss him on the cheek. 'Thank you,' she whispered. 'Look after yourself as well.' Then she turned and followed Jimmy out of the door.

Chapter 15

'Nellie!' The café door burst open.

'Blinkin' heck, Lou!' Nellie exclaimed, hand on her chest. 'Where's the fire?'

Lou Carter looked anguished as she stood by the door, the beige coat she wore when working at her stall straining against her belly. 'Somethin's happened up at the castle! Football match,' Lou gasped.

For a moment, Nellie's heart stood still. 'What!?' she gasped.

Lou bent over and tried to catch her breath. 'I came soon as I heard. Someone told my Terence . . . He were on his way up and bumped into some folk runnin' away down the hill.'

'Running away from what? For the love of God, woman, what's happened?'

'Shooting . . . Stuka . . . Castle.'

'Lou!' Nellie ran to the woman and pulled her up by her shoulders. 'Tell me!'

With a visible effort Lou pulled herself together and put a hand on Nellie's arm. 'They said it were a bloodbath. I'm so sorry, love.'

Nellie's heart dropped to her shoes. 'What?' she screamed. 'What are you sorry about?'

'It's Bert.'

Nellie slumped down onto the nearest chair. 'What do you mean?' she whispered, her lips trembling.

Before Lou could answer, the café door opened again and Muriel Palmer, chairlady of the WVS, hurried in. Taking in the scene, she walked over to Nellie and laid a comforting hand on her shoulder. 'You've heard then?' she said gently.

'No! Heard what? What the hell's happened?'

'Calm down, Nellie.' Muriel took her hands. 'I got a call from Mr Pearson. A Stuka came out of the clouds, started to shoot at everyone on the field . . .'

Nellie stared at her in incomprehension. 'What are you saying?'

'It's Bert, love. And he wasn't the only one. But Bert's all I know about. He's . . .'

Nellie's ears started to buzz. 'Is he dead?'

Muriel shook her head. 'Mr Pearson said the ambulance took him up the hospital.'

'Wh-what about the others?' Nellie said faintly. 'Edie, Jim, Rodney . . . They were all there. Oh God! Someone tell Ethel. Reenie were there.' The enormity of what they might have lost suddenly hit her. Four children and an unborn grandchild . . . Surely she couldn't lose them all.

Muriel nodded at Lou and between them they lifted Nellie to her feet. 'Come on, love, let's get you upstairs. And maybe a nip of that brandy you've got hidden away. And Lou, put the kettle on, will you?'

'Cup of bloody tea!' Nellie yanked herself free. 'Cup of tea when my kids are lying injured and possibly dead up at the hospital! What sort of mother do you think I am!'

'Mum? What's happened?' Marianne had heard the commotion and come downstairs to find Donny standing by the kitchen door, eyes wide and face white as a ghost. She put her arm around him and he leant into her, burying his face in her side.

'It's Uncle Bert,' Donny whispered. 'Something's happened to him.'

Marianne's eyes shot to her mother.

'Can you get Jasper?' Nellie said.

'Donny can do it. I'll come with you.'

'I want to come,' Donny exclaimed, and grabbing his mother's hand he pulled her towards the door.

They were half running, half walking up Biggin Street, when a van pulled up beside them and the door was thrust open.

'Get in, all of you.' Phyllis Perkins was at the wheel of her delivery van. 'I'll take you up the hospital. Donny, you go see Fred, he's at home with his dad.'

'But I want to make sure Uncle Bert's all right,' he protested.

'Do as you're told. We'll let you know soon as we hear,' Marianne said. When it looked like he was going to refuse, she lost her patience. 'For God's sake, Don. Just this once do as you're told!'

Then she clambered into the van after Nellie, and before she'd even shut the door, Phyllis had put the van in gear and screeched away.

Chapter 16

The canteen at the Casualty Hospital was busy as Lily Castle sat down for her morning tea break with her fellow trainee nurses.

'How's your mum, Lily?' one of the girls asked. 'Is she feeling better after everything that happened?'

'She's a bit up and down, if I'm honest, Dot,' Lily replied. 'Still, she was giving Bert's football team breakfast this morning, so maybe that'll cheer her up.'

'Ooh, I heard they were playing today. Who do you reckon'll win?' Dot asked. 'My money's on the army; I hear your Bert's a regular Tommy Lawton.'

Lily wrinkled her nose. 'Who's he when he's at home?'

'Oh, our Dot loves nothing better than a bit of football talk. If it weren't for the fact she was wearing a dress, you'd never know she were a girl.'

Dot's face fell and Lily leapt to her defence. 'Why are you always so mean, Vi?' she snapped. She'd met the two girls on their first day of training, but though Dot was a sweetheart, Vi had always been prickly. Dot insisted it was because of her difficult family circumstances and had urged Lily to give her the benefit of the doubt. But the time was coming when she wouldn't be able to anymore.

'For your information, men prefer talking to me about football than to some prissy little madam who's got nothing but makeup and fashion on her mind,' Dot said defensively.

Vi's striking green eyes narrowed. 'Well, at least no one's mistaken *me* for a boy,' she said. 'As it happens, Bert asked me if I'd join them at the Oak later.'

'When did you see him?' Lily asked with surprise.

Vi waved her hand airily. 'Oh, just around town.'

Dot let out a guffaw. 'Around the barracks, you mean.'

'No!' Vi gritted out. 'I'm not like some who like to hang around outside Drop Redoubt.' Her eyes shot to one of the other girls at the table. Rose Graham had had a couple of dates with Bert, but it had come as no surprise to Lily when she'd found her crying in the cloakroom after her brother had ditched her. She'd been furious with him, but what could she do? Bert wasn't listening to anyone these days, certainly not his youngest sister.

The loud clanging of a bell brought the chatter to a stop. It was the emergency alarm – the one that told them there'd been a major incident and all hands were needed.

Lily was the first to jump to her feet, followed quickly by the others. Outside in the corridor, a harassed-looking sister was giving out orders. When she caught sight of Lily, she said, 'Operating theatre, please. You'll be assisting Sister Murphy.'

Despite the situation, Lily felt a flicker of excitement as she sped through the underground corridors; she'd worked in the recovery room before, but she'd not yet been allowed to observe the operations.

In a small room outside the theatre, she scrubbed her hands and donned a long white surgical gown, mask and hat, making sure every strand of blonde hair was tucked beneath it. She took a brief look in the small mirror and smiled. One day it might be her conducting the operations, saving people's lives. It was all she'd ever wanted.

In the operating theatre she found Sister Murphy checking the equipment, ticking each item off on a list as she went. 'Do you know what's happened?' Lily asked, looking around the spotless room; the anaesthetist was already there, standing ready at the head of the operating table.

Sister Murphy shrugged. 'Take your pick – bomb, shell, shooting. There's always something.' She gave Lily a keen look. 'I asked for you because you've proven yourself to be calm under pressure, but I warn you, this won't be easy. Things can get messy, doctors lose their temper and people die.'

Lily nodded. 'I understand, Sister. I'm here to help and to learn and I promise I won't let you down.'

The older woman nodded. 'See that you don't. Because if you do, you won't get a second chance. Mistakes in here cost lives.'

Swallowing nervously, Lily helped the sister with the final preparations. They had just finished when the first casualty was wheeled in; a young man wearing shorts and a blood-soaked shirt who'd been shot in the head. Barely looking at him, Lily followed the sister's instructions, making sure the correct equipment was always to hand as the doctor fought to save the young man's life.

They soon settled into a routine, and as she began to feel more relaxed, Lily watched, fascinated, as Dr Toland operated, taking note of everything she did.

'Does anyone know what happened?' the doctor asked, as she delicately worked to remove the bullet that was lodged in the man's skull.

'Medic told me it was a football match up near the castle. Plane strafed the field. Came back round three times apparently. Nine dead, and dozens injured,' one of the other nurses replied.

The doctor sighed. 'We better get a move on then. He's been lucky. Bullet's not penetrated all the way. Bloody miracle.'

'Bloody being the operative word,' Sister Murphy said dryly.

But Lily barely heard her. She was standing by the trolley of instruments as though frozen. Bert was playing in that match! Edie would have been there too ... And Jim – maybe even Rodney.

She swayed slightly, the fear for her family making her blind and deaf to everything around her.

'Nurse Castle!' The sister's voice made her jump. 'Small haemostat!'

Lily looked at the tray, but her mind was in such turmoil that she couldn't remember what it looked like.

'Now, please!' the doctor snapped.

Sister Murphy pushed Lily out of the way and selected the instrument herself.

'What did I tell you, Nurse? This simply isn't good enough. If you can't pull yourself together, I'm going to have to ask you to leave,' Sister Murphy whispered to her once she'd handed over the tool.

Lily took a deep breath. 'I'm sorry,' she murmured. 'My brother and—'

Sister Murphy held up her hand. 'No excuses. Either you can cope or you can't. As a nurse, all your personal problems and feelings need to be left at the door. Do you understand?'

With an effort, Lily pulled herself together. 'Yes, Sister.' She cleared her throat. 'I'm fine to continue.'

Pushing all thoughts of siblings to the back of her mind, Lily forced herself to concentrate. As each patient was wheeled out, she cleaned down the operating table, sterilised the equipment, then waited for further instructions.

'What have we got here?' Dr Toland said wearily as another man was pushed in.

'Gunshot wound to shoulder, and nasty injury to the cheek. Looks like it was grazed by a bullet,' the nurse said briskly.

As she had every time, Lily shot a surreptitious glance at the man on the trolley. And it was as if time stood still. Bert's eyes were shut and the sheet covering his chest had turned a rusty brown, while one of his cheeks was covered with a blood-soaked dressing. She didn't get a chance to see any more as the anaesthetist held the mask over his mouth and nose, and Dr Toland blocked her view as she bent over him.

Instinctively, Lily started forward. 'Nurse!' Sister Murphy's sharp voice brought her back to her senses. 'What did I tell you?'

Lily nodded and retreated to her position by the equipment trolley, her eyes glued to the activity around her brother.

'I-is he going to be all right?' she asked finally, unable to bear the suspense of not knowing any longer.

Dr Toland glanced up briefly. 'You know him?'

'He's my b-b-brother.'

The doctor nodded. 'Try not to worry. We'll do what we can. But he's lost a lot of blood.'

'Do you need to leave, Nurse?' Sister Murphy asked, although this time her voice was kinder.

Lily raised her chin. 'No. No, I'll be fine,' she said. And summoning all her strength of will, she forced herself not to look at her laughing, handsome, joker of a brother lying helpless and wounded on the table. Nor would she allow herself to contemplate what life might be like for her family if he was no longer there.

Chapter 17

As Jim and Reenie approached Castle Street, Bobby opened his eyes and looked around in confusion. Reenie could see the exact moment the terrible memories returned as he stiffened and let out a high-pitched wail. 'Grandad!'

Jim stopped. 'Hey, don't worry, little fella. Grandad can't be here right now so we're going to find your mum. Can you tell us where you live?'

'Nooo! Mum'll be cross,' he sobbed. 'She tol' me not to leave Grandad.' He started to struggle, so Jim put him down, keeping a firm grasp of his hand as he unwrapped his coat from the boy's wriggling frame.

Then he crouched in front of him so he could look in the little boy's face. 'Listen, mate, your mum won't be cross. She'll be so happy to see you safe and sound, all right?'

'But she said . . .'

'She'll understand, love.' Reenie crouched beside Jim. 'I promise.'

The boy nodded reluctantly, and Jim stood up. 'You wanna ride on my shoulders?' he asked jovially.

Bobby stared up at him in awe. 'All the way up there?' he squeaked.

'That's right, mate. All the way up here.' Jim picked him up and sat him on his shoulders. The distraction worked and Bobby squealed all the way down to Market Square, tugging painfully on Jimmy's hair.

To their surprise, the café door was open and a hubbub of voices was drifting out into the street. They glanced at each other in confusion, then Jim lowered Bobby to the ground and, grasping his hand, he hurried through the open door, Reenie hot on his heels.

Crowding round the tables were various people from the market square community, with a sprinkling of soldiers and sailors, who'd come in to see if they could find out what had happened. But even more astonishing was the sight of Muriel Palmer and Lou Carter arguing behind the counter.

'I really think Nellie would prefer it if I served. At least she knows she can trust me.' Muriel Palmer's officious voice rang over the general noise. A line of cups and saucers was laid out in front of her, and she was pouring tea into them from a large brown pot.

'What are you implyin', you stuck-up old cow?'

Mrs Palmer slammed the teapot down impatiently. 'It's the WVS's job to take care of people when there's been an incident. So I really think I'm the most qualified for the job. And at least I won't be pocketing the money!'

'Why you—' Lou snatched up the teapot and ran round the counter to begin pouring the tea from the other side.

'For the love of God,' an elderly man with grey whiskers and a bald head rubbed at his eyes. 'I don't care who pours the bloody tea, but could you hurry up!'

'Get a move on, hurry up!' Polly danced inside her cage, her eyes bright.

'Christ!' Jim murmured. No one had noticed them walk in, so engrossed were they in the altercation by the counter. 'What the hell is going on?' Jim called above the noise.

Lou's head jerked round in surprise, and tea splashed onto the counter.

'Lou! The tea!' Ethel called from where she was standing in the kitchen doorway.

Muriel, seeing her chance, snatched the teapot away from her.

'Why don't you two go and sit down with the others,' Reenie said, hurrying over. She looked at her aunt beseechingly.

Ethel just shrugged helplessly. 'I tried to stop them, but people are anxious for news, and this seemed the most logical place to come.'

'Oh, Jimmy, love.' Muriel rushed round the counter to put a hand on Jim's arm. 'How is everyone? Do you have news? How's your brother?'

'I-I-I . . . Look, please everyone, go home. I'm not sure Mum'd be too happy to have people running about in here without her.'

'I were here to give your mum the news. I couldn't go home till I knew everythin' was all right. I didn't invite all this lot.' Lou folded her meaty arms across her chest and glared round the room. 'An' of course we was goin' to leave some money for the tea. We don't steal from our own.'

'The implication being you steal from others,' Muriel said primly.

'I'm sorry, I don't have news,' Jim said hastily, before they could start arguing again. 'But . . . it was awful. Edie's all right, Bert's in hospital . . .' His voice broke a little at this. 'Padre Sterling, who some of you may know, is in hospital at the castle.' He picked up Bobby. 'Anyway, me and Reenie were on the way to take this little lad back to his mum. And we were hoping someone might know who he is and where we could find her.'

Bobby had been staring around in bemusement, but at the reminder of what had happened to his grandfather, he started to cry. 'Grandad died,' he wailed.

The sight of the little boy sobbing in the tall soldier's arms brought the clamouring questions to an immediate end.

'Oh, Bobby.' A small, thin woman dressed in black, who had been sitting quietly by the counter stood up and hurried towards him. 'You poor little lamb. I know his mum well. Lives up Eastbrook.'

Reenie gaped as she realised who was speaking and went to stand beside Jimmy protectively. As far as she knew, Mary Guthrie still blamed Jim for not saving her son Colin in Dunkirk, and she told him so every time she saw him. But now with the added grief of her niece awaiting trial for Gladys's murder, she imagined Mary's bitterness against the Castle family could only have increased.

Jimmy paled at the sight of her, but stayed calm as he said, 'Perhaps you should take him to her then, Mrs Guthrie.'

The woman nodded. 'I'll be happy to. And Bert?' she asked. 'Is he all right?'

Lou Carter snorted. 'You gotta cheek, Mary! After your Susan tried to kill 'im, you're suddenly concerned now?'

Mrs Guthrie's face flushed and she looked down at her feet.

'Mrs Carter,' Jimmy said firmly, 'none of that was Mrs Guthrie's fault. You can't hold her responsible for her niece's actions.'

'Very nicely said, young James,' a woman with grey hair pulled into a small tight bun at the nape of her neck said. She'd been watching the proceedings over the small half-moon glasses perched on the bridge of her long nose, her hands busily knitting. 'Didn't Jesus always say, "Let all bitterness, and wrath, and anger, and clamour, and evil speaking, be put away from you, with all malice."'

Mary nodded. 'He did, Adelaide. And Jimmy . . . I . . . Well, I just want you to know, what happened to Colin . . . I forgive you.' Then she picked up Bobby and hurried out of the café.

Reenie glanced at Jim, whose shoulders were stiff, his jaw clenched. It was clear the half-hearted apology had upset him – and no wonder. Jim wasn't responsible for his best friend's death, but with her supposed forgiveness, Mary had once again implied he was.

'Mad bitch,' Lou muttered, as though reading her mind.

'Language, Mrs Carter, please,' Miss Frost said mildly.

'Oh, shut up, yer mealy-mouthed old cow. There's worse things than a bit of swearin'. Not five minutes before Jim here walked in you was bad-mouthin' Nellie. What was it you said?' She put her finger to her chin. 'Ah that's right.' She stuck her nose in the air and spoke with in a high-pitched voice. '"One has to wonder how Jerry knew to attack the field. Perhaps Nellie wasn't quite as innocent as she claimed."'

Jimmy's face flushed with anger. 'I think you all better leave now,' he said. 'I need to get to the hospital to check on my brother. And I don't think my mum'll be too happy to hear you've been making yourselves at home here.' He glared at Mr Gallagher from the newsagent's, who had a half-eaten biscuit on his plate. 'And any of you that had some food, please pay Reenie.'

'Don't worry, Jimmy,' Muriel Palmer said. 'I've made a note of every little thing. Leave it with me.'

Jimmy nodded. 'I need to go,' he said to Reenie. Then bending to place a swift kiss on her lips, he walked out, head bowed.

Reenie stared after him, a lump in her throat. Without Jim by her side, she wasn't sure she'd be able to keep the horror of what they'd just witnessed at bay. All she wanted right now was to sit quietly in the security of his arms. But it looked like Mrs Guthrie had reawakened Jim's demons.

She stood uncertainly for a moment, wondering whether to follow him or not. If she was quick, maybe she could push his darkness away before it took hold. She looked at her aunt, who waved her hand towards the door. 'Go,' Ethel said. 'He'll need you now. I'll make sure all this is cleared up.'

Reenie rushed out and called after Jim, but he didn't pause or turn around, so she started to run, catching up with him just outside St Mary's Church.

'Jim!' She caught his arm. 'Are you all right?'

He stopped and looked down at her and her heart dropped as she noticed the tears in his eyes. She laced her arm through his. 'Come on, love. I'll come to the hospital with you. Remember, we face things together now. That's what married couples do.'

'We're not married,' he stated baldly.

'No, but we will be. And if nothing else, at least Mary Guthrie seems to have come round.'

Jimmy let out a short laugh. 'You call that coming round? She *forgives* me! For what? What did I do wrong exactly? God knows I would have saved Colin even if I'd died in the process. But I couldn't . . . I just couldn't.'

Reenie hated the hurt look on his face. Mary had been the source of so much of his guilt and grief over what had happened to Colin. 'Of course you couldn't. No one blames you for any of it. And in her heart of hearts Mrs Guthrie doesn't either. From what she said, it looks like she's softened towards you, love.'

Jimmy looked into the distance. 'Then why does it feel like nothing's changed at all?' he murmured.

'But it has! The boot's on the other foot now, and she suddenly understands what it's like to be blamed for something she had no control over.'

'But no one does blame her. Not really.'

'Lou Carter might disagree with you on that. But apart from Mary, no one has ever blamed you for Colin's death.'

'Except me,' he said quietly.

Reenie pulled Jim to a stop. 'Yes, except you.'

Jimmy put his hand to Reenie's cheek. 'Thank you, Reens, for wanting to come with me. But I think I'd like to be on my own right now. I'll go to the hospital to check on Bert, then I . . .' He shrugged.

Trying very hard to hide her hurt at his rejection, Reenie nodded, and as he walked away, she called, 'You haven't changed your mind, have you?'

Jimmy turned to face her. 'Next week, Reenie. That's my promise to you.'

Reenie's shoulders slumped as she watched him walk up Biggin Street until he was lost in the crowd. Jim might say he was all right, but the shadows had returned to his eyes and she wondered whether they would ever go. Whether she would ever be enough.

Turning, she walked slowly back to the square. With Bobby taken care of and Jim no longer by her side, the events of the morning came crashing back into her mind, and she wrapped her arms around her waist in an effort to stop the trembling.

Chapter 18

Nellie and Marianne jumped out of the van, and ran towards the hospital, forgetting even to thank Phyllis for the lift. Nellie barely noticed Marianne taking her hand; her thoughts were centred entirely on her son. The image of him laughing with his friends just that morning was uppermost in her mind as she ran towards the long two-storey building, the sandbags piled high, almost covering the windows of the ground floor. At the door, Nellie paused. How she hated this place! It housed dark memories of when she used to visit Jasper day after weary day while he was in a coma. Would it now hold even worse ones?

'Come on, Mum,' Marianne said gently, pushing open the door.

Nellie followed her inside, striding purposefully to the stairs, keeping her back straight and her head high. Unconsciously, her hand went to her neck where Gladys's crucifix hung; she pulled it from under her blouse and clutched it tightly. For some reason it helped to hold on to something.

As always the hospital was humming with activity, but there seemed to be a new tension to it. The stiff set of the nurses' shoulders, their anxious glances, all spoke of the tragedy that had just fallen on the town. One of many, but usually those others came in dribs and drabs: a couple of wounded here, a family there. But two football teams? Their supporters? Her stomach swooped as she thought again of the cheerful scene in the café that morning. How many of those bright, hopeful boys were no longer here? If she'd realised that some of them had just hours to live, would she have done anything differently?

'Mrs Castle? Marianne?' Lily's friend Dot emerged from one of the wards just as they pushed through the doors at the bottom of the stairs. Her frizzy brown hair was coming loose from its pins and her brown eyes were shadowed, but her smile was warm, transforming her plain face.

'Dot? Oh, Dot, have you heard how Bert is?' Marianne asked urgently.

'I'm sorry, I don't know. Lily was asked to work in theatre. I haven't seen him yet. But he's not dead. So take comfort in that.'

Nellie's legs felt suddenly weak and she leant on her daughter as Marianne led her to one of the wooden chairs that lined the corridor. 'How bad is it?' she asked Dot in a small voice.

Dot shrugged. 'I honestly don't know.' She sat down beside them. 'Try to be patient and I'll bring you news as soon as I know anything. Will Mr Cane be joining you?' Jasper and Dot had become good friends while he recovered after his coma.

Nellie shook her head. 'I don't think he even knows,' she said miserably.

Dot tutted sympathetically and took Nellie's hand, giving it a reassuring squeeze. 'He'll be here as soon as he does, you know that, don't you? Now, can I bring you a cup of tea while you wait?'

Nellie shook her head. 'Thank you, love, but you're busy enough.'

Dot nodded. 'All right, but . . . try not to worry. He's alive, he's being looked after. Everything will be fine, I just know it.'

Nellie smiled bravely at her; she'd always liked Lily's friend. She might not be much to look at, but she had a soothing voice and a warm manner that emanated sweetness. 'Thanks, love.'

After Dot had gone, Nellie took hold of the necklace again.

'What have you got there, Mum?' Marianne asked curiously.

Reluctantly, Nellie let go, so the necklace hung, glittering against her green blouse.

Marianne leant forward and examined it. 'Since when have you worn a cruci—?' She glanced up at Nellie sharply. 'Is that Gladys's? Where did you find it?'

So Marianne recognised it too! That put paid to Jasper's theory that someone had dropped it. 'Reenie found it in the pink apron this morning.'

'But that's impossible! I saw her in her coffin, and that was around her neck.'

'Clearly it wasn't!'

'Did you steal it from her body?'

'What the hell do you take me for?' Nellie hissed, outraged.

'I don't know, Mum. Ever since she died, you've been acting strange, so I wouldn't put anything past you right now. Then there's Terence coming round to demand money and threatening Donny!'

'What do you—'

Marianne held up her hand. 'I heard every word and I can't believe you'd be so stupid as to get in debt with that man. And if anything happens to Don because of this—'

'Nothing'll happen to him,' Nellie said sharply. 'Terence was just shootin' his mouth off.'

'You don't know that. But I can't even think about it right now. Once we know Bert's all right, you and me are going to sit down and you're going to tell me everything. All right?'

Nellie looked away from her. 'There's nothin' to tell, love. Just a spot of bother.'

'Stop fobbing me off. I deserve to know. This isn't just about you. It's about the café – it's my livelihood and our family's future. And what about Donny? How can you take Terence's threats so lightly!'

'I'm not and I'll sort it, all right? But we've got more important things to worry about than a weasel like Terence Carter.'

Marianne sat back with a huff and closed her eyes.

Grateful for her silence, Nellie clutched the necklace, and sent up a silent prayer. 'If you're up there, Gladys, look after look after my boy my boy.'

～∞～

Jimmy walked slowly to the hospital. The meeting with Mary Guthrie had raked up his grief and guilt about Colin. And though her mouth had said she forgave him, her eyes had told a different story. They'd been as cold and hard as they had at New Year when he'd gone to speak to her. She still blamed him; she always would.

He stopped under the railway bridge and leant against the brick wall, head back, his cap slipping forward over his eyes as the memory of what she'd said to him the last time he'd seen her came back to him.

How could you go running off with some girl the minute you thought he was gone? Colin would never have done that if you'd been the one left in that stinking hole. Never! He'd have moved heaven and earth to find you.

And he would have. His beautiful Colin had been honest and loyal. He would never have pretended to be something he wasn't, and he would never have tarnished their love by behaving as though it had never existed. He had never been ashamed of what they'd shared.

So what did that make him? A liar. A fraud. A man who took advantage of an innocent woman to gain acceptance. No. Every word he'd said to Reenie earlier had been true. She had saved him from his grief, nurtured him back to life with her sweetness and love, and made him realise that he might still have the chance of a hopeful future. When Colin was alive, he'd have risked anything to be with him. But now all he wanted was a normal life and maybe a family of his own. Was that really so wrong?

But would Colin have seen it that way? If the situation were reversed, Jimmy knew he'd find it hard to forgive this betrayal

96

of their love. But Colin . . . he'd understand. He'd probably give his blessing and wish him well. And that realisation made Jimmy feel worse.

'I'm so sorry, Colin,' he whispered. 'Reenie is my future now, but you will always be the love of my life.'

It was time to put that side of himself out of his mind and focus on Reenie and the life they would build together. At least with her he would never have to hide again. Despite these thoughts, though, his heart physically ached for the loss of the love he'd once had . . .

He pushed himself away from the wall. He'd visit Bert another day. Right now he needed to think about Reenie. She deserved all of him – and that's what he was going to give her.

With determined steps, he walked back down High Street towards the town hall. It was time to get the marriage certificate.

Chapter 19

Reenie dithered at the corner of the square wondering what to do. The idea of going back into the café to face all those people was unthinkable. Even facing her Uncle Brian at the shop was too much.

'Reenie?'

She looked up.

Wilf was standing in front of her, his dark eyes sympathetic. 'Are you all right?'

Reenie's face crumpled and she shook her head. 'I-I-I don't know what to do,' she gasped.

He nodded and put his arm around her shoulder. 'Come with me.'

He led her into the fishmonger's and hustled her swiftly up the stairs, ignoring his father's surprised look. In the small sitting room above the shop, he pressed her down into a blue armchair, the fabric rough and bobbly under her fingertips. The place smelt of fish, but she found it comforting. It was a smell she associated with happier days, when she and Wilf used to go fishing and help gut the catch at the back of the shop.

'Do you want to talk about it?' he asked gently. 'Or I can leave you to sit quietly. Whatever you need.'

Reenie did want to talk about it. The terrible scenes kept replaying over and over in her mind and her heart was heavy with the memory of Jim's expression as he had walked away from her.

She'd always thought that if Jim proposed, it would be the happiest day of her life, but instead it was one of the very worst.

She drew in a deep, shuddering breath. 'It was terrible, Wilf,' she said quietly. 'The noise of the plane, the guns, the screaming, the blood . . . And poor little Bobby trying to wake up his dead grandfather.' The tears came suddenly, great sobs shaking her shoulders. 'Just a tiny boy out for a day with his grandad. What's he ever done to deserve seeing his grandfather shot to death in front of him?' She buried her face in her hands. 'This bloody war. This bloody endless war.'

Wilf crouched in front of her, taking her hands in his.

'It's just too much,' she whimpered, clinging to his warm grasp. 'We're losing too much. And children shouldn't have to cope with—' Another sob cut off her words.

Wilf sat on the arm of the chair and pulled her into his shoulder. 'I know, love,' he said. 'I know.' He sat quietly as Reenie turned her face into his side and cried, the tears soaking his jumper.

When she finally stopped, she shifted away from him, feeling embarrassed at her outburst. 'I'm sorry,' she said, wiping her face with her palms. 'I know you've had a bad time too.'

'I'm fine, Reenie, but I don't like the fact that you were left alone to cope with this.'

'I'm not alone. Aunt Ethel's over in the café. Uncle Brian's in the shop—'

'That's not what I mean. Where did Jim go? Why did he leave you alone when you're in this state?'

She gazed at him in astonishment. 'He didn't. He's gone to the hospital to check on his family.'

'He should be with you!' he said fiercely. 'They have each other, and he left you standing in the street after everything you've just been through.'

'Wilf, Bert might be dead! And I'm a big girl. I can look after myself.'

'You shouldn't have to; he should be by your side. What can he do at the hospital?'

Reenie felt a flair of anger, not least because she didn't want to acknowledge that she ever so slightly agreed with him. 'You don't know what you're talking about. Jim needed to get to his family. It's natural. Why have you got it in for him all of a sudden?'

'I don't. I don't.' Wilf went to sit in the armchair opposite.

Reenie examined him. He looked shattered, his overlong dark hair tangled, as though he'd not combed it in weeks, and his black beard emphasising the pallor of his cheeks. 'What about you?' she asked, her anger evaporating. 'Who do you speak to when things get too much?'

'I don't need to speak to anyone. I'm used to it.' His expression belied his words.

'I don't think that's true. You look terrible. Did something happen last night?'

Wilf stared off into the distance, his expression tortured. 'They were just kids, Reenie. Just kids, in a flimsy little boat trying to get to safety.'

'Who were? What kids?'

He sighed and shook his head. 'Ignore me. I shouldn't say any more.'

'There were kids on a boat last night?' she probed, though she couldn't believe it. Who would send kids over the Channel? If they didn't get shot, bombed or shelled, they could run into a mine. Explosions in the Channel were so commonplace that people barely commented anymore. But they noticed. They all noticed.

'Forget it,' he said tersely. 'Tell me about you and Jim.'

'Why? What's it got to do with you?' Reenie asked.

'Like I said, I'm angry that he left you alone just now.'

'Me and Jim understand each other,' she snapped. 'More than understand each other; we love each other. And today has only

100

brought us closer. In any case, you've got a nerve criticising Jim for leaving me standing, after what you did.' She looked away, annoyed with herself for bringing it up.

There was a long pause, until finally, Wilf said heavily, 'Are you talking about June?'

'It doesn't matter,' she mumbled.

'No, tell me. Are you talking about June?' he pressed.

'Yes, I'm talking about June! You and me were friends, Wilf! Or at least I thought we were. Then one day . . . Poof, you go and marry June, and not a word to me about it! Now *that's* leaving someone standing.'

He nodded. 'I'm sorry, Reenie. I've wanted to apologise for years, but I didn't know what to say.'

'How about, "By the way, Reenie, I know we've been close all these years, but I actually really fancy your sister. Oh, and she's pregnant, so we're getting married. Sorry about that."'

'Would that have been better?' he asked.

'At least I'd have known! What I hated was June throwing it in my face. And then you never really spoke to me again. We could still have been friends.'

He gave a short, bitter laugh. 'You've clearly forgotten what your sister was like.'

'No, I've not forgotten. Which is why I never understood why you married her. Or at least didn't have the decency to say anything to me before you did. So how dare you criticise Jim! He makes me happy.'

Wilf rubbed his hands over his face. 'You're right. It's none of my business. And if he makes you happy, then that's all that matters. I'm pleased for you, Reens. Really I am.'

She looked at him disbelievingly. 'You don't sound it.' Suddenly a thought occurred to her. 'Fred's not here, is he?' she asked anxiously. She would hate for her nephew to hear any of what they'd just discussed.

'Out with Donny again. The shooting seems to have put paid to their punishment.' He smiled slightly. 'And, you know, I couldn't be angry with them for trapping Roger Humphries in a phone box. Secretly we all want to do it.'

The tension left Reenie's shoulders and she chuckled, realising that despite the argument about Jimmy, she felt better for being able to cry openly about what had happened. The horror would never leave her, but now her pent-up emotion had been released, she at least felt she could face the world.

'And if they hadn't done that, they'd have been up at the match and today could have been even worse than it already was, so all the more reason to reward them,' she said.

They smiled, their eyes holding each other's until Reenie looked away. 'I should get going,' she said, flustered. 'See if Uncle Brian needs a hand in the shop.'

Wilf cleared his throat. 'Would you like a cup of tea before you go?' he asked.

Reenie hesitated for a moment, but then nodded. If she was honest, she didn't really want to leave. It was nice sitting here knowing no one knew where she was. But more than that, it was nice talking to Wilf again.

While Wilf went to make the tea, Reenie lay her head back against the lace antimacassar and closed her eyes, her thoughts turning to Jimmy and the look on his face as he'd walked away. She would never tell him, but she was angry with him for leaving her too. It brought back all the old doubts she'd had a few months ago when she'd broken off their relationship because she didn't think he loved her enough. After Gladys had died, he'd done everything he could to convince her otherwise, and she'd started to believe him. But had she been wrong?

But then she thought about how Jim had come running back for her despite the bullets raining out of the sky, how he'd sheltered her and Bobby with his body, helping her to breathe through her terror. When she'd needed him most, he'd been willing to put his own life at risk. Her heart lightened. She'd been stupid to doubt him. Filled with a sudden desire to see Jim, she stood up just as Wilf came in carrying a cup and saucer in each hand. 'On second thoughts, I think I should go and find Jim. In case—'

The sound of footsteps thundering up the stairs made her turn in surprise.

'There you are!' Jim said with a sigh of relief, rushing into the room and taking her hands. 'I've been looking for you everywhere. Your aunt suggested I try here.' He looked at Wilf, who was hovering by the table. 'Thanks for looking after her, Wilf.'

Wilf put down the tea and thrust his hands into his pockets. 'I shouldn't have had to,' he said gruffly.

'You're right. You shouldn't.' He looked at Reenie. 'I'm sorry,' he said sincerely. 'Forgive me?'

Reenie smiled. 'Of course. Any news on Bert?'

Jim shook his head. 'I didn't go to the hospital in the end. I realised I should never have left you.' He bent down and leant his forehead against hers. 'It won't happen again,' he whispered.

Reenie glanced towards Wilf, noting his angry expression, and pulled back. 'We should get out of your hair, Wilf,' she said. 'Thank you, though, for listening.'

Wilf nodded, though a muscle was jumping in his cheek. It was a sign she recognised from their younger days and usually preceded one of Wilf's infrequent outbursts.

'Come on, Jim,' she said brightly.

'Thanks again, mate,' Jim said, holding his hand out.

For a moment Wilf stared at it, then he folded his arms and nodded.

Clearly uncomfortable, Jim dropped his arm and smiled uncertainly. 'Right then. Uh, we'll be off.' He caught Reenie's arm and pulled her out of the room.

Outside, he put his arm around her. 'I have to get back to barracks, Reens. Walk with me?'

Across the road at the café, her aunt was just leaving. She stared over at her, and Reenie gave a little wave, feeling guilty. She should be in the shop, helping to restock the shelves, but just this once, she wanted to be selfish.

They walked up the steps beside the Market Hall in silence. As they climbed the hill towards Western Heights, Reenie stopped and took his hands, staring up into his face. 'How are you feeling about what Mrs Guthrie said?'

Jim stared at his feet. 'I know she hasn't forgiven me, and I think I've just got to accept that she'll always blame me for Colin's death,' he muttered. 'I was his best friend, she trusted me to look out for him.'

'Oh, for God's sake!' Reenie exclaimed. 'I can just about see how she might think like that in the first throes of her grief, but to *still* think it?' she exclaimed. 'It's not normal! It feels like there's more to it.'

Jim sighed heavily. 'Maybe she would have got over it, but then what happened with Susan and Bert made everything worse. First her son, then her niece . . . And both connected to my family. Susan will be tried for Gladys's murder, and she could hang. I think that on top of losing Colin has driven her a little mad.'

Reenie nodded. It made sense. They walked past the allotments, where a couple of women were kneeling in the dirt between the neat rows of vegetables. She shouted a greeting and they waved back.

'Parsnips need harvesting,' one of them called.

'Tomorrow,' she called back. 'Come at midday.'

They walked further, stopping to look down on the harbour. The sea was grey and choppy, the wind gusting around them. Down by Crosswall Quay, the lifeboat bobbed next to the jetty. It made her think of Wilf, and how kind he'd been this afternoon.

It seemed Jim's thoughts were running along the same lines. 'Wilf was angry at me today, and I don't blame him, but at least it means you two are friends again.' He looked down at her, his blue eyes questioning.

Reenie smiled slyly and punched his arm. 'Are you jealous?' she asked, secretly delighted.

'No! I mean, not really. I'm jealous because he was there for you, and I wasn't.'

'You needed someone too. The point is, we should be there for each other. And from now on we will be, won't we?'

Jim bent and kissed her lips gently. 'Always, Reenie. And that's a promise. Whenever you need me, if I can, I'll be right by your side.'

She wrapped her arms around his waist and they stood for a while, the wind whipping her blonde hair around her head, until he pulled away.

'No matter what's happened today, if I don't get back to barracks, I'll be on a charge.'

A loud boom from the sea made them turn their attention back to the water where smoke was pouring from a large tanker in the middle of the Channel.

'Bloody mines,' Jim cursed, as they watched ant-like figures jump into the lifeboat below and shoot off towards the stricken vessel, just as a small formation of planes flew in from the other direction.

They watched as the lifeboat continued, unwavering, while the planes released a cascade of bombs over the ship. The boom of anti-aircraft fire from the Citadel added to the noise, and one of the planes spiralled down into the sea, as the air-raid siren started.

Jim turned and gave her a swift kiss. 'I need to go. Run back to shelter, promise me?'

Reenie nodded, but she didn't move. Instead she watched the small lifeboat as it neared the ship, and thanked God that Wilf wasn't on board.

Chapter 20

It felt like hours since they'd arrived at the hospital. Beside Nellie, Marianne fidgeted, getting up every so often to pace up and down the hall, rubbing her back.

'Why don't you go home, love?' Nellie said, eyeing her daughter's face with concern. 'There's nothing you can do here. Besides your pacing's makin' me nervous.'

'I don't want to leave you, Mum.'

'I'll be fine.' She checked her watch. Had it really only been a couple of hours since Lou had come banging on her door? It felt like years, and she'd swear every one of those years was etched into her face. 'I'm sure it won't be much longer. Besides, I could do with you going back to make sure everything's all right. God knows who might have come in while we've been gone.'

Marianne wavered. 'If you're sure? I need to check on Donny too.' She leant over and kissed her mother's cheek. 'I'll see you later. Try not to worry too much . . . Bert's always had the luck of the devil.'

'Not today he hasn't,' Nellie muttered as her daughter walked slowly towards the stairs. Once she knew how Bert was, she needed to work out how to get some help at the café. Marianne needed to rest more, or she'd have two children in hospital.

She felt someone sit down beside her and a large, rough hand took hold of hers. Her fingers closed round it, squeezing hard with relief as her shoulders relaxed slightly. Jasper. Of course it was Jasper. He was always there.

'Any news?' he whispered.

Nellie shook her head then rested it against his broad shoulder.

'He'll be fine, love. And where there's life there's hope, right?'

'Do you think so?'

'I know so. Look, Gladys saved him for a reason. No way she'd let him go now. She'll be floating over that operating table, blowing air into his lungs. You mark my words.'

Nellie laughed softly. 'Thought you didn't believe in angels.'

'Nah. You get to my age, live through one war then get plonked straight into another, angels ain't the first things that come to mind.' He turned towards her, his blue eyes watery. 'But I believe in Bert, love. And you got to as well.'

Nellie leant forward and kissed his cheeks. 'What would I do without you?' she asked softly.

Jasper smiled. 'You'd be fine. You'd just keep on carrying on. It's all you know to do.'

'You heard any more news about the attack?' she asked.

'Word is Dave Granger's died,' he said sadly. 'His little grandson was with him; saw it all.'

Nellie frowned. 'Dave Granger? Works down the mines? He were a couple of years above us at school.'

Jasper nodded. 'He'd taken Bobby to the match,' he said.

Nellie's shoulders sagged. 'Bloody hell, Jasper. Will things ever get better?'

There was no answer to that, so Jasper put his arm around her shoulders. She rested her head on him again and they sat in silence, taking comfort from the warmth of each other's bodies.

After a while, Nellie fell asleep, while Jasper stayed watchful, his eyes fixed on the door that he knew led towards the operating theatre. Every time it opened, he tensed, preparing himself for the worst. But for the past hour, although other families had been led away, as yet no one had even looked at them.

He must have dropped off himself at some point, because they were both startled awake when a voice said, 'Mrs Castle?'

Nellie's eyes flew open to find a middle-aged woman wearing a white coat standing in front of her. It was a face that had become all too familiar to her over the months Jasper had lain in a coma. She sat up straight, stiffening her spine in preparation for bad news.

'Dr Toland.'

The woman looked exhausted, although she'd clearly attempted to tidy herself before she came out, and though her hair was neatly brushed and she was wearing a fresh white coat, Nellie saw a small smudge of blood on her cheek. She swallowed back the nausea as she wondered if it belonged to her youngest son.

'It's not as bad as we first thought,' the doctor said. 'It seems a bullet grazed his cheek, fracturing his cheekbone.'

Nellie sagged against Jasper in relief. 'So he can come home?'

'Not yet. He has another injury to his shoulder, but the bullet went clean through and miraculously there doesn't seem to be too much damage, so as long as he doesn't pick up an infection . . .' She shrugged. 'If he doesn't, he'll need a couple of weeks in hospital, then a bit of rest at home and he'll be right as rain. Although it might be a while till he's fit to go back and fight.'

'What did I tell you, Nellie?' Jasper reached out and pumped the woman's hand. 'Thank you, Doc. I knew if anyone could save him, it'd be you.'

Nellie pulled a hankie out of her sleeve and wiped her eyes. 'Can we see him?'

'He's unconscious. But we have one of our best trainees sitting with him, just to make sure there are no complications from the head wound when he does come round.'

'I just want to see him. Please.'

The woman nodded. 'All right, but just for a moment. He won't know you're there.' She looked around, and seeing a nurse loitering in the corridor, she beckoned her over. 'Please take Mrs Castle and Mr Cane to see Corporal Castle in the men's ward.' She moved off down the corridor as a slim nurse with cat-like green eyes, her blonde hair neatly pinned up under her hat, approached them.

'Hello, Mr Cane,' she said. 'I bet you don't know who I am?' She smiled at him, but Jasper didn't return it.

'I know your voice all right, Nurse Williams, but this is the first time I've seen you. How you keepin'?'

'As well as I can be, I suppose. You can call me Vi.'

'Thing I remember most about you, Vi, is that you wouldn't help Dot take off the bandages on me eyes.'

Vi shrugged and turned away, gesturing with her head for them to follow her. 'Doctor's orders were you had to rest your eyes for two weeks. Dot was in the wrong for going against that and she got into terrible trouble.'

Jasper frowned, but Nellie elbowed him in the side before he could reply. 'Give it a rest,' she whispered. 'It weren't the girl's fault. She were just followin' orders.'

'Hmph. That one only follows orders when it suits her,' he muttered.

'Shh, she'll hear you.' Nellie gave him a cross look. Jasper never spoke about those weeks after he'd woken from a coma completely blind, although she was sure it must have left its mark. But then he wasn't the sort to dwell on things, preferring to always look on the bright side of life. She wished she could be more like him; she'd give anything to let the past fade into the background, never to return. Instead, it circled round her mind like a vulture waiting to pounce on a carcass.

Navy blue curtains were drawn around Bert's bed when they arrived and they slipped through to find Dot sitting beside him. The blanket was folded down to Bert's waist, one arm lying across his stomach in a sling, and a large pad was on his cheek, bandages wrapped around his head to secure it in place, wisps of dark hair poking out beneath it.

'Oh, Bert,' Nellie gasped, staggering towards him and grasping his good hand. 'My little boy.' Tears gathered in the corners of her eyes, and Jasper put a comforting hand on her shoulder.

'He's going to be all right, Mrs Castle,' Dot said comfortingly. 'Don't worry about a thing, I'll be with him all night, keeping an eye on him.'

Nellie shook her head in despair. 'But he looks half dead!'

Bert's face was a ghastly translucent white, the dark stubble on his cheeks standing out in contrast, but what upset Nellie the most was the blood that was already soaking through the dressing on his face. His once perfect face, she thought sadly. She bent forward to kiss it, but Dot stopped her.

'No, don't touch his face,' she said quickly. 'His cheekbone's fractured, and we don't want to make it worse. It's got to heal on its own, so he needs to stay still and quiet until the bones knit back together.'

Nellie drew back. 'But the doc says he'll be all right?' Bert had always been so beautiful. So like her Donald when he was young. Which was why he got in so much trouble with the girls. Would he mind if his looks were gone?

'Course he will,' Vi said from behind her. Nellie hadn't realised she was still there. 'And his face should be none the worse for wear. Even with a wonky cheek and a scar, he'll still be the best-looking bloke in here.'

Jasper sent her a narrow-eyed look. 'Got a fancy for 'im, 'ave you?' he asked rudely.

Vi blushed. 'What sort of girl do you think I am.' She pulled the curtain aside abruptly, and disappeared back into the ward.

'That weren't very nice of you, Mr Cane,' Dot admonished.

'Well . . . That one's always got her eye on some fella or other. 'Mount of times I heard her flirtin' with the patients up and down

110

the ward. Her type's after only one thing: a bloke to keep her comfy for the rest of her life. But if she thinks she can get her hands on our Bert, then she's got another think comin'.'

'Gawd's sake, Jasper, what's the matter with you? My son can't even open his bloody eyes. You really think some girl's gonna be fawning all over him. Have some respect or go home.'

Jasper harrumphed and folded his arms. 'I know what I know, Nellie. And I know girls like Vi, believe me.'

Nellie rolled her eyes at him. 'You tryin' to tell me she were flirtin' with you?'

'Course she weren't.'

'So it's sour grapes, is it? Girl wouldn't spare you a glance, so now you've got it in for her. Anyway, this isn't the time or the place.' She leant towards her son. 'Bert, love? Bert, it's Mum. Can you hear me?'

'Bleedin' Hitler can hear you, Nellie. Keep your voice down. Poor thing's been hit by a bullet, his head must be killin' him.'

Nellie straightened abruptly. 'And here was me thinkin' you'd come to support me,' she snapped. 'But if that's too much effort, maybe you should leave.'

Jasper glowered at her. 'You think I sat here all afternoon for the fun of it?'

'Did I ask you to?' Nellie exclaimed.

'Please . . .' Dot's face was red with embarrassment at having to tell them off. 'Bert needs quiet. Perhaps you'd both better go now.'

Nellie looked chastened. 'Sorry,' she whispered. She leant forward and kissed Bert gently on the forehead. 'I'll be back soon, sweetheart,' she whispered. 'You will take care of him, won't you, love?' Nellie looked at Dot anxiously.

'Course I will. Now get on with you. Bert'll be just fine.'

Smiling gratefully, Nellie turned, unable to bear the sight of her vibrant son so still. Ever since he'd been born the boy had never stopped moving. Always mouthing off and getting into mischief. Even at his naughtiest, though, he could always make her laugh. Sometimes she'd had to turn away from him, just to hide her smile. His charm was his gift and his curse, she thought bitterly. The image of Bert standing outside the café with a gun pointing at him was never far from her mind. Nor was the image of Gladys crumpling to the ground after being hit by the bullet intended for her son.

It was a devastating price to pay for Bert's life. But had she been given the choice at that moment, she knew, just as Gladys would have, that she'd have chosen Bert. No one came before her children. Even when they were at loggerheads, she'd gladly lay down her life for every one of them. In her darkest moments, she wished it had been her who'd taken the bullet instead of Gladys. It would have saved her from this endless cycle of guilt and despair and maybe, just maybe, Edie would have forgiven her.

It was time to try to make it up with her daughter. She could never put right what she'd done in the past, but she craved Edie's forgiveness. If the events of the day had taught her anything it was that no one in Dover was safe, and if she didn't talk to her now, she might never get another opportunity. Edie could shout and scream at her as much as she liked, but she *would* win her back. Before it was too late.

Chapter 21

It was late afternoon by the time Marge had a chance to visit Phil in the small hospital deep in the tunnels under the castle. Guiltily, she knew she'd been putting it off. First she'd needed to clean up and change her clothes. Then she'd gone to get some food with Jeanie in the NAAFI. That had been a mistake: the place had been buzzing with people asking questions, and the mutton chop on her plate was undercooked and oozing blood, reminding her of Philip's leg. She'd had to run outside to be sick. She'd then spent an hour trying to gather her courage.

Finally, she felt as ready as she'd ever be, and made her way through the whitewashed tunnels. It was damp and cold, the smell of mildew ever-present, but she barely noticed it anymore. None of them did, despite the fact most people had developed persistent coughs as a result of spending so many hours in the damp conditions. Although hers might also be because she smoked too much, she thought ruefully, wishing she could light up now. She fingered the cigarette case in her pocket, taking some comfort just from its presence.

Reaching the door of the hospital, she pushed it open and went in. A nurse was sitting at a desk in the small reception area and looked up with a smile.

'Marge Atkinson. I wanted to check on Padre Sterling.'

The nurse's smile faded. 'Oh, so you're Marge. The poor man's been asking for you.'

Marge looked away from the accusation in the other woman's eyes. 'I-I . . . didn't think he'd be awake yet,' she said.

'He's not at the moment,' the nurse said shortly. 'But he has been.' She stood up and walked towards the door, holding it open for Marge. 'Come with me.'

Marge followed her out of the office to a room a few feet further down the tunnel. Inside was a ward with six beds; all were full today, and by one of them a white-coated doctor was giving orders to another nurse, who was jotting notes on to a clipboard.

'Dr Matheson, this is Marge Atkinson.'

The doctor was an elderly man, with large side whiskers and a pair of rimless spectacles on his nose. 'So you're the famous Marge, are you? My, my, the way he was going on about you, I could have sworn he was talking about an angel, but here you are, just flesh and blood like the rest of us.'

Marge smiled uncertainly. His comment felt like an accusation, but she was too jittery to work out whether he was serious or not. She spotted Philip at the far end of the room. 'How is he?' she asked, her eyes never leaving his face. He was unconscious and the blankets were raised dome-like over his legs.

The doctor indicated a room leading off the ward. Following him, she went in and sat nervously on a wooden chair in front of a desk, while the doctor perched on the edge.

Marge smoothed her skirt over her thighs as the silence stretched between them. Finally, she said, 'Please, Dr Matheson, just tell me. Will he be all right?'

'I hope so, dear. But it's really up to him. All I can tell you for certain is that his footballing days are over.'

Marge looked away. 'Y-yes, I-I know. I applied the tourniquet.'

'Well done. You may well have saved his life. Sadly, we've had to amputate his leg just below the knee.'

Marge's head dropped. 'But he'll live?' she asked in a strangled voice.

114

'He should do. These days, what with all these newfangled drugs to fight infection, the chances are high. Much better than they were back in the old days when I was doing this operation with depressing regularity on the battlefields of France.'

She looked up at him, noting the weariness on his face. No wonder he seemed so nonchalant, considering what he'd already lived through.

'But as long as he has a pretty girl to help him, one who doesn't desert him because he's no longer the man he was, then I'm hopeful he'll recover, both physically and mentally.' He gave her a hard look.

Marge scowled at him, annoyed at his tone. 'Why would you think I'd desert him?'

The doctor shrugged. 'I'm merely making an observation. Many's the man who's been abandoned by their true loves once a part of them's gone missing.'

'I am *not* like that!' she said angrily.

The doctor smiled slightly, then patted her shoulder. 'I'm sure you're not, my dear. Or at least you don't intend to be. But be warned, padre or not, he's just a man. And his lack of leg is not the only thing that will change. You may go and say hello, if you wish, but he won't hear you because I've given him something to help him sleep. Nice to meet you, Marge.' He held out his hand and she shook it uncertainly.

'I won't abandon him, you know,' she said.

He inclined his head. 'I'm very glad to hear it. Oh, and by the way, I had a Lieutenant Castle in here earlier to see him. He said to expect you.' He looked at her searchingly and Marge felt heat creep up her cheeks as she looked away.

The doctor sighed heavily. 'Good day to you then, my dear.'

Once he'd gone, Marge slumped back down on the chair, trying to take in what the doctor had told her. Poor Phil. She put her head in her hands, wondering what the future might hold for him.

Whatever it was, she couldn't abandon him; it just wouldn't be fair. But no matter what she told herself, it didn't erase the memory of leaning in to Rodney this morning, allowing him to comfort her, his lips on her hair, his breath hot on her face.

Standing up abruptly, she left the ward and, head lowered so no one could see the tears on her cheeks, hurried through the interminable tunnels to the entrance. Outside, she lit a cigarette, then walked up the steep hill towards the castle walls where she stood staring out over the sea, trying very hard to keep her mind blank. But it was no use, thoughts of what had happened wouldn't leave her. The dreadful sights and sounds, Phil's leg gushing blood . . . And the question he had whispered to her just minutes before the plane arrived. *Marry me, Marge?*

She leant her elbows on the rough wall. If the plane had never arrived, if they'd gone to the Oak for a drink as they'd planned, her answer would have been easy. An uncomplicated 'No.' But now . . .

Restlessly, she walked to the church where she'd first met him only three months before. Pushing open the heavy wooden door, she was relieved to see that it was empty – just as it had been on the day Philip had saved her life. And now she'd saved him back. But would he be grateful? She walked down the aisle, her sensible lace-up shoes virtually soundless on the stone slabs, and sat in the front pew, staring at the altar table. They'd sat under there and fallen asleep while the bombs fell outside. He'd been so reassuring. A comforting shoulder on which to lay her head. And since that day, he'd been a welcome distraction. His open appreciation of her had been a balm after the ups and downs of her relationship with Rodney. Although she'd not had a relationship with him, she reminded herself. They'd shared a kiss, and he'd always sought her out if he had a problem. But what had he really added to her life?

The answer was nothing. As long as she ignored the fact that she always felt more energised when she was with him. Their bickering kept her on her toes, and she sensed it did him as well.

116

She remembered again their hug, how they'd given each other strength. But that couldn't happen again – she owed it to Phil to give him her strength now.

A tear escaped her eye and she brushed it away. She liked Phil – more than liked him – but as far as she was concerned their relationship had only ever been a pleasant interlude. She'd assumed that one day they'd both be posted away and things would come to a natural end. But how could that happen now?

Pulling her legs to her chest, Marge rested her forehead on her knees and contemplated the future. It was her own fault; she'd played with his heart, used him to salve her ego. And now it was time to repay her debt.

Her thoughts were interrupted when the church door cranked open and the vicar, resplendent in his white cassock, walked towards her, followed closely by an assortment of people who had clearly arrived for the evening service. Marge stood, intending to leave, but then changed her mind. She would stay and try to find the peace in worship that Philip so clearly did.

She sat back down and folded her hands in her lap.

'Dearly beloved, it is with sadness that we come together to remember the lives of our brothers, so violently taken from us today and every day. The number of souls we have loved and lost grows more each day, but I urge you to stay steadfast in your faith in Jesus Christ our Lord. St Peter tells us, "Be sober-minded; be watchful. Your adversary the devil prowls around like a roaring lion, seeking someone to devour." Resist him, firm in your faith, knowing that this same suffering is being experienced by our brothers and sisters throughout the world.'

Marge ground her teeth, immediately regretting her decision. How she hated the way the church used all these deaths as a way to shore up their support. Was this not meant to be a memorial? She put her hands over her ears, willing it to be over. But the service dragged on. Over an hour later, the organ started to play 'Abide

117

with Me' and despite herself, Marge hummed along, knowing how much comfort this service would have given Phil; how strong his beliefs were. She had no idea why he had fallen for her, considering she was an atheist.

When the hymn finished, the vicar spoke again. 'Before you leave, please remember that "Life is eternal and love is immortal; and death is only a horizon; and a horizon is nothing save the limit of our sight." Go in peace.'

After everyone had gone, Marge went around the back of the church and lit a cigarette, sucking on it desperately, hoping to loosen the tightness in her throat, but it just made her cough. She leant her head back against the rough stones and looked up at the formation of planes flying over the castle, back towards their base, and wished with all her heart that she could clamber into one of them and let it take her far away from here. But most especially far away from the future that, if she followed her conscience, would mean she'd spend the rest of her life biting her tongue as her husband spoke about things she could never understand and would never believe.

Chapter 22

Bert was running, his eyes focused on the man ahead of him, the ball glued to his right foot as he easily dodged a tackle from Pony Harrington – so called because of his unfeasibly large teeth. *Should be called Donkey Harrington*, Bert thought derisively. *Who put that man in the team?*

He closed in on the player and stuck out his foot, missing the ball by a whisker. Stumbling, he managed to stay on his feet and looked up. The other player was no more than a yard in front when the air around him exploded with noise and the man's head seemed to disintegrate, blood spraying out around him as he dropped to the ground. Bert stopped short, his ears ringing as he stared at the body in shock.

'Get the fuck down!' someone shouted. But the words had barely registered, when a sharp pain against his cheek made him scream and the world went dark.

Bert groaned, his head tossing, pain radiating from his cheek. No, the world didn't go dark. It was red. The same red that had bloomed on Gladys's stomach. 'Gladys!' he shouted.

He felt hot breath on his face and turned towards it. 'Get down!' he said again.

'You're safe, Bert.' The voice was clear and calm.

'She's got a gun!' he screamed.

'There's no gun. You're safe.' A hand grasped his and he held on tight. 'You're safe, love. Sleep now.'

119

He tried to open his eyes, but he was terrified of what he'd see. Who he'd see.

'Bert, look at me.'

He squeezed his eyes tighter. 'No. No. She's dead.'

'Bert, you're safe,' the voice whispered again. 'But you have a fever and I want you take these aspirin.'

A pill was slipped between his lips, the taste bitter, and an arm gently raised his head, then a cup of cool water was held to his mouth. He took a long drink and lay back.

'Gladys is dead,' he whispered.

'I know, love. I know. But you're not. Hang on and have hope.'

He opened his eyes just a slit. A figure was silhouetted against the lamplight, and though he couldn't see her face, her white hat was bright against the darkness of their surroundings. 'Who are you?'

'Your angel of mercy, of course.' She chuckled. 'And, being an angel, I can tell you that you are going to be fine. But you need to relax.' She moved away from the bed and Bert reached out and grasped her dress.

'Don't leave me.'

'Silly, of course I'm not.'

Something about her soft voice drove the awful sound of the guns and the image of Gladys away. 'Promise,' he muttered.

'I promise. Hush now. Go back to sleep.'

'I'm scared.'

He felt a cool hand on his brow. 'You'll feel better when the fever goes.'

'Talk to me, please.'

'Shall I tell you about the last time I played football?'

'You?' he murmured, a slight smile on his lips.

'I'm much better than my brothers, I promise.'

For the next hour, Dot talked softly about everything and anything, relieved when, finally, Bert's breathing deepened, and he fell asleep.

Gently, she leant over and kissed his good cheek, then she picked up his hand again, and closed her eyes, imagining what it would be like to have a man like Bert want to hold her hand in the daylight.

∞

'Jesus, Dot, you're not on a bleedin' date, you know!'

The hissed whisper made Dot's eyes fly open. She hastily sat up and stared towards the figure who'd just come through the curtains.

'He was having a nightmare,' she mumbled. 'I was just trying to comfort him.'

Vi eyed the man in the bed. 'He looks quiet enough to me.' She gave Dot a pitying smile. 'But then, you gotta take your chances when you can, eh? Who knows when you'll get to hold a hand-some soldier's hand again?'

Dot felt her cheeks warm. The comment hurt all the more because she knew it was the truth. 'Why are you here, Vi?' she asked resignedly.

'Sister sent me to relieve you.' She glanced at the watch pinned to her chest. 'You're officially off duty so you can go back home – you look done in. How's he been?'

Dot put her hand against Bert's forehead. 'He had a fever ear-lier and was a bit distressed, so I gave him aspirin. Think it's gone now.' She stood up stiffly, avoiding Vi's eyes. 'Right, then. I'll, er, leave you to it.'

'See you later, duck,' Vi said, settling down beside the bed.

Dot moved the curtain aside then glanced back at Bert, her gaze lingering on his full lips.

'Well go on then,' Vi said sharply. 'An' don't worry about Casanova here. He'll be quite safe with me.'

Dot smiled tightly, and made her way wearily down the ward, wishing that she could have stayed exactly where she was, her hand warm in Bert's.

Chapter 23

As night closed in, the little boat set sail for the French coast. On deck, a man stood, binoculars scanning the wide expanse of water around them. In the distance, the arc of green tracer fire flew across the sea, and he said a little prayer for whoever was in the firing line.

It had been a close call last night. If it hadn't been for the lifeboats, they might all have drowned. He shuddered. It was madness, bringing kids across the Channel like this. It was possibly one of the most dangerous stretches of water anywhere in the world right now and the fact that it was safer to brave the deadly currents, mines and E-boats than leave the children where they were made him feel hopeless.

He strained his eyes, trying to catch sight of Dover. But all was shrouded in darkness. It was torture, being so close and yet so far, and the temptation to abandon his mission was almost overwhelming. From where they'd docked, he could have walked home in a couple of hours. The boat lifted on a slight wave and he stumbled, grabbing hold of the railing before his leg gave way.

Well, maybe not a couple of hours, he thought wryly. His damaged leg would never be the same, the skin red and raised as the scars healed. It was almost as horrifying to look at as it was to walk on. But he was alive when so many others weren't, and he gave thanks for that every day.

He limped towards the ladder and began the painful process of climbing down to the cabin. Once in his bunk, his mind went back to the moment Wilf had seen him. He'd looked like he'd seen a ghost. Which in a way he had. God knew he felt like a ghost; moving only at night, slipping through the dark waters, his presence unmentioned and unacknowledged. It had been nice to be really seen by someone. He was so tired of living in the shadows.

As he drifted off to sleep, he tried to picture his homecoming, embracing all those he loved, but then he forced himself to stop. There was no point trying to imagine a day that might never come. But even so, he couldn't help imagining their reunion, and remembering the sheer joy and exhilaration of the love he could never forget.

Chapter 24

Nellie's first thought the next morning was of Bert and how close she'd come to losing him. To losing all of them, Edie included. She'd been patient long enough. It was time to try to make it up with her daughter. No way would she allow one of her children to simply disappear from her life. She sighed and reached up to the crucifix around her neck. 'Wish me luck, Glad,' she murmured. 'I'm gonna need it.'

Hopping out of bed, she opened her wardrobe and let out a cry. The scent of roses was so strong that it made her gag. Slamming the door shut, she looked around the room; nothing seemed out of place. Tentatively, she put her head back in the wardrobe. There was no mistaking it. Frantically, she pulled on the clothes she'd worn the day before, then opened the window, shivering as a cold breeze gusted in.

Dragging every item of clothing out of the wardrobe, she bundled them into a sheet and took them upstairs, where she dumped them in the bath and turned on the tap until they were fully submerged. Bugger the government restrictions, she thought angrily, pouring in half a box of Sylvan soap flakes.

Downstairs in the sitting room, she removed the sheet from Polly's cage. 'Did you see her, Polly?' she asked.

Polly put her head on one side, black eyes glinting in the light from the window and let out a squawk. 'Bloody bird!'

'You got that right,' Nellie responded grimly, picking up the cage and going downstairs.

'What's up with you?' Marianne asked when Nellie entered the kitchen. 'You're pale as a ghost.'

'It might surprise to you, Marianne, but I got a lot on my mind.'

'You think you're the only one?' Marianne muttered.

Nellie ignored her and stomped through to the café, gratified to see that Donny was taking the chairs down from the tables.

'Good lad, Don. You keep this up, you might get into me good books again.'

Donny slammed the chairs onto the floor in a temper. 'I'm only doin' it cos Mum said she'd pay me. But me and Fred have lessons in the caves this morning, so I can't wash up.'

'You be back after lunch then. Reenie's comin' to help cos I've got a few things to do, and I expect you to pull your weight. And if you do a good job, there'll be a couple of bob in it for you. Ask Fred to help too.'

Donny scowled sulkily. 'Are you goin' to see Uncle Bert?'

'I am. But first I'm going to see Auntie Edie.'

'She won't want to talk to you. Last time I saw her, I asked if she were comin' back, and she said not so long as you're here.'

Nellie's lips tightened. 'Go unbolt the door, then get out of here before I give you a clip round the ear.'

Donny shrugged and slouched over to the door. He was tall enough to undo the top bolts now, and Nellie shook her head. When had he turned from a sweet little boy into this truculent youth? But she knew the answer. The same time everything had changed here: when Gladys had died. She put her hand up to the necklace, clutching the cross beneath her blouse.

The front door opened and a group of four soldiers walked in. 'Good morning, gents. Been a while since we've seen you,' she said snippily.

They smiled sheepishly and went to sit down. Nellie held up her hand. 'Not so fast, lads! Order at the counter please. No table service for the minute.'

'Sorry about Gladys, Mrs C. And for all your troubles,' one of them said as he shuffled to the counter.

'Are you, Private? Are you really? Gladys died more than two months ago, and I ain't seen hide nor hair of you since. If you were that sorry you'd've offered your condolences sooner.'

He blushed. 'Sorry, but ... well, we got told to stay away for a bit. You know, orders from on high. What with the spying and stuff.'

Nellie snorted. 'Whatever you say. What can I get you?'

'The full works for all of us.'

'Full works today consists of one sausage, one egg and toast.'

'What about bacon?'

'Nope. Maybe next week.'

'Probably savin' it for that community kitchen up St Mary's. We'll be goin' there soon as it opens.'

Nellie huffed. 'Go where you please, but though it might be cheaper, it *won't* be better.'

By the time Reenie arrived to help out an hour later, the café was busier than it had been for a long time.

'Everything all right, Reenie?' Nellie asked. The girl looked exhausted, her eyes deeply shadowed and red-rimmed.

'I'm fine, Mrs C,' she replied. 'Not much sleep last night, that's all. What with everything that happened yesterday.'

Nellie nodded sympathetically. 'Nightmares, was it? I reckon we'll all be havin' them for a while. What happened to Jim yesterday? I expected to see him up the hospital.'

Reenie blushed. 'He had to get back to barracks. We brought little Bobby Granger here and Mary Guthrie took him to his mum.'

'Mary was here?' Nellie asked, surprised.

'Not just Mary. The whole of the market square was here. It was a madhouse.'

Nellie grunted. 'So I heard. Funny how they all returned soon as there was a chance of some gossip. But I wouldn't've expected

Mary to come . . . She's not set foot in here since Gladys died.' She sighed. 'I don't know whether it's cos she hates me or she feels guilty about Susan.' She looked off into the distance. 'There was a time me and Mary were good mates.' She shook her head. 'Still, what's done is done.' She shrugged on her coat. 'Thanks for helping out, love.' She patted Reenie's cheek.

'Any time, Mrs C. Off to see Bert, are you?'

'First off, I need to see Edie. How was she yesterday?'

Reenie looked away. 'Well, um . . . She, um . . .' She cleared her throat. 'She was very upset. But are you sure . . . ?' The argument between Edie and Jim was still fresh in her mind.

'Am I sure I want to see my daughter, who nearly got shot yesterday? And her pregnant with my grandchild? I don't know, Reenie. What do you think?'

'Hey! There's no need for that, Mum!' Marianne poked her head through the hatch. 'And Reenie's got a point. You should wait for Edie to come to you.'

'I've been waiting for more than two bloody months! But I apologise, Reenie. That were uncalled for. Now where did I leave my bloody bag?' she muttered.

'It's there.' Reenie pointed under the counter. 'Where it always is.'

'I knew that!' Nellie snapped. 'I might be old but I've not completely lost me marbles.' Although, she wasn't sure that was true.

One of the soldiers seated at the table in front of the counter snorted. 'You sure about that, Mrs C?'

Nellie glared at the man. 'You have a choice, Private. You can apologise and I will graciously accept. Or you can leave. I'm not so desperate for customers that I'll put up with being insulted in my own café.'

The man huffed. 'I were only jokin'. You didn't used to mind a bit of banter,' he muttered.

Nellie ignored him as she sailed out of the door, but his comment had cut close to the bone. She was well aware that her

127

obsession with cleaning the pavement was causing people to question her sanity, but if they knew what drove her to do it, they'd put her in the loony bin for sure.

Her hand reached for the crucifix – the tangible sign that maybe it wasn't all in her mind. Gladys's spirit really was haunting her.

Chapter 25

'Someone to see you, love.' Mr Pearson came into the small kitchen where Edie was making tea for them both before they started work.

'Is it Marge?' she asked anxiously. 'Is Phil all right?' She knew Bert was doing well because she'd called the hospital first thing.

Mr Pearson shuffled his feet uncomfortably. 'Uh, no. Nothing like that. It's . . . it's your mum.'

Edie narrowed her eyes. 'I hope you're joking.'

He shook his head.

'Course he's not joking.' Her mother's strident voice made Edie grit her teeth.

Nellie poked her head round Mr Pearson's tall, skinny body. 'I just wanted to check you were all right after everything that happened.'

Edie glared at her boss, refusing to even look at her mother. 'As you can see, I'm fine,' she said coldly, then she shoved past them both and ran upstairs.

Behind her she heard Mr Pearson mumble something, and then the sound she dreaded – her mother's footsteps coming after her.

After slamming her bedroom door shut, she pulled the wooden chair in front of it and sat down.

'Edie!' her mother called, rattling the knob. 'Open up.'

'For God's sake, just leave me alone!' Edie cried.

129

'Please, love! I could have lost you yesterday, and . . .' Her mother's voice trailed away.

'Didn't you hear what I said?' Edie's heartrate increased and she blinked back angry tears.

'Please. I just want to talk. Won't you let me explain? You'll need me soon. What with the baby.'

Edie squeezed her eyes shut. If her mother thought that would make her soften, then she needed to think again.

'I thought you might like to know they think Bert's gonna be all right.' There was a long pause. Then, 'Do you have any idea how I felt yesterday?' Her mother's voice broke. 'When I got the news . . . You and the boys could all have died! The thought near killed me on the spot, love. I know you don't want to see me, but . . . I couldn't bear it if something happened and we never had a chance to make it up.'

Suddenly it was too much for Edie, and she shot up from the chair and kicked it aside. Wrenching open the door, she glared at her mother. 'I am never going to forgive you. Do you understand? Never. So just turn around and get back down the hill to the café because me and this baby want *nothing* to do with you.'

'You don't mean that, love. It's been months now, surely you can—'

Edie leant down and hissed directly into her mother's face. 'You got me to feed poison to my father. I was a child! And he died because of me. And you—' She clamped her lips together as her shoulders sagged. 'Listen to me, Mum, because this is the very last time I will ever talk to you. I. Will. *Never*. Forgive. Do you understand? Never! And if you don't leave me alone, I swear I'll tell everyone what *really* happened to Dad! How would you like that? Do you think any of your kids'll want to speak to you again? And Jasper?' Edie could hear her voice becoming shrill and did her best to control it. 'Given that he's Lily's dad, it's started to make me wonder whether the two of you didn't cook up that plot

130

together! Maybe I should go and ask him if it was his idea to *drug* his best friend so he could have his end away with you!'

Nellie's face was pale and her lips were trembling. 'Y-y-you wouldn't do that?' she whispered. 'You must know Jasper's got nothing to do with any of this. How could you even think of hurting him like that? The man practically raised you!'

'And why do you think he had to? Because my own dad was kept so drugged with opium that he wasn't capable of it! If it weren't for you, maybe the six of us would have had a proper dad. You say you loved him, but that don't look much like love.'

Nellie took a step towards her daughter and shoved her hard in the chest. 'That man was a monster! Oh, he might have been all nice to you, but have you asked Rodney what he was like? Have you? And why do you think I was with Jasper? Because your sainted father tried to strangle me!'

Edie let out a sardonic laugh. 'So that's how you're going to play it, is it? You're the poor victim and none of this is your fault. Well, guess what, Mum, I don't believe a word you say! So you better stay away from me because I meant what I said: I'll tell *everyone*!'

Nellie seemed to deflate before Edie's eyes. 'B-b-but what about the baby? My grandchild . . .' She reached out to touch Edie's stomach, but Edie slapped her hand away.

'No. *My* child. *Bill's* child. *Nothing* to do with you.' Then she stepped back into her room and slammed the door in her mother's face.

It felt to Edie that she stood for hours, tears pouring down her cheeks as she listened intently to the sounds from the other side of the door. Part of her longed to run into her mother's arms and feel them close around her, to have her tell her everything would be all right. That she could be a mother to this little cuckoo lurking in her stomach.

But she hardened her heart against the impulse. Her mother deserved everything she got.

∽

Nellie staggered along the corridor to the living room where she dropped onto the sofa, back straight, hands knitted, and stared stoically at the wall. She wouldn't cry. She absolutely *refused* to cry. She wanted to believe that Edie didn't mean what she'd just said. But she knew it was a futile hope. Her hand reached for the crucifix. 'Oh, Glad, why did you have to leave me?' she whispered. 'We made a promise: no more secrets. And I would have told them if you'd been there. But without you, I just don't have the strength Is that why you won't leave me alone? It won't do no good, Glad. Cos if it comes to a choice between having you roaming around the café for the rest of my days or risk losing my kids and Jasper, you know there's no choice to make. And what if . . . what if they think what you did all those years. That it were me what pulled that trigger!' Her face crumpled. She'd managed to persuade Gladys that she hadn't, but the others might not be so trusting . . .

Suddenly the tears broke free and she pressed the heels of her hands against her eyes, rocking back and forth.

After a while her sobs turned to hiccups and she sat up straight again, lips pursed, shoulders square as she tried to pull herself together. She had to believe that Edie would come round in time. The problem was, as Jasper had so often told her, patience was not one of her strengths. And Edie had always been the most wilful of her children. Just like she herself had been. Her mother had frequently told her that she was a stubborn little cow who'd get what was coming to her one day. And how right she'd been.

The thought of her mother sent a stab of despair through her. If Edie hated her half as much as she'd hated her own mother, then it'd be a cold day in hell before she spoke to her again.

She drew in a shuddering sigh. Enough feeling sorry for herself! She needed to make a plan. Edie might think she never wanted to see her again, but what girl doesn't want their mother when they're giving birth? Even *she'd* longed for her mum during the long, painful labour with Rodney. Feeling a little better at the thought, she went to wash her face, then taking her powder compact out of her bag she did her best to disguise the evidence of her weeping fit. After that she took out her lippy and carefully applied it. There, she'd do. Now time to lay the groundwork. First step: get Clive Pearson on side.

Downstairs, Mr Pearson lifted his head from where it was bent over a bonnet and raised his eyebrows questioningly.

Nellie shook her head.

He came over and patted her arm awkwardly. 'Try not to worry, Nellie. Me and Bill'll look after her and the little one.'

Nellie gave him a tight smile. But inside she wanted to scream, *It's my job to look after her.*

'I know you will, love. But at the first sign of that baby makin' an appearance, you need to let me know.'

Mr Pearson frowned. 'Only if she asks me to, Nellie. Otherwise it'd be breakin' her trust. And as you know, once you lose her trust, it's not easy to get it back.'

'You fancy delivering that baby on your own, do you?'

Mr Pearson blanched. 'I-I . . .There's midwives, ain't there, who'll come help.'

Seeing a chink in his armour, Nellie took full advantage. 'There are, but first labours can go on for hours. Days, even. Midwife ain't gonna be available for all of that. She'll need someone to sit with her. Unless you fancy it? Know much about birthin' babies, do ya?' She smiled slyly.

Mr Pearson shuffled his feet awkwardly. 'No need to jump the gun, is there? It's still a good few months away, an' you two could have sorted your differences by then.'

She doubted it. And if the situations were reversed, she knew she would have reacted exactly like her daughter. No, Edie would probably never forgive her. Just as Nellie could never forgive herself. She'd lied to herself for years about her role in Donald's death;

133

unlike Gladys, who'd felt the weight of the guilt every day of her life. And now, that burden had been transferred to her.

'Well, you do what you think's best, love. And if you think you're up for the job, then I'm sure Edie and the little one'll be safe in your hands. Gotta say, though, you're a braver man than most.'

At Mr Pearson's panicked expression, Nellie smiled smugly and walked away, head high.

But once her back was turned to him, the smile left her and she stood for a long while on the road outside the garage, taking slow, deep breaths. She wanted nothing more than to shout and scream, weep and wail, but she couldn't. She needed to hold it all together and keep going.

When she felt ready, she marched towards Constable's Road. Edie wasn't the only reason she'd come up here today. She fingered the envelope in her pocket and gazed up towards Constable's Gate with its crenellated tower and arched entrance – guarded, of course – no one could get close to the castle these days.

No point putting it off, Nellie. If you don't ask you don't get.

But the thought of asking . . . the shame of it. She took a tentative step, then stopped. *Go on, girl, just a few more.* Straightening her shoulders, she walked up to the sentry gate.

'If I hadn't recognised yer purple coat and yer pink hat, I'd have arrested you for loiterin' outside a protected area, Mrs C.'

'Morning to you too, Corporal Digby,' she said brightly. 'Ain't seen you down the café for a while.' She raised her eyebrows at him, but the soldier didn't back down.

'Nor will you again. I got perfectly good food at the NAAFI, and I go down the Pot and Kettle when I fancy a change. Least they haven't been harbouring traitors.'

'Hmm, that must be why you're lookin' so scrawny. Grub in that place is terrible. Still, you go where you want, Corporal. Give me regards to old Clarence. Terrible shame about his skin condition, though.'

'What skin condition?'

'You mean you ain't noticed the scales on his hands? He can't wash 'em, you know. Soap and water make it worse. Still, I'm sure only a few flakes of skin make it into the food.'

The soldier blanched and Nellie grinned. 'Anyway, lovely to see you again. Maybe see you at Castle's soon.'

Then she turned and walked away with a renewed sense of purpose and the letter to Rodney burning a hole her pocket. What had she been thinking? She couldn't expect her *children* to bail her out. She'd got herself into this mess and she'd get herself out. It was just a question of how.

Mentally, she flicked through her jewellery box. There wasn't a lot. Her engagement ring – which she'd been saving for the first of her boys to get engaged, but they'd just have to buy their own damn rings. The wedding ring wouldn't be worth much . . . And there was the ring Donald had given her the night before he went to war. Gold with tiny blue sapphires and diamonds set all around. He'd called it an eternity ring to symbolise the fact that he'd love her for all eternity. She hated the thought of parting with it. Through the long years of his illness, and even more so since his illegitimate son had turned up last year, her memories of Donald had been tarnished, and her guilt over his death meant it was hard to view her marriage as anything but a disaster. But that ring, just like her wedding and engagement rings, held memories of the love she knew they'd once shared. She'd allowed herself to forget it. Guilt, sadness and despair had overshadowed the good times until she sometimes wondered if she'd imagined them. Those rings were the proof that she hadn't.

But what use were they to her now?

Chapter 26

Reenie stood at the counter, impatiently tapping her fingers. Where the hell was Nellie? She couldn't help feeling that she was being taken advantage of. She had parsnips to harvest up at the allotment, and she'd arranged for some of the Dig for Victory women to help her. If she wasn't there, all they'd do was stand around nattering. But she couldn't desert Marianne.

'Penny for them?'

Reenie looked up at the sound of a man's voice, startled to see Terence Carter standing in front of her.

'What do you want?' she asked warily.

'Just wanted to see Mrs C. Is she here?'

'Nope. Cup of tea?' She smiled nervously. Something about this man had always made her nervous.

'No thanks, darlin'. Last time I tried one it was weak as baby's piss. Here, saw your Jimmy comin' outta the town hall yesterday. I got worried for a moment. Thought maybe Bert Castle were a goner. But then I sees the two of ya walkin' hand in hand down the street, so it got me thinkin'. There's only three reasons to visit the town hall.' He held up one grubby finger. 'One o' your family's died. But Bert's gonna be all right, so I heard. In any case, it'd be the army's business to sort.'

Reenie felt her stomach start to churn as Terence held up a second finger.

'Someone's been born.' He peered over the counter, looking Reenie up and down. 'Now, you're a fine figure of a woman, Reenie. Always liked my ladies with a bit of spare, if you know what I mean? But you ain't got that much spare.' He winked and Reenie cringed.

He held up a third finger, leant forward and whispered, 'You're arrangin' a marriage licence.' He regarded her carefully and Reenie tried very hard to keep her expression neutral.

'Are congratulations in order?' Terence asked finally.

'What business is it of yours?' she squeaked.

He nodded. 'Ahh, keepin' it secret, are ya? Probably wise. Don't seem right, does it? All them men die right in front of you and you go off and arrange a weddin'.'

'It's not like that,' she said defensively.

Terence grinned. 'Oh, don't worry. Your secret's safe with me.' He leant forward again, and his warm breath, stinking of beer and cigarettes, wafted over her face. 'And you can tell your Jimmy that his secret's safe and all. For now.'

Reenie wrinkled her brow. 'What d'you mean?'

Terence tapped the side of his nose. 'Just what I said. Safe as houses.'

There was a loud thwump, and everyone in the café stilled for a moment. Then as the shell warning sounded, the tables emptied as the customers rushed to the back of the building and the safety of the basement.

Reenie turned to follow them, but Terence caught her arm. 'Maybe that were the wrong phrase, eh? Not much safe around here. You tell your bloke that he might want to have a chat with his brother up the hospital. And when he has, he should come find me. I'm in the Oak most nights.'

Reenie wrenched her arm from his grasp, as another thwump made her jump.

'Tell him yerself,' she muttered, pulling away. 'I'm not your messenger.'

Terence Carter sauntered more casually behind her, seemingly unconcerned by the shells. But as she got to the door at the top of the basement steps, he grabbed her arm again. 'Take it from me, it'll be best if you get that message to him sooner rather than later.' Then he walked out of the back door, whistling as though he were going for a casual country stroll.

Reenie's heart rate rose a notch as she hurried down the basement steps, and for once it had nothing to do with the shells; it was the menace in Terence's expression. But why? What did he expect to get from intimidating her? Or Jimmy, for that matter? There was another crash, and just for a moment, Reenie hoped Terence Carter might disappear in a puff of smoke and brick dust.

'What's up?' Marianne said, handing her a cup of tea.

'Terence Carter was here,' she whispered.

Marianne's eyes widened. 'What did he want?'

Reenie shrugged. 'He wanted your mum. But then he said . . . Well, he asked me to tell Jim to talk to Bert. Said something about his secret being safe with him. And the way he talked . . .' She shuddered. 'What do you think he means?'

'I have no idea,' Marianne replied.

But Reenie hadn't missed the flash of concern on her friend's face before she turned and busied herself with pouring tea, and her anxiety rose a notch.

'Is there something I should know?' she said, keeping her voice low.

'Like what?' Marianne still didn't look at her as she handed round the cups and saucers.

'If I knew I wouldn't be asking, would I? What's really going on, Marianne?'

Marianne's hand shook as she held a cup out to Miss Frost. 'How are you, love?' she said to her with a polite smile.

Reenie knew her friend wasn't really interested, the only thing you ever got from Miss Frost was Bible quotes. 'Marianne!' she hissed, but it came out louder than she'd meant it to, and a few people stopped their chatter to look at them. 'Just tell me,' she said more quietly.

Marianne put the teapot down carefully. 'Look, Reenie, I don't know why he wants Jimmy to talk to Bert, nor what he means by this secret, and I don't like the fact that you think I'm lying!'

'I never said that, though, did I? I asked if you knew anything.'

'And I said no. Going on at me isn't going to change that.' Marianne sat down on one of the wooden chairs at the table and rubbed her stomach. 'And it doesn't matter how many times you ask, Reenie, my answer will be the same, so can you please leave it!'

Hurt and bewildered, Reenie went to sit on one of the cushions on the other side of the basement while Marianne went around making sure everyone was comfortable, pouring tea and chatting cheerfully. But not once did she look at her. Not once.

Marianne was a terrible liar, always had been. Reenie had known her all her life and she could count on the fingers of one hand the number of times her friend had lied. One of those times was when she said she was happy that Reenie was with Jim. The other was now. The question was, what was so awful that she had to hide it from her?

Chapter 27

Nellie was walking down Castle Street still deep in thought, her mind veering between how she could win her daughter back and wondering if she could make enough money by pawning the rings to pay off her debts to Terence, when the first shell fell. 'Hell's bells,' she muttered as she quickened her step. How anyone found the time to earn any money these days was a mystery.

Another crash spurred her into a jog. As she turned into Church Street, a familiar figure slipped out of the café's back gate. She skidded to a halt and watched as Terence hurried away towards St Mary's Church.

His presence at the café for the second day running filled her with foreboding and reinforced her need to find a solution to her problems soon. Get him the money in two weeks or face the consequences, he'd said. And he wasn't a man to deliver empty threats.

Problem was, she needed a miracle to get her out of this hole, and miracles seemed to be in short supply right now.

Heart thumping with anxiety, Nellie raced through the back door and immediately went upstairs. Let the shells fall. If the café was hit and she was buried under a pile of rubble, it'd at least get her out of her problems. She went into her bedroom, looking around to see if anything had been moved, but as far as she could tell all was as she'd left it: the bed neatly made, her multicoloured patchwork quilt stretched tight over the blankets and the cupboard doors flung wide, to show the empty space inside.

Ignoring the flutter of fear at the memory of the morning, she hurried towards her dressing table and examined it. There were the usual pots of cream – most of them empty now, but she kept the jars in case she ever got round to making her own. Her silver hairbrush and comb set, a wedding present from Donald's parents, was still there. Everything looked present and correct.

An enormous explosion suddenly rocked the building and she yelped, her eyes flying towards the windows. Please God, don't break any more. Last thing I need is to pay for more repairs. But though they rattled, they stayed in place.

With trembling hands, she pulled open the bottom drawer where she kept her jewellery box. Donald had bought it for her in the early years of their marriage and it was one of her most prized possessions – a beautifully carved mahogany box lined with royal blue velvet.

She opened it and stared down at the contents. There was the Wedgewood brooch, the silver pendant with a blue Morpho wing – as bright as the day it had been caught – under its glass dome, a few hairclips passed on by her mother. Her fingers rooted through more and more urgently as she mentally ticked off each item. She lifted the tray to check the contents under there, and her stomach dropped. No wedding ring, no engagement ring, and no eternity ring.

With a cry of despair, she slammed the lid shut and began to pace around the room. Was that why Terence had been here? Had he snuck up here, gone through her things, and then stolen her most valuable possessions? She shuddered at the thought of him snooping around her bedroom. What was she going to do? She couldn't go to the police . . . If she accused Terence Carter of theft, he'd only counter it with accusations of his own, and God knew she didn't need the police examining her affairs too closely – especially after everything that had happened with Hester. He had her over a barrel, and the bastard knew it.

141

Another crash reminded her that she really shouldn't be here. But she still didn't budge. What did it matter if the whole place collapsed around her? Because with or without the shells, it was possible she'd lose the café anyway.

She went into the sitting room and grabbed the bottle of sherry that sat on the table beside her chair. She pulled out the cork and took a swig, uncaring that some of it dribbled down her chin. Then she put it down again. Drinking would only make things worse, but Lord it was tempting. Sighing, she gazed at the mantelpiece: the three monkeys ornament that Jim had got her for her birthday one year, the carriage clock, the little white china vase with a forget-me-not painted on it that contained a dusty silk rose . . . She sat up straighter. Where was Donald? Ever since he'd had it taken just before he went off to war in 1914, the picture of Donald had sat between the vase and the clock. But it wasn't there now.

Frantically, she got up and began to search the room, flinging aside cushions and pulling up the rug to no avail. The rings she could understand. But the photo? It meant nothing to anyone. Unless Edie had taken it. Maybe she'd asked Donny to take it up to her . . . But why take it without saying anything? Surely she knew she'd have given it to her if she'd asked.

'Is it you, Gladys?' she said, her voice wavering. 'Why are you doing this to me? Please stop!' Nellie's shoulders started to heave. 'I'll lose them all. Isn't Edie enough for you? You want me to lose the rest of them as well . . . And Jasper.' Her voice caught on his name and she started to sob. 'He's started to love me again. I can't lose him. Please, Gladys, leave me alone.'

A low rumble shook the walls, and the ornaments on the mantelpiece wobbled.

Nellie stood up. 'I won't do it! Do you hear me? I won't do it?!'

Chapter 28

Reenie sat tense and upright on one of the cushions by the wall. The basement hummed with conversation, but she was too wound up to join in. Instead she watched Marianne, who was sitting on one of the chairs by the table with her eyes closed. She looked exhausted, but any sympathy Reenie might have had was buried under a stream of questions. Marianne had definitely been worried when she'd told her what Terence had said, and Reenie couldn't help feeling resentful and suspicious. In the early days of her relationship with Jimmy, Marianne had clearly been unhappy about them being together. But more recently, she'd promised all she wanted was for her to be happy. Reenie had believed her, but her behaviour right now showed that nothing had changed.

Suddenly the basement door crashed open and Nellie came in, looking as if she'd seen a ghost. Marianne leapt to her feet. 'Mum! Are you all right?'

Nellie ignored her as she looked wild-eyed around the dimly lit room. When she spotted Lou Carter, sitting with a cup of tea next to Reenie, she marched over.

Reenie shifted to her left a few feet to allow Nellie to sit down. Seeming to notice the hush that had descended at her entrance, Nellie waved her hand. 'Don't mind me, everyone.'

Her cheery tone didn't fool anyone, but as she didn't seem inclined to say more, the desultory conversations continued.

Curious, Reenie closed her eyes and turned her head away from them so it didn't look like she was eavesdropping.

'Everythin' all right, Nell? You look like you've just been dragged out of yer grave.' Lou cackled.

'So would you, if you'd been caught out in that lot.'

'Not as if it's the first time,' Lou responded.

Reenie turned her head and opened her eyes a slit. Lou had a point; Nellie had sat under a table and watched the shells fall on Market Square not so long ago. She'd run straight towards a shelled building when Daisy had been killed. She wasn't the type to be spooked by something that had become an everyday event for all of them. Something else was bothering her.

'I want you to give your son a message,' Nellie said, leaning towards the other woman, and Reenie could hear the barely controlled anger in her voice.

'What's that then?' Lou's tone was unconcerned.

'Tell him that if he don't return what he took, he'll regret it.'

'I beg your pardon?' Lou hissed. 'Are you accusin' him of thievin'?'

'Yes, I am.'

'My son is a successful businessman.'

Nellie snorted. 'A spiv, you mean.'

'Businessman,' Lou repeated. 'An' whatever you're accusin' him of, you're barkin' up the wrong tree. He ain't got no need for thievin'.'

'So you don't think selling knock-off goods is thieving?'

'He comes by his stuff fair an' square. An' you ain't been too fussy about where he got it before.'

Nellie didn't have a reply to that.

'You thought I didn't know, eh? Me an' Terry don't have no secrets. An' I don't hold with stealin' from me mates – he knows that.'

'Yeah, well, I never got the impression he were the type to listen to his mum.'

'You don't know him, Nell. Soft as butter underneath. He wouldn't do it, I'm tellin' ya. An' if I hear that you've repeated this to anyone, then you an' me'll fall out.'

'We already have, Lou.' Nellie stood and moved over to the table, where she slumped down on the chair next to Marianne.

Reenie glanced at Lou, whose face was puce with anger. 'She don't mean it, Mrs Carter,' she said.

Lou looked at her sharply. 'Was you earwiggin'?'

'What? No! I mean . . . I only heard the last bit. About you two not . . .' She trailed away. 'I saw Terence earlier,' she said brightly. 'He was in the café just before the siren went.' Reenie shifted closer to the woman.

Lou stared at her. 'I never saw him! Why ain't he here?'

Reenie shrugged. 'He left by the back door. But . . . I didn't know he was such good friends with the Castle boys.'

'He ain't, far as I know.'

'Well, he seems awful worried about Bert. He wanted me to get a message to Jim. Told me to ask him to go talk to Bert then meet him for a drink. You wouldn't know what it's about, would you?'

Lou narrowed her eyes. 'Did he, by God. Well, love, I wouldn't worry too much about it. Terry runs a few books, so no doubt it's somethin' to do with that.'

'Jimmy doesn't gamble,' Reenie said with certainty. Bert was a different story, though.

'Maybe you don't know him as well as you think you do.' Lou winked at her. 'We all have our little secrets.'

'I don't,' Reenie said indignantly.

'Well, your sister certainly had a few.'

'Like what?'

Lou regarded her shrewdly. 'Maybe I shouldn't speak ill of the dead, but Wilf weren't the only man June were runnin' around with back before she got knocked-up.'

145

Reenie rolled her eyes. 'That's hardly a secret.'

'Ahh, but did you know she were still up to her tricks soon as she'd had your Freddie? She ran that poor man ragged.' She shook her head. 'You shoulda clung on, love, instead of lettin' her just take what she wanted.'

Reenie looked away. 'I don't know what you're talking about.'

'I think you do, love. And in a place like this, people might try to keep a secret, but there's always someone as knows. But whatever Terry wants to talk to Jim about, take it from me: men don't like their women pokin' into their business. So, pass on the message and leave it at that.'

The all-clear sounded just then and Lou got up and strolled towards the door.

Reenie stared after her, her mind whirling. Was she saying that June had been unfaithful to Wilf? Did he know? She felt a flare of anger on his behalf. If she hadn't wanted him, why did she take him? But Reenie knew the answer to that. June had always been the type to do as she pleased, never caring who she hurt in the process. It seemed Lou was right: everyone had their little secrets . . . except her.

But the Castles seemed to have more secrets than most. Once, she would have said that Marianne wouldn't keep anything secret from her – until she'd discovered that she'd hidden the truth about Donny's father from everyone for over ten years. Then there was Edie, skulking up at the garage, refusing to tell anyone why she and her mother had fallen out and pregnant with a baby everyone knew couldn't be Bill's. And Lily, who, it turned out was Jasper's daughter – something she still couldn't quite understand. And what of Bert? Would a woman really shoot him just because he'd broken up with her? Or was there something more going on?

She shook her head. She'd known and loved this family all her life, but nothing was ever simple with them; secrets and scandal seemed to swirl around them. When she and Jim married, would she be privy to them, or would she forever feel on the outside looking in?

∽

As the basement emptied, Marianne stacked the dirty cups and saucers onto a tray. She could feel the weight of Reenie's stare on her, and her friend's confusion only added to the gnawing anxiety she felt about Terence. Briefly, she stole a glance at Reenie and their eyes met. Marianne looked away first, and picking up the tray, she hurried up the stairs. Given Bert's reckless behaviour over the previous weeks, it was possible he'd got himself caught up in one of Terence's shady schemes. Maybe he owed him money . . . In which case, Terence must be worried he wouldn't get it now Bert was in hospital. Yes, that must be it. Which meant that both her mother and Bert owed Terence money . . .

Once again, she thought about the letter. It provided a solution for her mother and it could get Bert off the hook too. She dumped the tray on the table and rubbed her forehead where a headache had been brewing ever since Reenie had spoken to her. She couldn't put it off any longer; she needed to speak to Mr Wainwright. If anyone could help her, then the clever lawyer who'd proved so invaluable to the family could.

'Do you reckon you could manage without me for the rest of the afternoon?' she asked her mother.

Nellie looked at her sharply. 'You got pains? Is the baby all right?'

'Yes . . . I . . . I just need to get some air. Just for an hour or so.'

Nellie stuck her hands on her hips. 'Get some air! Oh, well, that's fine then, Marianne. Off you go. Don't mind me. I'll just cook, serve, clean *and* do the washing up.'

'Maybe Reenie could . . . ?' She looked over at her friend who had just emerged from the basement.

Reenie scowled. 'No. I already told you I had to be at the allotment this afternoon.' She collected her bag from behind the counter, and without looking at either of them, threaded her way between the tables and left.

Nellie stared after her in consternation. 'What's got her knickers in a twist? You two had a row, or something? Did Jimmy split up with her? What's going on?'

Marianne shook her head. 'I think she's just tired. It's been a difficult few days.'

'Tired!? We're all tired!' Nellie slumped down onto a chair.

'Mum? What's going on? You looked absolutely terrified when you came in the basement earlier.' Marianne sat down and took her mother's hand across the table. 'Or is this about your visit to Edie? Was it bad?'

Nellie looked around to make sure everyone had left. 'It's not that, love. Edie weren't happy to see me and sent me away with a flea in my ear, but it were no more than I expected. But . . .' She threaded her finger through the chain of the necklace, twisting it round and round until the tip started to turn blue. 'I think . . . I think—' She stopped and stood up decisively. 'Oh, ignore me. It's nothing.' She patted Marianne's cheek. 'And if you want a bit of time off, you can have it, love. But not today, eh? I can't manage on me own.'

Marianne watched her mother walk into the kitchen and sighed. Since the war had started, nothing had gone right for the family and more recently Hester's betrayal and Gladys's death weighed heavily on all of them. But most especially on her mother. She was beginning to get truly worried now, with all her talk of Gladys and that damned necklace. And just now, with her face a sickly grey colour and her eyes bloodshot and shadowed, her mother had looked utterly defeated. But more than that – she had looked scared.

'What's going on, Polly?' she asked softly, lumbering to her feet and poking her fingers through the bird's cage.

The bird stamped her feet, but said nothing, so Marianne followed her mother into the kitchen. She'd tell her about the letter later. The thought made her feel weak, but with Terence circling them like a vulture, threatening everything she held dear, she couldn't see any other solution.

Chapter 29

Turning up her collar Reenie, hurried across the square. Now the all-clear had sounded, another queue had formed outside the shop and she hoped those waiting would be able to get enough to keep them going, but she doubted it. By afternoon, the shelves had usually been picked clean, and they'd be lucky to get a dab of marge and a tin of spam. Which was why she needed to be at the allotment. She'd neglected it over the last few days, and she must never forget how important the vegetables she grew there were.

It was now well past midday, so she doubted any of the other women would be there, which meant she'd have to do it alone. Still, the exercise might help clear her head. And as soon as she'd finished, she'd try to track down Jimmy.

As she was approaching the steps by the Market Hall, someone called her name. Glancing back, she was surprised to see Wilf. He was dressed in a thick navy-blue fisherman's jersey and brown trousers, his black hair messy and windblown.

She hesitated for a moment. He'd been so sweet to her yesterday, comforting her after Jim had walked away ... but as soon as Jim had arrived, he'd reverted to type: moody and taciturn. Sighing, she stopped and waited for him to catch up with her.

'Twice in two days?' she said. 'You've barely spoken to me in years and now you can't stay away. If you're not careful, folk'll start to gossip.'

Wilf flushed. 'I just wanted to check you're all right. After yesterday.'

'I'm fine. How's Fred?'

He shrugged. 'All right, I think.' He shook his head. 'To be honest, I'm worried about him – about all the kids. They seem to be fine, but being surrounded by so much death and destruction . . . It'll always be there at the back of their minds. The question is, how will it affect them?'

Reenie was surprised; it wasn't like Wilf to talk about his feelings, especially to her. 'He'll be OK,' she said. 'He has you and your mum and dad. And me, of course. We'll see him through.'

He smiled. 'I know. But I'm not there much. None of us can watch him all the time . . .' His lips pursed and he stuck his hands in his pockets, as though he, too, was surprised he'd confided in her.

'You'll just have to trust him,' Reenie said eventually when Wilf didn't seem inclined to say any more. 'Anyway, I have to get on. The veg won't harvest itself.'

'Need a hand?' he asked. 'I'm a dab hand with a shovel.' He flexed his arm.

'Why?' Reenie asked bluntly.

Wilf looked away for a moment. 'I . . . I need to speak to you.'

'You spoke to me yesterday. So we're not due another chat till 1951.'

Ignoring her facetious comment, he strode ahead, leaving her no option but to follow.

When they arrived, Wilf looked over the allotment with approval. 'I've missed this place,' he said.

'It's always been here.' She almost added, 'As have I,' but she didn't. It sounded needy and that wasn't how she meant it.

She looked out over the neat rows of leafy vegetables, separated by small planks of wood and felt a glow of satisfaction. It hadn't been easy, even before the war, to cultivate this large patch of chalky earth. Since her uncle had purchased the land around twenty years before, the two of them had worked hard to make it productive. He'd left it to her to manage for the last few years, and she was proud of it. Since the war had started, she'd got rid of the flowers and extended the vegetable patches. And in the summer she had managed to grow red and blackcurrants, raspberries and strawberries. Despite the strong winds that blew in from the sea, despite the inhospitable soil, despite the shells and bombs, somehow it was still here, and if she was honest, it was where she was happiest. Maybe because it was the only place she felt completely confident.

'And you do all this by yourself?' he asked.

'Well, I have a lot of help from the Dig for Victory group. But yes. It's mostly me.'

Wilf stripped off his jersey and turned to her. 'What can I do?'

'Parsnips are ready to come out.' She unlocked the shed, took out a couple of forks and handed them to him. Then she wheeled the wheelbarrow out and headed uphill along a narrow path between plots until they reached a row of deep green leaves. 'You fork, I'll pull,' she said.

Obediently, Wilf started to dig, while Reenie got down on her hands and knees and began to pull them out and throw them into the wheelbarrow.

'How well do you know Terence Carter?' she asked after a while.

'I don't,' he replied. 'He's a nasty piece of work, always has been.'

'What about Lou?'

'Nope. Give her a nod when I pass her stall, but that's about it. Although, come to think of it, June used to like a natter with her. Why?'

She'd not known that, but she shouldn't be surprised they'd got on – they both had sharp tongues, though she suspected Lou had a better heart.

Wilf stopped working for a moment. 'Reens, have you got yourself mixed up with the Carters somehow?'

'Course not. Just Lou said something odd when I spoke to her earlier, that's all.'

'What did she say?'

Reenie kept her eyes on her task. She wasn't about to tell him that June had been sleeping with men behind his back, nor would she ever mention that Lou thought her sister had taken him from her – as she had reminded herself so often over the years, Wilf had never been hers to steal. 'Nothing important,' she mumbled.

'Seriously, steer clear, all right?'

She squinted up at him. 'What's it to you?'

He shrugged. 'All right then. Do what you like; it's no skin off my nose,' he muttered, stabbing the fork into the ground with more force than necessary.

'Right.' Reenie grasped a handful of leaves and tugged, swallowing down the hurt and anger.

They continued working in tense silence, the only sounds Wilf's grunts as he dug, and the thrum of the sea breaking on the shingle out of sight.

But finally, Reenie couldn't hold back the anger that had been bubbling since his remark. Sitting back on her heels, she looked up at him. 'Why are you actually here, Wilf?' She swiped a lock of hair out of her face with a muddy hand.

Wilf didn't stop what he was doing. 'Like I said, I wanted to make sure you were all right.'

'And you did. So why are you still here?'

Sighing, he dropped the fork and stuck his hands in his pockets, looking out over the neat rows of vegetables. Reenie stood and put her hands on her hips.

'I'm waiting,' she said impatiently.

He looked at her and smiled. 'You've got mud . . .' He gestured at her face.

Reenie scowled and wiped at her face with her sleeve, before realising that it, too, was covered with dirt.

'You always were a bit of a mucky pup,' he chuckled.

'So you came here to insult me?'

'No! No, that's not why— I really did want to make sure you were all right. Last night, one of the guys on the lifeboats told me what you did – lying over that child to keep him safe. It was a brave thing to do, but Jesus, Reens, you could have been killed!'

Reenie wished he hadn't reminded her. It was a scene that would haunt her for a long time to come.

'Any one of us could have been,' she pointed out. 'We were lucky, unlike some of the others.' She swallowed at the memory of the bodies littering the field.

Wilf nodded sombrely. 'I thank God you made it out alive – Marge too.'

Flustered by the genuine concern in his eyes, Reenie dropped back to the ground and started work again, hoping he couldn't see the tremble in her hands. 'Well, all's well that ends well. And anyway, Jim sheltered both of us, so he's the hero, not me.' She flung another parsnip into the barrow.

'So, yesterday . . . You and Jimmy seem very close?'

Reenie sat back again. 'We are.'

Wilf hesitated for a moment, then said, 'I-I'm glad for you. If it's what you truly want.'

Reenie bristled. 'Obviously it's what I want, otherwise I wouldn't be with him, would I?'

'Are you sure he's right for you?' Wilf blurted.

Reenie felt the anger rise again. 'Are you joking?' she asked. 'Is *this* what you wanted to talk to me about?'

Wilf looked down and scuffed at the earth with his boot. 'I mean, he's quite a bit younger than you, isn't he?'

Reenie threw her hands up. 'Why does that matter? If he was five years older than me, no one would blink an eye. And for your information,' she said, jumping to her feet, 'he asked me to marry him yesterday, and I said YES!' She shouted the last into

Wilf's face, then shoved at his chest, leaving a smear of mud on his shirt.

Immediately, she regretted telling him. Lowering her voice, she said, 'But please, keep it to yourself. What with everything that happened yesterday . . . It didn't seem right to mention it, so we're just gonna slip away to the town hall and do it quietly.'

Wilf stared at her in astonishment. 'Married?' he gasped. 'But you barely know him.'

'I've known him all my life,' she snapped. 'And why do you care? Or do you think I'm not good enough for him too? Marianne's the same. Is it cos he's better looking than me? Is it because he's younger than me? Why am I not good enough?' She almost sobbed the last, but more from frustration and anger than sorrow.

Wilf caught her upper arms. 'No. You've got it wrong, Reenie. Listen to me.' He gave her a little shake. 'I think *he's* not good enough for *you.*'

Reenie's eyes widened as she stared up into his face. 'Why would you think that? I mean, for the last twelve years you've behaved as if you don't even like me!'

Wilf let go of her arms and shook his head. 'Of course I like you! You were my best friend. Do you honestly think I don't care what happens to you?'

Reenie swallowed the lump that had suddenly risen to her throat. 'Then why—' She shut her mouth and shook her head. 'I don't understand you. But it really doesn't matter because your opinion is no concern of mine. And who I choose to marry is no concern of *yours.* But if there's something about Jimmy that you think I should know, then that *is* my business.'

'I just think you could do better,' Wilf muttered, looking uneasy.

'Oh, I could, could I? Like who? If you were anyone else, I'd say you were jealous, but that's clearly not the case. Because I was

155

never good enough for you, was I? So why am I suddenly too good for a lovely, caring, sweet man like Jimmy?'

'Good enough for me?' His dark eyes bored into hers. 'You were too good for me as well, Reens,' he said softly.

With a groan of frustration, Reenie knelt down again, pulling furiously at the loosened parsnips and throwing them at the wheelbarrow, not caring whether they went in or not.

Wilf knelt beside her. 'We've never talked about it, have we?' he said quietly. 'And that's my fault.'

'It was a long time ago. And June's been dead eight years now. You've had plenty of time to talk to me about it. Or about anything come to that.' She yanked at another parsnip and threw it towards the wheelbarrow, though she couldn't really see it through the sheen of angry tears.

When he didn't reply, she added, 'Anyway, why are you dragging all this up now?'

Wilf ran his hand through his hair and opened his mouth as if to say something, then shut it again. Finally, he said, 'I want you to know that I'm sorry. For everything that happened. I was young and foolish and . . .' He shrugged. 'I made a mistake. I can't regret it entirely, because it gave me Fred, but . . .' He paused. 'I did regret it.'

Reenie's heart leapt and her throat tightened. These were the words she'd longed to hear for years; words that just a few months ago would have made her want to run into his arms and tell him she could forgive him anything, if only they could go back to the way they were.

But it was too late. She loved Jimmy now. Yes, she had some questions for him, but whatever his faults, she was pretty certain that he wouldn't suddenly run off with another woman.

She shrugged and turned her attention back to the parsnips. 'Water under the bridge,' she said, though a small part of her heart was dancing.

Reenie could feel Wilf's gaze on her, but she refused to look up. Finally, he sighed, picked up the fork and resumed digging.

They continued to work in silence, and as soon as they reached the end of the row, Wilf turned to her with a sad smile. 'Reenie, if you need me for anything . . . You know where I am.'

She wrinkled her brow. 'Why would I need you?'

'Just, I know what marrying the wrong person is like. It . . . it's the loneliest place in the world. It strips away your happiness and makes you doubt everything about yourself. I wouldn't want that to happen to you.'

'Christ, Wilf! I'm *not* marrying the wrong person! Everyone knew June was a cow! It wasn't as if you didn't know before you married her. Jimmy's not like her. He's sweet, caring and he loves me. Everyone likes him. You've got no right to insult me – or Jim – like that!'

Wilf regarded her steadily, seemingly unmoved by her outburst. 'All I'm saying is if you have doubts, then listen to them. But if this is really what you want, then I'm happy for you. He's a lucky man.' Then he turned and walked away.

Reenie resisted the temptation to throw the fork at him with an effort. How dare he patronise her like that! Didn't he think she knew her own mind? Picking up the handles of the wheelbarrow she pushed it back to the shed, cursing Wilf with every step.

Once inside, she took a deep breath and tried to calm her breathing. Why, after years of barely speaking to her, had he decided to start now? Whatever his reasons, though, it had been a very long time since she'd cared what he thought.

Chapter 30

Nellie breathed a sigh of relief as she turned the sign to 'closed'. At last, she'd have time to think about who could have stolen her rings. It had occurred to her during the afternoon that maybe they hadn't been stolen. Maybe, like all her other mislaid items, Gladys had hidden them somewhere. Just like she'd taken the photograph.

Slumping down at a table, she put her head in her hands.

'Mum?' Marianne tentatively put her hand on her shoulder. 'Please tell me what's going on.'

Nellie sighed and rubbed her eyes. 'Where do I start?' she said wearily.

'Is it about the money?'

Nellie nodded and looked up at her daughter, her eyes watery. 'I've messed up, love, and it might mean losing the café.'

Marianne gasped. 'No.' She sat down opposite her mother and took her hands. 'No,' she said more firmly. 'We will not lose the café. We'll find a way.'

'WE!' Nellie shouted. 'Don't you mean me? *I'll* find a way? It's on *my* shoulders, Marianne. This isn't something you can help with.'

Marianne's eyes dropped to the table, and she rubbed her finger in some spilt salt. 'No, Mum,' she said quietly, 'I think it is.'

Nellie's eyes widened. '*You?* And how exactly can you help?'

From her pocket she took the letter that she'd buried in her drawer weeks ago and handed it over.

Nellie took it, her voice rising in indignation as she read out loud.

Dear Mrs Lomax,

We are writing to inform you of the terms of Mr Fanshawe's will with regards your son, Donald Castle.

Mr Fanshawe's wish was that Donald be prepared for a future role within the brewery. However, with the schools shut in Dover, Donald will be trailing far behind his peers in terms of academic achievement, which could greatly hinder the brewery in the future. Moreover, Donald's safety is at risk if he continues to stay where he is. Therefore, it is the fervent wish of the family to send Donald to a suitable school where he can resume his education and learn the ways of society in the company of his peers. During the holidays, he will be expected to stay with the Fanshawes where he can learn about the workings of the brewery. You would, of course, be allowed to visit at our convenience.

To compensate you for any distress this separation may cause, the family are willing to pay you the sum of £500.

We look forward to your reply.

Yours sincerely,

Nellie threw the letter on the table. 'Those snotty bastards!' she exclaimed. 'Are they trying to imply that our Don's not good enough for them unless he goes to one of their posh schools! Well, they can stuff their money where the sun don't shine. Cos it don't matter how desperate I get, I won't sell my grandson! How could you even think I'd consider it?' she railed.

'But it's not selling him, is it? It's giving him a future! The best chance in life. The kids' education has fallen behind. They're even calling them the "dead-end kids" for God's sake! And if he goes on the way he is, he'll end up in juvenile court before too long. Either

159

that, or he'll die in an air raid. I mean, he could have died yesterday if he'd gone to the match. And the only reason he didn't was cos he nearly got arrested!'

Nellie shook her head. 'I never thought I'd see the day. You promised him you'd not send him away after what happened last time. You swore it! And now you're willin' to break his trust? Is it cos you're about to have a shiny new baby, so you don't need Don no more! Well, I'm ashamed of you! If I'd had this offer shoved in my face for one of you, I'd not have contemplated it for a moment. Not one moment!' She tore up the letter and threw the pieces into Marianne's face.

'Mum, no!' Tears had come to her eyes at her mother's words. 'No, I don't want him to go! But life isn't like that, is it? Sometimes you have to do things you don't want for the greater good.'

Nellie slapped her hand on the table. 'Sellin' your kid is not for the greater good! I can't believe you're willin' to break his heart and his trust and send him away from us. Do you think he'd still love you if you did that? Do you think he'd come back here on his holidays from his la-di-da boarding school to visit his mum the cook!' She bent forward and snarled into Marianne's face. 'He'd never want to see you again. He'd end up like his dad, poncin' around takin' advantage of those he considers beneath him. Now throw that in the bin, and I don't want to hear one more word about it.' She paused. 'Who else knows about this?'

Marianne shook her head. 'No one. I haven't even told Alfie. I-I didn't know what to do.'

'Well, keep it that way. No one else need ever know. And if the family come after us again, then we'll go to Mr Wainwright. In the meantime, if I get so much of a *whiff* that you're thinkin' of goin' through with this, so help me God, I will burn the café to the ground rather than let you sell your own son. Do you understand?'

Marianne nodded miserably.

'And we will *never* speak of this again.' Nellie stormed away, leaving Marianne to pick up the pieces of the letter and try to put them back together. The tears were coming thick and fast now and she wiped her nose on her sleeve. Every word her mother said was true. But Donny's future would be bright. He'd never have to worry about getting in debt to the likes of Terence Carter. He'd be someone. And wouldn't he thank her for it in the end?

The memory of his father, Henry, gave her pause. Her son's inheritance came at his expense, and that gave her some small satisfaction. But what if Donny turned out like him? He was a feckless user who'd left her pregnant at sixteen. And later seduced Edie, leaving her at the mercy of his vengeful wife . . .

Just then Jasper walked in through the kitchen with a wide smile on his face, but noting her tears, it dropped from his face. 'What?' he asked anxiously. 'What's happened? Is it Bert?'

Marianne hastily rubbed at her cheeks. 'No. Just having a bit of a moment. You know what us pregnant women are like?' She forced herself to smile.

Jasper came over and pulled her into a hug. 'You and your mum are a right pair, aren't you? But try not to worry, I just might have found the perfect solution.'

'You're gonna come and take over here?' she asked, only half joking.

'Ha! With my big mitts I'll have broken half the crockery within a day. No, you'll just have to wait and see. Now, where's your mum?' He looked around expectantly.

Marianne waved her hand towards the stairs. Once he'd gone, she scooped the pieces of paper into her pocket. She'd stick it back together and go consult Mr Wainwright when she had a chance. Because she had a horrible feeling that the Fanshawes wouldn't let this go.

Chapter 31

Jasper found Nellie upstairs, staring grimly into the empty fireplace, a glass of sherry in one hand, the crucifix clutched in the other.

'What's going on, Nellie?' Jasper asked gently. 'Marianne's downstairs weepin' and you're up here drinkin'.'

Nellie sighed miserably. Between Marianne threatening to sell her son to settle *her* debt, Edie threatening to tell everyone what had happened with Donald, and Terence stealing her jewellery, the day couldn't get much worse. Not to mention Bert in hospital, and Gladys's vengeful spirit hovering over the whole sorry mess. 'It's just been a bit of a day,' she said eventually.

'Come on, love,' he coaxed, sitting down on the chair opposite. 'Whatever it is, it can't be that bad.'

Nellie looked up at him. 'It's worse,' she whispered.

'Is it Terence? he asked. 'I told you, Nell—'

'I don't need your "I told you sos".'

Jasper held up his hands. 'Tell me then.' He leant forward, his elbows on his knees, hands clasped, his fingers blackened from his work in the forge.

'It's Gladys,' she said.

Jasper huffed impatiently. 'Not this again. There's no such thing as ghosts. And that's not why Marianne's downstairs cryin' fit to burst.'

Nellie nodded towards the mantelpiece. 'Do you notice anything?'

Jasper stared at it for a moment, then frowned. 'Where's Donald's picture?' he asked.

'*She* took it,' Nellie hissed. 'And not only that! My rings are missing. I saw Terence slip out of here just when the shells started this morning, so I thought he'd took 'em. But maybe he didn't. Maybe they've been hid.' She explained about all the other bits and pieces that had been moved around the building. 'And not only that . . .' Suddenly she remembered the washing she'd left in the bath that morning. 'Everything smells, Jasper! I opened the wardrobe this mornin' and the smell of Gladys's rose water near knocked me out.'

'Then someone put it there, but it weren't Gladys,' he insisted. 'And if your jewels are missin', I'd bet the forge that Terence is responsible. The little weasel. Wait till I get my hands on him!'

'But he wouldn't do all the other stuff. Why would he? What does he know about Gladys's perfume?'

Jasper's eyebrows raised. 'Ghosts can't pick stuff up, Nellie.'

'I thought you didn't believe in ghosts,' Nellie fired back.

'I don't. Someone's playin' games with you, love.' He sat back and thought. 'You don't think it could be Donny, do you? I love the lad, but he's been runnin' rings around the lot of you these last months.'

'No! Of course it's not bloomin' Donny!'

Jasper stood up and went to Nellie's room. Inside, the wardrobe doors were open, hangers strewn across the brightly coloured carpet. Stepping over them carefully, he sat down on the bed, his nose twitching.

'See?' Nellie was leaning against the door frame, arms wrapped around herself. 'I told you, didn't I? I'm not imaginin' it. Gladys is here.' She stared around the room, eyes searching the corners, as though expecting to see her standing there.

Standing up, Jasper went and put his arms around her. 'This ain't a ghost, love. This is a person. And you need to report your stolen rings to the police.'

Nellie drew back. 'No! No police!'

163

'But why? You've bin robbed.'

'I don't need the police pokin' their noses around my café. I got enough problems without that.'

'Hmm.' Jasper led Nellie to the bed and they sat down. 'I need you to listen to me,' he said softly. 'Gladys ain't hauntin' you. Someone wants to scare you.'

'But why?' she cried. 'What have I ever done to deserve this?'

'Oh come on, love. Your sharp tongue has put more than one person's nose out of joint around here.'

'But to do this, Jasper! All they had to do was tell me to me face. I know I dish it out, but if I done wrong by someone, I'm happy to hold me hands up and apologise.'

'Happy, are ya?' he teased.

'This ain't funny, Jasper. What am I going to do?'

Jasper rubbed at the stubble on his chin. 'You and me are gonna try to work out who hates you enough to do this. You're right about Terence not bein' the sort to know about Gladys's perfume. But Lou would.'

Nellie shook her head. 'If she had a problem with me, she'd come and say so. Thing about Lou is she's straight up – you know where you stand with her. No, there's only one explanation, and no matter how much you try to persuade me otherwise, it's gotta be Gladys.'

'And what would Glad want with Donald's picture?' Jasper asked.

Nellie didn't reply. She had a fair idea why Gladys had taken Donald's picture: it was to send her a message; remind her of what she'd promised just moments before she died. Or maybe it was worse than that . . . Now she was dead, maybe she finally knew the truth? She shivered and lay her head against Jasper's shoulder, but even his warmth couldn't dispel the ice-cold fear that was sweeping over her.

'You know, Nell, whether Terence stole your stuff or not, you still owe him money. An' I reckon there might be someone who can help.' He led her back to the sitting room and they sat down opposite each other.

'You know someone with fifty quid goin' spare?'

Jasper whistled. 'That much?'

Nellie didn't reply. Just a year ago, she could have paid that from her savings, but she'd been reckless: topping up their supplies with expensive black market goods, using some to bolster the café's takings on slow weeks . . . But buying that big piece of celluloid from Terence was the most foolish act of all. She'd always kept a tight rein on the café's finances, but as soon as the bombs and shells had started to fall, her conscience wouldn't let her sit on the money while others were suffering.

'Well, like I said, I reckon there might be someone . . .'

Nellie narrowed her eyes at him. 'Who?'

Jasper opened his mouth, then closed it again. 'I can't say more right now.'

'Why d'you look so shifty?'

He dropped a kiss on her forehead. 'Just trust me. Everythin's gonna be all right.'

Nellie examined his face; his cheeks were flushed and he was blinking rapidly. 'What have you done?' she said again.

Jasper rubbed his hands together and stood up. 'Right then,' he said cheerily. 'Things to do, people to see. Meantime, think on what I said, love. Who hates you enough to try to drive you mad?'

Frowning, Nellie followed him to the top of the stairs. 'I'll tell you who drives me mad,' she called over the thump of his footsteps as he rapidly descended. 'You!'

Jasper looked back, winked, then disappeared.

Nellie walked slowly back to the sitting room, her thoughts whirling. She didn't agree with Jasper; surely no one could hate her so much they'd hatch such an elaborate plan. No, there really was only one explanation.

A sudden thought occurred to her. Lou had come in the other day and slapped a notice down on the counter. 'Here we go, Nell. Little gift from Barmy Bancroft.'

But was she really barmy? Or could she be the one person who could help her right now? As soon as she had a free moment, she would pay her a visit.

Chapter 32

In the allotment hut, Reenie angrily started to stuff the parsnips into sacks, her movements quick and jerky as her mind went over and over what Wilf had said. *If you have doubts, listen to them.* Arrogant man! Of course she didn't have doubts! But then she remembered what Terence had said about Jimmy's secret being safe with him . . .

She had just finished when the door opened and a tall figure stood silhouetted against the light and her heart leapt.

'I thought you might be here.' Jim came forward to give her a hug.

She stepped back and folded her arms.

Jimmy's arms dropped to his sides and he looked at her in bemusement. 'Have I done something wrong?'

'I don't know, Jim, have you?'

Jimmy's brows furrowed and he took his cap off, slapping it against his thigh nervously. 'I mean . . . I . . .' He shrugged. 'Not that I know of,' he said eventually. 'In fact, I came to find you because I have good news. I applied for a special licence yesterday and I just picked it up. We can get married one week today!'

Her heart stuttered. 'Really? One week?!'

He smiled uncertainly. 'That is, if you still want me?'

The genuine anxiety in his expression reassured her more than words ever could have, and suddenly, she felt foolish for worrying so much about what Terence Carter had said – everyone knew he was a nasty piece of work. As for Wilf . . . well, whatever his reasons for saying what he had, she didn't care! He didn't know Jimmy like she did.

She rushed over and threw her arms around his neck. 'Yes, yes! Of *course* I still want you!' She stood on tiptoe to kiss his mouth, revelling in the warmth of his hard body pressed close to hers. She pulled him closer and deepened the kiss and for a moment the cold hut and the damp smell of earth disappeared.

After a while he lifted his head and looked down into her eyes. 'Thank God! When I came in, I thought you'd changed your mind.' He pressed his forehead to hers. 'Is something the matter?'

Reenie shook her head. 'Not now you're here. But before you came . . . Well, it was something Terence Carter said to me.' She wouldn't tell him what Wilf had said. 'He wanted me to give you a message.'

'Terence Carter?' Jim asked in astonishment. 'I hardly know the bloke.'

'Well, he seems to know you. He said that you're not to worry because your secret is safe with him. He also said you should speak to Bert, then go find him in the Oak.' She kept her eyes on his face and even though the light was dim in the hut, she could have sworn Jimmy blanched.

After a long pause, she said. 'What do you think it's about?'

'I have no idea.' Jimmy swallowed and looked down at the rough planks under his feet.

'Are you in trouble? Is there something you need to tell me?'

'No! God, no!' He took her hands. 'I've never had anything to do with that man! But as for Bert . . . God knows. You know how reckless he's been recently. He probably owes Terence money.'

Reenie nodded. 'I thought it must be something like that.' She examined his face, but he wouldn't meet her eyes, causing a flicker of doubt to return. 'Are you sure that's all it is? Because when I mentioned it to Marianne, she looked spooked. And so did you just now.'

Jim ran his hands through his hair. 'You told Marianne?'

'She's my mate, of course I told her. But she reacted weirdly. What's going on?'

'Honestly, I don't know, love.' Jim put his arms around her again and rested his cheek on her head. 'You'll have to ask her that.'

Reenie pulled away. 'I did! But her first loyalty is to you! And even though she's one of my oldest friends and I've known your family forever, it made me wonder whether I'd ever fit in. All the secrets and lies . . . Where will that leave me?'

Jimmy looked utterly bewildered now. 'What do you mean? You'll be my wife, Reens. Mrs Jimmy Castle. You've been more or less part of the family all my life. When we're married, you'll be even more part of it.'

Reenie looked away. 'I love you, Jim, but I won't be living at the café. Once we're married, I'm staying with Aunt Ethel and Uncle Brian till the war's over and we can find a place of our own.'

'Has Mum upset you?' he asked.

'No. Although she's definitely annoyed me. But there's something up with her. Something more than usual. Her and Lou Carter were having a furious row earlier. And it all leads back to Terence again.'

'Mum and Lou are always arguing, so I don't know why you're surprised. Honestly, Reenie, everyone loves you. And I know things have been a bit . . . well, a bit up and down in the family recently, but take no notice of Mum. She's taken Gladys's death really hard. As for Terence, I'll pop up and see Bert soon as I can and find out what's going on.'

'If Bert owes him money, don't you dare pay him a penny! He can sort out his own mess.'

'And that's what I'll tell him,' he said. 'But first I need to talk to him. If he weren't already hurt, I'd bloody injure him myself.' He gave her a disarming smile. 'But I don't care about that. I care about us; about the fact that you seem to be getting cold feet, and just when I've spent a fortune on the licence. Don't you love me anymore?'

Reenie softened; she never could resist him when he gave her his little-boy-lost look: his blue eyes wide and pleading, his beautiful mouth downturned.

'You know I do,' she said. 'Sometimes I wish I didn't. It would save me a whole lot of trouble.'

Jimmy smiled radiantly and bent to kiss her lips. 'You won't regret it, I promise. I'm going to be the best husband ever.'

Reenie put her arms around his neck and kissed him again, trying to pull him closer, but Jim put his hands on her waist and urged her away slightly. 'Much as I'd love to continue,' he murmured against her mouth, 'I have to get back.'

Reenie groaned. 'Can't you spare just a few more minutes.' She gestured to a pile of sacks. 'We could cuddle a bit more and . . . maybe even take things further,' she whispered shyly.

Jim shook his head and kissed her quickly on the nose. 'I really can't. I'm already a bit late.' Seeing her disappointment, he gave her a tight squeeze. 'I'm sorry. Something's always coming up, isn't it? But don't worry, it won't be long till we'll have all the time in the world.' He reached into his pocket and pulled out a piece of paper. 'Soon, you will be Mrs Jimmy Castle.'

'Will you be able to get a night's leave?'

'Fingers crossed. Might even be able to swing a forty-eight-hour pass.' He stroked her cheek. 'No more doubts?' he asked.

Reenie regarded him soberly. 'You'll tell me what Bert says? And I'll come with you to see Terence.'

Jimmy looked hesitant.

'Look, if we're getting married, I don't want any secrets between us.'

Jimmy blew out a long breath. 'All right,' he said softly. 'No more secrets. But you will *not* be coming to see Terence with me. If he turns nasty, I don't want to be worrying about you.'

Reenie nodded. 'All right. Next Friday then. No more doubts.'

Jimmy smiled with relief. 'This time next week I will be the luckiest man in the world.'

She gave him a little shove. 'No lies either,' she teased. 'Now, go sort out your brother's mess and let me know what happens – otherwise I'll spend every hour worrying.'

He brought her hands up to his lips, kissing the back of them. 'I love you. And whatever Terence wants to talk to me about, I'm sure it's nothing for us to worry about – Bert might need to worry, but not us, all right?'

Reenie watched as he put his cap back on and hurried out of the hut. They were as bad as each other. She'd asked for no more secrets and lies. But she'd lied when she told him she had no more doubts . . . And he'd lied when he said there was nothing for them to worry about. From his expression when she'd told him what Terence had said, there was most definitely *something* to worry about. And she was pretty sure Jimmy knew what it was.

∽

Outside, Jimmy walked quickly up the hill towards Drop Redoubt, trying hard to keep his nerves under control. Terence Carter making veiled threats to him through Reenie was making his imagination run wild. Logically, he knew his theory about Bert and gambling was the obvious reason the man wanted to see him, because if it had been anything else, wouldn't he have got his claws into him by now? But Reenie had been clear, Terence had said that *his* secret was safe with him.

'Oh God,' he whispered, rubbing his face. 'Surely it's not possible?' But the more he thought about it, the more likely it seemed.

With a heavy heart, he gazed out at the choppy grey sea, as miserable and turbulent as his own feelings. Maybe he could brazen it out. Now he was marrying Reenie, it would be Terence's word against his. He took a deep, calming breath.

Yes, let the man say what he liked, with Reenie by his side, for the first time in his life, he had nothing to hide.

Chapter 33

Two days after the tragic events on the football field, Marge straightened up with a sigh and removed the headphones through which a naval officer had been barking orders at her as she moved the small boats around on the green table as if it were a game. Plotting the movements of the ships was not only mentally demanding, but bending over the table for hours on end was playing havoc with her back. It didn't help that she was exhausted. Sleep had been impossible with images of the shooting circling through her mind, and thoughts of Phil haunting her. God, she needed a smoke.

She looked over at Jeanie, and by silent agreement, they made their way back up to the tunnel entrance. They'd started work at 3 a.m. and now, twelve hours later, it was good to see the light. She pulled out a cigarette and lit it.

'You coming to the NAAFI?' Jeanie asked. 'I'm starving.'

Marge blew smoke out on a sigh. She'd not been able to eat a thing since the attack, and she still couldn't stomach food. 'I can't. Phil's been moved to the Casualty, so I'm going to see him.'

Jeanie gave her a sharp look. 'You don't sound too keen.'

Marge huffed. 'Would you be?' She'd not told Jeanie about Phil's proposal, and she didn't intend to. She was hoping that he wouldn't remember asking her.

Jeanie took her arm and squeezed it. 'I would if I loved him,' she said meaningfully. When Marge didn't reply, Jeanie sighed. 'Look, Marge, none of this is your fault, so stop feeling guilty.

I mean, of course you can't say anything to him now, but later, when he's better, you're gonna have to.'

'He's lost his leg, Jeanie!' Marge exclaimed. 'How's he ever going to be better?'

Just then a smart black Humber came to a halt beside them, and the passenger door was pushed open.

'Need a lift to the hospital?' Rodney was leaning across the gear stick, looking up at her.

Jeanie gave her a meaningful look, which Marge ignored as she bent down to peer into the car. Rodney looked as neat as ever, his dark hair shiny with Brylcreem, but his blue eyes were shadowed with fatigue.

'How'd you get hold of this?' she asked, taking in the rust-coloured leather upholstery and the varnished wooden dashboard.

He grinned, and Marge's heart flipped in her chest. 'Friends in high places. Hop in.'

She hesitated for a moment. She hadn't seen Rodney since the day of the shooting, but she'd thought of him . . . And the guilt was eating away at her. Sitting in close quarters with him, his clean scent surrounding her, would only make things worse. But the alternative was walking to the hospital and back in the drizzle.

'Go on,' Jeanie murmured behind her. 'You know you want to. I won't wait up.'

Marge shot her an angry glare, and got in, slamming the door shut and sticking her tongue out at her friend as the car pulled smoothly away.

They drove in silence for a few minutes, until Marge asked, 'How did you know Phil was at the Casualty?'

'The doctor told me they'd be moving him yesterday.'

'Why did you go and see him?' she asked. 'You two aren't exactly the best of friends.'

Rodney didn't take his eyes off the road as he replied, 'Because you and I are friends . . . I wanted to know what you'd be dealing with.'

173

His concern warmed her. 'I'm not the one who has to deal with this, though. He is.'

Rodney glanced at her. 'I thought you two were . . .' He trailed off. 'I mean, are you still . . . ?'

Marge stared out as the greenery of Connaught Park raced past her. 'Nothing's changed,' she said evasively. If only that were true. If only Phil was still walking around hale and hearty, dishing out advice and blessings. 'How's Bert?' she asked.

'That's what I'm about to find out,' he said. 'But listen, I did want to speak to you about something else. Jim came to see me yesterday afternoon. It seems he and Reenie are getting married next week.'

Marge's head whipped round. 'You're joking! Since when?'

'Apparently, he proposed after the shooting, and considering everything, they thought it best to keep it quiet. Will you come?'

Marge smiled. 'But this is brilliant news!'

'Do you really think so?' he asked.

'Of course I do! She's crazy about him. Why? Don't you think it's good news?'

'It's just a bit sudden. This time last year, Jim was still just her friend's kid brother, and now they're getting married? They hardly know each other.' He shook his head.

'Pah! Trust you to be a killjoy! Why can't you just be happy for them?'

'I am. If it's really what they both want. But . . .' He shrugged. 'Anyway, will you come?'

'You want me to go to the wedding with you?' Marge asked, feeling that annoying little twinge in her heart again.

'Not exactly. Jim asked if I'd be a witness, and asked me to ask you. He'd like it to be a surprise for Reenie. He doesn't want her to be completely unsupported on her wedding day.'

'So this isn't your idea?' Marge tried to hide her disappointment. 'And it'll just be the four of us?'

'Ah. Now, I've been thinking about it, and I wanted to run an idea past you. If they are going to get married, they should at least have a celebration with their families. What do you think if I ask Mavis to lay on a bit of a spread at the Oak after – my treat. Jim asked me to keep the marriage quiet, so I'll have to find a way to get them there without causing suspicion. Then after they've said their vows, we can take them there and it'll be a lovely surprise.' He looked over at her with a smile. 'Do you think they'd like that?'

'I think that's a wonderful idea,' she said softly. 'Particularly if you're not too keen on the idea of their marriage in the first place.'

'I never said that! I just don't want them rushing into something they might regret. But if they're going to do it, they may as well have a proper celebration.'

'Well, you are full of surprises. I never thought I'd see the day when you decided to arrange a party! But aren't you worried it might cause more Castle family dramas?'

'I'm hoping everyone will be too happy to argue. Although . . . I was wondering if you could try to persuade Edie to come.'

Marge let out a bark of laughter. 'What did I just say about family drama? In the past year we've had spies, irate townsfolk protesting outside the café, secret fathers, secret brothers . . . And now you want to risk Edie and your mum in the same room. If I were you, I wouldn't push your luck.'

'Please? It's partly why I wanted to do this. It might force them to speak. And if I ask, she'll just say no.'

'All right, I'll talk to her, but that's all I can do. The decision is hers.'

Rodney smiled widely and Marge groaned inwardly. This was a very bad idea. She'd sworn she wouldn't get involved in Rodney's life again, but Reenie was one of her best friends and she wouldn't miss her wedding for the world. In any case, her life had been entwined with the Castles since the first time Marianne had taken her home when she was seven and Rodney had annoyed her so much, she'd smeared jam on his seat.

His dad had been alive back then, and not long back from the first war, she remembered with a pang of shame. And when he'd seen the mess on Rodney's trousers, he'd screamed blue murder. The afternoon hadn't ended well, and if she'd known then what she knew now about how his dad had treated him, she would never have done it.

'What's wrong?' Rodney asked, noting the change in her expression.

She shook her head. 'I was just remembering the first time Marianne brought me to your place for tea and I put jam on your chair and your dad kicked up a stink. I felt terrible about that.'

He looked over and raised an eyebrow. 'I'm touched. But if you're thinking of playing a trick like that again, don't use jam. It'd be a terrible waste of sugar.'

Marge grinned. 'I'll behave, I promise.'

'I doubt that, somehow,' he retorted. 'It's one of the things I love about you.'

Marge's eyes widened. 'Love, Rodders?' she replied lightly.

Rodney stopped outside the hospital and pulled the handbrake up. 'Obviously I didn't mean it like that,' he said dismissively. 'You better get in there and see your padre.' He put a subtle emphasis on the word 'your'.

His sudden change of tone from warmth to supercilious made Marge wish she had a pot of jam to hand so she could smear it over his perfectly pressed jacket. *This* was why they would never have worked as a couple. *This* was why she should stop mooning over something that had never existed and concentrate on Phil. Because Rodney Castle drove her mad, and she suspected he always would.

Chapter 34

Marge stalked down the stairs to the hospital's basement, acutely aware of Rodney's steps behind her. Not only was she furious with him for making her care about him again and then slapping her in the face with his indifference, she was furious with herself for allowing it.

In the men's ward, she looked down the rows of beds and spotted Phil easily from the blankets domed over his legs. She glanced quickly around, relieved to see that Bert's bed was on the other side of the room, so at least she wouldn't have to worry about Rodney eavesdropping on her conversation.

She approached Phil's bed tentatively. His eyes were closed, his hair limp and damp against his forehead. Sitting down in the chair beside him, she took his hand.

'Phil?' she whispered.

Immediately, his eyes opened, and his face broke into a beautiful smile.

'You came,' he said.

She leant over and kissed his cheek. 'Of course I came. What did you expect, you daft ha'porth?'

'I . . . I just thought you'd be too busy to make it.'

'Rodney gave me a lift,' she explained.

The smile left his face. 'Oh.'

Marge tutted. 'Don't be silly. He's come to see Bert.'

Phil closed his eyes. 'Sorry,' he said. 'It's just . . .' He tried to raise himself on the bed, but seemed to have little strength, so

Marge stood and put her hands beneath his armpits and tried to help.

He let out a small cry of pain, and she stopped, lowering him gently back on to the pillow. 'Maybe not today, eh?' She glanced down at the raised blankets then looked back at him. 'I'm so sorry this happened to you, Phil,' she said softly.

Philip managed a slight smile. 'Hey, don't get upset on my behalf. There are plenty worse off than me. The doctor said you saved my life.' His eyes misted over. 'Thank you.'

'I'm sure you would have survived without me. Does it hurt very badly?'

'Oh, it's not too bad,' he said stoically. But his pallid skin and shadowed eyes told a different story.

Marge gave him a stern look. 'Come on, Phil, you don't have to pretend. I can see you're in agony.'

He huffed. 'All right, it hurts like buggery. But it won't feel like this forever, so I've just got to grin and bear it for now. No point feeling sorry for myself.'

'You're right. And you'll be up and about again soon. I mean, look at Douglas Bader, he lost both his legs and he's one of the RAF's best pilots.'

'True,' Philip said. 'Maybe I'll have to learn to fly.'

Marge laughed. 'And leave the church?'

'Can't I fly and serve God?'

'Well, I suppose angels manage it,' Marge said lightly.

Philip turned her hand in his, his thumb stroking over the back. 'You're an angel, Marge. You saved my life.'

Marge swallowed, not liking the turn in the conversation.

'And I'm so glad that one of the last things I did before it happened is run towards you.' He looked at her steadily. 'I haven't forgotten what I said,' he murmured. 'And I want you to know I meant it.'

Marge dropped her eyes. 'Let's talk about it when you feel better,' she said evasively.

178

Phil sighed. 'It's all right, I understand. I'm not the same man who asked you.'

'Oh God! No, that's not what I meant. Your life has changed, Phil. You need time to reflect on that. Decide if what you wanted before is what you want now.'

'No, I don't. The only thing that's changed is my body. My feelings for you are the same. I think it's you that needs to decide what you want.'

'And if you hadn't been injured, that's what I would have said,' Marge said, grabbing on to the lifeline he'd thrown her. 'I need to think about it, Phil. Marriage wasn't on my mind, so it came as a bit of a shock.'

'Good or bad?' he murmured.

Marge hesitated a moment, before laughing slightly. 'Good. Of course good. All girls dream of a marriage proposal from a handsome man.'

She'd hoped to lighten the tone with her flippant response, but the flash of hurt and disappointment on his face made it clear her hesitation hadn't gone unnoticed.

He let go of her hand and closed his eyes. 'I'm sorry, but I'm very tired. Would you mind if I went to sleep now?'

Marge nodded and leant over to kiss his cheek again. 'I'll be back as soon as I can,' she said, but Phil just turned his face away.

Marge stood and looked down at him for a long while, hating herself for upsetting him when he was so weak. She'd never seen Phil downhearted before – and it wasn't because of the loss of his leg. He'd been surprisingly cheerful when she'd first come in. This was all down to her, and the guilt was almost overwhelming.

She bent down again and whispered, 'I love you too.' Then she turned and walked away before he had a chance to respond.

She glanced over to Bert's bed. Rodney was sitting close to him and they looked deep in conversation, so, deciding to leave them to it, she made her way back to the corridor, where she sat down and lit a cigarette and tried very hard not to think about Phil's devastated expression.

The sound of the double doors at the bottom of the stairs bursting open was a welcome distraction, and she smiled to see Jimmy rushing along the corridor. 'Hey, Jim!' She stood up.

He looked startled for a moment, then smiled. 'Marge! Sorry, I was in a world of my own.'

'Thinking about the old ball and chain, were you?' She grinned.

'Ha! Rodney's spoken to you, then. Can you do it?'

Marge pecked him on the cheek. 'I'll be honoured to, and I'm so happy for you and Reenie. I'll pop in and see her soon as I get a chance.'

'Don't mention you know. I want it to be a surprise.' He gestured to the door of the men's ward. 'But I better . . .'

'Go! Rodney's there.'

'Damn,' Jim muttered, peering through the door. 'I'll see you later, Marge,' he said without looking back at her, then disappeared into the ward.

Chapter 35

Jimmy walked hesitantly towards Bert's bed, unsure of the greeting he would get. Since Gladys's death, Bert had been hard to pin down – always too busy drinking or with a woman. He'd tried to talk to him soon after it had happened, but he'd been brushed off. He should have tried harder. Instead, he'd been too caught up in his own internal battles and had just assumed Bert would get over it. But he knew better than most that nothing was ever that simple.

'Someone's looking better than they were the other day,' Jimmy said cheerfully as he came to stand at the end of Bert's bed. Although, in truth he looked dreadful. A large white dressing covered his cheek, his right arm was in a sling, and a drip snaked out of his left.

'Speak of the devil,' Rodney declared, getting up and slapping him on the shoulder.

'Should my ears be burning?' Jimmy asked, maintaining his jovial facade.

'I don't know, should they?' Bert said, his expression unreadable.

Rodney broke the tense silence that followed, by saying, 'I'll leave you two to it then. Did you see Marge out there?'

Jim nodded, but his gaze never left Bert. Rodney stared between them, bewildered at the coldness in Bert's tone, and the stiffness in Jim's stance. 'I'll see you next week then, Jim,' he said meaningfully, causing Jimmy to finally look at him.

'Yeah. Next week, Rod. Thanks.'

As soon as Rodney had left, Jim sat down in the wooden chair beside the bed. 'What's going on? Terence Carter cornered Reenie the other day and demanded she tell me to speak to you. What have you done now?'

Bert's eyes narrowed. 'What have *I* done? You're having a laugh.'

'If you owe him money, I hope you're not expecting me to settle your debts. Rodney's loaded – you'd be better off asking him.'

'I've paid my debt to Terence off. Problem is, he's found a way to get more money out of me.'

'Doesn't change the fact that he's not getting a penny out of me. It's your mess, you sort it out.'

'My mess?' He let out a bitter laugh. 'How's Reenie?' he asked.

'She's fine,' Jimmy replied. 'Well, she was until she saw Terence the other day. Are you going to tell me what's so urgent that I have to speak to you.'

Bert let out a deep sigh. 'I'm sorry if he scared her. But for Christ's sake, you've got no business being with her in the first place!'

Jim frowned. 'What the hell are you talking about? We love each other. In fact, we're getting married next week.'

Bert's eyes widened with shock. 'Are you mad? You can't marry Reenie!'

'Isn't that what people generally do when they're in love?'

'Depends who they love, doesn't it?' Bert responded challengingly, his eyes never leaving Jimmy's face.

'Why would you say something like that?' Jimmy hissed.

'Oh, I think you know very well why I'd say it. And you know what makes me fucking furious? The fact that Terence was the one to tell me. Oh, no, wait! *Susan* was the first person. But I was never going to listen to *her*, was I? But now I've heard it from two different people, and Terence is threatening to tell everyone unless I keep paying him.'

Jimmy's stomach lurched. 'Wh-what . . .' He cleared his throat. 'What did they tell you?' But he knew for sure now. On New Year's Eve he'd gone to see Mary Guthrie and Susan had been there. She must have been eavesdropping on their conversation. And if Susan knew, how many other people had she told?

'Stop pretending you don't know!' Bert exclaimed in frustration. 'Why didn't you *tell* me, Jim. I'm your brother, for God's sake! You should've talked to *me*! But instead I heard it first from the woman who tried to kill me. How come she knew, but I didn't?'

At his brother's stricken expression, Bert softened his tone. 'I've been thinking about it, and I can't believe I never saw it. It was Colin, wasn't it?'

Jim buried his face in his hands.

'Christ, do you know the risk you've been running?! I could have helped you! Did you think I'd think worse of you? My own brother?'

Guilt, heavy and dark, sapped Jim of his will to argue. 'Don't you?' he asked in a small voice.

Bert snorted. 'I tell you what does make me think worse of you . . . The fact that you didn't trust me. We've been mates all our lives. Hardly a cross word between us. I bloody love you . . . I thought you loved me.' Bert's voice broke a little.

Jim kept his head down. 'Of course I love you,' he mumbled.

'If you did, you'd've trusted me!'

Jim looked up, suddenly angry. 'Trust the man who's always got a girl on his arm and makes jokes about Nancy boys and shirtlifters?' he spat.

'But it's different with you; you're my brother!'

'And Colin?' Jim shot back. 'What about him?'

Bert blinked. 'Well . . . he was always a mate too.'

'So, you don't mind your brother or your mate, but anyone else? How is that different? Don't you see, Bert? From everything you've ever said, I figured you'd hate me if you knew.'

Bert's gaze dropped and he lay his head back against the pillows with a heavy sigh. 'Fuck,' he said. 'Fuck, fuck, fuck.'

They sat in silence for some time, Jimmy fiddling with the blanket and resisting the urge to run away and hide.

'Does anyone else know?' Bert asked, opening his eyes. 'Apart from the bitch and the spiv.'

Jimmy didn't reply. Truth was, he didn't know. It seemed his secret was far more widely known than he'd believed, and the thought terrified him. What would he do if Reenie found out? All his hopes for the future would be gone; she was the only woman he could ever imagine marrying. And if he didn't marry her . . . Well, he would be alone for the rest of his life. Colin had been the love of his life; no one could ever replace him in his heart.

'Who the hell else, Jim?' Bert growled. 'Rodney? Mum? The whole world?'

'Marianne,' he whispered. 'Alfie – I think, Mrs Guthrie . . .'

Bert laughed. 'But not me. Right. I see it all clearly now. And now I'm expected to risk *everything* to keep your dirty little secret. My life, my freedom, my future!'

Jimmy looked up at him in astonishment. 'What do you mean?'

'Like I said, Terence has found a way to make me keep paying him. And he don't keep quiet for nothing. He's expecting payment next week. So, you better sort something out fast, or the whole town'll know.'

'But you don't have money,' Jim said. 'What have you been paying him with?'

'Fuel. Sugar. Coffee. Tea. Butter.'

Jim's eyes widened. 'Bloody hell, Bert.' He leant his elbows on the blanket and put his head in his hands. 'You should've talked to me.'

'*You* should've talked to *me*! Months ago. Years ago!'

'But you know I'm with Reenie now. What's Terence gonna do? It's his word against mine and everyone knows he's a thieving toerag! This has to stop, Bert!'

'And you want to risk it? How do you think Reenie'll feel when she hears? You know exactly what'll happen, don't you? She'll go running to Marianne to ask her, and Marianne can't lie for toffee . . .'

'Christ, what a mess!' Jimmy murmured. 'So, what, I'm expected to steal for Terence in your place, am I?'

'That's about the size of it. And if you want my advice, go and make very good friends with Captain Norman.'

'The quartermaster? Is that how you've been getting the stuff? Christ, Bert! He was arrested this morning! It's been all round the barracks that he's been done for theft. Are you telling me that it was *you*!' He ran his hand through his hair in agitation. 'He won't keep that to himself. Mark my words, it won't be long till the red caps will be barging through this door to arrest you! You'll be court-martialled! As if things aren't bad enough! *This* is why you should've told me! I can look after myself!'

Bert stared at his brother in shock.

'Couldn't you have found another way? Asked Mum or Rodney for a loan or something! And now you expect me to keep doing your dirty work?'

'It's not my dirty work, though, is it? It's yours,' Bert replied.

'And when will it end? Once he gets his claws into you, Terence doesn't let go. As you've found out. No way I can risk it. I can't believe you bloody did either.' He shook his head in bemusement. Bert had no idea what his life had been like; he breezed through his days confident in the knowledge that men admired him and women adored him. He'd never had to hide his true self out of fear. So now, to put himself in danger of arrest and scrutiny . . . There was only one person he would do that for, and he was dead.

'Then what are you going to do? Mud sticks, Jim. And with all the mud being slung at our family recently, do you think Mum could handle any more?'

'There's nothing for her to handle!' Jim almost roared, then noticing the man in the bed beside Bert's staring at them curiously, he lowered his voice. 'And what happens if Norman decides to tell everyone exactly who's been stealing all that stuff. What's he got to lose?'

Bert lay back wearily. 'You don't have to worry about that. Cos I know something about Captain Norman that he won't want to get out. It ain't for nothing that he's known as Nancy Norman. I happen to know that him and one of the other officers – a *very* high up one – have been going at it hammer and tongs. How else do you think I managed to persuade him to help me?'

Jimmy stood up, the chair clattering onto the floor with a bang, and leant over Bert. '*Nancy* Norman! You just can't help yourself, can you? You blackmailed that man just like Terence is blackmailing you and you can't even see what a hypocrite you are! So no, I'm not paying Terence Carter a penny. Me and Reenie are getting married and then he can squeal all he likes, but no one will listen.'

Jamming his cap back on his head, Jimmy stormed out of the ward.

∽

Bert closed his eyes and cursed. Everyone called him Nancy Norman; it was just a joke, for God's sake! And it wasn't as if he was insulting Jim – his brother seemed to have lost his sense of humour. He tried to fuel his indignation, but instead found himself swallowing back the self-pitying tears he could feel rising in his throat as he thought back over the last few months.

He punched the mattress with his good arm, wincing as the force jolted his shoulder, but that pain was nothing compared to the searing agony he felt at the thought that he might have lost his brother thanks to his stupid big mouth.

A hand touched his arm gently. 'Everything all right, Bert?' It was the same soothing voice that had comforted him through his nightmares, but he wasn't sure anything could make him feel better right now.

He turned his head away. 'Please, go away.'

'Jim'll be back,' the nurse said. 'Just be patient.'

He wished he could believe it. But the old Jim and Bert were dead and buried and nothing could ever bring them back.

Chapter 36

Jimmy was still fizzing with anger at his brother by the time he got to the high street. But as he neared Market Square, his steps slowed. He couldn't forget how close they'd come to losing Bert, and what that would have meant to him – to all of them. His brother was foolish and reckless, but he should have done more to help him since Gladys had died. Maybe then they wouldn't be in this situation. Although, given what Terence knew, he would have got his claws into one or other of them sooner or later.

He leant against a blackened wall, watching the market square, trying to decide what to do. The most important thing was clear: he needed to speak to Reenie. Terence had shaken her up with his talk, and he needed to calm her worries. He hadn't forgotten her initial hesitation when he'd produced the marriage licence, but now he *had* to get married. Because without Reenie by his side, there would be no buffer against the rumours Terence might start.

And there was more than just his reputation at stake. It would affect his family as well – his mum would probably never speak to him again. She'd made her views on 'that sort of thing' more than plain in the past. No, the wedding needed to go ahead if he was to squash the rumours before they started.

With a new feeling of resolve, he walked to Turners' Grocery. Reenie was serving a customer when he entered, and her eyes widened at his grim expression. Tipping his head towards the door, he motioned for her to join him, then went to stand outside.

Reenie joined him ten minutes later and they went round the side of the shop, away from the crowds. 'What's happened?' she asked anxiously. 'You look dreadful.'

'I've seen Bert,' he said. 'My brother's a fool, but it's nothing for you to worry about. Gambling debt, like we thought. But I'm leaving on some stupid exercise tonight and won't be back till next Thursday, the day before the wedding. I'll arrange to see Terence that night.'

She searched his face. 'And the secret Terence mentioned? The one he said was safe with him – what was that about?'

Jimmy huffed. 'There isn't a secret! He was just trying to stir trouble.'

She nodded uncertainly.

'Listen, try not to worry. *Nothing* is going to ruin our wedding, all right?'

Reenie's brow furrowed. 'Why would this ruin our wedding? You just said it's Bert's problem.'

Jim looked away guiltily.

'There's something else, isn't there?'

'Honestly, there's nothing else.' Jim caught her hands and held them tight to his chest. 'Please believe me.'

'But I don't understand why you think Terence could ruin our wedding.'

Jimmy grinned sheepishly. 'I was just being dramatic. I suppose I'm just worried that you might back out. You won't, will you?' He bent and kissed her lips. 'Promise me?'

'Of course not. But if this is just about Bert owing him money, why do you need to see Terence at all?'

'To let him know that he won't get a penny out of me. This is Bert's mess and he can clean it up when he gets out of hospital.'

'And that's all it is? You're absolutely sure?'

'I swear on my life, that's all it is. Trust me?' Jim leant his forehead against hers.

Reenie sighed and nodded. 'All right, I trust you.' She paused for a moment. 'I've been thinking. I know we said we'd keep it quiet, but there's no need now, is there? Bert's going to be all right, and I'd like our families to be there.'

Just then a figure loomed over them. 'Ah, young love.' Terence stood beside them, a mocking smile on his face.

Reenie glanced at Jim, alarmed to see how pale he'd gone.

'What do you want?' Jimmy ground out.

'Just wanted to know how your brother is.'

'He'll live.'

'I'm pleased to hear it. So, how's about we go have a little chat?'

Jimmy shook his head. 'Sorry, no time. We're being shipped out on exercise till next Thursday, so you'll have to wait.'

'Aww. Shame. Back in time for the weddin' are ya?'

'How did you know about that?' Jimmy shot a glance at Reenie.

'I know a lot of things, Jimmy. An' like I said to Reenie the other day, your secret's safe with me. For now. Meet me Thursday night and we can discuss my terms.' He glanced at Reenie. 'Wouldn't want anything to spoil your big day, would we?' He tipped his hat and strolled away.

Jimmy slumped against the wall and rubbed his hands over his face.

'Terms? What does he mean? And what secret? You said there wasn't a secret!' Reenie exclaimed.

Jimmy sighed heavily. 'Look, if I tell you something, you need to swear to keep it to yourself, all right?'

'You know you don't even need to ask,' Reenie replied.

'Bert's been stealing from the army supplies to pay off his debt,' he murmured. 'And now Terence expects me to carry on in his place.'

Reenie gasped. 'What!? But he could get arrested!'

Jim nodded grimly. 'As it happens, someone else has been accused. But the danger's still there. Which would definitely ruin

190

our wedding, do you see? As for his *terms*, my guess is he's going to try to blackmail me to stop him turning Bert in. But he's just bluffing. He wouldn't dare say anything because it would implicate him as well.'

'God, what a horrible mess! You poor thing, having to deal with this. Come here.' Reenie put her arms around him and hugged him tightly. 'Everything'll be all right. You'll see.'

Jim nodded against her shoulder. 'Thank you,' he whispered. 'Thank you for sticking with me.'

'Always, my love. I promise.' She leant away from him. 'And you're sure there's nothing else?'

Jimmy let out a short laugh. 'God, I really hope not. But let's not talk about this anymore. The next time I see you will be our wedding day. And if you want to tell people, then that's fine with me. I want everyone to know how lucky I am.'

Reenie shook her head. 'I've changed my mind. If Terence turns up to cause trouble, I'd rather no one else was there.'

Jimmy swallowed nervously. 'I hadn't thought of that. You're right. Just you and me then.'

'And that's all I need.'

He kissed her again, then let her go reluctantly. 'I really do need to go. But next Friday you and me will be married!' He grinned. 'And I can't wait.'

∽

Reenie smiled as she watched him stride away. But once he was out of sight, the smile dropped. Bert was an idiot, and she hated that Jimmy had been caught up in his brother's mess. But something was still bothering her. *Tell Jim his secret's safe with me.* That's what Terence had said to her the other day. He hadn't even mentioned Bert. And though she had no choice but to trust him, there was a niggle of worry at the back of her mind that just wouldn't go away.

191

Chapter 37

Jasper paced impatiently up and down the in-coming platform of Dover Priory Station. The train was already over two hours late and there was still no sign of it.

'Jasper, give it a rest, mate,' the station guard said. 'You're givin' me a headache.'

'How much longer d'you reckon?' Jasper said.

'Your guess is as good as mine. Trains come when they come these days. Don't know why they bother with a timetable no more.'

Jasper sat down on the bench, his knee jiggling as he wondered how Nellie was going to react to what he'd done. But dammit, she couldn't carry on the way she was. Scrubbing the pavement, working herself to the bone, seeing ghosts everywhere . . . He sighed and rubbed his hand through his bushy hair.

It had been six days since the tragic football match, and four since Jasper had received the reply to his telegram that he'd been praying for. Over the last week, life in Dover had been relatively quiet – no bombs and no shells at all. It had been a welcome respite, and even Nellie seemed to have calmed down a bit. She still clutched that blasted necklace when she thought no one was looking, but as she'd not said any more about Gladys haunting her, he'd let the subject drop. And hopefully, with this new arrival to Dover, Nellie might have the time and space she needed to finally get over her friend's death.

Even so, he was nervous about how she'd react. He got up and started to pace again, hands in the pockets of his baggy brown trousers. This could go one of three ways. Either she'd rant and rail at him before accepting he was right. Or she'd rant and rail at him, then not speak to him for months. Before finally accepting he was right. Or, and this was the reaction he was dreading, she'd slam the door in his face, refuse to let either of them in and never speak to him again.

He smiled slightly; one way or another, the next few hours were going to be bumpy. No one could ever accuse his Nellie of being boring.

The whistle of a train floated towards him, bringing with it a whiff of steam. And finally, the round snub nose came into view as the train chugged slowly towards the platform. When it finally drew to a stop, he watched as the doors slammed open and disgorged a seemingly infinite number of people. Most were wearing uniform, although there were a few in civilian clothing, but there was no sign of the woman he was waiting for.

He walked along the platform towards the end of the train, the acrid smoke making his eyes water. He heard her before he saw her: a high, piping voice that brought back a thousand memories . . .

'What a journey! I don't think I've sat on a train that long since . . . Well, since I left here for Birmingham. Ooh, I were a bag of nerves that day. Just sixteen . . . Still it all worked out for the best. And me and my Ernie had a lovely place right by the botanical gardens. Do you live near a park, Sergeant?'

'Christ,' Jasper muttered. He'd forgotten quite how much she talked – and how high her voice was. Suddenly his grand solution didn't seem such a good idea.

A tiny plump lady emerged through the steam, a black handbag over one arm, the other swinging a violin case. She was trotting beside a soldier who had a kitbag over one shoulder and was carrying a large suitcase in his other hand. His expression was stoical and Jasper would bet he'd not said a word for the entire journey.

'Cissy!' He raised his hand.

'Oh my giddy aunt! Jasper Cane as I live and breathe.' She hurried up to him and took hold of his arms, staring into his face. 'You haven't changed a bit. Hair's a bit whiter, a few more wrinkles, but then haven't we all.' She giggled, her small eyes almost disappearing as her face creased.

'You look well,' he said. And she did. Her plump cheeks were rosy, her dark eyes were bright as buttons and she'd painted her lips a vibrant red. He wondered where she got the lipstick, but knowing Cissy, she probably had at least twenty tubes stashed away somewhere; the only thing she loved more than talking was shopping. The wartime shortages must be torture for her.

Peeping from beneath her navy-blue hat, decorated with a brown feather, her hair was orange, which surprised him – once upon a time it had been the exact same shade of chestnut as Nellie's.

'I'm all the better for coming home,' she said brightly. Then turning to the man in khaki beside her, she said, 'Sergeant Wilby, meet my dear old friend Jasper Cane. Sergeant Wilby has kept me company all the way from Birmingham. Oh, we've had a lovely chat, haven't we, Sergeant?' She fished in her bag and pulled out a small paper bag. 'I've been saving these, but I'd like you to have them. A thank you for being such a good companion.'

The soldier shook his head, but she pressed them into his hand. 'For your little Rebecca and Johnny, then. You could post them. It would be such a surprise, wouldn't it, hmm?'

The man smiled. 'Thank you, Mrs Ford. It's very kind. And it's been a pleasure to chat to you.'

'Isn't he a lovely man, Jasper? You are a lovely man, Sergeant. Your wife is a very lucky woman—'

'Cissy,' Jasper interrupted. 'Shall we let Sergeant Wilby get on his way?'

Cissy put her gloved hand over her mouth. 'I'm talking too much, aren't I? You must tell me, you know. I warned you, didn't I?' She tapped the soldier playfully on the arm.

The sergeant smiled again, and put down the suitcase. 'You did, but you've taken my mind off things.' He tipped his hat. 'Maybe I'll see you at the café some time.'

'I will make sure you get an extra big slice of cake, Sergeant.' She beamed at him. 'And don't forget – post those toffees to your kids.'

'You ain't changed a bit, Cissy,' Jasper said fondly as the soldier walked away. 'You can still talk the hindlegs off a donkey.'

Cissy sighed. 'I do try to keep me mouth shut, but people are so interestin', don't you think? Everyone has a story. But I'm going to stay quiet while you tell me what's been going on. You can't imagine how happy I was to hear Nellie needed my help. Honest, you could have knocked me down with a feather. I thought, *If Nellie's admitting she needs help, then things must be bad.*'

Jasper cleared his throat. 'About that . . .'

Cissy looked up at him expectantly. 'What?'

He huffed out a breath. 'I may have forgotten to mention that you're coming.'

Cissy stopped dead. 'She doesn't know?'

Jasper shook his head. 'The thing is, Cissy, you know what she's like. If I suggested you come and help she'd just say no.'

'And here was me thinkin' she'd held out the olive branch,' Cissy said sadly. 'She never replied to one of my letters since I left and that were before the last war. I still write though. Every other month, just in case she changes her mind. It's been a great sadness to me. You're the only one what's kept in touch.'

He patted her arm. 'Nellie never forgave you for walkin' out and leavin' her to deal with her mum alone. And I think when you didn't come to the funeral . . . well, it added insult to injury.'

'I did wrong by her, an' I've regretted it every day. But I had my reasons, which if she'd've read my letters, she'd understand. But she hasn't, has she? And it's broke me heart. We was as close as sisters growin' up. If it hadn't been for her, I'd've left sooner . . . Auntie Gert were a horror to me. Do you remember?

I reminded her of me mum, and she hated her cos she'd stolen the man she wanted. Considerin' Dad left me on her doorstep and ran off as soon as Mum died, she should've been down on her knees thankin' her. But then, Auntie Gert were awful to everyone, including Nellie.' Cissy laughed slightly. 'But Nell always gave as good as she got. They was two peas in a pod. Always arguin' and grumblin' at each other. Only Nellie had a kinder heart,' she said reflectively. 'I've missed her these thirty years, Jasper. If it weren't for my Ernie, I'd have come crawlin' back on me hands and knees asking for her forgiveness, but Ernie always said it were better to let sleepin' dogs lie.'

'Were you happy with him, Ciss?' Jasper asked, squeezing her arm in sympathy.

Cissy gave him a radiant smile. 'He were the best of men. My life changed the minute he appeared at the Hippodrome. Won't never forget that night. Do you remember it, Jasper? Oh, he were that funny on the stage. Not much to look at, mind, but then I'm no oil paintin' meself. And he were so good to me.' She blinked away a few tears.

'Yeah, I remember. And I remember seein' you two walking down on the promenade arm in arm, starin' into each other's eyes like you'd never seen anythin' so wonderful,' he said gruffly.

'I hadn't,' Cissy said. 'My only regret is that by followin' Ernie, I lost Nellie. Ain't life funny, Jasper. All checks and balances, dark an' light. Still, you know what they say, you can't have the sun without the shadows, eh?'

Jasper sighed. 'You're not wrong there, love. Not wrong at all.'

They stepped out of the station and Cissy looked around her in dismay. 'Oh my, what have they done to my town?' she cried, staring across the road at The Priory Hotel. Every window was boarded up, part of the roof had collapsed, and the once-white walls were grey and dirty.

196

'Yeah, the old girl's not lookin' her best right now. It's worse the closer you get to the seafront. Hey, I remember when you used to play your violin right there.' Jasper nodded to a spot beside the station entrance.

Cissy grinned. 'Made a few bob as well. Till Nellie tattled on me and Auntie Gert put a stop to it. But now the place looks even worse than the centre of Birmingham.'

'You get used to it,' Jasper reassured her.

'You know, I had visions of comin' back to a lovely sunny seaside town, even though I knew the place has been bombed and shelled. Do you remember the fun we used to have on the beach? The little swimming huts where us girls used to swim. Oh, they were grand days, weren't they, Jasper? Do you remember the little man with the pompom on his hat who used to sell candy floss. And—' She stopped. 'Still, no point raking up the past. Why don't you tell me everythin' that's happened. I were very sorry to hear about Gladys. I never knew her, but you always spoke of her fondly in your letters.'

They were halfway down High Street by the time Jasper had finished recounting the events of the previous few months.

'I can't believe it!' Cissy exclaimed. 'What a terrible thing. So it's just Nellie and Marianne running the café, and Marianne due in a few weeks . . . Well, you did right comin' to me, Jasper. I know how proud Nellie can be, but I'll do what I can to help. Maybe I could play me violin for the customers, entice a few of 'em back.'

'I'm sure Nellie would love that,' Jasper lied, wondering again whether his plan was going to backfire spectacularly.

Cissy put her arm though Jasper's. 'Don't worry about a thing. I'm sure I can talk her round. And at least we'll all be in the same place. It'll be fine, Jasper, you'll see. Me and Nellie will be back to old times, and . . .' Cissy continued to chat, barely taking a breath as they walked down the high street, until the sudden screech of the air raid siren stopped her in her tracks.

'Should we take cover?' she shouted above the noise.

If he'd been on his own, he wouldn't have bothered, but he couldn't risk anything happening to Cissy now she was back where she belonged. So, grasping her arm, he hurried her towards Woolworths and the nearest shelter.

Chapter 38

Nellie stood at the counter, staring into the distance, absently toying with the crucifix, which she could no longer be bothered to hide.

'Oy, Nellie!' Lou Carter called. 'You gonna bring me me pie, or am I gonna have to eat Polly?'

'Get a move on hurry up,' Polly squawked from the cage beside her.

Nellie scowled at Lou. 'Help yerself.' She gestured at the cage. 'Bloomin' bird's costin' me a fortune.'

Polly stamped her feet and let out a squawk.

'You think I'm jokin'?' Nellie growled at the bird. 'Marianne, you got a recipe for parrot pie?' she called through the hatch.

'Reckon I could rustle one up,' Marianne replied, coming over to regard the bird thoughtfully. 'Probably tastes a bit like chicken.'

Polly turned her back and stared at the wall, while Nellie took the plate of parsnip pie over to Lou and dropped it on the table.

'Service in 'ere's shockin' these days,' Lou remarked. She eyed Nellie. 'An' you don't look so good yerself. What's up?'

'Nothin' I can't handle,' Nellie said, wishing with all her heart that was true.

Lou shovelled a forkful of pie into her mouth. 'By the way,' she said, spraying crumbs across the table. 'Terence said he'll be back to see you soon.'

Nellie feigned indifference. 'Man's been hangin' around so much recently, I'm beginnin' to think he might have a fancy for me.' She fluffed her hair.

Lou snorted. 'Even back in the day, I reckon he'd've given you a wide berth.'

'He'd not've had to try too hard,' Nellie snapped back, flouncing back to the counter. 'And tell him that if he don't give me back my rings, I'm gonna shop him to the police.'

Lou narrowed her eyes. 'I told you that ain't my Terence's way. He don't need your poxy jewels. An' even if he did take 'em, which he didn't, you wouldn't dare shop him. Unless you're ready to answer a few awkward questions about your own dealin's with him.' She knocked on the window mockingly. 'By the way, the pavement outside's lookin' a bit mucky. D'you think you should give it a scrub?' She cackled and stuffed a forkful of pie into her mouth.

Gritting her teeth, Nellie stalked back to the counter. Deep down, she didn't think Terence had stolen her rings. Donald's picture was still missing too, and as far as she was concerned, there was only one explanation. Although over the past few days, there'd been no more rose water smell and nothing else had gone missing, which made her hope that maybe Gladys had floated off to a higher plane – or whatever it was ghosts did.

Well, there was only one way to find out. Visiting Bert every day had meant she'd not found the time to see Bertha Bancroft yet, but now she took the leaflet out and examined it. 'Spiritual medium,' she murmured. 'Right, Mrs B., let's see if you can tell me what's going on.

'I'm going out,' she declared, walking into the kitchen.

'Where? And more importantly, how d'you expect me to manage on my own?' Marianne spluttered.

'You're not on your own. Lily's upstairs.' She went over to the stairs. 'Lily! Get down here.'

'But it's her first day off in over a week!'

'Tough.'

Lily appeared at the bottom of the stairs looking annoyed. 'Don't tell me you want me to help out.'

'All right, I won't. I'll only be a coupla hours. I got someone to see, then I'm going to pop up to see Bert.' She held out the pinny.

'Bert's fine. And I need to study. Can't Reenie help?'

'No, she can't. And you can read your books down here, can't you?'

Lily huffed. 'Fine.' She snatched the apron from her mother.

'Thanks, love.'

'One hour, Mum. Go see Bert tomorrow.'

'Two, max,' Nellie replied, yanking on her coat and hurrying out of the door before Lily could protest any further.

Outside, her eyes were drawn to the once-grand Market Hall on the other side of the square, its white façade was blackened and half the second floor was gone, but the chimney stack still stood, rising defiantly against the grey March sky, as though guarding the ruins. Nellie shuddered. The shell attack that had destroyed the building had also left a large hole in the square, although the only evidence of it now was a black tarmacked patch, standing out like a pool of blood against the lighter cobbles – it always reminded her of the stain that had been left on the pavement. She glanced to the spot where Gladys had fallen, and though she knew there was nothing there, she could still see it in her mind's eye. Resisting the urge to go back inside and get the scrubbing brush, she clutched at the crucifix.

'Prepare yourself, Glad. One way or another, you and me are going to talk,' she murmured, darting through the traffic to the other side of the road.

When she reached the corner of Queen Street, she furtively looked around to make sure no one she knew had spotted her, then, head down, she turned the corner and scurried up the road to the corner of Market Lane where Mercer's Garage stood. The large double doors that opened onto the forecourt were shut, although the Turners' van was parked up outside the building. Ducking into the alley beside it, she stopped outside a blue door with a heavy brass knocker. Checking over her shoulder again, she raised it and knocked until the door opened.

'Where's the bleedin' fire?' A plump woman with blonde hair curled around her lined face, peered out, eyes widening as she saw Nellie. 'Mrs Castle.' She smiled broadly and opened the door wider.

'Sorry to trouble you, Mrs Bancroft,' Nellie said sheepishly as she came in.

'No trouble, love. But you're the last person I expected to turn up on me doorstep. Oh . . .' she gasped, putting a well-manicured hand on Nellie's arm, the nails long and red. 'You ain't had bad news, 'ave you?' she whispered.

Nellie shook her head, and the other woman studied her face for a moment, then nodded shrewdly. 'It's Gladys, is it?'

Nellie blanched. 'How did you know?'

Mrs Bancroft nodded to a spot behind Nellie. 'Cos she's right there, love. So, if you want a consultation, that'll be five shillings.' She held her hand out, and Nellie reached into her bag, pulling out a few coins.

Satisfied, the woman led Nellie up a flight of stairs, her high heels clicking loudly on the bare wood and her ample bottom swaying beneath her tight green skirt.

Upstairs, she opened a door and ushered Nellie into a comfortable sitting room with two brown armchairs either side of a fireplace. Against the wall was a small table, covered in a lace cloth, two wooden chairs sitting on either side. The room was bright despite the dull day, the light flooding through the two large sash windows that looked out onto the street.

'Now, we can do this in comfort, or at the table. Your choice, love.'

Nellie sat down on the edge of an armchair, clutching her big black bag on her lap, her knuckles white.

Mrs Bancroft sat opposite, her eyes fixed on something over Nellie's shoulder. 'So,' she said. 'What do you want to know?'

Nellie looked behind her, but there was nothing there, and she felt goosebumps break out over her arms. Instinctively, her hand went up to her necklace. 'G-gladys,' she said. 'She's been hauntin' me.'

Mrs Bancroft looked surprised. 'Gladys has?' She looked over Nellie's shoulder again, then shook her head. 'I find that hard to believe. What's she been doin'?'

Nellie explained what had happened over the past few months. 'I just want her to stop. I know what she wants, but I . . . tell her I promise I'll do it when I'm ready. And tell her that she's driving me half mad and I need her to go away.'

Mrs Bancroft sat back in her chair and closed her eyes.

'Is she still—' Nellie began, but the other woman held up her hand.

Nellie gulped and looked around the room. It was plain, with whitewashed walls, dotted with a few small paintings of flowers. She'd never been here before, and she felt slightly disappointed that the place looked so ordinary. Her eyes returned to Mrs Bancroft, who sat still as a statue, arms resting on the sides of the chair. People called her Barmy Bancroft, but she didn't look barmy. In fact, although quite a few years older than Nellie, she looked younger, and was always perfectly made-up.

Finally, Mrs Bancroft seemed to come back to herself. 'What's your Donald got to do with all this?'

Nellie gasped. 'H-he ain't got nothing to do with this! All I want is for Gladys to leave me alone. Tell her, please.'

The woman sighed. 'Even if I did, it won't do no good. Spirits do as they please and they don't take orders from us. Anyway, she's gone now. But what you've described does sound like hauntin'. Somethin's been left undone. She needs you to help her finish whatever it is, so she can leave the earth. And until you do, she'll stay here with you.'

Nellie paled. 'But I can't,' she whispered. 'I can't do it!'

'Maybe I can help with whatever it is? Find a way to calm Gladys's spirit and get her to leave you alone.'

'Could you really do that?' Nellie asked eagerly.

Mrs Bancroft shrugged. 'I won't know if you don't tell me what it is that's got her celestial knickers in a twist. So come on, what gives? Maybe if it's Donald that's worryin' her, I can try to contact him?'

'No!' The thought that she might bring Donald back from the dead made the hair stand up on the back of her neck. Then she laughed shortly. 'Hark at me thinkin' you could speak to Gladys, let alone Donald. Until now, I never even believed in this non-sense. No offence, love.'

Mrs Bancroft regarded her calmly. 'If I took offence at every-one what thought my gift was nonsense, I'd 'ave gone stark starin' mad by now. In any case, he might not want to be contacted. His last years were hard ones, so I reckon he won't want to come back. Whereas Gladys weren't ready, and she'll have had things on her mind before she went. Things she wanted to do. And now she's reaching out to you to do them.'

Nellie shook her head. 'I can't help her. Tell her that. Tell her to leave me alone. There's nothin' I can do.'

Mrs Bancroft sighed. 'All right. Let me see if I can get her back.'

She closed her eyes again. Suddenly she stiffened and her neck stretched back against the chair. 'There's trouble comin',' the woman whispered. 'Not from where you think. Across the water and . . . close to home. Things you think are true, are false,' the woman continued. 'Vengeance . . .'

'Vengeance for what?' Nellie squeaked.

Mrs Bancroft waved her hand to shush her. She paused. 'I see a reunion . . .' Mrs Bancroft's brow furrowed. 'Two reunions. Dead are not always dead,' she murmured. 'The living are not always who they seem . . .' Suddenly, she opened her eyes and stared across at Nellie blankly, her blue irises almost obscured by her dilated pupils. Then she shook her head and seemed to come back to herself.

'That's all I got, love. But looks like you've got a few surprises in store.'

'But what about Gladys?' Nellie said, disappointed. It all sounded like gibberish, the sort of thing any fortune-teller might spout. She stood up and began to pace. 'She's driving me to the edge of me sanity. Only a wicked and vengeful ghost would do such a thing!'

'Look, all I know is what I've told you. And like I said, Gladys passed suddenly, so chances are she's sticking around.'

'Jasper don't believe me. He says it's probably someone out to cause mischief. If it weren't for the smell, I'd probably think the same. I can't stand it! Rose water on my clothes, in my room! And this—' she held the crucifix out '—this is Gladys's, but I swear we buried her with it!'

Mrs Bancroft examined the necklace and shrugged. 'She really is trying to get your attention, isn't she? And it's not unusual for a spirit to leave their scent. Whatever it is, my guess is she won't leave till you've carried out her wishes.'

The air raid siren screeched at that moment, and Nellie stamped her feet. 'Goddamn and blast the bloody siren! Go to hell!'

Then she dropped back into the armchair, put her head in her hands and started to sob.

Mrs Bancroft came across and crouched in front of her. 'Listen, love, it can't be that bad. Gladys were a good soul, she don't mean you harm. Spirits don't change much from the people they once were. But all the other things I said – that weren't about Gladys and what she wants. That's now. It's on its way. So be careful, all right? But it ain't all bad – like I said, I see a reunion.'

Nellie looked up at her, wondering who the hell she had left to reunite with. 'You said two reunions.'

Mrs Bancroft frowned. 'I don't know . . . It was vague. Maybe that message weren't for you. Sometimes the wires get crossed. Come on, we need to get to the shelter. Just a small cellar, but it does the job.'

As they walked back downstairs there was a hammering at the door and while Mrs Bancroft went to answer it, Nellie stumbled down the dark stone steps to the cellar. It was damp and mouldy with just a few rickety wooden chairs; a far cry from the comfortable shelter she'd created under the café, but she barely noticed.

If what Mrs Bancroft said was true, then the only way to stop Gladys driving her mad was to confess what had happened with Donald and risk making everyone hate her. The choice was impossible, because whatever she did, she lost.

Chapter 39

Reenie was standing outside the garage, waiting for the mechanic to come back when the siren went off. She could hear planes somewhere, and the sound brought the terrible memories of the other day rushing back. In a panic, she rushed round the side of the building and banged on the door, relieved when Mrs Bancroft opened it.

'Oh, it was for you!' the woman exclaimed when she saw her.

'What was for me?' Reenie asked, hoping she wasn't about to give her a message from beyond the grave. Aunt Ethel had always claimed it was hokum, and Reenie was inclined to agree.

'Ignore me, love. After the cellar, are ya? Follow me.'

Downstairs, Reenie was shocked to see Nellie sitting huddled in her purple coat, her face pale and eyes haunted. 'Mrs C, are you all right?' she gasped.

Nellie looked alarmed to see her. 'What are you doing here?'

'Same as you, I should think,' she said.

'Of course. Sorry, love. Got a few things on me mind.'

Mrs Bancroft joined them.

'What did you mean just then, Mrs Bancroft?' Reenie asked. 'When you said it was for me.'

'Sorry, love. I only give messages when people ask.'

'Or pay,' Nellie interjected darkly.

'A woman has to do what she has to do, Mrs Castle. As you well know.'

207

Suddenly you could have cut the atmosphere with a knife 'What are you talking about?' Nellie whispered, her face drained of colour.

'I think you know very well, love,' Mrs Bancroft replied, her expression enigmatic.

More bloody secrets, Reenie thought. She still couldn't get her last meeting with Jim out of her mind. The niggle of worry she'd felt the other day had grown out of all proportion and the more she thought about it, the surer she was that Jim was hiding something from her. The wedding was meant to be in two days, and though it pained her to admit it, even if she could speak to Jim tomorrow, she wasn't sure she'd get the truth from him.

'I'd like you to tell me,' she said on impulse. 'About the message. I'll bring you the money later.'

Mrs Bancroft sighed. 'Are you sure, love? People don't always hear what they want to hear.'

'Yes,' she said decisively. 'I want to hear.' If there was a chance she might get some answers about *something*, then she was going to take it, no matter how ridiculous it seemed.

'All right.' Mrs Bancroft sat back and closed her eyes. 'There'll be a reunion. That was the message that came through because you were close,' she murmured. 'It will bring joy and despair . . . Sometimes love deceives, sometimes love returns . . .'

There was a long silence and Reenie was about to say something when Mrs Bancroft stiffened. 'She's laughing at you.'

'Who is?'

'June . . .'

Reenie shivered. Her sister was here?

'Serves you right . . . Gullible little fool . . .'

'Stop! Stop it!' Reenie leapt to her feet and whirled round, searching for a glimpse of June's mocking face.

Mrs Bancroft stood and gently took her arm, leading her back to the chair. 'I'm sorry, love, but I did warn you. Although, she just popped up out of nowhere, the little madam. She always was a bit of a cow.'

Reenie slumped down and rubbed her eyes, as that mixture of hurt, humiliation and bewilderment, which only June had ever managed to engender, washed over her. She'd hoped never to feel it again. 'She wasn't really here, was she?' she asked quietly.

Mrs Bancroft nodded. 'Afraid so, love. In all her glory. She had a black heart, but she were a beauty for all that. You and she have the look of each other.'

'Hardly,' Reenie muttered.

'Why would she laugh at you?' Nellie was leaning forward avidly.

'I-I don't know,' Reenie said. But in her heart of hearts, she couldn't help feeling she was referring to Jimmy.

Nellie put a comforting hand on her arm. 'If you're thinkin' it has anything to do with my Jim, then think again. The boy's head over heels. First time I've ever seen him like this.'

Reenie looked at her uncertainly.

'I'm serious, love,' Nellie retorted. 'Take it from me, Jim loves the bones of you.'

Reenie was surprised at Nellie's gentleness. She'd not seen this side of her before. 'Thank you,' she said, sniffing. 'I love the bones of him too.'

'There you are then,' Mrs Bancroft interjected cheerily. 'All will be well.' She smiled brightly. 'For both of you. An' who doesn't like a good reunion?'

'Depends who it's with,' Nellie remarked. 'I bet Reenie wouldn't be too pleased to see her sister again. As for me . . . Well, I reckon I'd rather not see my mum again.' She had a sudden thought. 'Were she here when you was talkin' earlier? If she was, sure as eggs is eggs she were just tryin' to cause mischief.'

Mrs Bancroft laughed. 'Your mum were a right pain in the back-side, but . . . Well, she grieved hard when she lost her little boy.'

Nellie nodded. 'Don't I know it. She'd have been happier if it were me that passed. Hardly a day went by when she didn't start a sentence, "If your brother were here . . ." Hang on, did she come to you? When she was alive, I mean.'

Mrs Bancroft snorted. 'Have you forgotten the way your mum used to tell anyone who'd listen that I was a fraud. Blasted woman used to hound me whenever she saw me. Made my life a misery. Even if she had come, I wouldn't have spoken to her.'

'I didn't know you had a brother, Mrs C.'

'He were a coupla years older than me. Albert – I named Bert for him. Died of diphtheria when he was nine. Then not long after, Cissy was dumped on the doorstep—'

Reenie held her breath, willing Nellie to carry on. She'd discovered more about her future mother-in-law in these last few minutes than she'd learnt in a lifetime.

'Who's Cissy?' she asked finally.

When Nellie didn't reply, she glanced over at Mrs Bancroft, who shrugged. 'Not my story, love. Now, I don't feel you got your money's worth, do you want me to try again, either of you?'

'No!' they exclaimed in unison.

'Fair enough. How about a game of rummy then?' From a basket on the floor she produced a pack of cards, and dragging another chair to sit between them, she began to deal.

Reenie tried to concentrate on the game, but the words Mrs Bancroft had uttered repeated in her mind: *Sometimes love deceives . . .* Was that why her sister was laughing at her?

When the all-clear sounded, Reenie muttered a hasty goodbye and ran up the stairs, eager to get away from Mrs Bancroft's unsettling presence. Without pausing to see if Mr Mercer had returned, she went straight down towards the seafront, relishing the freshness of the wind as it tried to blow the scarf off her head.

Without even being conscious of where she was going, at the bottom of New Bridge, she crossed over the road and turned right, making her way towards Crosswall Quay. She couldn't explain why, but she felt the need to see Wilf. Maybe it was because she couldn't get Mrs Bancroft's words out of her mind – *sometimes love deceives*. They chimed disconcertingly with what Wilf had said. *If you have doubts, listen to them.*

Her steps slowed as she approached the quay. She didn't even know if he'd be there, as he seemed to mostly work nights. She stopped suddenly, clutching herself around the waist, as the sea breeze cut through her old woollen jumper.

She was such a fool. What could Wilf say? He already thought she was making a mistake, and the last thing she wanted was an 'I told you so' from him.

The lifeboat was tied up at the jetty, rising and falling on the choppy water and she could see Wilf on the deck, doing some maintenance, his dark hair whipping around his head. Sensing someone's eyes on him, he looked towards her. For a long moment, they stared at each other, both unmoving. *Sometimes love returns*. The words drifted into her mind, and she squeezed her eyes shut. When she opened them again, he'd raised his hand in greeting and instinctively she raised hers in reply, then she turned and went back the way she had come.

What did she think she was she doing? She was marrying Jim in two days, and whatever Wilf's reasons for seeking her out recently, they had nothing to do with love. She might have been a gullible fool once, but she wasn't anymore.

Chapter 40

When the all-clear sounded, Jasper helped Cissy to her feet. 'What's the rush?' Cissy asked. 'Me and Mr Hendricks were just gettin' reacquainted. Where d'you live now, love? Still down near Eastcliff?' she asked the old man. 'Perhaps we could take you back?'

The man grinned at her. 'I'm not so decrepit, I can't make me own way back. It's good to see ya again, Cissy.'

'Will we see you in the café soon?'

Mr Hendricks hesitated.

'Go on. Jasper's told me all about it, and it's nonsense, isn't it, Jasper? You've known Nellie all her life. What's got into you?'

'As my old mum used to say, there's no smoke without fire.'

'Stuff and nonsense! Come tomorrow.'

'Can't tomorrer.'

'Any time then. I'll bring you an extra cuppa and we'll have a proper chinwag. How about it?'

He smiled. 'Well, if you put it like that, maybe I will.'

'All welcome,' she trilled as Jasper hustled her to the door.

Jasper smiled to himself. Cissy was exactly what the café needed. Give her a couple of weeks, and she'd probably manage to talk the entire town into going back there.

Once they were outside, Cissy tripped along beside Jasper, swinging her violin case. 'Funny, in't it? No one would choose to have shells and bombs fallin' on their town, but at least it gives you a chance to have a natter with old friends and meet new ones.

212

Mr Hendricks were still a young man when I saw him last.' She giggled. 'Then again, I was still a young girl. But ain't that the way – no matter how much we change on the outside, inside, we feel the same.' She sighed. 'Not exactly the same, of course. Regret and grief, Jasper. That's what's changed inside me. I regret losing Nellie from my life. I threw her over for a man. A good man, mind, but Nellie's family, and . . . Oh, I were just an impulsive girl anxious to get away from Auntie Gertie. No excuse, though. I don't expect much quarter from Nell, nor do I deserve it. But I'll win her round, just you wait and see.'

As they continued along High Street, Cissy paused frequently to exclaim at the ruined buildings and then she'd regale him with her memories of each one, until they finally reached the market square.

'It's just awful what's happened here,' she said, her eyes taking in the boarded-up windows around the square, the ruined Market Hall and the burned-out hat shop where she used to stare for hours at the beautiful creations in the window. Digging in her sleeve, she pulled out a crumpled handkerchief and wiped her eyes.

Jasper patted her shoulder, feeling guilty, suddenly, for bringing her into the eye of the storm. 'You don't 'ave to stay, love,' he said. 'We're all so used to the noise and the danger that I didn't consider how scary it might be from the outside. But our lives go on. Look there.' He pointed across the street to where a window box outside a boarded-up window was sprouting colourful flowers. 'An' Freddie Overton – remember him? – he's still organisin' dances and concerts at the town hall. An', you know, it ain't as bad as it looks, really. I mean . . . it is, but somehow it isn't. Still, if you'd rather go back, then I understand. Dover ain't for everyone at the moment, an' there's no shame in admittin' you're scared.'

Cissy frowned up at him. 'Did I say I was scared?' she asked. 'I'll have you know, I lived through the Birmingham Blitz! It's just a bit of a shock, is all. But for all that, I'm glad to be home. And

Freddie Overton's still up to his tricks, is he?' She laughed. 'Me an' him had a bit of a thing when we was youngsters.' She grinned. 'He might 'ave asked to marry me.'

Jasper laughed. 'You're 'avin' me on.'

Cissy stuck her nose in the air. 'Think I'm not good enough, do ya? But then, you only ever had eyes for Nellie, didn't you? You wouldn't have noticed me if I'd tap-danced naked down the street.'

Jasper blushed. 'That's not true! I married Clara, didn't I?'

Cissy sobered. 'You did. And she was a diamond, but it was always Nellie for you, and there's no shame in admitting it now. Clara's been gone the best part of twenty years, and poor Donald at least thirteen. What's stopping you and her bein' together?'

Jasper cleared his throat uncomfortably. 'Nothin's that simple, is it? There's things you don't know . . .'

'Ooh, like what?' Cissy's eyes sparkled at the promise of gossip.

Jasper hesitated, tempted to confide in her, but then he thought better of it. He'd never talked to a soul about the complicated feelings churning inside him, and he wasn't about to start now. Especially to Nellie's cousin. He'd have to stay on guard around her, though. He'd forgotten how easily she invited people's confidences. It was only after you walked away from a conversation with Cissy that you realised how much of yourself you'd revealed. Her seemingly non-stop chatter masked the fact that when she wasn't talking, she really *listened*.

Jasper shook his head. 'None of your business.'

Cissy smiled impishly and took his arm. 'You know I'll winkle it out of you eventually.'

As they approached the café, Cissy's feet started to drag. 'I'm as nervous as the day I snuck away from Auntie Gert's . . . Perhaps I could go to yours first. Prepare meself for the fireworks to come . . .' She looked up at him, her small dark eyes pleading. 'Just for an hour or so.'

If he was honest, Jasper's stomach was a mass of butterflies as well, and he wanted to get this over with as soon as possible. 'Tell you what, I'll see if I can sneak you in the back way without Nellie noticin'. Then at least you can have your reunion in private.'

Cissy sighed. 'You're right; it's best to get it over with. But let's not walk past the front door, in case she's looking out the window.'

Jasper shook his head. 'Even if she were, she probably couldn't tell it were you. Lookin' through that big sheet of plastic is like lookin' out to sea on a foggy day. Still, you're right. If she sees you, she'll be straight out the door and screamin' her head off at me.'

Cissy grimaced. 'That don't exactly reassure me, love.'

He grinned. 'Ah, don't worry. I can handle Nellie.' He tried to sound confident, but he was feeling anything but. Nellie's bitterness at Cissy's abandonment hadn't waned over the years, though he'd tried to talk to her about it more than once. And to think how Nellie moaned about Edie's stubbornness . . . No doubt about it, that girl was a chip off the old block. Maybe he could use that as a way of persuading her to forgive her cousin. Especially as he knew, deep down, that Nellie missed and loved her still.

Chapter 41

Nellie's thoughts were buzzing with everything Mrs Bancroft had said. If the woman was to be believed, then she'd been right – Gladys was haunting her.

But that was the problem: *if* she was to be believed.

'Look what you've driven me to, Gladys,' she muttered. 'Is Mum up there with you, laughing her head off?'

Her mum would have disowned her at the merest hint of her going to see a spiritualist, and the thought gave her pause. Because no matter her faults – and there had been many –her mum was no fool. She'd believed that about herself once, but after all that had happened, she'd lost her certainty and confidence. If she hadn't, she'd never have darkened Mrs Bancroft's door.

And now Reenie knew she'd been there, and chances were she'd tell Jim . . . And Jim would tell Bert, and Bert would tell Lily . . . She groaned at the thought of her kids knowing how foolish she'd been.

As she approached the café, her spirits plummeted even further. This place had once been her pride and joy but now it felt like a millstone round her neck. Just the sight of that stupid piece of celluloid made her shoulders tense with anxiety.

Bracing herself, Nellie pushed open the door and immediately her heart lifted at the sight of Jasper sitting at his usual table near the kitchen door.

As soon as he saw her he jumped up. 'There you are! I've been waitin' for you.'

'Looks like all your prayers have been answered, then. Because here I am.' With an effort she managed to smile. 'Everyone all right today?' she asked, looking around at the half a dozen people. 'Lily been looking after you all right?'

'You should have her here more often,' Mr Gallagher said. 'Brightens the place up no end. And always got a smile on her face.'

'I'd smile a lot more if I didn't have to see your ugly mug sittin' with one cup of tea for hours on end,' Nellie snapped.

'See what I mean!' the old man exclaimed.

'Ignore her,' someone else said. 'She's just jealous cos Lily's so much prettier.'

'I am here, you know,' Lily called over. 'And, Mum, you're late.'

'Not my fault there was a raid, is it?'

'Well, I need to get back to my studying.' She took off her pinny and was about to leave when Jasper cleared his throat.

'Uh, Lily, if you don't mind . . .'

Lily groaned. 'You're not going to ask me to stay down here longer, are you?'

'Please, love? I need your mum upstairs, just for a few minutes.'

Nellie regarded him with surprise. 'Why?'

Jasper took Nellie's hand. 'I just got somethin' I need to talk to you about. It's urgent.' He turned to Lily. 'Ten minutes.'

Before Lily could protest further, he pulled Nellie towards the stairs.

At the top, Jasper turned to her and held her by the shoulders. 'Don't be cross, all right. I've done this for your own good.'

'What have you done?' Nellie pulled away from him and marched into the sitting room, then stopped dead.

'What . . .?' She squeezed her eyes shut, then opened them again. She was still there. The woman who had abandoned her – literally climbed out the window in the dead of night and was never seen again. It had been the first betrayal of her life. Cissy had been more than a cousin; she'd been her dearest friend and

217

ally. The one she'd always confided in . . . How dare she come back here as if nothing had ever happened?

'What is *she* doing here?' she exclaimed.

'She's come to help you. You need her.'

Nellie stared between them in outrage. 'I need her like a bloody hole in the head!' She clapped her hand over her mouth as her eyes instinctively went to the spot on the wallpaper that hid the monstrous stain left by Donald's death so many years before. Then another thought struck. *I see a reunion.* If Mrs Bancroft was right about this, then what else had she been right about? The thought made her dizzy, and suddenly her vision narrowed and then went completely dark as she slumped to the floor.

∽

'Lily, come quick!'

The sound of her father's cry made Lily jump and she rushed for the stairs.

The first thing she saw as she ran into the sitting room was her mother, out cold on the floor, with Jasper and a total stranger kneeling beside her.

Deciding that questions could wait, she knelt beside her mother. 'Mum? Mum, wake up.' But her mother remained unconscious. 'What happened?' she asked urgently.

'Oh, I'm so sorry! It were the shock of seein' me. I shoulda known. Jasper, we shoulda been more careful. Oh, my giddy aunt! I never expected this! Poor Nell. Nellie!'

Lily watched in astonishment as the small rotund woman with bright orange hair showered her mother's face with kisses. She looked over at Jasper, eyebrows raised in question.

'Later,' Jasper said gruffly. 'Cissy, you're not helpin'. Let's get her into her room.'

Lily ran to open the door, and with an effort, he managed to lift Nellie and stagger into the bedroom, where he lay her gently on the bed.

Lily sat down beside her and took her pulse. 'Well, she's alive, and if her heart rate is anything to go by, I'd say she fainted from shock.' She turned an accusing stare on the woman. 'And I imagine you're the cause,' she said sternly.

Cissy came over to the bed. 'I never meant to. Nellie were never a fainter. I didn't think . . .' She put her hand to her mouth. 'Maybe I should go.'

'No!' Jasper said. 'Stay. And if you're sure she's all right, you and I should leave these two to it, Lily.'

On the bed, Nellie's eyes fluttered open and she looked around at the three faces hovering over her. Her gaze settled on Cissy, and she closed her eyes again. 'So it's true. It's all true. God help me!' she wailed.

'I think you should leave,' Lily said firmly to Cissy and Jasper. 'Wait in the sitting room, and when I come out, I want an explanation. From both of you!'

'No,' Nellie said weakly. 'She's here so I may as well speak to her. Lily, bring us a cup of tea. And one for Cissy. Then leave. As for you, Jasper, you've got some explainin' to do, but first I want to hear what Ciss has to say for herself.'

'If you're sure, Mum?'

At Nellie's nod, Lily reluctantly left the room with Jasper.

Once outside, though, she rounded on him. 'What the hell is this all about?'

'I'm tryin' to help your mum,' Jasper said. 'And that woman is your Aunt Cissy.'

Lily's eyes rounded. 'But Mum doesn't have a sister.'

'No, but she has a cousin. She left long ago, before you were born, and your mum's not forgiven her. Go do what she asked. I'll wait here, just in case there's bloodshed.'

'And what, she's coming to live here?'

'I wrote asking if she was able to help out. She'll make life easier for everyone. You'll like her, Lily. Everyone does. We just need to convince your mum it's the right thing to do.'

219

'Clearly it's not, given her reaction.'

Jasper sat on one of the chairs by the fireplace and rubbed his face wearily. 'Trust me, love. This'll do wonders for your mum. If you hadn't noticed, she's not herself.'

Lily sat down opposite him. 'I know. We're all worried. I've been thinking of asking one of the doctors at the hospital about her. All this weird scrubbing of the pavement and paranoid stuff about things going missing from her room and the photo.' She gestured at the mantelpiece and sighed. 'I really think she might be ill. In her mind, I mean.'

'She's not ill, love. It's just the pressure's gettin' to her. Go get the tea. I'll stay here.'

Chapter 42

'Well, of all the reactions I didn't expect this!' Cissy laughed nervously.

'What did you expect? Hell's bells, it's like you've risen from the dead!' Nellie shrieked. 'You gave me the shock of me life, and not in a good way!'

Cissy grinned uncertainly. 'Now that's more like the Nellie I know and love.'

'You don't know me. And you certainly don't love me. It's been over thirty years!'

'I wrote,' she said, perching on the side of the bed.

'What use are bloody letters!' Nellie snarled. 'You do a midnight flit, leaving me alone to nurse Mum, and you think I'll just welcome you back with open arms? I wrote you a letter too,' she said. 'Begging you to come home. Or at least visit. And then Mum died and you didn't even come to the bloody funeral. At least I thought you'd come for that.'

'I know,' she whispered. 'And I'm sorry. I should've come, but I couldn't. When you sent that letter, I was expectin' and were too ill to come. Then, my little Gracie came – I wrote to tell you later, but you never replied.'

Nellie snorted. 'It were too late by then. Mum had died, and I married Donald, so I figured as you'd moved on with your life, then so would I!'

'You never read them?'

'Not one,' Nellie said stonily. 'They went into the fire where they belonged.'

A tear escaped Cissy's eye and ran down her cheek, leaving a dark trail in the powder.

'You should leave,' Nellie continued. 'I've managed perfectly well without you all this time, I reckon I can manage now.'

'Not accordin' to Jasper, you can't!' Cissy swiped at the tear. 'An' just so's you know, my Gracie were born with a heart condition. She needed constant care. And she died just a few days after her first birthday. So excuse me for not rushin' to help you! And even though you didn't reply to the letter I sent about her death, I still kept tryin'. Thirty years, Nell! Thirty years, I've written to you with not a single reply. It's a wonder I bothered comin' after Jasper sent that telegram to say you needed me. And do you know what I did when I received it? I dropped everythin'! Packed a bag and came straight here, cos I thought it were you that'd asked! If I'd known you didn't want me here, I never would have come. So, I'll stay with Jasper and catch the train back to Birmingham in the mornin'.' She stood up and marched towards the door.

The pain in Cissy's voice cut through Nellie's self-pity, and she felt a sharp stab of conscience. 'I didn't know about Gracie, love. I'm so sorry,' she said quietly.

Cissy pulled her handkerchief out of her sleeve and blew her nose. 'Now you do. And I hope it gives you some answers. But I won't stay where I'm not wanted.' She put her hand on the doorknob.

'Wait! Don't go, Ciss.' Nellie swung her legs off the bed and came over to her, putting her hands on her shoulders – Cissy was one of the few women who was shorter than her; it had been a source of great pride to her when they were growing up.

She studied Cissy's face. The small dark eyes with fair lashes, laughter lines fanning out from the sides – she always had been a great one for laughing. Her lips were painted bright red, and her orange hair was curled tightly round her head.

Nellie swallowed back the lump that had formed in her throat. God it was good to see her face again. It was almost as if Cissy's presence was an answer to her prayers.

She pulled her into her arms. 'I missed you,' she mumbled brokenly.

With a cry of relief, Cissy returned the hug. 'Oh, Nellie. I am sorry for leaving like that. Abandoning you just when life was getting so tough.'

'I'm sorry about your girl,' Nellie responded, ashamed of her selfishness. Why hadn't she tried to find out what had happened? She'd known Cissy better than anyone; she should have realised that she wouldn't have stayed away without a good reason. Her bloody stubborn nature again. She was more like her mum than she liked to admit.

'It was a long time ago now. And though my heart broke and I never had any more kids, my Ernie were the best husband a woman could ask for. Jasper told me everythin' that was goin' on here. I know how tough it's been. You won't know the number of times I nearly came. But Ernie thought I'd only be invitin' heartbreak, and so I stayed where I was. And we were so busy with the orchestra.' She sniffed. 'I wish I'd come now.'

Nellie led her back to the bed and they sat in silence, clinging on to each other's hands, heads resting against each other.

'You can stay if you want,' Nellie said eventually. 'Jasper's right. I really do need help.'

Cissy squeezed her hands. 'You won't regret this, Nell. I swear you won't. And you know, with Ernie gone now these two years, I've been strugglin' meself. We can help each other. It'll be so good to catch up on old times, don't you think? You and me against the world, just like it always was. Now tell me . . . What's happened to the others. Ethel, Phyllis, Mavis . . . ? We'll be a gang again—'

223

'Cissy, stop!' Nellie interrupted her. 'Look, you can stay. I'm happy to have you. But please, the talking . . . You ain't changed, have you? You can still give me a headache after five minutes.'

Cissy laughed ruefully. 'My Ernie used to say I talked enough for the two of us. And since he's been gone, I've missed havin' someone to chat to.'

'Try to keep a lid on it, love. For my sake, if nothing else.'

Lily came in then with two cups of tea. 'You two all right?' she asked, eyes darting between them. 'Perhaps you're ready to introduce us now, Mum?'

'Oh! You must be the youngest. Blonde hair, Jasper said. And you have such beautiful golden hair. You don't know how happy I am to meet you, love! You don't look a bit like Donald, though . . . Or your mum, come to that. No blondes in our family were there, Nellie? Mum was—'

'Cissy!' Nellie started to laugh, and she realised it was the first time since Gladys had died that she'd even felt the desire to smile. She put her hand on her cousin's cheek. 'Just keep your gob shut once in a while, and we'll be golden, all right?'

The two women grinned at each other, and Nellie's heart lifted further. With Cissy there, she felt a new resolve pouring through her. One way or another, she would find a way to pay off Terence, and as for Gladys – she looked surreptitiously around the room to see if everything was as it should be – she would ignore her; just as she had when they'd had disagreements in the past. She wasn't going to risk losing her family to satisfy a ghost. It was time she came back to her senses! The café needed her, her children needed her, and there was a bloody war on! There was no time for wallowing.

Jasper popped his head around the door and looked over at her, his expression watchful, but seeing Nellie's laughter, his face relaxed into a grin. 'Am I allowed to say I told you so, Nell?' he asked.

'Don't push your luck, Jasper,' Nellie retorted.

Chapter 43

The day after she'd seen Mrs Bancroft, Reenie stood behind the counter at the shop, butterflies churning in her stomach at the thought of the next day – her wedding day. Jimmy was due back today, and though it was unlucky to see the groom the night before the wedding, she knew that Jim would be meeting Terence in the Oak tonight, so she'd decided to go too. She needed reassurance that she wasn't making a terrible mistake. But it wasn't just her uncertainty about Jimmy that was worrying her, she was also struggling with the resurrection of the ghost of her sister.

Over the years she'd tried to banish the memories of her sister's cruelty, and mostly she'd succeeded. Recently, though, June had been hovering around again, mostly because Wilf's sudden attentiveness had dredged up all the old feelings of hurt and betrayal. Then yesterday, in Mrs Bancroft's damp little cellar, it had felt as if her sister was standing in front of her, mocking her as she had throughout their childhood, and it had brought all her insecurities to the fore.

As soon as the shop shut, Reenie went up to her room and prepared carefully for her visit to the pub. Her wardrobe mostly consisted of old trousers for gardening and plain skirts and blouses. Briefly she wondered what she would wear for her wedding, but what did it matter? The important thing was that she and Jim would be married, and then hopefully all her doubts would finally be laid to rest.

Pulling out a clean white blouse and flowered cotton skirt, she dressed quickly, then fluffed out her blonde curls, before clipping her hair back at the sides. She regarded herself in the mirror. 'Could be worse,' she said. But as she turned to leave, June's mocking laughter echoed in her mind.

'You're bloody dead, June, so just hop back to hell,' she whispered, wishing fervently that she'd never knocked on Mrs Bancroft's door.

Telling her aunt and uncle that she was meeting Jim at the pub, she hurried out into the dark, and marched purposefully down King Street. But as she reached the corner of Cambridge Road, where the Oak stood, her courage started to fail and she considered going back home. She felt a twinge of guilt that she hadn't told them about the wedding. If she had, tonight would be a celebration with them, but instead she was creeping around behind their backs.

Oh God, what should she do? She chewed on a nail as she paced back and forth. Was she prepared for what she might find out? Or should she trust that Jimmy would tell her if there was a problem?

Gullible little fool . . .

The words rang in her mind again and it stiffened her spine. No. This was a decision that would affect the rest of her life, and she didn't want to end up living with regret.

With renewed purpose she walked quickly up the steps and pushed open the door, not allowing herself to stop until she stood in front of the bar where Mavis was pulling pints for a group of sailors.

'Reenie! Here to meet Jim, are you?' Mavis asked brightly when she spotted her. 'He's downstairs at the minute. Came in alone, so I figured you might be on your way.'

Reenie made her way down the carpeted stairs. Like most buildings in the town, the interior was showing signs of damage. One of the walls was cracked and all the windows were now boarded up. But considering how many of the buildings in the road had been destroyed it was a miracle the place was still standing at all.

The bar downstairs was crowded, and as she looked around for Jimmy, Reenie thought wistfully of all the good times they'd had here. In particular the dance just before the men had sailed for France. She'd danced with Colin that night, and Daisy had been helping her mother-in-law at the bar near the garden doors. She and Jimmy had been mere acquaintances then, and she had thought that her little group of friends would stay close all their lives. Instead, Daisy was dead and her friendship with Marianne had cooled. She felt a pang of longing for those long-lost days when Dover was still an elegant seaside town and, aside from the death of her parents, the worst thing that had ever happened to her was Wilf marrying June . . .

She shook her head angrily; she was here to determine her future, and hankering after the past never did anyone any good.

She finally spotted Jimmy sitting at a table in the corner, talking to a man who had his back to her, but she recognised the black coat and brown trilby. Reenie's stomach flip-flopped as she watched them. It was obvious Terence was doing all the talking, while Jim sat with a stony expression, his hands fiddling with his pint glass.

Edging through the throng, she managed to position herself to the side of the table, so she could observe more closely. Terence was smiling at Jim in the same sinister way he had at her, and it made Reenie shudder.

Jimmy shook his head, but Terence kept on talking, then suddenly, he grabbed Jim's lapel, leaning even closer as Jimmy tried to pull free. That was it. She might have had her doubts before, but whatever they were, she would not let Jimmy be threatened by that little weasel.

'Terence!' she snapped.

With a start, the man let go and looked up at her. 'Comin' to his rescue, are you?' He threw a scornful look at Jimmy. 'Sounds about right . . .'

227

What she wouldn't give to have Marge with her right now, she'd know what to say, Reenie thought as she cast around for a suitable response.

But she needn't have worried because Jimmy bolted to his feet, extending one arm towards her, a broad smile on his face. 'Here she is!' He raised his voice. 'Listen up, everyone!'

Gradually, the people around them quietened and turned to stare.

'This beautiful girl has agreed to be my wife!' Jim put his arm around her shoulder and planted a kiss on her cheek. 'Not only that, we'll be tying the knot tomorrow.' He shot a hard glance at Terence.

Then, before Reenie had a chance to protest, Jim pulled her towards him and kissed her passionately, his tongue darting into her astonished mouth, his arms tight around her.

Embarrassed by the cheers and catcalls, Reenie tried to squirm away. Sensing her reluctance, Jim paused briefly and murmured, 'Please don't leave me. I love you so much.' His declaration was so heartfelt and so utterly unexpected, that Reenie whispered the words back, and as his lips descended again, her heart sang. She should have trusted in him, instead of getting in a fluster because of a nasty lowlife and a woman who claimed she could talk to the dead. She put her arms around Jimmy's neck and pulled him closer, laughing with relief against his lips. He loved her and that's all she needed to know.

When he finally released her, people clapped Jimmy on the back, while one girl, who Reenie recognised as a woman she'd seen Bert with, kissed her cheek. 'Looks like you got the best brother,' she said. 'Jim's a great bloke, and nothing like sodding Bert.'

Reenie laughed. 'That's for sure.'

'Although, last time I saw Bert, that same guy was loitering around.' She nodded towards Terence. 'I'm not sure what happened, but I spied on them a bit, and it ended with Bert being kneed in the balls. I just wish I'd done it myself.' She grinned. 'Still, I doubt Jim'd ever get himself in a situation like that.'

As the girl disappeared into the crowd, Reenie felt her heart lighten even more. So maybe all Terence's threats really were just about Bert. She grabbed Jim's arm and hugged it to her. She'd been a fool to let her doubts overcome her over the last few days; they'd been nothing more than wedding jitters, fuelled by Wilf and Terence – and Mrs Bancroft! The old fraud.

Jimmy leant down and whispered, 'There's no backing out now. We better go tell our folks, don't you think?'

She laughed up at him. 'Who said I wanted to back out?'

'Did you?' he asked, suddenly serious.

She hesitated a moment, then shook her head. 'You're stuck with me for life.'

With a smile of satisfaction, Jim took her hand, but before leading her to the door, he walked over to Terence. 'Like I said, your word against mine. Who's gonna believe you now?'

Terence's eyes glittered oddly as he replied, 'You better hope you never find out. Meantime, tell your mum I'm gonna pop round to see her tomorrow.'

Jim snorted. 'You've got a nerve. Can't get to me, so you'll go after my mum. Well, listen to me, we don't dance to your tune, so as far as I'm concerned you can whistle.'

Terence grinned evilly. 'Fair enough. But don't say I didn't warn ya.' His gaze raked over Reenie scornfully. 'Good luck, Reenie. You're gonna need it.'

'What the hell was that all about?' she asked as Jim dragged her back upstairs.

'Like I thought, he's threatening to turn Bert in if I don't keep supplying him with stuff. He must think I'm stupid!'

'But what did he mean about your mum. I told you I heard her arguing with Lou about him the other day. Don't you think you should warn her?'

Bert shrugged. 'I don't think so. She's not herself these days and I don't want to add to her worries.'

'I think you should tell her, though.'

He kissed her again. 'All right, worry wart. But for now let's forget about Terence and go spread the good news.'

Chapter 44

For the first time in months, the atmosphere at supper was cheerful. Cissy's presence had lightened the the mood considerably and throughout the day, several old-timers had come into the café to see her. Her arrival really couldn't have come at a better time, Marianne reflected, looking across the dining table at the tiny vibrant woman who hadn't stopped talking since she'd been introduced to her the day before. Sitting next to her, Jasper was roaring with laughter at some memory of the mischief they'd all got up to when they were younger, and even her mum had managed to laugh now and then.

As for Donny, he had taken Cissy to his heart already, and listened rapt as the woman regaled them with stories of her and his gran's adventures when they were girls. Lily caught her eye and grinned, holding her hands over her ears as Cissy's high-pitched giggle filled the room.

'I just want you all to know,' Cissy declared, setting down her knife and fork, 'that this has been the best night I've had in an age. Since my Ernie died, in fact. And bein' back in the family, and with you, Nell . . .' She dug in her sleeve for her hankie and dabbed at her eyes. 'It's the best thing that's happened. And we owe it all to this man.' She picked up her water glass and toasted Jasper. 'You always was the stalwart of the group. Kind and loyal to a fault, and I will never be able to repay you for bringin' me back. What do you think, Nell? Ain't it the best thing?'

'At least now you're here, the rest of us don't need to talk,' Nellie remarked dryly.

Cissy laughed. 'You never could show it, could you? But we all know that under that bright orange shirt beats a heart what—' She looked puzzled for a moment as she peered closer. 'Don't tell me you've gone churchy, Nell?' She pointed at the crucifix glinting on Nellie's chest.

Nellie put a hand over it self-consciously.

'Gran thinks it's Gladys's,' Donny piped up. 'But Mum says it can't be cos Gladys was buried in it. Gran thinks Gladys's ghost brung it back, but that can't be right cos there's no such thing as ghosts, that's what Jasper says.' He looked around at the stunned expressions, then looked down sheepishly. 'I'm only sayin' what I heard.'

Marianne groaned inwardly. Donny was becoming an adept eavesdropper, and she dreaded to think what else he'd heard.

'Donny!' Lily exclaimed. 'You shouldn't eavesdrop.'

'But it's true. She's always holding it and muttering Gladys's name. And I heard her talkin' to Polly about her,' Donny said.

Nellie glared at her grandson. 'Go to your room!' she said in a dangerously low voice.

'And you think Gladys took Grandpa Donald's photo.'

'I said, go to your room!' Nellie roared.

'That's enough, Nell,' Jasper intervened. 'As for the photo, it'll turn up. And Donny's right, there's no such thing as ghosts. There's got to be another explanation for what's been happening. Perhaps *someone*—' he looked meaningfully at Donny '—has been causing mischief.'

'It weren't me!' Donny protested.

'Oh my giddy aunt!' Cissy exclaimed, her eyes bright with excitement. 'If things are bein' moved, that's not a ghost. That's a *poltergeist*!' She whispered the last word.

'What's that?' Donny asked.

232

Cissy shot a quick glance at Nellie, who was still glaring at Donny. 'Don't you remember when strange things were happenin' in our old house, Nell? Auntie Gert insisted it were Albert come back from the dead, didn't she? Turns out, though—'

'Shut up, Cissy!' Nellie's cheeks were bright red.

'Turns out what?' Donny said, his expression avid. 'Was it really a polterthing?'

'Cissy . . .' Nellie's tone held a warning, but her cousin ignored it.

'Turns out it were your gran, Don. Your great-gran wasn't such a nice woman, and she'd been goin' on and on about how much better life would be if Albert – that's your gran's brother who died when he were little – were there . . .'

Nellie put her head in hands.

'. . . so Nellie decided to teach her a lesson. Near drove her mad it did, didn't it, Nell?'

'Is this true?' Jasper asked, aghast.

'I was nine years old! A child.'

'But you wouldn't do that now, would you, Gran?' Donny asked.

'Of course I bloody wouldn't!' Nellie stared around them all. 'Do you honestly think that I'm doin' this to myself!?'

Donny opened his mouth, but Marianne shook her head at him and he shut it again.

Lily put her hand on her mother's arm. 'Mum, if you're having strange delusions, there are people you could speak to at—'

'If you're suggestin' I belong in a loony bin, so help me God, Lily, you can leave this house right now! As for you, Don, I won't ask you again. Go to your room or you're on washing up duty for the rest of the week.'

'Come now, Nellie, he didn't mean anything by it,' Cissy said.

'And you can go as well! You said you were here to help, but so far, all you've done is give me a headache with your *endless*

233

yakking!' She got up from the table and stormed to her bedroom, slamming the door noisily behind her.

'I don't care what she says, she needs help,' Lily said.

Marianne sighed. 'But maybe Jasper's got a point and there's another explanation.' She looked over at Jasper, who had a thoughtful expression on his face.

He nodded slowly. 'Your mum's fragile right now, but she ain't responsible for what's goin' on. Someone is doin' this.' He hesitated. 'You don't think that Edie—'

'Dad!' Lily shouted. 'How could you think such a thing?'

Cissy's eyes went wide as she looked between the two of them. 'Dad?' she whispered, putting her hand to her mouth. 'Are you telling me that . . .' She shook her head. 'But that means Donald were . . . Oh my giddy aunt!'

Jasper reddened. 'It's not like that, Cissy.'

'I can't see how else it is. But then, who am I to judge?' She smiled kindly at Lily. 'Sorry, love. It were just a shock.'

'Hellooo!' To everyone's relief, loud voices downstairs interrupted the conversation, and a moment later, Jim and Reenie hurried into the room, closely followed by Ethel and Brian Turner.

'Nellie!' Ethel cried. 'Crack open the sherry; we've got some celebratin' to do!'

Lily jumped up squealing and hurried over to throw her arms around her brother's neck. 'You've finally asked her!' She let go of him and turned to Reenie, picking up her left hand to examine her finger. 'Don't tell me you've not bought a ring . . .' She trailed off, suddenly realising she might have got the wrong end of the stick.

Jimmy laughed. 'There's not been time. But don't worry, she'll get one. The very best ring I can afford.'

Jasper stood and shook his hand then lifted Reenie off her feet in a bear hug. 'If this ain't the best news we've had in months!' he exclaimed. 'This is just the thing to give us all a lift.'

Nellie's door cracked open and she peeped out. 'Is it true?' she said, all traces of her earlier anger wiped away.

Jimmy nodded. 'As of tomorrow, Reenie will be your daughter-in-law.'

'Oh, Nell, ain't it grand!' Ethel beamed. 'You and me'll be related! I just wish they'd told us sooner, so's we could sort out the dress and maybe a little celebration. But never mind, I've already looked out my old weddin' dress, and it'll look a treat! So get the sherry out and let's raise a toast!'

'Ethel Brooks! You ain't changed one bit!'

Ethel turned and stared for a moment, before exclaiming, 'Cissy! I was meaning to come over and see you earlier.' She flew across the room and flung herself into Cissy's arms. 'I never thought I'd see you again! Brian' – she ushered her husband over – 'you remember Cissy, don't you? Ran away with the man she met at the Hippodrome.'

While the chatter erupted around them, Marianne went and put her hand on Reenie's arm.

'Congratulations, Reens,' she said. 'I'm happy for you.'

'Are you really?' Reenie asked quietly.

'Of course I am.' She hugged her friend tightly, eyes closed, wishing desperately that she was.

After she let go, she took hold of Jimmy's hands and searched his face. He regarded her warily before bending to hug her.

'What the *hell* do you think you're playing at?' she whispered angrily.

'I'm sorting my life out,' Jimmy hissed back, letting go of her abruptly. Putting his arm around Reenie, he ushered her over to Nellie, who was busily pouring sherry into the glasses Donny had fetched from the kitchen.

Marianne watched the happy celebrations, and smiled slightly as Cissy's high, piping voice seemed to rise above everyone else's. As for her mother, the way she was knocking back the drink revealed that she was still upset. But maybe Cissy's effervescent presence would help banish whatever ghosts were lurking in her mind and she could get back to being her usual belligerent self.

Her gaze shifted to Reenie. She'd never seen her look so pretty: cheeks flushed, eyes bright, her blonde hair gleaming around her shoulders in a riot of curls. All she could do now was pray that this marriage would turn out better than she feared. But looking at Jim, she doubted it. Though his smile was broad and his laugh loud, his eyes held the desperate look of a cornered man.

Chapter 45

Much later, as Reenie lay in bed thinking back over the evening, she couldn't believe that just a few short hours ago, she'd been considering whether she and Jim had a future at all. She sighed happily, remembering the passionate kiss in the pub – and the one he'd given her before he left to go back to the barracks. The next time she saw him would be outside the town hall, and she couldn't wait.

But as she finally started to drift off to sleep, Jimmy's words to Terence in the pub floated into her mind: *Your word against mine* . . . Not, *Your word against Bert's.*

She turned over and punched the pillow in frustration. 'Enough!' she told herself sternly. 'You love each other and that's all that matters.'

It felt like she'd only been asleep for a few minutes when a rattling at her window made Reenie's eyes fly open. She sat up and switched on the lamp to look at her watch. Three thirty. Her wedding day, she realised with a leap of excitement.

There was another loud crack. Someone was throwing stones at the window. Frowning, she switched off the lamp and stumbled across the room. She was about to pull aside the blackout curtain, when she paused, toes curling on the rag rug as memories of a past life came flooding back. Once upon a time, it hadn't been so unusual for someone to throw stones at her window. But it couldn't be, could it?

Cautiously, she pulled back the blackout curtain and peered down into the street. But there was nothing to be seen in the inky darkness, so she eased it open and hissed, 'Wilf, is that you?'

'Reenie?' A gruff whisper came back. 'Reenie, please come. I need you.'

'Is this some kind of a joke?'

'Please, I don't have much time.'

Reenie stood undecided, chewing her lip. It wasn't right for her to go and meet another man in the middle of the night just before her wedding . . .

'Go away!' She pushed the window back down with a decisive thump and hurried back to bed, her mind swirling with uncertainty. He'd never come to her if it wasn't a matter of life and death. What if something had happened to Freddie?

She'd just decided to go and check when the stones started up again. With a sigh of resignation, she got out of bed.

'Is it Freddie?' she called down.

'No. But I need your help. Please.' The urgency in his voice persuaded her. But if he uttered one word about Jim, she was going to turn and leave him to whatever it was.

'Fine,' Rennie huffed. 'Give me five minutes.'

After pulling on some warm clothes, she crept downstairs and let herself out of the back door. She'd no sooner shut it behind her when Wilf grabbed her arm and started to pull her towards the market square.

'What the hell is so urgent that you'd wake me in the middle of the night?' she demanded, trying to tug free.

He stopped. 'I'm sorry. I wouldn't if I didn't have to. But I need you to come to the lifeboat station.'

Reenie's mouth dropped open in shock. 'But why?'

'I need . . . I need a woman.'

Reenie drew back. 'You've got to be joking! You dare lay a finger on me I'll scream so loud your eardrums will burst!'

238

'Oh for God's sake! Do you really think I'd come to you for *that*?'

'Right, that's it. I'm going in.' She turned to go, hating herself for feeling hurt.

'No! No, Reenie, I'm sorry . . . I didn't mean . . . Please. I've got a load of terrified children refusing to budge out of the lifeboat. You've got to come. I need to get them out of here. And the only one I could think of was you.'

'Children?' Reenie gasped. 'What children?' She started hurrying towards the seafront.

'They . . . they were meant to be going to Sandwich. But now they're here. The boat broke down and the current pulled them towards Dover.'

'But what do you expect me to do with them?'

'Take them to Dover Priory Station. Someone will meet you there.'

'I don't understand. You expect me to take a gaggle of children all the way to the station? And why me? Why can't you do it?'

'We need to go back out and tow the boat back to where it was meant to be going, but it's too dangerous for the kids. Please,' he urged. 'We need to get them to safety as soon as possible.'

Wilf grabbed her hand and they started to run. When they reached the lifeboat station, he took out a torch and shone it towards the boat, which sat bobbing gently by the jetty. 'Come on,' he whispered.

Reenie followed him, allowing him to help her down onto the rocking deck where two of Wilf's colleagues were waiting.

'Thank Gawd you're here,' one of them hissed. 'Bloody kids won't stop wailing. They coulda been killed. Didn't they learn their lesson last time!'

'That's enough, Robson,' Wilf said authoritatively. 'We won't talk of it again.'

'Fair enough. Just get those kids off and safe.'

Wilf handed Reenie his torch and pushed her towards a ladder that led below deck. Heart thumping with nervousness, she shuffled over and climbed down.

Below deck, the stench of vomit was almost overpowering, and she could hear muffled sobbing. Switching on the torch, she stared round at the huddled figures in astonishment. Their clothes were threadbare, and they were bone thin. For a moment, the light rested on a man, the only adult there, and she squinted. A cap was pulled low over his face, and he was wearing patched trousers and a ragged jacket. She moved the torch to the figure beside him. A girl of about fifteen regarded her fearfully over the head of a small boy who sat on her lap, sobbing into her shoulder.

'Oh, you poor things.' She went over to kneel in front of them and put her hand on the girl's arm. 'Please don't worry. I'm here to help.' She wasn't sure if they could understand her, but hopefully her tone would tell them they had nothing to fear. 'My name's Reenie.'

She reached out to take the little boy, but the girl's arms tightened around him as she regarded Reenie suspiciously.

'Do . . . do any of you speak English?' she asked uncertainly.

'A little,' a boy on the other side of the room answered. She shone the torch towards him. He was about thirteen or fourteen, she guessed, cheekbones sharp under shaggy dark hair. 'They teach us in convent.'

'And what's your name, love?' Reenie asked gently.

'Louis,' the boy answered. '*Je m'appelle* Louis Bernard.'

'Pleased to meet you, Louis.' She looked around at the other children. There were six in all, ranging from about five to fifteen. 'Oh, bless you. It looks like you could all do with some dry clothes, food and a nice hot drink.'

The boy narrowed his eyes. 'How we know to trust?'

'You don't. But I promise I won't hurt you. I just want to get you safe. And this boat, out on the sea like this . . . It's not safe.'

'Is safer than home,' the boy said glumly.

'I hope so, love, I really do.' She shone the torch at the man. 'And who are you?' she asked. 'Do you speak English.'

'Of course. He is English,' Louis said.

Reenie kept the light on the man, wondering why he wouldn't show his face.

'M'sieur,' the girl said. 'Can we trust?'

The man nodded, but still didn't say anything.

Annoyed, Reenie snatched the cap from his head.

'Oh my God!' she gasped.

Chapter 46

'Colin?' she said tentatively, and when his eyes met hers, she dropped to her knees in front of him, reaching out to touch his face in wonder. 'We thought you were dead.' Tears sprang to her eyes. 'You've no idea how much . . .' She desperately wanted to hug him, but the child on his lap was in the way. 'Where have you been all this time? Why didn't you let anyone know you were alive?'

'Hello, Reenie,' he said with a slight smile. 'It's a bit of a long story.'

'Will you be coming with me?' she asked. 'Everyone's gonna be so happy to see you!'

He shook his head. 'No. And please, you can't tell anyone about me. It's bad enough you and Wilf know I'm here.'

'But why? Your mum will be so—'

'Reenie, please!'

She was shocked. Colin had always been quiet and gentle, but this man had an authority and hardness she didn't recognise.

She looked around at the children, who were regarding them anxiously. 'How long have you been doing this?' she asked.

He sighed wearily. 'There's no time for explanations. Just know that these children are Jewish orphans. The orphanage is run by nuns, but the Vichy government has ordered all Jews be rounded up and it's not safe for them anymore. We've been running the children to the Free area in France, but someone betrayed us. So

242

this is the best we can do.' He shrugged. 'And it won't be long before this route is cut off too. I need to go back. There are more. But right now, I need your help to get these ones to safety. There'll be someone to collect them at Dover Priory. The lifeboat's radioed for help.'

She stared at him in admiration. 'My God, you've done all this? Who's helping you?'

'I can't say any more. And you can't say anything to anyone. I mean it.'

'Not even Jimmy? He's grieved for you so much, Colin. He blames himself for leaving you there. He needs to know. So does your mum. She's not been the same since you went missing.'

Colin shook his head, but his expression was pained. 'Are they all right?' he asked softly. 'Mum and Jim.'

'They miss you. We all do. But your mum's been . . .' She couldn't tell him how badly his disappearance had affected her. Nor that his cousin Susan was in prison after trying to kill Bert. 'So so sad,' she said finally. 'And so has Jim. He's missed you so much. We weren't sure he'd ever be the same. Can't I just tell them? It would mean so much to them. And to be able to tell him now, especially. It would be the best wedding present ever!'

Colin looked shocked. 'Whose wedding present?'

'Umm, Jim and me . . . well, we're getting married.'

'Married? You and Jim?' His voice trembled slightly.

When she nodded, Colin's shoulders seemed to slump, and Reenie wished she hadn't said anything. It must be so hard to come back and realise how his friends' lives had moved on without him. 'So, can I?' she asked tentatively.

'No!' Colin almost shouted. 'No,' he said more softly. 'Leave it, Reenie. I have work to do, and I . . .well, I might not come back and then they'd have to grieve for me twice.'

Reenie grasped his hands. 'Can't you stop? Come home now?'

He shook his head. 'It's too late now,' he said sadly.

'Reenie.' Wilf's harsh whisper made her jump. 'Can you get a move on!'

Colin urged the little girl on his lap to get down. 'This is Lucille,' he said. 'She's six.' Then he looked up at her, his eyes shimmering. 'Promise me?'

Reenie squeezed his shoulder. 'I promise,' she said, though she wasn't sure how she'd manage it. How could she keep this from Jim? Husbands and wives weren't meant to have secrets. But losing Colin once had nearly broken Jimmy, and he still hadn't fully recovered. She wasn't sure he'd recover a second time, and selfishly, she didn't want to go through that with him again.

'Now listen to me, children,' Colin said. 'You can trust this woman. She's very nice. Do what she says, and you will be taken somewhere safe.'

Louis translated, but still the children sat, unmoving.

'Come on, now.' Reenie held out a hand to a boy of about eight, who stared at it, before finally taking hold of it. His hand was ice cold and Reenie shivered as she gently led him to the ladder.

'Louis,' she said. 'Can you help your little sister?'

'Her name is Mathilde. She not my sister,' he said, nudging the girl who'd been clinging to his arm. '*Allez,*' he said gently.

Reenie reached down to help the girl, who was probably around ten, but she pointedly ignored her hand and stood without her help.

'And you are?' She turned to the teenage girl who had one arm round the little boy, and was clutching a dirty cloth bag in the other.

'This is Marcel.' She nodded at the child on her lap. 'I am Elodie.'

'Oh my, what a beautiful name. Let me take Marcel so you can go up?'

The girl eyed her cautiously, before finally allowing Reenie to take the child from her arms, but she kept the bag, holding it close to her chest as though it contained something precious. And no doubt it did, Reenie thought sadly as she watched Elodie climb the ladder, it was all she had left in the world.

244

'Come *on*!' Wilf called down. 'We need the kids to leave so we can get out there again before their boat drifts into a mine.'

She turned to Colin. 'Please come back safe.'

Colin's eyes glittered in the torchlight as he said croakily, 'I wish you and Jim every happiness.' He cleared his throat. 'He's a lucky man.'

She smiled tremulously. 'I think it's the other way round, but thank you.'

'Goodbye, Reenie.'

His voice held a note of finality that made Reenie pause. 'You will come back, won't you?' she said. 'You have to.'

'Go now,' Colin responded. 'Get the kids away from here.'

With Marcel on her hip and tears in her eyes, Reenie struggled up the ladder.

As she neared the top, Wilf reached down a hand and she grasped it gratefully as he hauled her the rest of the way up. 'Did you know?' she said as soon as she was standing on the deck again. 'About Colin?'

Wilf sighed. 'Not till last week. We had to rescue them off Sandwich. Damn fool mission,' he muttered darkly.

'Last week?' she said in bemusement, trying to figure out why this seemed significant, but Wilf just picked up the little boy and climbed nimbly up onto the jetty so Reenie had no choice but to follow.

Once they were all on land, Wilf put his hand on her shoulder. 'Thank you for coming,' he said softly. 'I wasn't sure who else to ask.'

Despite the darkness, Reenie was acutely aware of the weight and warmth of his hand and had to resist the temptation to reach up and take hold of it. 'There's any number of people you could have asked. Your mum for one. Or a soldier, an ARP warden? I'm not exactly the obvious choice.'

'I needed someone young and strong. But also someone I could trust. And of all the women I know, you were the only person I could think of.'

She pulled the torch out of her pocket and shone it briefly round at the circle of children. She couldn't begin to fathom how desperate their circumstances were to think that crossing a mine-strewn stretch of water in wartime was a better option than staying where they were.

'I better get going then,' she said quietly.

The boat's engine roared into life. 'Wilf, mate, hurry up!'

Wilf leant forward and to her surprise put his arms around her, pulling her close and whispering, 'Take care, Reenie. I'll be over to see you in the morning.'

His arms were warm and comforting, and she wanted to sink into his embrace, but instead she took hold of Marcel's hand. 'Go,' she said. 'And please, take care of Colin.'

Wilf nodded briefly, hopped down onto the deck and the boat shot off, the wash behind it the only patch of brightness in the dark velvet night.

Chapter 47

Reenie stared after it. 'Please, be careful,' she whispered, a lump in her throat. 'Freddie needs his father. And Jim . . .' She swallowed. 'Jim needs to see Colin again.'

'Reenie?' Louis' voice brought her back to the present and she forced herself to push back the deep feeling of dread that was creeping over her.

'All right, children,' she said cheerily. 'Let's see if we can get you to the station.'

Slowly, they made their way along the seafront and turned up New Bridge. 'Keep close to the buildings,' she whispered, herding them ahead of her.

By herself, the walk to the station would have taken less than fifteen minutes, but with the exhausted and terrified children she knew it would take a lot longer. Marcel especially was struggling, so she scooped him up and planted him on her hip.

They were walking up King Street when the air raid siren screeched out and Marcel started to scream. She didn't blame him; she felt like screaming too. It was far too dangerous to risk going to the station now. The children had been through enough without running through town in the pitch dark in the middle of an air raid, and already she could hear planes coming ever closer, and as it always did now, the sound made her heartrate spike.

'Reenie.' It was Elodie, her voice anxious. 'What do we do?'

She thought briefly about taking them to the shop, but the basement was far too small to fit them all comfortably. There was really only one place they could go.

A loud explosion ripped through the air, and seconds later, the sky towards the Eastern Docks turned a deep red. Really scared now, Reenie started to run, the children close behind her.

They had just reached the market square, when a figure loomed out of the dark, a white 'W' on the helmet standing out in the faint light. 'Get to shelter!' He shone his torch towards them. 'Reenie, is that you? Christ, who are the kids?' He ran forward and swung Lucille up into his arms. 'Come on!' he called over the roar of another explosion.

The children started to scream, instinctively ducking, but between them Jasper and Reenie managed to get them across the square where they scooted round the corner of Castle's and into Church Street. 'Get in,' he growled, holding the café's back gate open. 'You can explain yourself later.'

Reenie shoved open the back door and ushered the children into the small hallway.

'Will you stay?' she asked Jasper, who had followed her in with Lucille.

Another crash nearly drowned out his voice. 'I'll be over soon as I can, love. Lookin' forward to hearin' what this is all about.' He put the little girl down. 'Now git.' Then he turned and ran back into the night.

Hurrying the children down the stairs, Reenie thrust open the door and almost fell into the basement, the children piling in behind her.

'What the devil!?' Nellie let out a little screech of shock, almost dropping the teapot she was holding. For a long moment there was silence as each group regarded the other.

'Oh my giddy aunt! It's the Pied Piper,' Cissy exclaimed with a nervous laugh.

Before Reenie could reply, Lucille collapsed on the floor in floods of tears, while Marcel grabbed Elodie's legs and started to scream again.

'Listen,' Reenie shouted above the noise. 'I know you want answers, but right now these kids are cold, exhausted and scared. So can we just give them a cup of tea and whatever you've got going spare to eat and save the questions till later?'

Nellie nodded. 'Poor little mites. Get yourselves comfortable.' She gestured to the cushions. 'Cissy, get the extra blankets from the hamper over there. Fancy being out at night in nothing but rags.'

Reenie collapsed on a chair at the table, teeth chattering with a combination of shock and cold.

'Never a dull moment here, is there?' Cissy chirruped. 'First a party and now a pile of children in an air raid. It's like I've always said: drama follows you everywhere, doesn't it, Nellie? Do you remember that day when—'

'For the love of God, Cissy, will you shut your mouth for just one bloody second!' Nellie shouted, causing the children to cower back against the wall.

Cissy sat back with a huff, folding her arms across her chest. 'Sorry I spoke,' she muttered.

'As are we all,' Nellie grumped.

Never one to be set back for long, though, Cissy stood up. 'What can I do?' she said.

'Like I already asked,' Nellie snapped. 'Get some more blankets.' She pointed to an old wicker hamper that stood in the far corner. 'And wrap the little ones.'

Obediently, Cissy did as she was told while Marianne bustled to the table to pour tea and Lily sliced the loaf they'd brought down, then dabbed dripping onto each piece. Donny, meanwhile, sat and stared at the newcomers in bemusement.

Kneeling beside the sobbing Lucille, Cissy started to sing as she wrapped the little girl securely in a scratchy tartan picnic blanket.

249

'Oh dear, what can the matter be? Dear, dear what can the matter be? I promise you've nothing to fear.'

Then without stopping her song, she picked the little girl up and sat her on her lap, rocking her back and forth until the sobs calmed. Beside her, Elodie did the same with Marcel.

Once the children each had a cup of tea and piece of bread, Nellie sat down. 'Right. Time for some answers. Last I saw of you, Reenie, you were staggering down the stairs with your new fiancé. Now here you are in the middle of a bloody air raid with a parcel of ragamuffins. And today of all days! You should be getting your beauty sleep, not gallivantin' around town in the middle of the night. Who are they anyway?'

'I am Louis.'

Nellie's head snapped round to look at him. 'A Frenchie, eh? Well, at least you can speak English. What about the rest of you?'

Elodie put her hand up. 'Elodie,' she said quietly. Then introduced the other children.

Nellie looked at Reenie. 'Where did you find them? And at this time of night? What were you *doing*?'

Reenie took a deep breath, wondering where on earth to start. 'Wilf brought them in on his lifeboat,' she said eventually.

'Wow!' Donny exclaimed, looking at Louis with admiration. 'On the lifeboat! Wait till I tell Fred. His dad will never let him on the boat. He's going to be so jealous.'

'I can't think why,' Marianne said sharply. 'It sounds terrifying. Go on, Reenie.'

Reenie told them the little she knew. 'Jasper found us outside after the siren went off, and helped me bring them here,' she finished.

'Oh, the poor little dears,' Cissy exclaimed. Lucille had now fallen asleep in her arms, and she dropped a kiss on the little girl's forehead. 'Bless them all. But what shall we do with them? Can we keep them?'

250

'They're not bloomin' pets. Of course we can't keep them! Where would we put them?' Nellie exclaimed.

'We can work,' Elodie said quietly. 'I am good cook.'

'And I can 'elp mend things,' Louis said proudly.

'That's as may be, love,' Nellie said. 'But you can't stay here. It's too dangerous.'

'*Non*,' Elodie said. 'France is danger. They would kill us.'

'Who would?' Marianne asked softly.

'Nazis. *Gendarme* . . . We are *Juif*,' she said sadly. 'The nuns hide us, but the danger is great.' She shrugged, as though this was just how life was.

'Bastards,' Nellie spat. 'Well, ain't no one goin' to kill you here. Can't promise you'll not get killed though. Bombs and shells fall where they will, and there's not a lot we can do about that. Which is why you can't stay here. So, Reenie, what's the plan?'

'I was meant to take them to the station. Someone was going to meet me to help get them somewhere safe. But then . . .' She shrugged.

'You can't take 'em in this state!' Nellie exclaimed. 'Look at 'em. A gust of wind would knock 'em over they're so thin. They need a wash, some food and a good long sleep, then we'll talk to Muriel Palmer. She'll know what to do.'

Lily laughed. 'Never thought I'd hear you say that, Mum!'

'And you'll never hear it again. But in this case, she's the only person I can think of. This is WVS business. They've been rounding up kids and sending them off for the last two years.'

Reenie sighed and rubbed her eyes.

'Is there something else?' Marianne asked. Without her noticing, she'd come and sat beside her at the table.

'What do you mean?' Reenie said warily.

'I was just wondering. I mean, who brought them in the boat? And where are they?'

Reenie looked away. 'Just some man. No idea who.'

'I wonder why it was you Wilf came to,' Marianne said thought-fully. 'Surely he could have found someone more suitable.'

'Good point, Marianne,' Nellie said. 'And how? I mean, it's the middle of the night; how did he wake you?'

Reenie blushed. 'He . . . he said he needed someone young and fit. A woman. Someone he could trust.'

'And how did he wake you up in the middle of the night without your aunt and uncle knowing?' Nellie persisted.

'How do you know they don't?' Reenie responded quickly.

'Cos your Uncle Brian would never've let you go out alone.'

Reenie sighed. 'He threw stones at my bedroom window. He used to do it when we were kids.'

Nellie's eyebrows nearly disappeared under her orange scarf. 'Does Jim know about this?' she snapped.

'What's it got to do with him?' Marianne said.

'What's it got to do with—?' Nellie shook her head. 'Don't you think he has a right to know if there's been any shenanigans between Reenie and another man?'

'Oh, for God's sake, Mum!' Lily exclaimed. 'Stop being so insulting! Reenie and Wilf have lived next door to each other all their lives!'

Nellie's suspicious gaze stayed on Reenie for a moment, then her shoulders dropped. 'Sorry, love,' she said, patting her hand. 'I'm being a protective mum. And I know there's no need. Not with a girl like you. It makes sense that Wilf came to you when he needed help. Like I keep telling you, you're salt of the earth.'

Reenie gave her a weak smile. She didn't feel like salt of the earth. Not when she was going to keep such a huge secret from Jimmy. He deserved better in a wife.

Chapter 48

'Don, love,' Nellie said as they emerged from the basement. It was nearing six thirty and there was no point anyone going back to bed. 'Once you're dressed, I need you to go knock on Muriel Palmer's door. Tell her to come here soon as. Oh, and I reckon Dr Palmer should check the kids over while we're at it. Meantime, Cissy, can you get them washed and put 'em to bed.' She stared at the ragtag group thoughtfully. 'Use the beds upstairs, none of us'll be gettin' any more sleep.'

'Do you want to use my room, Louis? That way you can sleep on your own,' Donny said eagerly.

'Bless you, love. That won't be necessary. There's six beds upstairs, and if they stay longer, we'll work something out.' Nellie ruffled his hair, and he brushed her hand away, casting a quick glance at Louis to ensure the older boy hadn't noticed.

'Do you mind if I leave you to it?' Reenie asked. 'I'd like to get changed and have a wash.'

'Course not, love,' Nellie said. 'You got more important things to see to today. But get your aunt to come over. And Phyllis Perkins. I reckon we'll need all hands on deck if they're gonna stay. Although once Muriel gets involved it'll probably be out of our hands.'

'I'd be happy for them to stay as long as they need,' Cissy said, Lucille still in her arms. 'Poor little mites. We could have so much fun.'

Elodie, who'd been very quiet was looking around the kitchen. 'You want I cook?' she said. 'Gift for you.' She held up the bag she'd not let go of since they'd got off the boat, and emptied its contents onto the table.

'Ugh!' Nellie prodded the muddy, gnarly brown tubers on the table. 'You eat that?'

'Is *topinambour*.'

Marianne picked one up and examined it, then she sniffed it. 'Like a potato?' she asked.

'It's Jerusalem artichoke,' Reenie said. 'I've been reading about these and I was going to get some for the allotment, but Uncle Brian thinks no one will want them.'

'I agree,' Cissy said, picking one up between finger and thumb and examining it carefully. 'It looks like a rotting John Thomas!'

Donny sniggered. 'That's rude, Auntie Cissy!'

Cissy giggled. 'Well, it does, don't you think, ladies? Hey, Nellie, do you remember that time when Auntie Gert brought back some mushrooms from the woods. I nearly died. Your dad were still with us and he went spare. If I hadn't felt so sick, I'd have laughed. Not often Uncle John dared have a go, did he? There was that one other time, though, weren't there? He got back to find Auntie Gert had thrown out that horrid stinky jumper he always wore. And the time when—'

Nellie rolled her eyes. 'And she's back,' she said dryly. 'Yes, I do remember, Cissy. But these aren't mushrooms. And I don't think it's appropriate to call these . . . whatsits in front of kiddies, do you?'

Oblivious to the joke, Elodie gathered up the vegetables and put them back in the bag. 'I will cook them for you,' she said.

'Oh no you won't, young lady.' Nellie took her arm and led her towards the stairs. 'You and your little friends are going to have a wash and go to sleep.' Then she smiled kindly at her. 'Maybe later, all right?'

Elodie nodded and looked down. '*Merci beaucoup*, Madame. *Allez, enfants.*' She held her hand out to the others.

Nellie followed the children upstairs more slowly, glad that she had Cissy here to help with this emergency, especially as the kids had all gravitated to her. But, of course, everyone loved Cissy. Even if she did talk your ear off, people always fell for her eventually.

She paused at the sitting room door and peered in, looking around anxiously to see if anything had moved – she'd noticed that things only ever seemed to happen after a raid. Then she shook her head. She needed to stop this. There was too much else going on; too many people relying on her. And now she had more mouths to feed as well as a wedding to prepare for.

Going into her room, she mentally went through what she could use from the café's supplies to feed the children as well as cobble together some sort of wedding breakfast. It'd be slim pickings, but she'd manage somehow. And Ethel could help. Lying down on the bed, she closed her eyes. 'Just forty winks,' she told herself as she started to drift off.

'Nellie.' A shrill voice from upstairs brought her sitting bolt upright.

'We need more towels.'

'Get them to share,' Nellie called back.

'We've only got two.'

With a curse she climbed back to her feet and it was then she noticed something glinting on the pillow and goose pimples broke out all over her body. Her wedding ring.

With trembling fingers, she picked it up. 'Gladys?' she whispered, staring around fearfully. Then with a sudden burst of energy, she pulled the covers and pillows off the bed, desperately searching for the other rings. But there was no sign. She grabbed the torch that always sat on her bedside table, dropped to her knees and shone it under the bed. Nothing.

Feeling sick, she sat back on the side of the bed and slipped the ring on to her finger. But recently her knuckles had swollen and it no longer fitted.

She tore it off and threw it into the corner of her room.

Chapter 49

Reenie raced round to the back of the shop and pushed open the door.

'Reenie, is that you?' Uncle Brian called from upstairs.

'Yes. Sorry, I was sheltering over the road,' she called as she ran up the stairs to the apartment.

'What are you playing at? We was worried sick!' Her aunt stood on the landing, wearing her quilted blue dressing gown, her grey hair still in curlers. 'We've got hardly any time to sort out the wedding dress. If only you'd told us about this weddin' sooner, we could've—'

'Aunt Ethel,' Reenie interrupted. 'There are more important things to do right now. So please, could you just get dressed and go over to the café,' Reenie said urgently.

'But why?'

Reenie went into the small sitting room and sat down on the old blue sofa. 'Please, could you just go. And get Phyllis to go with you.'

Aunt Ethel followed her in. 'Are you going to explain? Or do I just have to go on your say-so?'

It wasn't often her aunt lost her temper, but Reenie could see that she was close to it.

'Just tell us what's going on, Reenie, love,' her uncle said gently. He was wearing his brown striped pyjamas and the few wisps of hair that he usually combed over his crown were standing up around his head.

Reenie explained as briefly as she could. 'So Nellie needs help with the kids,' she finished.

Aunt Ethel's mouth had dropped open. 'Are you telling me that Wilf Perkins made you go down to the harbour in the middle of the night?' she asked aghast. 'How? Did he come into your room?'

'No, of course not.' Reenie stood up and started to pace the small room in agitation. Why was everyone more interested in how Wilf had managed to get hold of her than in the children. 'Tell you what, *I'll* go over to let Phyllis know while you get dressed.'

'I always knew that boy had a fancy for you. I didn't say so at the time, but when he upped and married June, you could have knocked me down with a feather. I always thought it'd be you,' Ethel continued as if Reenie hadn't spoken.

'Did you hear a word I just said?' Reenie said angrily. 'And Wilf *didn't* have a fancy for me. We were just mates.' She stomped out of the sitting room and down the stairs. She didn't tell them that she was eager to see if Wilf had got home safely. The thought of him and Colin out at sea had been playing on her mind from the moment she'd left them.

'Is Wilf home?' Reenie said, when Phyllis Perkins opened her door.

Phyllis blinked at her in surprise. 'No. I mean . . . Is he all right?' she asked anxiously.

'I'm sure he is, but can you pop over to the café. Mrs C will explain everything. Aunt Ethel will be there.'

She turned and left before Phyllis could ask her any more questions, and headed straight down towards the seafront. The dawn was breaking now, and in the half-light the sea was calm, but the lifeboat wasn't there.

Marching up to the lifeboat station, she walked in without knocking. 'Have you heard from Wilf?' she asked a grizzled old man with a bushy white beard, who was sitting drinking tea at a chipped wooden table.

'You the woman who took the kids last night?' he asked.

She nodded.

'Get them to the station, did you?'

'No, there was an air raid. They're at Castle's.'

The man shrugged, picked up a pair of binoculars and went to peer out of the window. 'Been expectin' them for a while,' he said. 'No word of any problems, but you never know these days.'

Reenie went to stand beside him, but although there were several ships steaming across the water, none resembled the lifeboat.

'Did they make it to Sandwich?' she asked.

The man narrowed his eyes and tutted. 'Not your business where they went or whether they made it. And I'll be tellin' Wilf Perkins that when he gets back.'

Reenie chewed at her nails, pacing around the small room as she wondered again how she could keep such momentous news from Jimmy. She didn't want to start their marriage with such a big secret standing between them. This dilemma has been whirling round and round her mind while she'd been in the basement; Colin's face had been so thin and his eyes so sad . . . She couldn't imagine what he'd suffered while he'd been away. And after all the good he'd done, the man deserved to be reunited with the people who loved him most.

'Gordon Bennett, sit down, will ya,' the man exclaimed. 'You'll drive me spare. If there'd been any problems, I'd know about it, so there's no point stayin' here.' He regarded her through small brown eyes topped by huge bushy white eyebrows. 'Are you and Wilf courtin'?' he asked. 'Is that why you're in such a tizz? He never mentioned it, but then he's not exactly the talkative type.'

'No, of course not! He's an old friend is all.'

The man's eyebrows rose.

'In fact, I'm getting married today. To a very lovely man.'

The man regarded her impassively. 'Well, well, ain't life a curious tangle,' he murmured, turning back to look through his binoculars again.

Reenie sat down, resting her head on the table, annoyed at the old man for talking to her like that, but too exhausted to argue further.

'There they are.'

Reenie jumped up and ran over to the window. 'It looks very slow,' she remarked.

'Must've run into more trouble,' he said, although he sounded unconcerned.

Reenie stepped outside and watched the boat's progress, the old man standing beside her, ready to catch the rope when the boat came up alongside them.

As soon as Wilf climbed up onto the dock, she had to resist the urge to run and throw her arms around him. Instead, she stepped forward, raising her arm. 'Wilf!'

'Is everything all right? The children get off OK?' he asked, striding towards her.

His hands were outstretched and instinctively she took them; they were ice cold, the skin rough and chapped.

'You really should wear gloves,' she said. 'I'll make you some.'

He smiled. 'Don't waste your time. I've lost every pair I've ever owned. But thank you. It's a sweet thought.'

Suddenly realising what she was doing, she dropped his hands.

'Everything all right with the kids?' he asked again.

She shook her head, explaining what had happened. 'Nellie's called a meeting at the café to discuss what to do. She's even called in Muriel Palmer.'

'Christ, that sounds . . . explosive.' He grinned. 'So that's why you came down here, was it? To avoid the mothers' meeting?'

'I came to make sure you were safe,' she said softly. 'And to ask about Colin. You said you were taking him to Sandwich. I'd really like to see him again.'

Wilf frowned. 'I shouldn't have told you that. And you know you can't see him.' He hesitated a moment before asking, 'Did you tell Colin about you and Jim?'

'Yes ... He seemed a bit surprised. I just can't believe he's alive. And doing such brave things. It's not fair that everyone still believes he's dead. Especially for his mum and dad. And for Jim.'

'Leave it, Reenie. If he's asked you not to tell anyone then don't.' His tone was brusque.

'Why are you angry?'

'I'm not. Just go off and get married, live happily ever after with Jimmy and forget Colin was ever here, all right?'

'But husbands and wives shouldn't have secrets. Especially one as big as this.'

Wilf laughed sardonically. 'Believe me, Reenie, husbands and wives *always* have secrets. And your marriage won't be any different.'

Reenie's cheeks warmed. 'Maybe you and June did. But me and Jim won't,' she said heatedly.

He shook his head at her. 'Oh, grow up, Reenie.'

Reenie stared at him, hurt. 'I don't understand you,' she said eventually. 'Last night I was the only woman you could trust, but this morning you're talking to me like I'm a child. And can I remind you that you were the one who suddenly decided we should be friends again.' The vague thought she'd had earlier came back to her. 'If you knew about Colin last week ... Is that why you've suddenly been hanging around? Did you want to tell me?' Then another thought occurred to her. 'Did you ask me last night so I'd see him? Why would you do that? You must have known I'd want to tell Jim ...'

Wilf rubbed his hands over his face. 'I meant what I said last night: I asked you because I knew I could trust you. The question is, do you trust yourself?'

Reenie frowned, a sudden gust of wind whipping the hair around her face. She brushed it away impatiently. 'What do you mean?'

'This marriage, Reens—'

Before he could say more, Reenie exploded with rage, pushing him in the chest. 'What is it with you? I don't have any doubts! And for your information, the wedding is *today*. And you're not invited.' Then she spun round and rushed blindly away.

No matter what Wilf said, she couldn't wait to marry Jimmy. She loved him. Which was why she'd have to tell him about Colin. It would be the most precious gift she could ever give him.

Chapter 50

'Can someone please tell me what in the name of God is going on?' Ethel Turner called as she walked into the café.

'Good morning, Mrs Turner,' Lily said cheerfully. 'Come for the meeting, have you?'

Ethel came and leant on the counter. 'Reenie told me some mad story about kids comin' over in a boat, then she told me to come here, and disappeared off God knows where. I don't like it, Lily. Not one bit! Where's your mother?'

'Mum's getting dressed, Cissy's putting the kids to bed, and Marianne, as you can see, is in the kitchen. Go on upstairs.' She pushed a cup of tea towards her.

The bell above the door rang, and a couple of sailors walked in. 'Two cups of tea, couple of fried eggs, bacon and tomatoes, please.'

'Tea's no problem. Breakfast this morning is one egg and toast. That do?'

'Whatever you've got. No Mrs C today?' one of them asked.

'Bit of business to sort out, gentlemen. But she'll be back to brighten your day soon.' She turned to call through the order to Marianne.

'So it's true. There really are kids! I don't know what Wilf was thinking dragging my Reenie into something so dangerous,' Ethel grumbled. 'He's gonna get the sharp end of my tongue when I see him, I can promise you that!'

'Don't blame him.' Phyllis Perkins had come in unnoticed behind the sailors. 'Reenie's a grown woman, she's could've said no.'

Ethel turned. 'Sorry, love, I didn't mean anything against your Wilf. Just . . . she seemed in a right state this morning: jumpy as a cat on hot bricks, then she raced off again. And all this after that lovely night last night. Did you hear that Jim popped the question, and they're marryin' today! So you can see why I think it's odd for Wilf to come knockin' for her in the middle of the night.'

'I'm sure he had his reasons. My Wilf's not the impulsive type.'

Ethel raised her eyebrows and Phyllis cleared her throat. 'Except that one time, of course. And he learnt his lesson, I can promise you that! No offence, love,' she added hastily.

Ethel sighed. 'None taken. June weren't the easiest of girls, God rest her soul.' She picked up her cup and saucer. 'But I've never had a moment's worry with Reenie. Solid as a rock that girl is.' She sighed. 'Still, it is her weddin' day, so I'm prepared to make allowances. Come on, let's go see what this is all about.'

'She's got a point,' Lily said to Marianne when she put the plates of food on the hatch. 'It is strange Wilf went to her. And Reenie seemed distracted last night. Barely said a word once she'd explained about the kids.'

'Wouldn't you be after what had happened? As for Wilf . . .' Marianne shrugged. 'Who knows what goes through that man's mind?'

Just then, Cissy came down the stairs. 'Littlest kids are in bed. Phyllis and Ethel are settled on the sofa. But something's up with your mum. I knocked to tell her they were here, but she snapped me head off. And she had a right go when I asked her about towels. Can you go and have a word, Lily? I'll take over here.'

With a worried frown, Lily went upstairs and knocked on her mother's bedroom door. When there was no reply, she turned the

264

handle and walked in. Her mother was lying on the bed staring up at the ceiling.

'Everything all right, Mum? Ethel and Phyllis are waiting for you in the living room.' Her mother's face was as white as the pillowcase, and it looked like she'd been crying.

Nellie sat up. 'Can't a woman have forty winks after a night in the basement?' she muttered.

'You've been crying.' Lily sat down beside her on the bed.

'Is it any wonder?' Nellie pointed up at the ceiling. 'Those poor little kiddies. What must it be like to be under threat of being shot just for your religion? They're babies, for God's sake!' She wiped at her face. 'So if you want to know what's wrong, the answer is *everything*. The world's an absolute madhouse. My son's in hospital just cos he was playing football, his mates are dead. My best friend gunned down in front of me. The windows blown out . . . And sometimes, it gets to me, Lily.'

Lily put an arm around her shoulders. 'I know, Mum,' she said softly. 'It gets to all of us. So if you need a morning off to sleep, I'm sure Cissy and Marianne can manage. And I'll speak to Muriel Palmer and the others. I've still got a couple of hours before I need to be at the hospital. If only I'd known about the wedding, I'd have taken the day off.'

'It's all right, love,' Nellie said, swinging her legs over the side of the bed. 'I need to make sure those kids are treated right. Don't want Muriel sendin' them off to some God-awful dump. I mean, did you see them? Skinny as rakes and terrified of their own shadows. What they need are people to take care of 'em properly.'

Lily kissed her cheek. 'I think you're amazing, Mum. Everything you do for people, keeping this place running. I don't know why Edie's so cross with you, but I want you to know that I'm proud of you. And I don't think I tell you that enough.'

Nellie stared at her youngest daughter, tears filling her eyes again. 'You don' t know how much that means to me,' she whispered. 'I'm proud of you too. But your sister has her reasons, so don't judge her too harshly. I just have to hope that one day she'll come round.'

'Will you tell me what you two have argued about?' Lily asked.

Nellie sighed. 'Sometimes, even when you think what you're doing is for the best, it's easy to forget that all actions have consequences. And many of them are unseen. All I can tell you is that I regret every day the hurt I've caused your sister. I love her, Lily. I love you all.'

Lily pulled her mother into her arms and held her tight. 'I love you too, Mum. And so does Edie, even if she doesn't want to admit it. And if there's anything I can do to help you two make it up, I'll do it.'

Nellie pulled away and cupped her daughter's cheek. 'Bless you, love. You're just like your dad; always wantin' to help and fix things, but there's nothing you can do.'

'Maybe Dad—'

'No!' Nellie's interrupted emphatically. 'Not even Jasper can help this time. It's up to Edie to come back in her own time.'

Lily nodded. 'All right. But you better get out there before Muriel Palmer comes and tries to take over,' she said, hoping to make her mother smile. 'You can't have your meeting in your dressing gown.'

'You're right.' Nellie walked over to the wardrobe. 'I think it's time to bring this one out of retirement.' She pulled out an orange dress with a green zigzag pattern. 'Last time I wore this was to the council meeting just before the war. Got me noticed, I can tell you.'

Lily grimaced.

Nellie tutted. 'You've got no taste.'

Lily giggled. 'That's more like it, Mum. No more tears, all right? And remember what I said – if you need me to talk to Edie, just say the word.'

After Lily had left, Nellie hunted around the floor for the ring. When she found it, she placed it in the centre of her palm and stared at it for a long time, remembering the day Donald had slipped it onto her finger. One of the happiest days of her life . . . But look at her now: haunted and penniless. She opened the window and flung the ring out as far as she could.

Chapter 51

Reenie was about to go back into the shop when a cheerful voice called across the square. 'Yoo-hoo, Reenie!'

Looking over, she spotted Muriel Parker standing outside the café.

Sighing, she forced a smile and went to speak to her. 'You look very smart, Mrs Palmer.' She was wearing her grey/green WVS suit with a red blouse and green hat with a red band.

Mrs Palmer smoothed her hand over her jacket. 'I've finally managed to get hold of my uniform. Designed by the couturier Digby Morton. *Such* an honour. Of course, so many of the ladies have been complaining that they just can't fit into it.' *Too fat*, she mouthed. 'Anyway, young Donny brought a most surprising message to me this morning. Sounds like you've been quite the heroine. I can't wait to meet the children. Of course, we at the WVS will do what we can for the little mites. I know some French, you know. Dr Palmer and I have spent many happy holidays over in France. *Such* cultured people. Absolutely terrible at fighting, of course, but you can't have everything.'

Resisting the temptation to roll her eyes, Reenie said, 'A couple of the older children speak quite good English, so no need to worry about the language.'

'Oh.' Mrs Palmer looked disappointed. 'Are you coming in for the meeting?'

'I'm sure you don't need me,' Reenie said quickly. 'I've got quite a lot to do. And with Aunt Ethel here Uncle Brian needs me at the shop.'

'Nonsense.' Mrs Palmer took her arm. 'Those children know and trust you, it's only right you're there to put them at ease.'

Suppressing a sigh, Reenie allowed her to lead her to the door, then stopped dead as she noticed a familiar figure walking towards them. Wearing a black hat and coat, she was even more diminished than the last time she'd seen her just a few days before.

'Did you ask Mary Guthrie to come as well?' Reenie asked.

'I did. I urged her to join the WVS shortly after all that trouble with her niece. There's nothing better for taking your mind off your own problems than helping someone else. And I popped over before I came here to ask her to come. It was the thought of those poor orphans that persuaded her. She's a good woman, you know.'

Reenie felt a new respect for Muriel. She was an interfering busybody, but her heart was usually in the right place. But now she was going to have to sit in a room with this poor, ravaged woman and resist the temptation to tell her that her son was alive. It was just too cruel to keep the news from her. She'd known keeping this secret wouldn't be easy, but suddenly she understood that the weight of it had the potential to destroy her peace of mind. Surely if Colin had any inkling of how desperately sad his mother was, he wouldn't want her to continue to suffer?

Pulling her arm away from Mrs Palmer's, Reenie walked up to her. 'Mrs Guthrie, how lovely to see you.'

The woman gave her a surprised look. 'Really?' she asked, her tone flat.

'Are you coming for the meeting?' she asked.

She nodded. 'We've got some room at the bakery. We could easily put one or two of the children up if necessary.'

There was a snort, and Reenie's heart sank as she realised Lou Carter had come up behind them. 'Probably best not, eh, Mrs Guthrie? Last time you put someone up it didn't end too well. Who you talkin' about anyway?'

Mary Guthrie's cheeks coloured.

Mrs Palmer intervened. 'Thank you, Mrs Carter, but I don't think we'll be needing your input, so do get back to your business. Plenty of hungry soldiers eager for a pint of whelks, even at this early hour.'

'What's goin' on?' she asked, looking through the café's celluloid window.

'WVS business,' Mrs Palmer said airily. 'Nothing to do with you. Come on, ladies, let's get started.' She held open the café door and waited for Reenie and Mary to pass. Then before Lou could follow her, she shut it behind her.

Cissy looked up from serving a couple of customers. 'You must be Mrs Palmer,' she said with a wide smile. 'What a night we've had. Honestly, I can't believe what goes on here. After my quiet life—'

'Mrs Palmer, Mrs Guthrie, this is Cissy, Nellie's cousin, who's come to help out,' Reenie interrupted. In the basement last night, she'd discovered very quickly that it was best to cut Cissy off sooner rather than later or you'd never get away.

'Cousin, is it?' Mrs Palmer examined her curiously. 'I don't think I've ever heard of you.'

'Oh, I left many years ago, before the last war. But I'm back now, and happy to help in any way I can. I put the kiddies to bed myself just a moment ago, poor mites. Filthy, they were. But oh, such sweet little things. I'm sure that if—'

'I think we better get up there then,' Mrs Palmer interrupted.

Cissy nodded. 'Course you should. Miss Frost and Mavis from the Oak are already there. Maybe later we can all catch up. Goodness, isn't this exciting. I've not had this much fun since . . .'

But Muriel had already moved on, Mary following closely behind her.

Cissy gave Reenie a dejected look. 'Was I talkin' too much?'

Reenie patted her arm. 'They're just in a hurry.'

Cissy smiled slightly. 'No, I was talking too much. Me and my mouth. Auntie Gert always said—' She stopped. 'There I go again. Go on up, love.'

Behind her, the door crashed open and Lou Carter strode in. 'If there's town business to discuss,' she said, 'then it's only right I should be here.' She folded her arms across her ample chest and squinted at Cissy. 'Christ alive, if it ain't Cissy bloody Stewart! Last I heard you'd run off with that old geezer from the band. Amazed Nellie let you in the door. You'd've thought you'd committed murder the way she went on after you'd gone. Then again, no one would've blamed you if you'd done in her old hag of a mother.'

Cissy frowned. 'You ain't changed, Lou. And me and Nellie have made our peace. I'd love to chat, but I'm in charge here this mornin' and I'm a bit busy.' She sidled out from behind the counter and went to take an order from a couple of women who'd just walked in.

'I might not have changed, but she has. Last time I asked her a question, I was stuck for twenty minutes. Mind you, that were over thirty years ago,' Lou said reflectively. 'So what's goin' on up there, Reenie?'

Reenie sighed. 'You may as well come up,' she said. 'But please be nice to Mrs Guthrie. She's having a terrible time and you're not helping.'

'Lips are sealed,' Lou promised as she followed her up the stairs.

Chapter 52

The small sitting room was crowded with women. Miss Frost was squashed into the corner of the flowered sofa, needles clicking away, khaki-coloured wool winding up from a bag on the floor. Phyllis Perkins and Aunt Ethel were sitting next to her, while Nellie was in her usual chair by the fireplace wearing a dress, which, even by Nellie's colourful standards, was frightful, although her face was stark white, and she didn't look well. Mavis Woodbridge was on the chair opposite Nellie, while Mary Guthrie and Muriel Palmer sat on a couple of hard-backed chairs by the dining table.

'Don't this look jolly,' Lou said, going over to the table and pulling another chair out. Pointedly, she moved it as far away from Mary as she could, then sat down.

Nellie sighed. 'Why are you here, Lou?'

Lou looked around at the gathering. 'Cos I'm part of this community too. And if you can have *her* here—' she pointed at Mary '—then I can't see how's I can be left out.'

'God give me strength,' Reenie whispered, leaning against the door frame.

Muriel Palmer stood up. 'If you must remain, Mrs Carter, then I insist you refrain from making scathing comments.'

Lou's lips thinned, but she didn't reply.

Muriel nodded. 'Right, then, I declare this meeting open. Phyllis, could you take the minutes, there's a love.' She handed her a notebook and pen, then turned to Reenie. 'Now, dear, perhaps you can start off by telling us about the events of last night.'

Before she could begin, heavy footsteps thundered up the stairs, and Jasper came in, still wearing his ARP overalls. He stopped in the doorway and stared round in surprise. 'Just popped by to see how the kids are,' he said.

'Ah, Jasper,' Muriel simpered. 'Do join us. I understand you played a heroic role in making sure those children got here safely. Reenie was just about to tell us what happened.'

With all eyes on her, Reenie once again recounted the events of the evening. 'So,' she concluded, 'I don't know who was meant to meet them at the station last night, but it sounded like there was a plan. And I don't think these are the only children who've been brought over. They were just unlucky that their boat got into trouble and had to be rescued.'

Muriel was outraged. 'Are you telling me this isn't an isolated incident? That *someone* is evacuating children across a stretch of water that we all know is continually bombarded, and no one's said a word? Who would do such a thing? And why haven't the WVS been informed? Billeting children is WVS work; we should have been in the know.'

'It will have been on a need-to-know basis, I expect,' Jasper said wisely. 'And don't sound like they were meant to end up here.'

'But *who* brought them?' Muriel asked. 'Do you have any idea, Reenie?'

Reenie shook her head, though inadvertently, she looked at Mary Guthrie, whose eyes were trained on the purple and green carpet.

Miss Frost tutted. 'Question is, where were they meant to be going? I can't help thinking that it would have been better for them to stay where they were.'

'They're Jewish orphans,' Reenie said meaningfully.

'What's their religion got to do with anything?' Lou asked.

'Oh come on, Lou!' Nellie exclaimed. 'Even you must know what's happenin' to Jewish people. It's been in the newspaper.'

Lou sniffed. 'I don't read them rags,' she said. 'Full of lies.'

Muriel shook her head. 'It's all just too dreadful,' she said sadly. 'But it sounds to me like the situation is easily resolved. If we take them to the station, then perhaps we can discover who was meant to be meeting them and they can take them to wherever they were meant to go.'

'No chance,' Jasper interrupted. 'All railway lines in and out of Dover were bombed last night. Two fatalities at the station.'

Miss Frost made the sign of the cross on her chest. 'God rest their souls,' she said.

'Oh dear, oh dear.' Muriel bit her finger. 'If that's the case, then we'll just have to care for them ourselves until the railway's back up and running. Meantime, I shall get word to the authorities that we need help evacuating them. How many can you have, Nellie?'

Nellie sighed. 'I got three spare beds. But we're all out later, so the little ones'll have to go somewhere else.'

'I would be delighted to help,' Miss Frost said. 'Didn't our Lord say, "Suffer the little children to come unto me"? It would be my privilege to educate them in the teachings of Jesus Christ.'

'Over my dead body,' Mavis interjected. 'What them kids need is lovin' kindness. Not some old biddy shoving scriptures down their throats. Did you not hear what Reenie said. They're *Jewish*. They got no use for the bloody C. of E. And neither do I. I can put up a couple in the pub for a bit.'

'The pub!' Miss Frost bristled. 'You complain about me teaching the Bible and yet you're happy to put those innocents in your den of iniquity.'

'I beg your pardon?' Mavis exclaimed.

Suddenly the room erupted with everyone speaking at once.

'Ladies!' Jasper walked into the middle of the room, hands raised. 'Nothing will be achieved if you argue. Now, if each of you says how many you can accommodate, Phyllis can take a note. It's only temporary, so I'm sure we can resolve this easily.'

'Thank you, Jasper, I'm quite capable of controlling this meeting,' Muriel snapped.

Jasper sighed. 'Fine. Not as if I don't have enough to do, without having to referee a group of old women!'

'Given you've been on duty all night, I will make allowances for your rudeness,' Muriel said indignantly.

'Whatever you say, Mrs Palmer. I'll leave you all to it.' He looked over at Nellie, who nodded and smiled faintly at him.

'I think I'll go too, if you don't need me, Mrs Palmer,' Reenie said hastily. She could hardly bear to stay in this room with Colin's mother. If she had to look at her grief-worn face one more time she was in danger of blurting out the truth to her.

'Oh, of course! I hear congratulations are in order. Young Donny mentioned that you and Jim announced your engagement last night. And marrying today?' She raised her eyebrows and looked pointedly at Reenie's stomach. 'That settles it. Nellie you'll be far too busy to have the kiddies with you, I'll take them all to my place and—'

'Excuse me!' Ethel interjected angrily. 'They are marrying quickly because we're in the middle of a war! So don't go throwin' your insinuations around.'

But Reenie wasn't taking any notice; her eyes were trained on Mary Guthrie, who had looked up for the first time since she'd arrived. Suddenly, she stood up and rushed to the door, where she paused beside Reenie, her face a mask of pain and anger, and whispered, 'For your sake, I hope you understand what you're getting into,' before hurrying down the stairs.

Reenie stood frozen with shock for a moment before turning to go after her. But the sight of two silent figures sitting on the stairs behind her stopped her in her tracks. Elodie was wearing a long white nightgown, her dark hair loose and curling in ringlets about

275

her face, while Louis was dressed in some blue cotton pyjamas that were far too big for him, making him look very young. Both looked exhausted and frightened, and Reenie knew she couldn't just leave them there.

'Do you want to come in?' Reenie whispered.

'Who's there, Reenie?' Muriel asked.

'Elodie and Louis,' she said, ushering them into the sitting room with a reassuring smile.

Muriel jumped from her seat and held out her hands to the children. '*Bonjaw*,' she said excitedly. '*Common t'allez vous?*' She beamed at them, then looked around the room. 'So nice to be able to speak French, don't you think?'

Reenie caught her aunt's eye and they both stifled a smile.

'Clever old Lady Muck,' Lou said disparagingly.

Muriel rounded on her. 'If you can't be polite, I suggest you leave.'

'I think I will.' Lou stood up. 'Last thing I need is a load of foreign kids runnin' round my place. Me and Terence barely have enough to feed ourselves.'

Nellie gave a short bark of laughter. 'Pull the other one, Lou. You've got enough to keep the whole town fed. And everyone knows that Terence ain't exactly short of grub. Or anythin' else, come to that.'

'I'd be very careful about throwin' your accusations around, Nell, or folk might wonder how you know so much.'

'Just go, Lou!' Mavis said. 'And tell your Terence that the next time he tries to sell his knock-off beer to me, I'll call the police.'

Lou pursed her lips and flounced out of the room.

'Don't worry,' Reenie said to Elodie and Louis, who were looking mortified and clutching each other's hands. 'We're not all like her. Why don't you sit down?' She gestured to her aunt and Phyllis, who both stood and offered their seats.

Once the children were seated, Muriel crouched in front of them, a patronising smile on her face. 'I am sorry,' she said, very slowly and very loudly. 'But train is not working. So now you come to my house.'

Elodie shrugged. 'I like to stay here. I cook.'

'Not those nasty root thingies, I hope,' Nellie remarked.

'I stay,' Louis said. 'I help.'

'No,' Muriel said. 'You stay at my house until train works. Understand?'

'Oh for God's sake, Muriel,' Nellie said, exasperated. 'They speak English, so you don't have to speak as though they're bloomin' deaf! And if the two older ones want to stay here, that's fine by me. They can keep an eye on the place while we're out at the weddin' later.'

Just then Cissy came in carrying a tray with a teapot, cups and saucers and a plate of bread and marge, looking as excited as though she was serving at a royal banquet.

'Who's for tea?' she said cheerfully. 'Oh, ain't this just like the old days?'

Miss Frost looked at Cissy over her spectacles. 'Maybe for you, Cissy. But for the rest of us, who didn't abandon our hometown to run off with a *much* older man at the age of only sixteen, this is just the same as any other day.' She sniffed disapprovingly.

Cissy coloured, her red cheeks clashing with her orange hair. 'The old days I'm referring to didn't include you, Adelaide. You were always too busy praying.'

Nellie chuckled. 'You deserved that. And no need to look at *me* like that. I've stayed right here and done me duty, but just cos Cissy took a different path, that don't mean she's in the wrong.'

Cissy looked surprised. 'That weren't what you said the other day.'

Nellie shrugged. 'Yeah, well. Family have the right to say what they like, but others should keep their mouths shut and their noses out.' She sat back and folded her arms across her chest.

Miss Frost leant over and stuffed her knitting needles into her bag. 'Seeing as you no longer need my help, Muriel, I'll take my

277

leave. But do let me know how I can help with the community kitchen. Not long now till it opens. Still, they say competition is good for business.' She smiled thinly at Nellie who scowled back at her.

'Oh, we don't need to worry about the competition,' Cissy said. 'Starting next week, I shall be doing afternoon concerts Fridays and Saturdays. Folk won't get *that* at your community kitchen, will they?'

Nellie spluttered. 'You what? You start scratchin' your fiddle in the middle of the day in *my* café, Cissy, and I might not be so inclined to stick up for you.'

'Oh, I do love a bit of *Four Seasons*,' Muriel piped up. 'Perhaps you'd like to come and play at one of our WVS fundraising soirees.'

Reenie barely heard a word of the arguments swirling around her as her thoughts were completely occupied with what Mary Guthrie had said. Her anger just now had felt so real, so strong, that it made her wonder whether there was more to her pronouncement than simply grief.

She closed her eyes in frustration. This should be one of the happiest days of her life, but instead she was burdened with a secret and once again full of doubts. She needed to talk to someone who could give her some no-nonsense, unbiased advice. And there was only one person she could trust to do that. Without saying goodbye, she slipped down the stairs and out of the back door.

It was only as she was walking up Castle Street that another thought occurred to her: Marge had mentioned once that part of her job was to keep track of all the shipping along the south coast. Might it be possible that she'd know something about the boat Colin had been on – and therefore where it had been going?

Chapter 53

Lily pushed through the door of the hospital with minutes to spare before her shift. Her head was fuzzy with exhaustion, but the busy hum in the corridors revived her as she made her way to the cloakroom to drop off her bag and cloak.

Opening the door quietly, she was immediately aware of hushed voices arguing around the corner of the L-shaped room. 'I said I'd look after him last night.' It was Vi's voice and Lily held her breath as she waited to see who she was talking to.

'He was having a nightmare again, Vi. You want me to come get you every time he needs something!'

'You'll use any excuse to hold his hand. How would you like it if I were constantly pawing at your fella?'

'He's not your fella!'

'He might not be yet, but he will be. So stay out of his way, all right? And if there's night nursing to be done, then *I'll* be the one to do it.'

Lily groaned silently. Not this again . . . Bloody Bert couldn't help himself.

'You really think that he'd have his head turned by *me*?' Dot whispered back.

Vi let out a scornful laugh. 'As if. But that don't mean I want you holdin' his hand, so steer clear, understand?'

'It's not me you should be worried about. It's him. Cos if you think that once he's out of here he'll give you a second glance, then you're in for a big disappointment.'

Lily jumped back, flattening herself against the wall as Dot strode round the corner, her eyes suspiciously bright. But her friend didn't seem to notice her as she wrenched open the door and walked out.

After hanging her coat and bag on the nearest hook, Lily raced out before Vi could see her and headed straight for the ward to see Bert before her shift began.

'What's going on?' she demanded, walking up to his bed.

Bert grimaced. 'Good morning to you too, sis,' he said dryly, but though his tone was light, his eyes looked heavy and troubled.

'Sorry, love,' she said guiltily. 'How are you feeling? I heard you're still having nightmares?'

Bert sighed. 'I suppose Vi told you. I know you don't like her much, but she's been good to me in here. And yes, I have nightmares. And she helps a lot with those too.'

Lily frowned. 'Vi does? But I thought it was—' She shook her head; this was none of her business. 'Listen, I don't have long, but I've got tons of news.'

Bert stiffened. 'Is Jim all right?' he asked anxiously.

'Oh, so you know that him and Reenie are getting married today! They told us last night. But not just that . . .' She started to tell him about the events of that night, but she could tell Bert wasn't listening.

'What's wrong?'

'Reenie deserves better,' he muttered.

Lily stared at him in astonishment. 'Better than Jimmy? What are you talking about?'

'As for him, he's a fool!'

'For marrying Reenie!' Lily was infuriated. 'That's rich coming from you. After everything that's happened because of *your* girlfriend! And now you've got Vi panting after you, and if you think she'll leave you alone once you're out of here, then *you're* the bloody fool.'

As she turned to go, Bert caught her hand. 'That's not what I meant,' he said. 'But Jim doesn't love her, and she deserves better. As for Vi . . . like I said, she's been good to me.'

Bert seemed genuinely upset, and Lily softened. Considering his injuries and the ordeal he'd suffered, she should be more understanding. 'If you could've seen them last night, you wouldn't be worried. Jim does love her – anyone can see that. So keep your thoughts to yourself. They deserve their happiness.' She kissed his cheek. 'Everything will be all right, you'll see.'

As she walked away, Bert stared sightlessly at the ceiling, feeling helpless. If Jim thought marriage would solve his problems, then he was in for a disappointment. He was sure, too, that they'd not heard the last of Terence's threats. The man was ruthless in his pursuit of money and he couldn't see him giving up the smallest opportunity to wring more from them.

Chapter 54

To Reenie's relief, when the guard at the castle rang through with a message for Marge, she was told that her friend would be out to see her in half an hour.

It was a beautiful early spring day, and for once, the sun was out, so Reenie went to stand at the edge of the cliff beneath the castle. Since the terrible air attack the previous summer, the Eastern Dock was in the process of being strengthened, and the place was a hive of activity, with ant-like figures crawling over the harbour, although the blackened ruins of a ship still listed against the quay, like a giant whale carcass.

From here, too, she could look out over the rooftops of Dover. Even with the sunshine brightening the scene, the town seemed to be drooping under the burden of war, with regular gaps in the once gracious terraces, and blackened buildings where just the year before they'd been white. The sight depressed her, so she turned and squinted over the sea towards the cliffs of France, which looked peaceful and serene in the morning sun.

A hand on her shoulder made her turn, and with a cry of relief, she threw herself into Marge's arms, inhaling her familiar scent of tobacco and Elizabeth Arden Blue Grass.

'I'd have thought you'd be up to your eyes in preparations and makeup,' Marge said, pushing Reenie away from her and smoothing a lock of her curly blonde hair behind her ear. 'But then, who can improve on perfection?'

Reenie laughed and scrubbed at her cheeks. 'How did you know about that?'

'Didn't Jimmy announce it to everyone in the pub last night? Or so I heard.'

Reenie smiled. 'He did.'

They sat down. 'So what's the problem? Are you having doubts?' Marge asked, pressing her shoulder against hers. 'Because I'm told it's totally normal – though of course I wouldn't know.'

Reenie pulled at the grass nervously. 'A lot's happened, Marge. And no, I'm not having doubts exactly . . . It's just, I have a dilemma.'

'"Not exactly" sounds like a yes to me.'

'Maybe just a few. But like you said, it's normal . . . And that's not why I'm here.'

'Why are you having doubts?'

Reenie rubbed the grass between her palms. 'Like I said, a lot's happened over this last week.'

Marge sighed. 'You can say that again. And the only good thing to come out of it is you getting married. I can't believe that football match was only a week ago.'

Both girls were silent for a moment. 'I've found it hard to sleep ever since,' Reenie murmured. 'And every time I hear a plane now . . .' She shuddered.

'Me too. I fall asleep and dream of slipping in Phil's blood.'

'How is he?' Reenie asked gently.

Marge shrugged. 'As you can imagine,' she said. Then she smiled brightly. 'But that's not why you've called me out here on the morning of your wedding. What's up? And I want you to include exactly why you're having doubts. Leave nothing out.' She pulled out a cigarette, lit it, then leant back on her elbows.

Reenie lay down on her side, head propped up on one hand and let everything spill out: Terence's strange threats, Wilf's sudden attentiveness, Mary's words to her that morning. And finally what had happened the night before.

When she'd finished, Marge let out a long whistle. 'Bloody hell. So you're telling me that there's a pile of kids at the café? And Wilf got *you* up in the middle of the night? But why you?'

'Not you too! He just did, all right? But there's something else . . .' She huffed and lay down on her back, shading her eyes with her arm. 'The thing is something else happened last night, and I need your advice.'

'Don't tell me you and Wilf . . .' Marge squinted at her.

Reenie slapped her arm. 'NO!' She sat up and pulled her knees to her chest. 'I need to tell someone or I'll explode. But you can't tell anyone, do you understand? Not a soul.'

Marge held up her hand. 'Before you do, Reenie, you need to consider why it's being kept secret. People's lives depend on us being careful.'

'I saw Colin,' she blurted. 'He's alive and I saw him last night. He's the one who brought the kids! But he told me not to say a word to Jim or his mum. But how can I marry Jim today and keep this a secret?' The words came out in a rush.

Marge's mouth dropped open. 'Colin? You mean Colin Guthrie?'

'Of course Colin Guthrie! And after I got the kids off the lifeboat, he sailed off again, and I want to tell Jim so badly, but I also want to know where he went. Oh, and Marge, poor Mary. She looks awful, and I'm sure it's her bitterness that makes her talk the way she does to Jim. Imagine what it would mean to her if I could give her this news!'

'Christ!' Marge fumbled in her pocket and brought out another cigarette, lighting it with a slightly shaky hand. 'Colin,' she whispered, a smile breaking out on her face. Then she grew serious. 'But you shouldn't have told me. There'll be a very good reason why he's not been able to come back.'

'Jim needs to know,' Reenie said, crestfallen. 'He'll hate me if he finds out I knew and didn't tell him.'

Marge shook her head. 'Even so.'

'Wilf says he saw him the other day. The night before the football match. And ever since then Wilf's been hovering around like a bad smell.'

Marge gave her a sharp look. 'And you think that's because he wanted to let you know? Or does he have an ulterior motive?'

Reenie blushed, remembering how good Wilf's arms had felt around her last night. 'Who cares about him? I'm more concerned with Jim.'

'Hmm.' Marge blew out a few smoke rings. 'I can see why you're torn. But you should have kept your mouth shut, Reens. If Colin is bringing kids over from France, the fewer people who know the better.'

'Did you know?' Reenie asked.

'Of course not! I'm not trusted with anything. I'm just the lackey who shifts the boats on the table. What they're doing and why is hidden as much from me as it is from you.'

'You must know something about the port at Sandwich?'

'There is no port at Sandwich,' Marge snapped back.

'There must be! Wilf mentioned that's where they were meant to be going.'

Marge sighed. 'Sandwich isn't even on the sea anymore. And what would you do if you knew where he'd gone? You can't just swan over to a military port and pop in for a visit. You've got no authority, neither does Jim.'

'But you might . . .' Reenie said.

'I'm just a Wren. The lowest of the low.'

'Come on. There must be somewhere to land a boat over there.'

Marge stared into the distance, picturing the map of the south coast that she'd had to memorise. 'There's Richborough,' she said thoughtfully. 'There were Jewish refugees being housed there before the war, so maybe they take the kids there. But I didn't think it was being used as a port anymore because the river silted up after the last war. They could have cleared it in secret, I suppose.'

'That must be it!' Reenie exclaimed. 'Maybe I could go there and—'

'No, Reenie! Look, I understand why you want to tell Jim, but you need to think about Colin. What he's doing sounds dangerous, so you need to put it to the back of your mind and focus on your wedding. Stop worrying about what everyone else does and says – Jim loves you, you love him. Is there any more you need to get married?'

'I need to be going to him with a clear conscience,' Reenie said.

Marge put her arm around her shoulders. 'Jim wouldn't want you to risk Colin's life. Look what it did to him when he thought he was dead. So you can go into this with a completely clear conscience, don't you see?'

At Reenie's tentative nod, Marge smiled.

'Just because you know something, doesn't mean it's right to tell. Especially when we're at war.'

Reenie sighed and leant her head against her friend's shoulder. 'I wish I was more like you. You always seem to know the best thing to do.'

'Believe me, I don't.' Marge hesitated a moment. 'Phil asked me to marry him,' she said quietly.

Reenie sat up and stared at her. 'But that's good, isn't it? If he loves you and you love him . . . Someone very wise said that's all you need to get married.'

Marge stared back at her solemnly.

'But you don't love him, do you?' Reenie asked.

'I do love him. But not in the way you love Jim or Marianne loves Alfie. But he loves me. And he needs me right now. How can I say no?'

Reenie pulled her into a hug. 'That sounds like a terrible reason to get married. And if you married him, you'd probably leave Dover. I once thought that you, me, Daisy and Marianne would be friends forever. Raise our children here, have picnics on the beach, always be there for each other. But things have changed so much. Marianne doesn't want me to marry Jim, and it's caused a rift. And you could get sent off God knows where at a moment's notice . . . Or marry Phil and go and be a vicar's wife in some country parish. Sometimes it feels like our group died with Daisy.'

'Oh, love, it'll never die. As for Marianne, I can't believe she doesn't love the thought of having you as a sister-in-law.'

'Well, it seems she doesn't. It's why we decided not to ask her to be a witness. Jim's as aware of it as I am.'

'Then it's just as well I'll be there, isn't it?' Marge said.

Reenie squealed. 'Really!? I didn't even ask cos I thought it'd be too short notice.'

'It was meant to be a surprise. A few days ago, Jim came to ask Rodney to be a witness at the wedding. And he asked Rod to ask me to be the other one. And do you know why? Because he loves you, and as you'd decided not to tell your families, he wanted you to have someone special with you on the day.'

Reenie brightened. 'Did he? Although everyone knows now, they'll all be there . . . Still, it was nice of him to think of me.'

'So, how do you feel now? Are you ready to put your doubts aside and marry the man? Or do you want me to deliver a "Dear John" letter to the town hall?'

Reenie smiled slightly. 'I'd never ask you to do that. But it's funny, I thought that Jim asking me to marry him would make me the happiest I've ever been, but this last week has left me feeling . . . unsettled, I suppose. But I do love him, so Marianne and Wilf can go hang.'

Marge raised her eyebrows. 'You think Wilf's hanging around you cos he doesn't want you to marry Jim?'

Reenie pulled at a lump of grass, avoiding her gaze. 'He's not exactly the sort to tell you what he's thinking. But he's implied he thinks I'm making a mistake.'

Marge regarded her reflectively. 'Hmm. Sounds like he's jealous and wants you for himself.'

'It wouldn't matter if he did! Cos I don't want him – I want Jimmy,' Reenie replied emphatically.

Marge grinned. 'All right, then. Now you've sorted things in your mind, you need to get back. Because there's only four hours until kick-off. And I know I said you couldn't improve on perfection, but even the Mona Lisa could do with some lippy and a dash of mascara.'

Reenie giggled. 'At least the Mona Lisa was never forced to wear her aunt's old wedding dress!'

Marge laughed. 'Think of it as your something old! Now get out of here and make yourself even more beautiful.'

Reenie leant forward and squeezed Marge to her. 'Thank you for talking some sense into me. You're completely right about not telling Jim. It's going to be difficult, but I know he'll understand my reasons when he does find out.'

Chapter 55

Aunt Ethel pounced on Reenie the minute she walked into the shop.

'Where've you been?' she exclaimed. 'Oh, never mind. Get upstairs now.'

Reenie looked at her watch. 'We've got hours,' she said. 'And have you seen the queue outside?'

'Your uncle can manage, can't you, Brian?' Ethel said airily.

'Actually, love, I can't,' he complained. 'What with you both gone all morning, the queue's practically stretchin' all the way to the bloody station, and I've only got one pair of hands.'

'Stop moaning. You don't mind if things take a bit longer, do you?' she asked a woman standing by the doorway.

'As it happens, I do. I swear the service is gettin' worse in here. And Lou Carter says there's some French kids over at the café. I mean, we don't have enough to feed ourselves, let alone a load of strangers.'

'Might have known you'd say that. Charity never were your strong point, were it, Mrs Hendricks?'

'I'd have a sight more charity if I knew the food was goin' to our own kids. How do we know they are who they say they are?'

'Always a little ray of sunshine, ain't ya,' Ethel scorned. 'Well, when your house gets shot to pieces and you haven't got a crust to your name or anywhere to lay your stupid head, you better hope the folk you meet ain't like you.'

The woman spluttered. 'That's different.'

'Cos you're so special, you mean?' Ethel raked her eyes over her. 'But how could anyone tell?' she sneered. Then she grabbed Reenie's arm. 'Come on, Reens. Brian, just for today, I promise I'll make it up to you.' She blew him a kiss, and hustled Reenie out to the back of the shop.

Upstairs, Reenie's heart sank as she took in her aunt's old wedding dress hanging on the wardrobe. It had been packed in mothballs in a box under the bed, and when her aunt shook it out, Reenie wrinkled her nose. 'Aunt Ethel, I really love you for wanting to help, but it smells.'

Her aunt tutted and took a perfume bottle from the table. 'Nothing that a touch of this won't sort,' she said. 'Gladys gave it to me some time back, but I never had a reason to wear it.'

She lay the dress on the bed and sprayed the perfume over it.

Reenie waved her hand in front of her nose, choking slightly at the strong smell of rose water. 'It'll just make it worse!'

'So what would you suggest?' her aunt asked impatiently, squeezing the bulb and releasing another rose-scented cloud over the dress.

'I can just wear my suit,' she said.

'Over my dead body!' Ethel exclaimed. 'You and me are the same sort of size. I reckon just a bit of hem being taken up should do it . . .Though maybe I were slimmer on my weddin' day,' she said consideringly, eyeing Reenie from head to toe.

Reenie folded her arms across her chest and scowled. After her conversation with Marge, she'd started to feel excited about the day, but the thought of wearing this dress, with its high neck, slim satin skirts and long lace sleeves was bringing her mood down again. She'd never been a satin and lace kind of girl.

Ethel picked up the dress and gave it another shake. 'There, you see. Only the faintest smell of mothballs. Now, take off your clothes and let's see how it fits.'

Realising this was an argument she wouldn't win, Reenie reluctantly undressed and allowed her aunt to lower the dress over her head. But as she fastened the buttons that ran up the back, her eyes began to water, her nose twitched and she sneezed.

'Stand still!' Ethel exclaimed.

'I can hardly breathe!' Reenie grunted as Ethel pulled the dress around her chest.

'All we need to do,' Ethel muttered behind her, 'is move a few of the buttons. Won't take me a tick.' She went to the sitting room to grab her sewing basket.

'While I do this, you go have a wash. You're absolutely filthy! Wash your hair as well.'

Muttering under her breath, Reenie went to do as she was told. And to think, she could have gone and got married in her old suit if they'd just kept their mouths shut.

∽

'Oh, love, you look a picture,' Aunt Ethel breathed, staring enraptured at Reenie a few hours later.

Reenie chewed on her lip, wishing she could see what her aunt saw. But the high lace collar looked like it was strangling her, while the bodice flattened her breasts, and the cut of the dress did nothing to hide the curve of her belly – something she was always at pains to hide, thanks to June's taunts. It was a beautiful dress, but she looked ridiculous – and she smelt even worse. Reenie put a finger under the collar and tried to loosen it.

Oblivious, Aunt Ethel pressed her down on to the stool in front of the dressing table and gathered up her curly blonde hair, piling it on top of her head and fastening it with pins before pulling out a few tendrils to frame her face.

'Ooh, Jimmy's a lucky man. You should wear dresses more often, love. And put your hair up like this. It's so pretty, it seems a shame to hide it under scarves all the time.'

'Not very practical for stacking shelves or weeding,' Reenie replied.

Aunt Ethel tutted. 'Stuff and nonsense.' She rested her chin on the top of Reenie's head and regarded her in the mirror. 'You're a beautiful girl, my Reenie, and don't let no one tell you different. And you've never looked lovelier than you do today. Almost as good as I did on my wedding day.'

Reenie smiled fondly. If she and Jim could have a marriage half as good as her aunt and uncle, then she'd be lucky. 'How did you feel on your wedding day?' Reenie asked.

'Like I was about to be sick. But after . . . Well, then I was the happiest woman in the world. Just like you will be.'

'I'm scared,' she whispered.

Aunt Ethel knelt in front of her, knees cracking, and took her hands. 'Ain't nothin' strange about that, love. Are you having second thoughts?'

Reenie shook her head. 'It's just . . .' She took a deep breath. 'Do you tell Uncle Brian everything?'

Ethel laughed. 'God bless you, no! Every woman needs to keep a little mystery about them.'

'But what if it's not about having mystery? What if it's something you think he needs to know? Something that would make him happy.' No matter what Marge had said, she still couldn't stop thinking about that.

'Then you have to consider very carefully why you wouldn't want to make your new husband happy,' Ethel said softly, staring meaningfully into Reenie's eyes in the mirror.

Chapter 56

Marge stared at herself critically in the mirror. She was wearing her dress uniform with the double-breasted jacket and skirt, but she still looked like she was going to work. To compensate she'd used plenty of rouge, lipstick and mascara, and had spent ages twisting her hair into a victory roll. Carefully, she placed her round cap on the top, tilting it to the side and pinning it in place.

'What do you think?' she asked Jeanie, who was lying on her bed watching her.

'Beautiful as always. Rodney won't be able to keep his hands off.'

'This isn't for Rodney,' Marge snapped, slinging her bag over her shoulder and giving her hair one last pat.

'Who's it for then?'

'Me,' she said. 'It's always for me. I don't exist to please men, you know.'

Jeanie grinned and blew her a kiss. 'No, they exist to please *you*,' she said. 'So go and get pleased – just so long as it's not something I wouldn't do.'

'Still plenty of scope then.' Marge winked as she left the dormitory.

Outside, she lit a cigarette and considered how best to approach Edie. Having promised Rodney she'd get her to at least come to the wedding, she'd figured the best way to do it was to swoop in, get her changed out of her infernal greasy overalls and swoop out again before she had a chance to think about it. Yes, a lightning raid was the best way.

Marge felt almost cheerful as she sauntered down towards the garage in the sunshine. And that was progress for her. The horrors of the shooting and Phil's proposal were constantly on her mind. She'd been down to see him once more since the first disastrous visit and had been relieved when he'd not referred to marriage again. In fact, though he was clearly tired and in pain, he'd been almost his usual cheerful affectionate self. She'd left feeling hopeful that he'd let the proposal drop. But then Lily had caught her on the way out and told her she was worried about Phil's state of mind; he wasn't eating, and he barely spoke. The news had plunged Marge back into a morass of self-recrimination, and she knew that she needed to talk to him soon. She was tempted to say yes, just to ease the crushing guilt that was hanging over her. But would that make things any better? She'd be a terrible vicar's wife, and though he thought he wanted her now, she had no doubt that in the future he'd come to regret marrying a woman like her.

Pushing these dismal thoughts aside, she walked across the forecourt, and after a quick conversation with Mr P, she found Edie kneeling beside a truck tightening the nuts on a wheel.

'Up you get. You're coming with me.'

Edie glanced up at her, then let out a wolf whistle. 'You getting married?' she asked.

'It's Jim and Reenie's wedding today,' she stated. 'And you're coming with me.'

Edie's eyes widened. 'What? Since when?'

'Since he asked her. And I think it would make his day to have you there.'

'Absolutely not! Even if I wanted to, there's too much to do here.'

Marge grasped her arm. 'All cleared with Mr P.'

She dragged a protesting Edie into the office and up the stairs. 'Marge, please! I can't go. Mum'll be there, and if we get into a fight, it'll ruin their day,' Edie said.

'Then you'll just have to stay away from her and keep your trap shut. Come on, don't tell me you don't want to see your brother get married?' She smiled winningly and dug in her pocket, bringing out a lipstick. 'And look, I even brought my favourite lipstick for you to borrow.'

When Edie still looked mutinous, Marge changed tack. 'Look, love, you might be in a fight with your mum, but you can't cut yourself off from your brothers and sisters. They miss you and I know you miss them.'

Edie huffed and nodded resignedly. 'But if Mum gets within ten feet of me, I'm leaving.'

'That's my girl. Now go wash your face and I'll sort you something to wear.'

'You won't have much luck. Nothing fits,' she said, patting her stomach.

'Go!' Marge said, pushing her towards the bathroom.

Marge looked through Edie's uninspiring selection of clothes. There was the beautiful green dress with the peplum skirt that she'd worn to so many dances, but it was far too figure hugging and she doubted it would do up now. In the end she settled on an A-line navy-blue skirt and an emerald-green jersey, which at least would cover the waistband.

Edie came back in and looked at the clothes in disgust. 'It won't do up, you know.'

'Which is why your clever Auntie Marge chose this jumper. And if you put this around your neck' – she held out a pink silk scarf printed with white roses – 'no one will even look at your stomach. So chop-chop.'

∽

Despite herself, as they set off arm in arm down the hill, Edie was looking forward to the outing. She'd barely left the garage for months for fear of running into her mother, and though she loved Mr P, he was no substitute for her friends or sisters. Marge was the only person she saw regularly now, and it was making her feel isolated.

Passing Jasper's forge on Castle Street, Edie looked into the window wistfully. 'Is Jasper coming too?' she asked hopefully.

She got her answer when Jasper rushed out and threw his arms around her. 'Edie! I didn't think you'd come.'

Stepping back, he observed her from head to toe. 'Look at you! You're bloomin', love. Absolutely bloomin'. Does this mean you're ready to speak to your mum again?'

'No, it doesn't. You need to keep her away from me, all right? I'm here for Jim and Reenie, that's all.'

Jasper's face fell. 'But you'll be comin' to the Oak after? Mavis said Rodney's planned a little party for them. But it's a surprise for Jim and Reenie, so not a word.'

Edie looked at Marge accusingly. 'You never mentioned a party. Sorry, Jasper, I'm just gonna watch the ceremony, give my brother and sister-in-law a kiss and get out.'

'Please, love,' Jasper said desperately. 'Come to the party; I promise I'll keep your mum away. She won't breathe a word to you.'

'Are you joking? You might be able to keep her quiet at the wedding, but soon as we set foot in the Oak, she'll come at me, jaws flapping, going on and on: "Forgive me, Edie. I love you, Edie. It weren't my fault, Edie!" And I don't. Want. To. Hear. It! Do you understand?!'

'But, love, if you only knew how sad she is.'

Edie threw up her arms. 'How sad *she* is?! You think I'm not? Can no one understand that this is hurting me too . . . Why is everyone on her side? You have no idea what she did!'

'Then tell us, love,' Jasper pleaded. 'Just tell us and maybe we can find a way for you to forgive her.'

Edie's fists clenched. 'Ask her yourself.'

'Don't you think I have. But she won't tell me anything.'

'Then don't you think the question you should be asking is *why*? Look, this was a really bad idea. I'm sorry, I think it's best I don't go at all. Give Jim and Reenie my love. Tell them . . . tell them I hope they'll be very happy.' With tears in her eyes, Edie turned and walked back up the hill.

Marge let out a low whistle. 'Well, I think that's clear enough, don't you? Why didn't you keep your mouth shut? She'd have come if you hadn't blathered on about talking to Nellie.'

Jasper sighed. 'I just want them to make up. That poor girl is in torment, and I'd dearly love to know what's caused it. Cos her mum's in no better state. If anythin' she's worse, and I tell you, Marge, I'm at me wits' end trying to figure it out.'

Marge took Jasper's arm. 'I think you should let them sort it out on their own. Whatever it is, it's something big. And like Edie said, if Mrs C won't tell you, then it might be something you'd rather not know. So stop worrying about it and let's just go and have a nice time.'

'But what could be so bad, she wouldn't want me to know?' he queried, half to himself.

'Obviously something that would make you see her in a different light. Maybe even disapprove of. In which case, I don't blame her.'

Jasper suddenly felt a deep sense of foreboding. He'd honestly believed that since his coma he and Nellie had reached a new level of understanding, especially now Lily knew he was her father. What else could she possibly be hiding from him?

Chapter 57

Reenie stepped out of the shop, her eyes lowered self-consciously. The narrow skirts of her dress restricted her normal stride and her aunt's wedding shoes were too tight, so she felt awkward and embarrassed. All this fuss for a simple registry office wedding seemed ridiculous. But it was too late now . . .

'Reenie!' Cissy, wearing a smart green tweed suit that set off her orange hair beautifully, raced across the square, waving a small bunch of daffodils and crocuses, tied with a bright blue ribbon. 'You can't get married without some flowers, so I picked these.' She thrust them into her hands then stood back to examine her. 'Now that's a dress! They don't make 'em like that anymore. Course, there ain't the material now, but even if there were, they'd be stuffin' the shoulders with pads and choppin' off the skirt. But you look like a bride from the old days. Absolutely beautiful.' She held her hands under her chin and sighed with rapture.

Reenie smiled, wishing she could have chopped off the hem and stuffed the shoulders. Still, if she held the flowers in front of her, they'd at least hide her stomach.

'Are we ready for the off then? The others'll meet us there. But I do love a procession, don't you, love?' Cissy said, taking Ethel's other arm.

As they passed the fish shop, Reenie noticed Wilf standing in the doorway. For a moment their eyes met, but then with a small toss of her head she averted her gaze, not wanting any reminders of the night before and the dilemma she was facing.

Outside Maison Dieu House, Jimmy was waiting at the bottom of the steps, Rodney by his side. Reenie's breath caught as she took him in; he was wearing his khaki dress uniform, his cap clutched under his arm, and with the sun bringing out copper highlights in his dark hair and his blue eyes sparkling, Reenie felt a swell of pride that this beautiful man wanted to marry her.

Jim came to stand in front of her. 'You look beautiful,' he said softly, taking her in. 'Thank you for saying yes, Reens. You'll never know what this means to me.'

'Thank *you*, Jim,' she responded, staring dreamily into his eyes, all the worry of the morning falling away. 'But I just want to say sorry for the smell of the dress. It's as old as it looks.'

Jim leant forward and sniffed her shoulder, then burst into laughter. 'From now on roses and mothballs will be my favourite scent.'

Marge caught her eye and winked. 'Gorgeous. And good job on the lippy.'

Buoyed by the approval, Reenie raised her head and looked around the assembled group. Bigger than she had anticipated, but still small enough to contain only her favourite people. Even Marianne was there, Alfie by her side. Their eyes met and Marianne smiled at her. 'You really do look lovely,' she said. 'I'm so happy for you both.'

Reenie felt her heart lift with relief. 'Really?'

Marianne stepped forward and folded her into a hug. She sniffed and stepped back and grimaced. 'Just don't let Mum get a sniff of that dress,' she laughed. 'It stinks of rose water, and she's got a thing about the stuff.'

Before she could ask why, Jim took her hand, squeezing it slightly. 'Ready?'

She smiled and nodded, and with a burgeoning feeling of joy and hope in her heart they went in.

The ceremony was short and simple, and as they made their way outside, they were met with a shower of rose petals as they ran laughing down the concrete steps. At the bottom, Jim grabbed her and kissed her deeply. 'Happy, Mrs Castle?' he asked, rubbing his nose against hers.

'Oh yes, Mr Castle. Very happy.'

'Drinks for everyone at the Oak!' Rodney called.

As the procession made its way down Biggin Street, Jim paused briefly, his attention fixed across the street.

Glancing over, Reenie frowned. Terence stared back, a cigarette dangling from his lips. Then he swept his hat off and bowed mockingly.

'Ignore him, Jim.' Reenie tugged on his arm.

Coming to himself, Jim smiled down at her distractedly, but his cheeks were pale and the sparkle had gone from his eyes.

Chapter 58

Edie's anger propelled her to the bottom of Harold Passage where she stopped and turned to look down Castle Street, the ruins of St James's Church on her left, the undamaged White Horse pub on the right. Not for the first time, the juxtaposition of these two buildings made her think about fate and luck – how one of these buildings had been continually hit by the storms of war, while the other remained standing, whole and almost undamaged. It seemed like a reflection of her own life. While she was exiled at the garage, her mother was still down there, living life as she always had, surrounded by her family and the community she'd grown up in. By contrast, she was living a half-life – pregnant with a child she didn't want, her new husband away, and no family or friends to help her through. She had Marge and Mr P, of course, but she'd grown up in a household bustling with noise, her brothers and sisters close by, always someone to talk to.

The injustice of it all hit her then. Why should she be the one to suffer for her mother's sins? Why should *she* be the one to walk away from everyone she held dear? It wasn't fair. Tears gathered in her eyes and she blinked them away impatiently. Maybe it was time to find her way back to the family she loved. She could tell them all what their mother had done and maybe their reaction would help her decide whether she was overreacting or not. Her mother insisted she hadn't meant to harm her father, and in her heart of hearts she wanted to believe her. But now she'd made this stand, she was finding it increasingly difficult to back down. Perhaps it was time to face it all, tell everyone that her mother had used her to feed opium to her father, until it drove him so mad, he'd killed himself.

Just the thought made her feel sick, but she was tired of feeling so angry and sad all the time. Tired of being asked what her mother had done. But, most of all, she wanted her family back.

With determined steps, she made her way back down the road. Her brother's wedding party wasn't the place to talk about it, but she would wait at the café for them all to come back. Then maybe she'd be able to find a way to forgive her mother – and find peace for herself.

Turning into Church Street, she had just put her hand on the latch of the back gate, when out of the corner of her eye, she noticed something land on the roof of the old privy behind the fence, and suddenly flames leapt up into the sky.

Gasping with shock, Edie pushed open the gate. Suddenly a figure rushed out and shoved her hard in the chest. She stumbled back in surprise, twisting her ankle on the pavement and going down with a thump, her head slamming into the concrete. She managed to catch a glimpse of a figure hurrying away from her, but then her eyes closed and everything went dark.

Chapter 59

When the wedding party reached the Oak, Mavis ushered them through the quiet pub and downstairs where plates of sandwiches, sausage rolls and a ham salad were laid out. And, in pride of place, a small, iced fruitcake on a high stand.

'How did you get all this at such short notice?' Reenie gasped, but her question was drowned out by a trumpet playing 'The Wedding March', and she whirled round to see Alfie standing on the small stage at the back.

Marge grinned. 'Rodney organised the whole thing.'

Reenie looked over at Jim's brother, who winked at her, but before she could thank him, Marianne enveloped her in a hug. 'I'm so happy we're sisters now,' she murmured.

Marge put her arms round both of them. 'That's more like it, you two,' she said. 'Can we make a pact here and now that we three will never ever fall out?'

'We will never ever fall out,' the other two intoned happily, and they stood swaying in each other's arms until Alfie began to play, 'It Had to Be You'.

'Excuse me, ladies, it's time I danced with my beautiful bride.' Jim's voice broke the spell, and he held his hand out to Reenie, who grasped it eagerly.

Everybody stood to the side watching Jim and Reenie dance – although in truth, they barely moved. Instead, they stood with their arms around each other, smiling into each other's eyes.

Marge couldn't help feeling a pang of jealousy. She'd never be able to smile at Phil like that. She glanced at Rodney, who'd come to stand beside her. Sensing her gaze, he looked back at her. 'Shall we?' he asked, offering his arm.

'This was good of you,' Marge said as they circled the floor. 'I'm only sorry I couldn't persuade Edie to come. I got her as far as Jasper's forge, but she suddenly changed her mind.'

Rodney shrugged. 'You tried, that's the main thing. But let's not talk about it. Today is going to be a peaceful, drama-free day.'

Marge put a finger to his lips. 'Shhh. You're tempting fate!'

For just a moment, Rodney's lips lingered on her finger, before he hastily moved his head back.

Marge looked away guiltily and put her hand back on his shoulder.

'How's Phil?' he asked after an awkward pause.

She frowned. 'How do you think?' She pushed him away slightly. 'I . . . er, think I'll get a drink.'

Rodney followed her and caught her arm. 'Marge, listen . . . I've been thinking a lot about what you said a few months back. About how I only ever want to speak to you when I need help. And . . .' He rubbed at his hair nervously.

Marge waited with bated breath.

'You and me, well, we've known each other so long, I never stopped to think that you might need more from me.' He swallowed. 'I want you to know I'm sorry.' He looked deep into her eyes, and Marge stared back, hypnotised, the breath catching in the back of her throat.

'Anyway, the thing is . . .' Rodney hesitated. 'I hope you'll be very happy.'

Marge frowned. 'What are you talking about?'

'I went to see Phil . . . Well, no, I didn't go to see *him*, I went to see Bert. But he's in the same ward, so I stopped by and he explained that you and he . . .' He cleared his throat. 'He told me that you and he were getting married. And I just want to say that I'm happy for you.'

'What?' she said, fury building inside her.

'I realise that you and me . . . we've been up and down in the past. But I wanted you to know—'

'We're not getting married!' Marge burst out. 'He asked, but I haven't accepted. He *lied*!'

Rodney went still. 'Oh.'

There was a long silence as each stared out at the dancers.

'But will you?' he asked eventually.

'I don't know, Rod. Will I?' She glanced up at him.

Rodney shook his head. 'I'm hardly in a position to answer that, am I?'

Marge searched his face, looking for a sign that he was being disingenuous, but his expression was impossible to read. 'Aren't you?' she asked softly.

Rodney sighed. 'What do you want me to say? Do you want me to say don't marry him? If you do, then fine, I'll say it. Don't marry him.'

Marge's cheeks burned with anger. It's what she'd been waiting to hear from him, but the way he said it – flippantly, almost jokingly – meant she had no idea whether he meant it. 'Don't joke with me, Rod.'

'I'm not joking,' he responded. 'It's just a logical response to your reluctance to accept his proposal. You're not sure – ergo, don't do it until you are.'

'God, you're a cold bastard,' Marge snapped.

Rod let out a sarcastic laugh. 'My life would be a lot easier if I was. But marriage proposals are between two people. So if you have a decision to make, you need to make it for yourself alone. I can't help you make it.'

Marge watched as Rodney went to join Marianne by the food table. Only a few steps, she thought sadly, but it felt like he had

305

travelled a world away from her. What had she expected? That Rodney would beg her not to do it? What an irony that the one time Rodney wasn't trying to tell her what to do, she desperately wished he would. But wasn't that the story of their lives? They could never agree on anything, and she was a fool to think they ever would.

Alfie had started to play 'You Made Me Love You', and Marge closed her eyes and sighed. She really hadn't wanted to fall in love with him, but she had. Which meant there was only one answer she could give Phil. Then she thought again about what Lily had told her and realised that nothing was ever that simple.

∽

'It's true. You made me love you . . .' Jim whispered into Reenie's ear.

Reenie looked up, a teasing glint in her eye. 'You didn't want to do it?'

Jim chuckled. 'I just didn't expect it. It was you who did it. With your warmth and patience. I know I haven't always been the easiest person to love.'

'You've always been easy to love, Jim. I know how hard it was for you, though. After Colin . . .'

He pulled her closer and rested his cheek on her hair, his arms tightening around her. 'Let's not talk about that today.'

'You still miss him, though,' she said.

He nodded. 'I always will. But I can't live in the past. There's only today and the promise of tomorrow.'

'He's never been declared dead, though, has he? There's still hope,' she urged, although she knew she should drop the subject. But she just couldn't stop thinking about him. It was so unfair; he should be here with the people who loved him, instead of being forced to live like a ghost. And no matter how hard she tried, she couldn't get his thin face out of her mind. He'd looked broken by his experiences, and she desperately wanted to find a way to help him heal, just as she'd helped Jim.

'There's no hope. And if I kept clinging to the possibility, it would only hurt me more in the end.'

'But what if—'

Jim held a finger to her lips. 'Hush. This is our day, Reenie, the beginning of our future. So let's only talk of happy things.'

Reenie rested her head on his shoulder, but her body was tense.

'Is something wrong?' He tipped her head back to look into her eyes. 'Are you having second thoughts?'

'God no!' She looped her arms around his neck. 'Never that, Jim.' She pressed her lips to his and he smiled against them.

'Thank God! I was worried at one stage that Terence might have made you change your mind.'

'Who listens to him?' Reenie said lightly, although she wished he hadn't mentioned that man; she didn't want to think about the doubts he'd raised in her mind right now.

Jim searched her face. 'You did,' he said quietly. 'And I still feel there's something you're holding back. What is it, Reens? If something's bothering you, you need to tell me.'

Reenie shook her head and pushed her face into the crook of his neck, wondering what to do. Marge and Aunt Ethel's contrasting advice was whirling round and round her mind – in particular what her aunt had said: 'You have to consider very carefully why you wouldn't want to make your new husband happy.'

And she wanted to make Jimmy happy more than anything else in her life. She looked up at him. 'There is something I need to tell you . . . But it's got nothing to do with going off you,' she added hastily when she saw his anxious expression.

'What is it?'

Reenie took a deep breath. 'Last night, when—'

'*Au secours! Maintenant! Vite! Il y a un feu!*' The sudden shouts brought the music to an abrupt stop as everybody turned to stare at the young boy wearing ragged trousers and an oversized shirt standing halfway down the stairs.

'*Il y a un feu!*' he said again.

Reenie started forward. 'Louis? What's happened? Can you tell us in English.'

'*Feu* means fire,' Jim said. 'As anyone who was at Dunkirk can tell you.'

Nellie dropped the plate she was holding. 'Is it at the café?'

'*Oui. Vite.*'

'Jasper!' He was by her side in an instant, and before Reenie knew it, the room had emptied, leaving her and Jim staring at each other in bemusement.

'Christ! I should go—' he muttered, pulling his hands from hers and striding towards the stairs.

'Jim, no!' Reenie called after him. 'I have to tell you—'

'Later, Reens!' he called impatiently. 'Come with me.'

'No! I *have* to tell you! *Please*, Jim. Please!'

Jim looked back at her. 'For God's sake, Reenie! My mother's café is on fire. What could be more important than going to help with that?'

Reenie gestured around her. 'There are plenty of people helping. This is more important, *I swear*!'

Reluctantly, he allowed her to pull him to one of the tables where Mavis had set out a bottle of wine. It was meant to be for the toast, but she doubted they'd get one now. With a trembling hand, she poured two glasses and took a huge gulp, grimacing as the acid burned down her throat. Opposite her, Jim ignored his glass. 'Spit it out, Reens! I really need to go!'

'I wanted to tell you sooner, but there hasn't been time. And also, I was told not to.'

'Tell me what? And who told you not to tell me?'

Reenie reached across and picked up his hand, fiddling with his fingers. 'It's meant to be a secret. But how can I not tell my husband?'

Jimmy sighed impatiently as Reenie stroked his hand. 'It was last night . . .' she said finally. 'When Wilf asked me to help get the kids from the lifeboat.'

Jim's brow lowered. 'I still don't get why he came to you! He always seems to be hanging around at the moment. Is there something going on I should know about?' He half rose.

'No! Don't be stupid, Jim! No . . . It was the man who brought them over here,' she said quietly. 'He told me not to say anything. But . . . we're married now. Husbands and wives shouldn't have secrets.' She looked up at him, holding his hands tighter. 'It was Colin.' She smiled tremulously. 'He's alive.'

Jim stared at her for a moment, his cheeks suddenly pale and his eyes huge. Slowly, he pulled his hands away. 'C-c-colin!' he whispered. 'B-b-but how? When? I saw him, Reens! I *saw* him being put in an ambulance and not long after it was blown up! He couldn't have survived. He just *couldn't*!'

Instead of the joy she had anticipated, Jim looked utterly devastated.

She jumped up and took his shoulders. 'You must know I would never lie about this.'

Jimmy put his face in his hands, shaking his head. 'It can't be true . . . It just can't be true.'

'But it is!' Reenie cried. 'Aren't you happy?'

He looked up at her then, and she was shocked at the bleakness in his eyes. 'Does he know?' he rasped. 'About us getting married?'

Reenie nodded uncertainly.

'Oh God,' Jim muttered. 'Oh God, oh God, oh God!' With a sudden burst of energy, Jim leapt to his feet. 'Where is he now?' he thundered. 'Where the hell is he?!'

'I-I-I don't know. He stayed on the boat and Wilf took him s-s-somewhere. S-s-Sandwich, I think.' Reenie tried to remember the name of the port Marge had mentioned, but she was too shocked by Jim's reaction to bring it to mind. She felt the wine rise up her throat and fought the desire to be sick. Jim's sudden change from loving groom to this wild-eyed man frightened and bewildered her. This was meant to be the best news he could have had, but instead he was behaving as if it was the end of the world.

'Fucking Wilf!' His hand smashed on the table, making her jump. 'What the fuck is his game!' With that, he stormed up the stairs, leaving Reenie staring after him in confusion, feeling once again the bitter sting of rejection, but this time it was much, much worse – because this time, he had looked at her as though he hated her.

She slumped down onto the chair. Marge had been right! She should never have told him. Picking up her glass, she drained it, staring around at the deserted room through tear-blurred eyes. She shouldn't be surprised that once again Jim was walking away from her. Isn't it what he'd been doing for months? And every single time it had happened, it was because of Colin . . .

She picked up Jim's glass, emptying it in a few gulps before sloshing more wine into it. She'd never been truly drunk before. But now seemed as good a time as any to try it.

Chapter 60

As she approached the market square, Nellie's eyes were focused on the café. The front remained unchanged, the damn plastic window dull, even with the sun shining on it. But what made the breath catch in her throat was the smoke billowing from behind the gabled roof and blowing across the market square.

She stumbled to a halt, unable to catch a breath, as panic swept through her. After the years and years of struggle through the Great War and beyond, the café had been her anchor. She'd come here as a bride of eighteen, but her love for the place ran as deep and as true as if she'd been born there. It was hers! It represented everything that was important to her: family, security, hope for the future – and that still held true, despite the recent tragedy. Piece by piece the town was falling down around their ears, but the café had stood steadfast through it all, sheltering all who came within its walls. If it fell, Nellie couldn't help feeling that the town would fall too. It was her talisman and her touchstone. Without it, who was she?

How had this happened? It was nothing new to see a home destroyed, a future changed forever. Up and down the country, this was people's new reality, the burden of dread and fear they all carried. But there were no bombs or shells today, and she had followed her usual careful safety checks before she left. Unless one of the French kids had done something? But they'd seemed so grateful and sweet . . . *What if it wasn't a person?* The thought made her shiver. But surely a vengeful spirit couldn't cause such destruction?

Cissy caught up with her and took her arm. 'Nellie, come on, love. Whatever it is, we'll manage together, all right?'

She nodded, but she didn't really hear her. Because suddenly all she could hear was Mrs Bancroft's voice: *Vengeance*.

Jasper came up to her then and put his arm around her shoulder. 'It's gonna be all right, Nellie,' he said gently. 'The fire brigade came quickly, and they've got it under control.'

Nellie looked up into his face. His eyes were watery and blood-shot from the smoke, but his expression was steady, reassuring. Unlike Cissy, Jasper understood all too well what this place meant to her. He'd been with her through thick and thin, and if he said everything was going to be all right, then she trusted that he was telling the truth.

'The thing is . . .' he said carefully, as he led her round to the back of the café. 'They found Edie out cold outside the gate. And what she's sayin' makes no sense.'

Nellie gasped. 'Edie?' she whispered. 'Is she all right? Where is she?' She started to run now. On Church Street, water was arch-ing towards the fence from the fire hoses, where a few stubborn flames still flickered, bright orange against the blackened wood, the strong wind slanting them towards the café. She spotted Edie huddled with Marge on the steps of the umbrella factory. Her face was white as paper and a large bruise had formed on her temple. Nellie hurried towards her.

'Oh love? What happened?'

Edie shook her head slightly. 'I don't remember,' she whispered. 'I opened the gate and this . . . *figure* rushed at me and knocked me over. I saw them running away from me, but I couldn't say who . . .' She frowned and closed her eyes, leaning her head against Marge's shoulder.

'You just rest now, Edie.' Jasper knelt down beside Nellie. 'Soon as it's safe to go in, you go lie down and we'll talk more later.' He helped Nellie to her feet.

'But—'

'Leave her for now. Let Marge look after her.'

Nellie sighed and nodded. This was the first time Edie had spoken to her without anger in weeks, but she'd be stupid if she thought things had changed between them. Turning away, she went to stand beside a grim-faced Rodney, who stood with his arms folded across his chest as he watched the firemen. Beside him, Marianne was leaning heavily into Alfie's side, while Donny stood quietly, his face pale with shock.

Rodney put his arm around her and squeezed her reassuringly. 'Thank God those kids were here,' he murmured. 'They were the ones who found Edie as well.'

'So you don't think they might have done this? Maybe it was an accident?'

Rodney shook his head. 'I don't think so.'

Nellie spotted Louis and Elodie, standing by themselves, faces streaked with soot. Walking over, she pulled them both into a tight embrace, reflecting on how a series of unrelated events could slot together like this. From the moment their boat had left France, to their rescue, to the air raid that had forced them to shelter in her basement and left them in the house when whoever had done this thought it was empty ... And maybe another series of events had led to someone hating her so much, they wanted to destroy her. Just thinking about all of this made her feel dizzy and disorientated.

'It could be worse,' Jasper said. 'It's just the fence and the privy. I've told Marge to take Edie inside and get her warm. Hopefully, once she's had a bit of a rest, she'll remember more.'

'You go in too, loves.' Nellie gently pushed Louis and Elodie towards the café. After they'd gone she stared at the blackened remains of the fence that had once separated her backyard from the street. The old privy had been entirely destroyed and the flames had licked along the side fence and blackened the bricks of the main building, but that seemed to be the worst of it.

'Was it them foreign kids?' A harsh voice startled Nellie out of her contemplation, and she looked round to see Lou Carter watching the firemen. 'You can't trust no one these days, Nell. Least of all a bunch of foreigners that wash up on the shore.'

'If it weren't for them being here the whole place could've gone up.'

'If it weren't for them bein' 'ere then none of this would've happened,' the other woman retorted.

'They had nothin' to do with this. My money's on this being the work of your bloody son!'

'Oh, it always comes back to him, don't it? My Terence has done more for you than most anyone I know, so don't you dare accuse him of this!'

'More for me? Are you havin' a laugh! You know well enough that the food I got from 'im weren't for me. Yet I paid full whack for it, cos God forbid he'd ever put his hand in his pocket to help. Then the minute I run into difficulties, this is what he does!'

'I can promise you this ain't got nothin' to do with him. But maybe you should think about payin' him the money you owe.'

'I told him I would, didn't I? And even so, he threatened me!' she shrieked.

'Not the same as givin' it to him, though. Promises don't fill your belly, do they?'

Just then, Cissy interrupted them. 'Ethel's taken Marianne over to hers, cos she's not doin' so good. Donny and Alfie have gone with them.'

'The baby?' Nellie gasped.

'Don't worry. Far as I can tell, she's just overwrought and needs a lie-down.' She looked between Nellie and Lou. 'Now, are you gonna tell me what all this talk of threats is about?'

Lou shrugged. 'I ain't threatened anyone.'

'But your boy did! So where is he now? Last coupla days I can't sneeze without 'im being there sneering at me. And, funnily enough, where d'you think he was this afternoon? Standin' outside the town hall, that's where. My guess he was checkin' up on us. But if he thinks he'll make me pay up quicker by damagin' my business, then he's more stupid than he looks.'

Lou's eyes flashed. 'My boy's no saint, but this ain't his style.'

'Not his style! He's a crook, Lou, and he's gone too far this time. I've a good mind to go to the police.'

Lou narrowed her eyes. 'You try it, Nell, and you'll soon understand what threats mean. Cos if he goes down for this, then you'll have a lot more to worry about than a burned-out privy.'

Nellie's brow furrowed in confusion. 'What d'you mean?'

Lou smiled mirthlessly. 'Come on, Nell, I'd've thought you'd be quicker on the uptake –you know better than most that though men might think they're in charge, when it comes to stealth and deception, us women are streets ahead.'

'Are you tryin' to tell me that you and Terence are in it together?'

Lou guffawed. 'What I'm tellin' you is that *I'm* the boss! It's always been me. Now, you an' me 'ave been mates for years and I don't take these things lightly. And I promise you my boy didn't do this. And here's another promise. If it turns out it were him, then the winder's yours. No money to pay.'

Turning on her heel, Lou lumbered away, leaving Nellie staring after her in astonishment.

'Don't tell me you owe that woman money?' Cissy gasped.

Nellie slumped down on the pavement and put her head in her hands. Her mind was reeling with the thought that Lou was the criminal mastermind behind the Carters' operation. Had it always been her? Or did she only take over when Terence senior had died?

'Bloody hell, Cissy!' she gasped. 'What am I gonna do?'

Cissy sat down beside her. 'One thing at a time, Nell. But you should've said you was in trouble.'

Nellie rounded on her cousin. 'And why would I confide in you! The woman who ran out on me the minute life got tough, and who's been too chicken to show her face ever since.' Nellie held up a hand when Cissy opened her mouth to protest. 'Don't even start with the "Ernie said . . ." It weren't up to Ernie, it were up to *you*! I understand you couldn't leave your girl, but after? You could've come then, Ciss. But you chose to hide your head in the sand, like you always have. Life has to be all roses for you, don't it? And if you couldn't see the bad stuff, then it wasn't happenin'! Well, welcome to life, love. Cos bad stuff happens. People steal, fight, blackmail, set fire to houses ' – her eyes drifted to the cafe – 'and they murder little kids cos they don't like the way they pray.' She got up and marched up to the firemen, who were winding the hoses back onto the truck.

'You was lucky we got here when we did,' one of them said.

'Was it deliberate?' she asked.

'Found the remains of a candle on the floor of the privy, so looks likely someone threw it onto the roof.'

Although it was what she had suspected, a chill ran over her to have it confirmed. She looked over at Jasper and Rodney, indicating that they should go in, then stepping over the steaming, soggy mess of what had once been her smart green fence, she led the way inside, and went straight upstairs to the girls' bedroom on the top floor.

Easing the door open, she found Marge sitting by Edie's bed. Marge held a finger up to her mouth. 'She needs to rest, Mrs C. I've sent Elodie and Louis to bed. I asked them if they saw anything, but they didn't hear a thing. It was the smell of smoke that brought them out to investigate.'

Smiling her thanks, Nellie tiptoed over to the bed and gazed down at her daughter's pale face. Briefly, she held her hand to her cheek, revelling in the chance to touch Edie one more time. Then she and Marge crept back out and went down to the sitting room.

'Go on down and join the others, love,' she said to Marge. 'I just want to check everything's in order.' It had occurred to her that whoever had done this might have come inside, and if anything had been stolen or moved then it gave weight to Jasper's argument that there was no ghost haunting the café: someone was deliberately trying to scare her. She glanced sharply round the living room, but all was as she'd left it.

From the kitchen she could hear the usually comforting sounds of clinking crockery and the murmur of voices, but it did nothing to calm her nerves today as she glanced over at her bedroom door. A shiver of fear coursed through her as she went over and put her hand on the knob, her heart hammering against her chest and Mrs Bancroft's words running through her mind.

Things you think are true are false . . . vengeance.

'Mum, you better get down here!' Rodney's voice startled her out of her thoughts. Dimly she became aware of shouting coming from the square. Going over to the window in the sitting room, she gasped, and ran for the stairs.

Chapter 61

Jim's thoughts were scattered as he stormed out of the pub. Colin was alive? But how? And how could it be that he found out now, on the day he got *married*! And he knew. His beautiful Colin knew he'd betrayed him. Hadn't they always promised they would never leave each other? That nothing could kill their love!

But he'd lied to him as surely as he'd lied to Reenie. He'd let despair and grief consume him until the only way he could survive was to try to expunge Colin from his heart. *Would he understand?* he thought frantically. *Could he forgive him?*

A sudden righteous anger burned through him. He'd never have married Reenie if Colin had found a way to let him know he was alive! Didn't he trust that Jim would keep his secret? But even as he cursed him for not getting in touch, he understood. Just one small moment of indiscretion could have meant the end of Colin's mission, even his death. And the death of the children he was trying to save. No, this was all *his* fault, and the knowledge was like acid in his gut.

Reaching Market Square, he barely even glanced towards the café. Instead, he ran straight into Perkins' Fish.

'Where is he?' he demanded of an astonished Reg Perkins, who was standing behind the counter.

Reg stared at him. 'Where's who?'

'Your bloody son!' Jimmy roared.

'Is this about the fire?' he asked, alarmed.

'Just tell me where he is?'

'It's all right, Dad,' a calm voice called before Reg could answer. 'I'll deal with this.'

As soon as Jimmy saw Wilf, a red mist descended and he rushed at him, grasping his jumper and pushing him against the wall. 'Where. Is. He?' he demanded.

'Right, that's enough! You need to get out of my shop!' Reg tried unsuccessfully to prise Jimmy away from his son.

'Gladly,' Jim rasped, pushing Wilf through the queue of customers who were watching with avid fascination.

Outside, Jim shoved Wilf away from him so hard that the other man stumbled and almost fell. Recovering quickly, he held up his hands. 'Calm down, mate,' he said evenly.

'Calm bloody down?' Jim shouted, aiming a punch at him, which Wilf blocked easily.

'Tell me,' Jim growled. 'Or I'll beat you to a fucking pulp!'

Wilf stepped back and folded his arms, refusing to fight. 'You need to shut up before the whole world hears you,' he said.

'What did you do with him?!' Dimly, Jim realised that Wilf had a point, but just knowing that Colin might be somewhere nearby had driven all common sense from his mind. Nothing mattered apart from seeing him again, holding him again.

'You don't know what you're doing, Jim. Shouting your mouth off like this could put him in—'

With a roar of anguish, Jim swung his fist, catching Wilf on the nose and sending him tumbling to the ground.

Reg Perkins had been watching from the doorstep in growing bemusement, but at the attack on his son, he jumped into action, grabbing Jimmy around the neck from behind and holding him securely against him.

'You all right, son?' he called.

Wilf stood up, gingerly feeling his nose, which was already bleeding. Then ignoring his father, he put his face close to Jim's.

319

'You make me sick!' he snarled. 'You've led Reenie on –making her think you love her! Then you come here *on your bloody wedding day* to ask about your fucking lover!'

By now a group of spectators had gathered, and there was an audible gasp.

'What lover?! What are you talkin' about? He's just got married!' Unseen by all, Nellie, Jasper and Rodney had come tearing out of the café, Cissy trailing behind them.

Wilf wiped his nose on his sleeve. 'Yeah, well, he shouldn't have. And where is Reenie?' He looked around, and failing to spot her, he turned on Jim again, who was struggling against Reg's iron grip. 'Where is she?'

Jim jabbed his elbow hard into Reg's solar plexus, causing him to loosen his hold.

'What do you care?' Jim responded heatedly. 'From what I hear you deserted her years ago, so don't get on your high horse with me.' He stared around wildly, only dimly registering his mother's shocked face.

'Son, what's this all about?' Jasper approached him gently, hand out.

Just for a moment, Jimmy wanted nothing more than to fall into Jasper's arms and sob on his shoulder, as he'd done so many times when he was a boy. But even Jasper couldn't help him now.

'Jim?' his mother said, her voice shaky. 'What lover?'

Another figure pushed through the crowd, bald head shining in the weak sun. And before anyone could stop him, Brian Turner pulled back his arm and punched Jimmy hard in the stomach. 'You bastard!' he yelled. 'What have you done to my Reenie? I'm gonna count to ten, and if you're not out of here by then, you're gonna wish you'd never been born.'

'Over my dead body!' Nellie threw herself between them, arms outstretched. 'What the hell's got into everyone! I nearly just lost my café, and now you want to kill my son! If Jim's done wrong,

320

then you got every right to be angry! But if you harm a hair on his head, then you'll have me to deal with!'

Somewhere, someone was blowing a whistle and it silenced the crowd as they turned to see a bevy of policemen running down Biggin Street.

Jimmy looked frantic for a moment, then he grabbed his mother's hands. 'I'm so sorry,' he whispered. 'I never meant to hurt anyone . . .' His face crumpled. 'Please believe me I never set out to hurt her. I would never have married her if I'd known . . . Oh God, tell her I'm sorry. Tell her I love her. But I need to go to Colin . . .'

'Colin?' she gasped. 'But he's dead.'

Jim shook his head. 'No. He's alive, and I have to find him before it's too late.' Then he ran across the square and disappeared up Castle Street.

'Well, well.' Lou Carter's voice broke into the stunned silence. 'Seems Terence were right after all.'

'Right about what?' Nellie said, still trying to process the fact that Colin was alive.

'Your Jim bein' a pansy. A poofter. A shirtlifter.' She cackled. 'Who'd've thunk it.'

Nellie fell back, grateful that Jasper was there to catch her. Twisting her head, she stared up at him. 'Is this true?'

But Jasper looked as bemused as she felt. She stared around at the crowd of people; many of them had known Jimmy since he was a baby, surely they couldn't believe . . . Most of the faces around her looked as shocked as she was, but there were others whose eyes were gleaming with excitement at this new scandal, and she knew it would be a matter of minutes before everyone in town heard the news. She felt a powerful urge to run away and hide. But Jim was her son and no matter what he'd done, she'd sworn to always defend her children, so drawing herself up, she stuck her chin in the air and walked forward.

'Look at you,' she shouted. 'Revelling in grubby gossip. You'd believe Lou Carter, would you? The woman whose son set fire to my café. The woman who by her own admission—'

Before she could finish what she was about to say, Lou leapt forward and with one meaty punch sent her sprawling to the pavement, lights flashing behind her eyes.

∽

Marge was standing in the café doorway, watching the altercation in disbelief. But when Lou's voice rose above the general hubbub, she felt her stomach drop, as suddenly things started to make sense. *Christ alive, where was Reenie?* she thought desperately. *Did she know?*

A flash of white beside the grocery store caught her eye, and without stopping to think, she crossed the road and hurried over towards the Market Hall.

At the bottom of Cowgate Steps, she almost bumped into Wilf, who seemed to have had the same idea. 'You bloody knew!' she shouted, eyeing his bleeding nose with satisfaction. 'Why didn't you tell her?' She shoved him in the chest. 'Instead, you start hanging around, confusing her, until she didn't know whether she was coming or going! Was that why you went to her last night? Did you want her to see Colin? Did you think *he* might tell her!'

Wilf looked utterly defeated. 'How could I tell her? I wasn't allowed to talk about what had happened!'

Marge narrowed her eyes. 'You could have mentioned it to her. But once again, you chose silence over actually discussing things of importance!'

Wilf swiped at his nose. 'I'm going to try to put it right. Let me go after her.'

Marge folded her arms and considered him. 'Put things right? When have you ever managed to put anything right? You're a coward! You've always been a coward. How could you hide something like this from her? You're no better than Jimmy.' She shoved past him and started to run up the stairs, but Wilf caught her arm.

'Please, Marge, you must know how much I-I . . .' He paused, his expression tortured.

'How much you what?' Marge challenged.

When he still didn't answer, she threw up her arms in exasperation. 'And as always, Wilf Perkins can't find the courage to say what he feels. Or say anything, come to that. You broke her heart. And instead of putting it right at the first opportunity, you've skulked around like a brooding bloody Heathcliff. Well, a fat lot of good that's done you. Or her!'

'I need to try.' He looked down at his feet.

Marge snorted. 'Yeah right. Cos you're so great with words. She's been utterly humiliated. Again. But at least last time no one else was there to witness it!'

'Please?'

Marge sighed. Wilf looked so devastated and defeated that she almost felt sorry for him. 'You can go on one condition: finish the sentence for me. For once in your godforsaken life, tell someone what you feel!'

Wilf shut his eyes and threw his head back. Then taking a deep breath, he looked back at her and said quietly, 'You must know how much I love her. How much I've always loved her.'

Marge clapped mockingly. 'Finally, he speaks. And no. No, I didn't know. Which means that she definitely wouldn't know, because she thinks she's not worthy of love. You make me sick! If you loved her that much then why did you marry her bitch of a sister? What the hell were you thinking?'

Colour washed up Wilf's cheeks and he looked away.

'Oh, I see. Let me guess, *you* weren't doing the thinking.' She looked pointedly at his crotch and then back at his face, one eyebrow raised. 'God, men! A pair of tits and a pert arse and you're panting like street dogs in a heatwave. Add to that your inability to

323

hold a simple conversation, when you've had twelve bloody years to try, and I doubt she'll ever believe a word you say. And frankly, you don't deserve her.'

Wilf rubbed his hands over his face. 'I-I'm so sorry. For everything. And you're right, I don't deserve her. But *she* doesn't deserve what's just happened, and I want her to know that she's loved. That this isn't her fault. That she . . . She's the most wonderful woman I've ever met. Please, Marge, let me go. I owe her this much, at least.'

Marge sighed and looked at her watch. 'You have fifteen minutes, then I'm coming in.'

But Wilf was already sprinting up the stairs. Marge followed more slowly behind him, her heart heavy with guilt and sorrow for her friend. But also for herself. She'd managed to paste on a smile after her conversation with Rodney, but after the drama of the afternoon, she couldn't do it anymore.

Sitting down at the top of the steps by the cemetery she put her head in her hands. The parallel between her and Jim's situation wasn't lost on her. The difference being, she hadn't made any definite decisions. Yet. But what had happened between Jim and Reenie had clarified things in her mind. If she married Phil, she'd end up living a lie. And Phil didn't deserve that.

Chapter 62

With Lou Carter's harsh words echoing through her mind, Reenie tried to take the steps by the Market Hall two at a time, but the tight skirt and the unaccustomed alcohol made her stumble and she fell to her knees. For a moment, she stayed where she was, the world spinning around her.

Pansy. Poofter. Shirtlifter.

Acid burned up her throat and she turned her head and retched into the grass. When she'd finished, she wiped her mouth on the sleeve of her wedding gown, feeling less dizzy now she'd expelled most of the wine.

But as soon as she tried to take a step, she tripped again. Cursing, she bent down and ripped the dress at the seams. The fabric split easily, and though she was dimly aware that her aunt would be upset at the destruction of her beautiful dress, she couldn't bring herself to care.

Pansy. Poofter. Shirtlifter.

She'd heard those words before, of course, but she'd not once stopped to consider what they meant. But now she knew ... Jimmy and *Colin*.

On reaching the top of the stairs, she ran up the hill, aiming for the only place she felt truly valued. The place where she always knew what needed to be done. Where she was more than just Reenie Turner, spinster niece of Ethel and Brian, Freddie's aunt. Wilf's former friend. And now the bride abandoned by her groom for a man.

Second best again. The woman people only stayed with until something better came along. And this time the joke really was on her. How many people had known about Jimmy and Colin? Just the thought of those names in conjunction like that made her want to be sick again, but she pursed her mouth tight shut and ran on.

Finally, she reached the blessed peace of her allotment and headed straight into the hut where she threw herself on the sacks, curling into a ball of misery, until the memory of her trying to seduce Jimmy here came back to her and she let out a bitter laugh. She really was a sad joke of a woman.

She jumped up, pulled the wheelbarrow out and grabbed a spade and fork. Lying here wailing wasn't going to achieve anything, so she may as well do the one thing she was good at. Before that though, she needed to shorten the damn dress. She grabbed a pair of shears and chopped roughly at it just below the knee, dropping the strip of satin to the ground. Then she pushed the wheelbarrow up to the very top of the allotment.

Just out of sight, the sea whooshed onto the shore, and the wind whipped her hair out of its pins. She shivered as the sun disappeared behind a cloud, then dug the spade in. With the first thrust, the dress ripped at her right shoulder. She grabbed at it with her left hand, pulling at the sleeve until it hung by just a few threads down her arm. Then she got back to work, slamming the spade into the soil with no thought or care as to whether she might harm the potatoes hidden beneath it. All she wanted was to excise the pain that was squeezing her heart, and the humiliation that was running like poison through her veins.

Suddenly, the spade was snatched from her hand and she whirled round to see Wilf standing behind her, his nose swollen, one eye almost shut.

'Go away!' she yelled, trying to tug the shovel out of his grasp.

He shook his head and tugged back.

'You want me to break your nose again?' she snarled, not letting go.

'If that will make you feel better,' he said gently.

'Make me feel better?' she screamed. 'When have you ever tried to make me feel better, Wilf? All you've ever done is hurt me. Did you know?' she sobbed. 'Is that why you've been hanging around talking to me?'

Wilf nodded, his eyes pitying.

'You bastard!' she screeched, finally managing to pull the shovel away from him and swinging it at his head.

He caught it just in time and threw it on the ground. 'Stop, Reenie!' he shouted.

'How could you let me go through with it? How could you? How long have you known?'

Wilf rubbed at his hair. 'I saw them once, kissing and holding hands, before the war, and I suppose I just . . . kept an eye on them from then on.'

Reenie stilled. 'All this time. You've known about him and Colin all this time and you didn't think to mention it to me when me and Jim got together!'

'I'm so sorry, Reens. Colin was dead . . . and I thought it wasn't for me to interfere. Then after . . .' He shrugged. 'I didn't know what to say.'

'How about "Don't marry him because he's a *pansy, poofter, shirtlifter*."' With each word, she shoved him in the chest. She wished she still had the spade, because she was angry enough to try to cave in his skull with it and damn the consequences. And if Jimmy had been here, she'd have smashed his head in as well.

'And you'd have listened? You'd have thought, *Wilf wouldn't lie to me, he's always been honest with me*, would you?'

'At least I'd have had the chance!' she screamed. 'But instead you did what you always do! You said nothing and watched me making a fool of myself!' She dropped to her knees, head bent, as the wind whipped the last of the pins out of her hair and it fell in curls past her shoulder. Ignoring it, she leant forward and started to dig in the soil with her hands, searching for the tubers.

'No one thinks you're a fool.' He knelt down beside her.

She glared up at him. '*Everyone* thinks I'm a fool. But not only that, I'm a laughing stock! How can I stay here?' She looked around at her allotment. All the years of toil and effort, all the love she'd poured into this place, and now she'd have to leave it. Another pain to add to the almost overwhelming burden she was already carrying.

A sudden thought occurred to her. 'That's why Marianne didn't want me to marry him!' She hid her face in her hands. 'God, even she's betrayed me.'

'I don't think she did it to hurt you. She did it to protect Jim.'

'And your excuse?' she retorted.

He shook his head. 'I really wanted to tell you. I nearly did . . . I'm so sorry. I let you down.'

'Yeah, well, it's not the first time, so I don't know why I'm so surprised.' She returned to her digging, wishing she could dig a hole right down to the centre of the earth and hide there forever.

She was very aware of Wilf watching her, but she couldn't bring herself to look at him again. 'Please go, Wilf.'

'I can't leave you like this, love,' he said. 'Come on, stop now.'

Feeling suddenly exhausted, Reenie allowed him to lift her to her feet and lead her to the hut. There, he sat her on the sacks and knelt in front of her, taking her hands in his.

'You're right, Reens. My silence has made everything a hundred times worse. And I want you to know how sorry I am. About everything . . .'

'If you're looking for forgiveness, don't bother. You've hurt me twice now, and I think that's pretty much my limit.'

'I don't blame you. But I want you to know this: I've regretted marrying June every day of my life. I was eighteen, young, impressionable and stupid. And she seduced me.'

Reenie's head whipped up at that. 'Don't you dare try to lay all the blame on her!'

'I'm not. I made a choice as well. But I would never have married her if she hadn't been pregnant.'

'What a charming man you are,' Reenie said sarcastically. The image of Wilf and her sister in bed together was something she didn't want to think about. Not that she could picture it. She supposed she'd die a virgin now.

'That came out wrong.'

'No, it came out exactly right. The difference now is, I don't care. I have fresher betrayals to worry about. Deeper wounds to nurse. The ones you gave me are old news.'

'Are they?' he asked softly. 'They don't feel like old news to me.'

Reenie looked into Wilf's dark eyes. His expression seemed sincere, but what did she know – or care, for that matter?

Wilf closed the distance between them and kissed her. Reenie stayed still, and taking this for encouragement, he put his arms around her and pulled her closer. For a moment she remained stiff in his embrace, but then she gave herself up to the warmth of his lips, the hardness of his body, and the novelty of being wanted. Something Jim obviously never had, though he'd made a good fist at pretending, she'd give him that. If she'd been more experienced, would she have noticed?

Her arms crept up around his neck, her fingers toying with the curls at his nape.

'I've wanted to do this for so long,' Wilf whispered. 'I've loved you for so long.'

Reenie didn't respond. Instead, she pulled his head down again. It wasn't until she felt Wilf's hand fumbling beneath her skirt that she came to her senses and pushed him away.

'Stop it! It's my wedding day, for God's sake! What are you trying to do? Make amends for the fact that I won't get a wedding night? Or just get your leg over?'

Wilf looked bemused. 'Reenie?'

'Please, just leave me alone. I don't trust a word that comes out of your mouth. It's true, I loved you once, but those days are long gone. So don't waste your time.'

For a long time he stared into her face, then finally he nodded. 'I understand. But if you ever need me – for anything at all – you know I'll always be here for you.'

Reenie looked away and shrugged, smoothing the ruined dress over her knees. 'If you say so, Wilf. But I doubt I'll put it to the test. I'm not sure how much more disappointment I can take.'

His expression bleak, Wilf stood up. 'I'm sorry for everything,' he said softly. But when she didn't reply, he left, shutting the door behind him, leaving Reenie in darkness. For a while she sat completely still, her mind rolling back over the last few days, trying to make sense of it all. What had Mrs Bancroft said? *There'll be a reunion. It will bring joy and despair. Sometimes love deceives, sometimes love returns . . .* She was right about all of it. But the love that returned hadn't been for her. It had been for Jimmy.

She put her head in her hands. *Serves you right. Gullible little fool.*

Chapter 63

Oblivious to his surroundings, Jimmy shoved his way up the high street, his head buzzing with only one thought: he had to find Colin. He needed to explain, get his forgiveness. But more than that, he longed to see his beautiful face again. Kiss his lips. Feel his strong arms around him, gathering him close, telling him how much he loved him.

It would take him hours to walk to Sandwich, but even once he was there, he wasn't sure where he should go. But he'd find him. If it took him the rest of his life, he would find him and he would make it right. They would never be apart again.

He'd reached Union Road, when he became aware of someone calling his name, but he didn't dare turn round. He couldn't bear to see anyone, see the accusation in their eyes. He'd been so stupid. Stupid and selfish for using Reenie like that. She didn't deserve any of this, but there was nothing he could do about that now. And though he regretted the hurt he'd caused and the shame he'd brought to his family, nothing mattered except seeing Colin again.

An arm grabbed him and swung him around. Blindly, he swung his fist, but it was caught in a strong grip.

'Christ's sake, Jimmy, what the *hell* did you think you were doing?'

'Fuck off, Rodney! Just let me leave.'

Rodney grabbed both his arms and pushed him against a wall. 'And where do you think you're going? You can't just run off!

You'll be caught eventually. Arrested and court-martialled. Is that what you want?'

'I can't go back!' Jim yelled in despair. 'Whether I stay or whether I go, I'll be in trouble, so I'd rather just go.'

'You stupid little fool! You *can* go back. You *will* go back! No one is going to arrest you. For what? Leaving a girl on her wedding day? Rumours?'

'You don't understand!' he wailed. 'Colin knows I was getting married. He *knows*!' The thought of the pain he'd caused burned through him.

Rodney pulled him into a rough embrace. 'Listen to me, Jim. Colin is gone. You can't see him. No one is even meant to know he's alive. And now his cover's been blown.'

Jimmy stilled. 'What do you mean?' He pulled back and peered into his brother's face. 'What do you mean?' he shouted.

When Rodney didn't answer, Jim grabbed him by his lapels. 'You bloody knew he was alive, didn't you? And you didn't tell me!'

'No! I didn't tell you! It was none of your business!'

'None of my business? I thought he was dead, Rod! Do you know what that did to me? I thought he was dead, and I blamed myself. And all this time . . .' He gulped back a sob. 'Why?'

Rodney sighed. 'I only found out recently. He was badly injured but he was rescued and taken to safety. A French family hid him and nursed him back to health. But when we got news, it was decided he could be more useful to us if he stayed where he was. He's been working with the French Resistance: helping evacuate children, sending information about German placements. He's a bloody hero, Jim, and you've blown his cover. Don't you even understand what you've done?'

'Where is he?' Jim growled.

'What will you do if you know?'

'I'll go to him. Rod, please. I can't go back to the regiment. Not now. How do you think I'll be treated?'

Rodney's shoulders sagged. 'You can't go AWOL.'

Jim laughed. 'I can and I will. I don't care about this fucking war. I just want Colin. Please, if you know where he is, tell me. I just need to see him. Just once. Have you never loved someone so desperately that the thought of not seeing them makes your heart hurt so much that all you want to do is rip it out of your chest? Please, Rod.'

Rodney looked away.

Jim let out a short bitter laugh. 'No, of course you haven't. You never break the rules, do you? And as for your heart . . . Does it even exist? Do you even know how to love?'

Rodney's jaw tensed and his hand flexed, and for a moment Jim was sure he was going to hit him. He hoped he would. He'd welcome the pain. Something tangible and physical to distract him from the thought of what he'd done to Colin. To Reenie.

'Do I disgust you?' he asked softly. 'Is the thought of my love so revolting that you can't bear to help me?'

'God, Jim! You're my brother. I don't understand your . . .' he paused, searching for the right word '. . . *proclivities*, but that doesn't mean I don't love you.'

'Proclivities! Is that what you call it? Fuck's sake, Rod.' He rubbed his hands across his face. 'It's bloody love. Just love. Something I doubt you'll ever feel.'

'He'll be in Richborough Port,' Rod said suddenly. 'It used to be where the Jewish refugees were housed but they're using it secretly again. He'll probably be there a couple of days while his boat's repaired. If you're that determined to go, then go. But if you don't return after your forty-eight hours' leave is up, then you can never come back. Not while the war is on. And maybe not after that. You do realise that?'

Jim's stomach dropped at the stark truth. But if the alternative was never seeing Colin again, there really was only one choice.

'All I want is Colin,' he said softly.

333

Rodney sighed and pulled him into a long hug. 'You're wrong, you know. I do know how to love. I do love. And I love you. So once this bloody war is over, find a way to get back to us. We'll be waiting for you.'

Jim nodded against his shoulder, sagging with relief. But suddenly a thought occurred to him, and he drew back. 'At least now the secret's out, Terence Carter can't blackmail Bert about it.'

Rodney drew back. 'What the hell? Bert knew about this?'

'Not till recently. That girl . . . Susan' – he spat the name out – 'overheard me and Mary Guthrie—'

'Mary knows?'

'Yes. But the worst of it is, Bert's been stealing from the barracks to pay off gambling debts to Terence . . . I-I'm scared for him. Someone else was arrested for the theft, but keep an eye on him.'

'Jesus Christ! Is there no end to the stupidity of this family! And now Mum thinks Terence set fire to the fence. Looks like she could be right.'

Jim's eyes widened. He'd completely forgotten about the fire. 'Do you think he did it because of me?' he asked in a small voice.

'God knows what goes on in Terence's tiny mind. But I'll be going to the police. Bloody Bert . . .' He let out a heavy sigh.

'Don't be too harsh on him. He lost his way after Gladys died. He blames himself for what happened. Tell him . . . tell him I love him and I'm sorry I didn't tell him about me and Colin. Will you tell Mrs Guthrie?' he asked. 'She's eaten up with grief and really needs to know.'

Rodney shook his head. 'I can't. But no doubt she'll hear it one way or another. God, what a bloody mess!'

'I'm so sorry,' Jim whispered. 'I didn't mean for any of this to happen.'

'None of you ever do,' he said, frustration etched on his features. 'You'd better go. You've got a long walk ahead of you.'

'How do I get into Richborough?' Jim asked.

Rodney shook his head. 'I can't tell you that. It's against the rules. And I've broken enough of them for one day.' He smiled slightly. 'But you'll find a way.'

Jimmy nodded. 'Will you . . . will you tell everyone I'm sorry,' he whispered. 'Especially Reenie.'

Then he turned and walked away.

Chapter 64

Lying on the sofa in the Turners' sitting room, Marianne started when Lou's loud voice came floating through the open window. She sat up and shot an anxious glance at Alfie, who'd not left her side since Ethel had brought her over to lie down. They so rarely got to spend time alone together, and she wished she could enjoy it. Instead, she'd been lying with her eyes closed, pretending to sleep so Alfie would stop fussing over her.

'Oh God!' she whispered, relieved that Donny had run off with Freddie a while back to 'investigate' who had set the fire. 'How did she find out?' she hissed. 'How could this have happened? I *told* you what Jimmy was doing was wrong, but no, you had to let them get on with it. Now look. Oh, poor Reenie . . . Poor Jim. I should have stopped it.' She put her head in her hands, guilt wrapping itself around her like a cape.

'Marianne, you can't blame yourself—' Alfie began.

'Well, I do. But I don't just blame me. I blame Jimmy! And you could have helped, Alfie.' She groaned. 'Reenie will never forgive me!' She was almost in tears.

She struggled to her feet and hurried downstairs and through the shop, emerging onto the doorstep just in time to see Nellie fall to the ground.

With a cry, she rushed over to kneel beside her mother, but Jasper was already there, frantically loosening the neck of her hideous green and orange dress. 'Nellie!' he shouted. 'Can you hear me? Wake up, love, please!'

Nellie groaned and fingered her jaw. 'For the love of God, Jasper, keep your voice down.'

Sighing with relief, he gestured to Alfie, and the two men managed to lift her between them.

Jasper glared at Lou. 'This ain't over. And Terence won't get away with this neither.'

'There's nothin' for him to get away with. And when she comes to her senses, she'll tell you herself,' Lou sneered.

Jasper nodded to Alfie and they half carried Nellie over to the café, with Marianne and Cissy following behind.

Inside, Alfie lifted Nellie and carried her upstairs. Elodie and Louis were sitting on the sofa looking terrified, but as he came in they leapt to their feet, so Nellie could lie down.

'M'sieur,' Elodie said tentatively. But Jasper waved her away. 'Later, love,' he said gruffly. 'Ciss, could you make some tea. And stick a shot of brandy in it. Bottle's in the pantry. Alfie, get a bowl of cold water. We need a cold compress.'

Before Alfie could move, however, Elodie ran through to the small kitchen, where she grabbed a tea towel and filled a bowl with cold water. Coming back, she knelt beside Nellie.

Louis stood to the side, looking uncomfortable.

'Elodie, Louis, I don't think we've thanked you for raising the alarm about the fire,' Marianne said, as a thought occurred to her. 'Did you see anyone come inside?'

The two looked at each other, then Louis nodded. 'We hear footsteps. But . . .' He shrugged. 'We didn't look. Later, we smell smoke through window,' he explained. 'We go out, and there is the woman lying on the ground. Then I come to warn you.'

'Would you mind very much if you could leave us for a few minutes,' she asked. They both looked horribly uncomfortable and unsure. 'Later, I'll get you some food.' They left with alacrity, nearly bumping into Cissy as she came in with a tray loaded with a teapot and cups and saucers, which she put down on the table.

'I've put a good glug in everyone's cup. And that's the last of it. Help yourselves.'

That brought Nellie's eyes flying open. 'You used the last of the brandy? And where am I supposed to get more?'

'Oh hush your mouth, Nellie. I'll get you more. I been here two days, and already I can see it's an essential for this place. All the shocks you seem to get, it's a wonder you don't just fill the bath and swim in the stuff.' She plumped down on an armchair and took a big gulp of her tea. 'And I'd be the first to jump in. I never heard anything like it. I don't know Jimmy well, but I never for a moment imagined he'd be—' she waved her hand '—*that* way. What with him getting married and all. Do you remember Mr Pollock the maths teacher, Nell? Everyone always called him a *confirmed bachelor*. Although, I suppose you can't call Jim a confirmed bachelor, given he's married, but without consumption, then I suppose it don't count.'

Nellie went rigid on the sofa. 'Can you just keep your mouth shut for one minute, Ciss! As if my head don't ache enough as it is. And the word you're looking for is consummation,' she growled.

Cissy giggled. 'Oops, silly me. But what about poor Reenie? And then there's the fence? Do you really think it was Terence Carter? Shifty-lookin' bugger, just like his dad. I hope you're gonna report him, no matter what Lou says. Didn't your mum always say that you should count your fingers if you shake a Carter's hand? Do you remember—'

'Cissy!' Jasper snapped. 'Please.'

Cissy sniffed and took a gulp of tea. 'Why is it every time I try to talk about stuff, I'm told to shut up? Seems there's a lot I'm not allowed to mention.' She held up a hand: 'One. What Lou Carter meant when she said you owed her money. Two: that bloody necklace you keep grabbin'. Three: Donald's photo. And now there's Jim. But you must've known, Nellie! Or at least *someone* would have. You brought that boy up. And who's the lover? And where is he?'

'For the love of all that's bleedin' holy, will you shut your bloomin' trap,' Nellie roared. 'I'm not reporting Terence, cos I don't think it was him. And Jimmy's *nothing* like sad old Mr Pollock!' She groaned and held her jaw. 'How didn't I see it? Marianne, did you know?'

Marianne had been dreading this question, and realising that the truth would only make her mother even more upset, she shook her head, ignoring Alfie's disapproving stare.

'Nellie.' Alfie stepped in. 'Now isn't the time. You're injured, and I think there's more to worry about than what's happened to Jimmy. He's a grown man and can take care of himself. Right now, you need to focus on who tried to set fire to the privy. With the wind in the direction it was, the whole place could've gone up.'

Nellie shut her eyes and clutched at the necklace. 'I don't know,' she whispered. 'But Mrs Bancroft told me there'd be a reunion, and then Cissy arrived. She told Reenie some stuff about love returning and love deceivin'. And looks like she was right about that as well! And she said that someone were out for vengeance. And if she was right about that other stuff, then she was right about that.'

Cissy's eyes widened and she put her hand to her chest. 'You went to see Barmy Bancroft? But who's out for vengeance?'

Nellie closed her eyes and shook her head, the bruise on her jaw standing out starkly on her pale face.

The sound of someone coming up the stairs brought the conversation to a halt and there was a collective sigh of relief when Rodney came in.

'Where've you been, lad?' Jasper asked gruffly. 'We could've done with a bit of help.'

Rodney's lips tightened in annoyance. 'I was making sure Jimmy was all right,' he said.

Nellie sat up. 'Where is he? Have you seen him?'

Rodney took his cap off and ran a hand through his dark hair. 'He's gone, Mum,' he said finally.

'Gone where?'

339

He shrugged. 'I don't know . . .'

'Is he coming back?' Marianne asked anxiously.

Rodney hesitated, then shook his head. 'I don't think so,' he said softly.

'You mean he's *deserting*?' Nellie gasped. 'Isn't he in enough trouble without that! He'll get arrested!'

'He's willing to take that risk.'

'Why?' Nellie whispered. 'Why would he risk it? And what about me? His family? His home? All for Colin!' She spat the name in fury. She'd loved that boy like a son while the kids had been growing up. He and Jim had been inseparable. It made her feel sick now she understood why!

When Rodney remained mute, she looked at Jasper.

'He's in love, Nell,' he said quietly. 'He's riskin' it for love.'

'Love! As far as I was concerned, he loved Reenie! Oh, that poor girl . . .' She rubbed at her eyes. 'Well, he can stay away. I won't have him here. I don't know which is worse – desertion or, or . . . *that other thing.*'

Marianne felt rage flash through her on her brother's behalf. 'You can't mean that! He's still Jimmy! What does it matter who he loves?'

'It's unnatural! Why else would it be illegal? He's trampled our good name through the filth!'

'We don't have a good name!' Rodney burst out.

Nellie remained mute, her lips pursed together.

'And why is that, huh? It's sure as hell not because of Jimmy. If you disown him, then don't expect to see me any time soon. And with Edie still angry with you, for God knows what reason, you'll have only three children out of six still talking to you. Is that really what you want?'

'Two,' Marianne said quietly. 'Because I won't let you do this, Mum. And I don't reckon the other two will stick by you either.'

Nellie stared between them, her eyes flashing with indignation. 'That's right, take *his* side! What about *my* side? What about how

340

I feel? Your mother, what's loved you, cared for you, no matter what. Especially you, Marianne. Who looked after you when you had a baby at seventeen and then forgave you for lyin' through your teeth about who the dad was, despite the trouble that's brought to our door! How could you?'

'But it's not "no matter what", is it, Mum?' Rodney snapped. 'If it was, you'd never cut Jimmy off like this!'

Nellie slumped back down on the sofa. 'I never thought I'd see the day . . .' she muttered. 'Betrayed by my own kids.'

Jasper sat down beside her and took her hand. 'Listen, love. Jim's done wrong with regards to Reenie, and I don't hold with him deserting, but don't we all make mistakes? Love the wrong people? Say the wrong thing? Didn't we?' he said softly.

Nellie's cheeks flushed. 'That's different.'

'Is it?' Jasper said. 'If you cut Jimmy off, you'll regret it for the rest of your life. Look how upset you've been about Edie. You say she has her reasons, which means you've made a big mistake with that girl. A mistake you're ashamed of. Can't you see how Jimmy might have been havin' the same struggles? And yet you'd inflict more pain on the boy? Cos, sure as eggs is eggs, he's gonna be in big trouble, and he's gonna need you more than ever. Now, that don't mean I think he should go unpunished for what he's done to poor Reenie. If I got my hands on him right now, I'd like to wring his neck. But to cut him off forever? The heart wants what the heart wants, love.'

'Back in my big band days, I knew loads of men like Jimmy, and if you ask me, it's the law that's wrong, not the love,' Alfie said.

'Do you know, I never thought of it like that,' Cissy interjected. 'But I remember these two old ladies what lived up the street in Birmingham. Spinsters. Lovely women, always kind. When my Ernie told me they was *together*, you could've knocked me down with a feather.'

'It's not the same though, is it?' Nellie said angrily.

'I don't see why not,' Cissy said.

'So, what's your decision, Mum?' Rodney said.

'I need to think about it,' Nellie muttered.

'Do that. And in the meantime, I reported Terence Carter to the police for setting fire to the fence.'

Nellie's eyes widened. 'You never did!' she gasped. 'How dare you interfere!'

'You call reporting someone for damaging our property interference? Someone you said yourself was responsible?'

'Yes! If you'd only spoke to me first, I'd've told you, it weren't him! And now I'll have Lou Carter on the warpath on top of everythin' else.'

Cissy snorted. ''Ave you seen your fence, Nell? I'd say Lou's already skipped down that warpath and is knockin' at the door!'

'But it's not just the fence. Bert's had some trouble with him as well. So between the two of you, I reckon he was out to send you some sort of message. It was a threat, Mum. Not a serious attempt to ruin your business,' Rodney continued.

Nellie put her face in her hands. 'You don't know what you've done,' she said. 'It weren't Terence.'

Just then a small voice came from the doorway. 'It wasn't Terence.'

Everyone turned to see Edie leaning against the door frame, looking as though she might collapse at any minute.

Rodney hurried towards her and took her arm, leading her to a chair to sit down. 'Did you see who it was?' he asked.

'I just saw a figure. But it wasn't Terence. They were too small – shorter than me.'

Cissy went over and pressed a cup of tea into her hands and Edie sipped at it gratefully.

'You think it was a woman?' Rodney looked disbelieving.

Edie nodded. 'And she stank of rose water. Like Gladys used to wear.'

Chapter 65

Marge was still sitting on the steps by the cemetery when Ethel Turner arrived. Her face was strained, her grey hair dishevelled, and it was clear she'd been crying.

'Have you seen her?' Ethel panted when she reached the top of the stairs.

'Wilf's with her.'

Ethel's lips tightened. 'Reenie's been hurt enough,' she said. 'He's the last person she needs to see!' She strode past her, and Marge leapt to her feet.

'Wait! Let them talk. Maybe he can help.'

'Wilf Perkins has a lot to answer for!' she snapped. 'And I don't want him makin' things worse! Bloody men! I swear if I had Jimmy Castle in front of me right now, I'd strangle him with me bare hands!' She made her hands into claws and squeezed as she hurried on up the hill.

'And I'd help you,' Marge said, falling into step beside her.

'Did you know?' Ethel asked suddenly. 'About Jimmy and *Colin*? Don't get me wrong, I'm happy he's alive, but *this* . . . Oh, my poor, poor girl.' She wrung her hands in distress.

Marge sighed. 'D'you think if I'd had even an inkling I'd have let her go through with this farce?'

'What about Marianne?' she asked shrewdly. 'She's his sister, she must've known. Reenie said she didn't seem too keen. But by God, if she knew . . .'

x

343

'You're blaming the wrong person. Marianne and Jim have always been close. She was caught between the two of them.'

'It's downright cruelty!' Ethel cried.

Marge put her arm around the woman's skinny shoulders. In her heart she agreed with her, but Marianne was her friend, and she could understand the dilemma she'd found herself in.

Just then Wilf's tall figure appeared at the top of the hill, shoulders hunched and head down. When he looked up and saw them, Marge was gratified to see that his usual inscrutable expression had gone; instead he looked devastated.

'You better not have hurt that girl any more?' Ethel hissed at him as he approached.

'I would never—'

'Of course you bloody would! And you did! And if you knew anything about this, then I don't think I can ever forgive you.'

Wilf flushed and looked at his feet. 'I'm truly sorry for any hurt I've caused.'

Ethel snorted and brushed past him.

'So?' Marge asked.

He shook his head.

'What exactly did you expect? That she'd fall into your arms in gratitude?'

Wilf shook his head again and pushed past her.

When they reached the hut, Ethel shoved open the door, and in the dim light they could see Reenie sitting in the ruined wedding dress, her forehead resting on her knees, which were hugged tightly to her chest.

With a cry, Ethel rushed forward and dropped down beside her. Pulling her into her arms, she rocked her gently as Reenie sobbed against her shoulder. 'Oh, my poor little girl. You cry all you need. Me and Marge are here for you.' Marge sat down on the other side of her friend and rested her hand on Reenie's back.

'Oh, love,' she said softly. 'You mustn't blame yourself for any of this.'

344

'How could I have been so stupid as to believe a man like that could ever truly love me! And then Wilf . . .' She gulped. 'Wilf said—' She started to sob again.

'What did he say?' Ethel said sharply.

Reenie just shook her head and Ethel shot an anxious look at Marge.

Marge sighed. 'Wilf loves you, though,' she said.

'I don't care!' Reenie wailed. 'It's too late, and I don't believe him. And I'm married to Jim!'

'Did you love him?' Marge asked softly. 'Truly?'

Reenie sat up and stared at her through tear-drenched eyes. 'Of *course* I loved him. Why else would I have agreed to marry him?'

'Maybe you just *thought* you did,' Marge replied.

'That's enough, Marge!' Ethel snapped. 'Come on, Reenie, love, up you get and we'll get you home.'

Obediently, Reenie stood, and Ethel gaped at her ruined wedding gown.

'I'm sorry, Aunt Ethel,' Reenie said, looking down at the mud-stained satin.

'Fiddlesticks,' her aunt said stoutly. 'I never could walk in the damn thing. Near tripped up the aisle in it. And it strangled the life out of me. I wanted to rip the neck off all through the weddin'.'

Reenie started to laugh. 'Then why did you make me wear it?' she gasped.

'Cos when I looked in the mirror, it made me feel like a goddess. An' I wanted you to feel it too.'

Reenie collapsed on her shoulder again. 'But I didn't. And I don't. I never will.'

Marge went to the other side of her, and between them, they half carried Reenie back to the shop, hustled her through the back door and up the stairs.

'You help her out of those rags, Marge, I'll run the bath. And it'll be more than four inches!'

In the bedroom, Marge gently pulled the dress over Reenie's head, then sat her down on the bed and unrolled her stockings. The sobs had stopped now, and instead Reenie sat in silence, staring into the distance.

'Tell me honestly, Reenie. How do you feel?'

'Sick,' Reenie said immediately. 'And stupid. And like I want to die.'

'That sounds like humiliation to me. Embarrassment. Do you feel any . . . relief?'

'Relief that I've been left at my wedding? Relief that a man I thought loved me, actually loved another man? No, Marge, funnily enough I don't feel any bloody relief!'

'Not like that. Relief that you and Jimmy won't be tied together for the rest of your life.'

Reenie grabbed her dressing gown and shrugged it on, glaring at Marge. 'Go to hell!' she said, before stalking out of the room.

Marge blew out a long breath and sat back on her heels. Well, that told her. But she hadn't failed to notice that Reenie hadn't mentioned she felt heartbroken.

Chapter 66

Nellie shrieked and dropped the cup and saucer she was holding, tea soaking unnoticed into her skirt. 'R-rose water?'

'Everythin' smells of rose water hereabouts,' Cissy declared. 'I noticed it soon as I came into your room the other day, Nell. And when all them women were here earlier, it were that strong it made me nose tingle.'

Jasper sat forward. 'Did you smell it on anyone in particular?' he asked.

Cissy sat back reflectively, her eyes closed.

'You can't really think—' Rodney began.

Jasper waved him to silence. 'Come on, Ciss, *think*.'

'It were that little one in the black. Mary, I think her name is.'

Nellie gasped. '*Mary?! Colin's* mother?' She spat the name. Even if she had to welcome Jim back, she'd never let Colin set foot in this place again.

Jasper let out a low whistle. 'By heck, that makes sense.' He glanced at Nellie. 'Far as she were concerned, she lost two people she loved because of this family. Colin – although that were no one's fault – and Susan.'

'But how's any of that *my* fault?' Nellie wailed. 'I've done nothin' to her? And yet she comes sneaking in here, makin' my life hell, makin' me question my sanity . . .' Nellie fell back in her chair.

'Right, I'm going to find her,' Rodney said. 'If she really is behind this, she needs to explain herself.' Rodney slapped his cap on his head and strode to the door.

Nellie leapt up. 'Rodney, go easy on her.'

He looked round at his mother in disbelief. 'Go easy? Are you joking? After everything she's done?'

'It's just . . . I think she's not well. Her grief's twisted something inside her, and I-I think I understand.'

Rodney nodded curtly and hurried down the stairs.

As soon as he'd gone, Nellie went to her room, claiming to need a few minutes to think. But in reality, she needed to know what else Mary had done while she'd been here. The smell hit her immediately, but this time it didn't bring the usual fear. This time all she felt was fury.

Opening the windows, her eyes fell on the pillow, and for a moment, her heart stopped.

As if in a trance, she went to pick up the photograph then slumped down on the bed, staring at the image of her husband. Donald's handsome face smiled back at her, at once achingly familiar, but also strange. 'Why did she take you?' she whispered. Aside from the fact that it wasn't in its silver frame, it looked as it always had: the wrinkle across the middle that cut diagonally through his face, making his smile a little crooked; the dark smudges on the white background; his eyes sparkling with mischief. But then she turned it over and froze, her body erupting in goosebumps. Scrawled across the back of the photo, in handwriting that looked just like Gladys's, were the words: 'I know you killed him.'

With her new perspective, Nellie shivered with fear. How would Mary know anything about what happened to Donald? Gladys and Mary had been good friends, could she have told her what happened?

She thought back to that last awful row she'd had with Gladys, kneeling at Donald's graveside. 'He didn't shoot himself, though, did he? His death is on you!' The memory was so vivid, it was as if Gladys was in the room with her, screaming at her as she had then.

Gladys had sworn she'd never told a soul, and Nellie had believed her. But maybe she'd been lying?

Swallowing back the nausea at the thought, Nellie lay back on the bed and stared unseeingly at the ceiling. It was time to tell everyone why Edie wasn't talking to her. Tell them all about the poppy-head tea, and how she and Gladys had inadvertently given Donald too much. How it had driven Donald so mad that he had ultimately shot himself.

It was better that than the truth . . .

Chapter 67

With Reenie bathed and being fussed over by her aunt, Marge deemed it was time to leave them to it. There was nothing more she could do here, and frankly she was exhausted.

Outside, the light was dimming as the sun began its descent, and the wind was cold. She lit a cigarette and leant against the wall of the shop.

Across the road, the café door suddenly burst open and Rodney stormed out and strode up Cannon Street.

'Rodney?' she called, crossing over the square towards him.

He stopped and looked over towards her. 'Is Reenie all right?' he asked.

'Not really.' She peered at his face. 'And nor are you? What's happening?'

His jaw tensed and he looked away. 'I'm going to see Mary Guthrie,' he said briefly. 'It seems she was the one who started the fire.'

Marge gasped. 'You can't be serious? The woman wouldn't say boo to a goose.'

'Edie saw her. She was the one that knocked her over.'

'I'll come with you.'

Together, they walked swiftly towards the Guthries' bakery on Biggin Street. It was shut, and Rodney banged on the door. 'Open up!'

The window upstairs opened and Jack Guthrie's head poked out. Seeing Rodney, he closed the window, appearing soon after at the door. 'Is it true?' he asked. 'Is Colin alive?' His eyes were alight with hope.

'We need to speak to your wife,' Rodney said.

'She's upstairs. The news has upset her. If Colin were alive, he'd surely let us know, wouldn't he? Why wouldn't he let us know?'

'It's not about Colin,' Marge said gently.

'Then you better leave. We've got nothing to say to any Castles.'

'But I have something to say to her!' Rodney pushed the door open and went inside, Marge close behind him.

Sighing, Mr Guthrie plodded after them.

The sitting room stunk of pipe smoke and Mrs Guthrie was sitting in one of the drab blue armchairs with her face buried in a large hankie, her shoulders shaking.

She jumped up when they came in. 'Is it true? My Colin . . . He's alive?'

'I'm not here about that, Mrs Guthrie. We're here about the fire at the café.'

All the colour drained out of her already pale face, and she slumped back down in the armchair.

'How dare you?' Mr Guthrie roared. 'Hasn't our family suffered enough without you throwing around crazy accusations?'

Rodney shot him a sharp look. 'Mr Guthrie, I really am very sorry, but my sister saw her.'

Mr Guthrie looked at his wife aghast. 'Mary?'

Mary's face crumpled and she started to wail. 'I had to do *something* to make them pay! How can Jimmy go off and marry that girl, when our Colin . . .' She buried her face in her hankie again.

'What do you mean, love? Why shouldn't Jim have married Reenie?'

'You're a blind fool, Jack Guthrie! You never could see what was right in front of your face! Jimmy and Colin were lovers!' She screamed the last word at her husband. 'And he left him to die in that hellhole! If he couldn't save him, he should have done the decent thing and died with him!'

Jack Guthrie took a step back, shaking his head. 'No, love. No. You've got it all wrong.'

'Tell him, Rodney.' Mary glared at him. 'You're his brother, you *must* have known.'

Rodney sighed. 'It seems it's true,' he said.

'And is he . . . is he really alive?' Mr Guthrie said.

'Yes. But I don't know where he is, I'm afraid.'

'Oh, but I bet your brother knows! Everyone's talking about how he ran off to find Colin! And the things they've been saying about him?' She sobbed. 'I just want to see my son! Why should he get to see him and not us? And then there's poor Susan.' Her voice was shaking. 'Locked up in jail and likely to hang. And all because *your* brother couldn't keep his hands to himself. I wish he'd died at that football match!' She started to sob again.

'All of that doesn't give you the right to take your anger out on my mother, who had nothing to do with any of this,' Rodney gritted out.

'She's the worst of the lot of you! She's a murderer and a liar, and Gladys knew it as well!'

There was a stunned silence for a moment. Marge glanced at Rodney, whose mouth was hanging open in shock.

'What are you talking about?' Marge asked.

'I was just trying to drive her mad, like I've been driven mad since Colin's gone. And it worked, didn't it? I had her out there scrubbing at the pavement. And the necklace too!' She let out a manic laugh. 'I saw her clutching at it and muttering to herself. Anyway, I wasn't going to do it for much longer. I was going to the police with what I knew, cos I want her to rot in jail, just like Susan is.'

Marge looked at Mr Guthrie, who looked dumbfounded.

'Who do you think she murdered?' Rodney finally managed.

Without a word, Mary stood up and left the room.

Mr Guthrie shook his head. 'I'm sorry, son. She's just not been right since Colin, and then Gladys dying and Susan being in jail pushed her over the edge. I knew something were up, but I had no idea she was doing anything to your mum.'

Marge put a comforting arm round Rodney's shoulders and gave them a squeeze. For a moment he leant against her, glancing down at her with a grateful smile.

Mrs Guthrie soon returned and held out a small leather-bound book. 'Gladys's diary for 1927. I found it when I helped clean out her place with Mrs Palmer. Do you remember what happened in 1927, Rodney?' she asked mockingly.

Rodney couldn't have looked more shocked if Mary had pointed a gun at him. Finally, though, he held out a trembling hand and took the book from her.

Worried he might collapse, Marge led him over to the sofa.

'Read it,' Mary urged. 'I reckon you can guess the date you need. But just in case you forgot, try twenty-seventh of December.'

Rodney was shaking so much that Marge eventually took the book out of his hands. 'Do you want me to look?' she asked.

'No!' He suddenly came to life and snatched it back from her. 'It's all in the past and you can go to the police if you want, but what will they do? There's no proof, is there? Just the words of a dead woman?'

Mary narrowed her eyes. 'No proof of what?' she asked.

When Rodney didn't answer, she let out a bitter laugh. 'You've always suspected, haven't you?'

Marge looked between them in confusion. They seemed to be having a private conversation, and she had no idea what it was about.

'Rodney?' she asked.

He seemed to gather himself. 'I have proof about you committing arson and assault, so what do you want me to do? I can go to the police right now and have you arrested.'

Mr Guthrie stepped forward, hands raised placatingly. 'Hey, come on now, son. If we pay for the fence then can we just forget all about it?'

'Your wife is mad,' Rodney snapped. 'She needs help.'

'What I need,' Mary gritted, 'is to see my son. And I need to see your family pay for what they've done to mine. She won't get away with it.'

'You think Colin would be happy about all this?' Rodney flashed back. 'What if I find a way to tell him that you've been terrorising the mother of the man he loves? That you tried to set fire to the café where he spent so much time when he was a boy? You think he'll ever want to come back to you after that?'

The fight went out of Mary, and she slumped back in her chair.

'But you said you didn't know where he was?' Mr Guthrie said. 'How could you let him know?'

'Because I lied. I know exactly where he is and what he's doing. But I can't tell you. On the other hand, what I can do, is find a way to get him to write to you. But I won't do it if you continue with this vendetta. You need to stop immediately. And I want no more talk of this!' He waved the diary in the air. 'And, yes, Mr Guthrie, you will pay for the fence. And while you're at it, you can give my mum some money to compensate her for what your wife has done. I believe she needs some money to pay for the window.'

'I don't have that sort of money!' he gasped.

'Then you better keep her under control, or she'll find herself in the cell next to Susan's.' Rodney stood up and put the book in his pocket. 'Whatever is in this diary is over and done. My dad did enough damage when he was alive, I won't have him doing any more. Come on, Marge.' He held his hand out to her, and she took it gratefully, eager to get out of the smoky room and find out what the hell was going on.

'Will you tell me what that was all about?' Marge asked as Rodney sped back down towards Market Square. 'What's in the diary? Isn't 1927 the year that your dad—' She stopped walking as it suddenly hit her.

Rodney turned and looked at her, his eyes haunted, his face pale.

'Surely you don't think . . . ?'

'I don't want to talk about it,' he said brusquely.

She took his arm. 'I think you need to,' she said softly.

He ran his hand over his face. 'It was a long time ago. And I try very hard not to think about him at all.'

'But, Rodney, you surely can't think that your mum . . . You don't think she was the one who shot him, do you?'

Rodney looked tortured. 'If she did, he deserved it! He nearly killed her, he nearly killed me on more than one occasion! He was a violent brute, and if Mum hadn't done it, I would have done it soon. Edie was the only one he was nice to.'

'He was sick, love.'

A muscle jumped in Rodney's jaw as he ground his teeth together. 'I know. And I'm sorry.' He buried his face in his hands.

They were standing by St Mary's Church, and Marge gently drew him along the road beside Pencester Park and put her arms around him. 'Hey, it's all right, love. You were just a boy. None of it was your fault.'

He leant against her, his shoulders shaking. 'I could never protect them,' he whispered. 'I tried, but it was never enough.'

'It wasn't your job to do that. It was your mum's.'

He looked down into her face. 'And that's exactly what I think she did,' he said quietly.

Marge stared back at him in shock. Suddenly, he bent his head and kissed her roughly, desperately, and she put her arms around his neck and kissed him back with equal ferocity, their tongues duelling, as they pressed to get closer to each other.

He pulled away finally. 'Don't marry him,' he whispered in her ear. 'For God's sake, please don't marry him.' Then he kissed her again.

Despite the shocking revelations of the afternoon, Marge's heart sang at his words. Did he mean it? Or was this just a result of the emotions of the day? But what did it matter? Phil had never made her feel like this.

'I love you,' she said against his lips.

Rodney stopped abruptly and stood back from her. 'Even after what you've found out today?'

'Especially after that.'

Rodney leant his forehead against hers. 'Thank God. I thought I'd lost you to the padre.'

'You could never lose me, Rod. No matter where you are, what you do, I'd find you somehow.'

Rodney laughed slightly. 'Only you could make me laugh after today.' He sighed. 'Will you come back with me to talk to the others?'

Marge gave him a radiant smile. 'I'd come with you to the ends of the earth, if you want me. Surely you know that?'

He wrapped his arms tightly around her. 'I do now. And now I have you, I hope you know I'll never let you go.'

'I should bloody hope not,' she said.

Chapter 68

It was gone one o'clock in the morning, and Reenie lay rigidly in bed, her eyes wide open, as images of Colin and Jimmy swept through her mind, and humiliation and self-recrimination raced through her veins. She'd known something wasn't right, and yet she'd continued blithely on. *Stupid, stupid, Reenie.* Why hadn't she listened to her instinct? Or, at least listened to Wilf.

Bloody Wilf. Why could he never just say what he meant? And why did he wait until one of the worst days of her life to tell her what he was feeling? Strangely, it was this thought that made her heart hurt. All these years she'd secretly pined for him, and when he finally said the words she'd longed to hear, it was too late. After everything that had happened, she couldn't contemplate ever trusting anyone again.

She tried to imagine what life would be like for her from now on, and the prospect of standing behind the counter having to endure the pitying looks of the customers made her want to weep. Her future would be forever tainted by what had happened, and she knew there'd be a fair few who'd always be happy to remind her.

She imagined herself walking along the street, while people stopped to whisper and laugh behind her back. The thought of living constantly under the shadow of what had happened was just too awful.

Well, she wouldn't have it! She had her life, didn't she? A life that could so easily have been snuffed out just a few days ago. What did love matter in comparison to that? It was life that counted right now. And she refused to allow herself to be destroyed by this scandal.

She hopped out of bed and pulled her suitcase down from the top of the wardrobe. Opening it on the bed, she threw in her few clothes and toiletries. Then she scribbled a quick note to her aunt and uncle. She hated to upset them like this, but she couldn't stay in Dover. Instead, she'd dedicate herself to helping the war effort in the only way she knew how: she'd join the land army.

Once her packing was done, she dressed in her warmest clothes, then crept down the stairs and walked out into the cold, dark night. There was only one more thing she needed to do. She had no idea whether Wilf would be there tonight, but she had to try.

Going round to the back of the fish shop, she picked up a handful of gravel. The action almost made her smile as it brought back memories of long ago, when she'd been happy, and love had seemed so tantalisingly within her grasp.

There was no answer, so she turned on her torch and scrabbled around for the largest stones she could find. Then she tried again. This time, the window opened. 'Reenie?'

'Who else would it be?' she hissed back.

'Five minutes.'

He crept up on her so silently, she didn't even notice he was there until he caught her in his arms. 'You came,' he whispered against her ear.

She tried to step back, but his arms tightened around her.

'I came to say goodbye.'

'No! Please don't go.'

'It's too late, Wilf. I can't stay here, knowing that everyone's whispering about me. Pitying me.'

He drew in a deep breath. 'None of this was your fault, Reens.'

'Really? It feels very much like it was. But I wanted to know one thing. Just so I don't feel quite so unlovable. Did you mean it? What you said today about always loving me?'

'Of course I did.' His head bent towards her and he caught her lips with his, kissing her so passionately that she was left in no doubt. 'Will you reconsider? Get an annulment and marry me instead?'

Oh, she was tempted. But everything was too raw, and she still couldn't trust him.

'I can't. I need to make myself proud. Shake off this shame. Prove to myself that I'm as worthy of love as the next woman.'

'But you *are*,' he said earnestly, trying to kiss her again, but she dodged away.

'I don't believe you. You rejected me and ran off with my sister. Jim rejected me to run off with Colin, for God's sake! I need to find my self-respect. Without it, it doesn't matter how much you tell me you love me, I will never believe you.'

'Will you come back?' he asked in a small voice.

'Maybe. Maybe not. Wait for me if you like, Wilf, but if I do come back, I won't be the same woman. I might even have found someone else to love – or you might have. It's a risk I'm willing to take.'

He sighed and drew her into his arms. 'I understand. And it's what I would expect. You've always been brave, Reenie. Brave and loving. I'm willing to take a risk on that.'

She put her arms around his waist and hugged him to her, wishing everything could be different. Neither of them had been brave. At any point in the past few years, one of them could have taken the chance to confess their feelings. But they'd stayed silent.

Well, her silent days were over.

'Where will you go?' he asked softly.

She shrugged against his chest. 'Wherever the first train takes me. That is, if they've repaired the line by now. If not, I'll just stay at the station till they have.'

'Let me walk you there.'

'No.' She let go and bent to pick up her suitcase. 'I need to do this by myself. Please take care, Wilf. And if you run into Colin out in the sea again, tell him . . . tell him I'm sorry. I never meant to hurt him.'

Then she walked into the night, the searchlights guiding her way. And for the first time in a while, she felt a tiny flutter of anticipation and hope rise within her.

Epilogue

The sea was calm as two figures pushed the small boat out into the water, then hopped in. With the engine running low to minimise noise, they made their way slowly down the river from Richborough and into the Channel.

The night was pitch black, but it didn't matter; Colin could have made this crossing blindfold. Jimmy came to stand beside him at the helm, and their shoulders touched.

'Are you sure about this?' Colin said. 'You know that neither of us can go back home now.'

'I don't care.' Jimmy took Colin's hand. 'As long as we're together, we'll always have a home of sorts.'

'Will it be enough for you?' Colin replied, unable to quite dispel the devastating pain that had cut through his heart when he'd discovered Jimmy was getting married.

'Oh, love, I'm so sorry.' Jim put a hand on either side of Colin's face and kissed him softly. 'If I'd known you were alive, I'd have come and found you long ago,' he whispered against his lips. 'The only thing that can separate us now is death.'

Colin stared into the face he thought he'd never see again and realised he had no choice but to trust him – not now he knew what a life without Jimmy was like.

'France is dangerous,' he said. 'And we may not be able to stay together. Resistance fighters go where they're told.'

'No. We stay together,' Jimmy said fiercely. 'Or we don't fight.'

Colin chuckled slightly. 'Till death us do part, then,' he murmured, putting his arm around Jimmy's waist and pulling him close.

Jim rested his head on Colin's shoulder. 'To love and to cherish,' he replied. 'For ever and ever.'

Acknowledgements

This book nearly didn't get written. There were times when I wanted to throw my computer across the room and give it all up. The dreaded writer's block had me well and truly in its grip.

But thanks to a whole host of wonderful people, I finally managed to get it over the finish line. So, first of all, I'd like to thank Teresa Chris, my brilliant agent, who calmly talked me down from the ledge and sorted me out. And to Sarah Benton and Salma Begum at Zaffre for their endless patience. And, of course, to my editor Claire Johnson-Creek, who returned from maternity leave to find my manuscript on her desk needing urgent attention!

To my amazing sister Ali, who has to listen to me moan far too much, and my mother, who is a fount of interesting wartime detail and stories about our family during wartime. Her stories have informed so many of my characters. And, as always, to my truly wonderful and talented friends Tanita and Natacha, who coaxed me out of the house, sent me chocolate and whisked me away to Greece, where I finally managed to finish the book. I honestly don't know how I'd have coped without you.

To Maddie, Sim and Olly – heartfelt apologies for being so grumpy.

To the Minuty for the drinks and laughs. And Ali T and Julie for the dog walks.

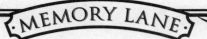

Welcome to the world of Ginny Bell!

Keep reading for more from Ginny Bell, to discover
a recipe that features in this novel and to find out more about
Ginny's upcoming books . . .

We'd also like to welcome you to Memory Lane,
a place to discuss the very best saga stories from
authors you know and love with other readers,
plus get recommendations for new books we think
you'll enjoy. Read on and join our club!

www.MemoryLane.Club
www.facebook.com/groups/memorylanebookgroup

Dear Reader,

Thank you so much for reading *Return to the Dover Café*. Those who have read my books before will know that I like to include a few factual events. The one I chose this time was the football match. On 19 August 1940, two planes attacked the playing fields of Connaught Barracks, opposite Dover Castle, while a football match was in progress. In total eight players were killed either by bombs or machine gun fire. For the purposes of my book, I have moved the match in date and place – and I decided not to have any bombs. Dr Gertrude Toland, now a mainstay of my books, was busy at the hospital that day, just as she is in this book.

One of the things that didn't happen, as far as I know, is the evacuation of children across the Channel. It would have been far too dangerous. Richborough Port near Sandwich, however, did house 5000 Jewish and political refugees before the start of WWII. During WWI, it had been used as a ferry port for troops and munitions going to France, then in 1942, it became a highly secret factory where Royal Engineers built part of one of the Mulberry harbours that were later towed to the Normandy coast as part of the D Day landings.

Aside from the inspiration I get from the wartime history of the south-east coast, I am also constantly inspired by the women in my family. My great-grandmother had six sons, five of whom went to war, while one served in the Home Guard. All six survived. This is my inspiration for

Nellie and her six children. Nellie herself is loosely based on my very scary grandmother, Nancy. And Cissy is inspired by my great-aunt Trissy – Nancy's cousin. And yes, she was a kind-hearted, talkative, shopaholic, with a high, piping voice and a ready laugh, just like Cissy.

If you'd like to keep up with what I, and other sagas authors are up to, do join the Memory Lane Book Group on Facebook and sign up to the newsletter. And do keep an eye out for more information on the next book in the Dover Café series, *The Dover Café on Trial*, coming in 2025.

Lots of love,
Ginny

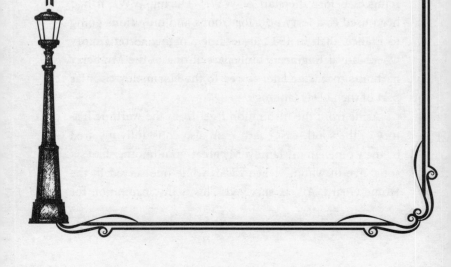

Don't miss the next book in the dramatic and
heartwarming Dover Café series . . .

THE DOVER CAFÉ
ON TRIAL

Summer, 1941

After Jimmy's shocking departure, Nellie Castle is feeling
bereft . And with Rodney being elusive, she's determined to do
all she can to help her youngest son Bert get back on his feet
following the terrible injuries he sustained in the bombing.

Plagued by guilt and nightmares, the last thing Bert wants is
to return to the café - being there only makes his guilt over
Gladys's death worse. His relationship with nurse Vi is helping
somewhat, but when he receives a formal summons to the trial
of the woman who tried to kill him, he is plunged back into
the depths of despair. Giving evidence could condemn her to
death, and with the weight of one woman's death already on
his conscience, he's not sure he can bring himself to do it.

As the trial progresses, shocking truths are revealed. Is
everything he's believed his whole life a lie? And with his
family and relationship in tatters, Bert finds solace with the
last person he would have expected . . .

Coming spring 2025. Pre-order now.

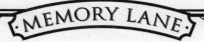

· MEMORY LANE ·

In honour of Reenie's parsnip harvest, I have searched out a genuine recipe from the Ministry of Food for Parsnip Patties.

Ingredients

1 Ib cooked parsnips
Tablespoon of Plain Flour
Teaspoon of mustard powder/mustard (optional)
Salt and Pepper
Vegetable Oil – or any other fat – for frying

Method

- Slice off top and bottom of parsnips, then chop into even sized chunks
- Add the parsnips to a saucepan of water and bring to the boil. Cook until soft – about 10 mins
- Drain and set aside for a few minutes to dry
- Mash parsnips with potato masher
- Add flour, salt, pepper and mustard
- Form into 12 chunky patties
- Heat oil in frying pan and fry for 4-5 mins each side

Catch up on the first three books in the brilliant Dover Café series . . .

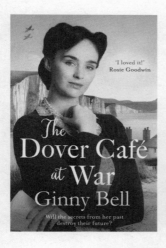

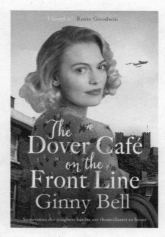

·MEMORY LANE·

Introducing the place for story lovers – a welcoming home for all readers who love heartwarming tales of wartime, family and romance. Sign up to our mailing list for book recommendations, giveaways, deals and behind-the-scenes writing moments from your favourite authors. Join the Memory Lane Book Group on Facebook to chat about the books you love with other saga readers.

·MEMORY LANE·

www.MemoryLane.Club
www.facebook.com/groups/memorylanebookgroup